ARIEL'S CROSSING

ARIEL'S CROSSING

Bradford Morrow

VIKING

VIKING
Published by the Penguin Group
Penguin Putnam Inc., 375 Hudson Street, New York, New York 10014, U.S.A.
Penguin Books Ltd, 80 Strand, London WC2R 0RL, England
Penguin Books Australia Ltd, 250 Camberwell Road, Camberwell, Victoria 3124, Australia
Penguin Books Canada Ltd, 10 Alcorn Avenue, Toronto, Ontario, Canada M4V 3B2
Penguin Books India (P) Ltd, 11 Community Centre, Panchsheel Park,
    New Delhi–110 017, India
Penguin Books (N.Z.) Ltd, Cnr Rosedale and Airborne Roads, Albany,
    Auckland, New Zealand
Penguin Books (South Africa) (Pty) Ltd, 24 Sturdee Avenue, Rosebank,
    Johannesburg 2196, South Africa

Penguin Books Ltd, Registered Offices:
Harmondsworth, Middlesex, England

First published in 2002 by Viking Penguin, a member of Penguin Putnam Inc.

10 9 8 7 6 5 4 3 2 1

The author wishes to express gratitude to the Bard Research Council, Bard College, for a grant
that was crucial to the completion of this novel.

Publisher's Note
This is a work of fiction. Names, characters, places, and incidents either are the product of the
author's imagination or used fictitiously, and any resemblance to actual persons, living or dead,
business establishments, events, or locales is entirely coincidental.

LIBRARY OF CONGRESS CATALOGING-IN-PUBLICATION DATA

Morrow, Bradford
    Ariel's crossing / Bradford Morrow.
        p.   cm.
    ISBN 0-670-03095-3
    I. Title.
    PS3563.O8754 A88 2002
    813'.54—dc21   2001046968

F MORROW

This book is printed on acid-free paper. ∞

Printed in the United States of America
Set in Fairfield with Perpetua
Based on a design by Brian Mulligan

The title page illustration was designed by Stella Teller of the Isleta Pueblo in New Mexico.
Based on traditional pottery designs, it represents an *avanyu,* which is Tewa for water-serpent. It
is trademarked by the Indian Pueblo Cultural Center in Albuquerque, New Mexico, and used
with the center's kind permission.

For Martine

and the Rochesters of Nambé

De la tierra fui formado,
La tierra me a de comer,
La tierra me a sustentado,
Y al fin yo tierra a de ser.

From the earth I was created,
The earth will eat me,
The earth has sustained me,
In the end the earth I'll be.

—Chimayó valley hymn

PART I

STRANGER BY THE GATE

Nambé

1820–1993

Doña Francisca de Peña never believed in ghosts, and even after she became one herself she couldn't help but have her doubts.

When she was young, Francisca already wore a weathered look in her dark eyes. Stronger than her brothers, she rode better than they did and worked the fields with a grown man's stamina. Her father, Trinidad Otero de Peña, a pioneer ranchero who settled three dozen hectares in Nambé valley before the midcentury pueblo land grants, taught her the names of animals and plants and stars. Showed her how to irrigate summer pastures and graft pear trees. Her mother, Estrella, schooled her in reading, writing, and numbers. They sensed Francisca was not like other children. Quicker, more awake, but at the same time given to curious reveries. Maybe she was a gentle *bruja,* they thought, a benign witch. They nicknamed her *Francisca esparaván,* little sparrowhawk.

On her seventh birthday, Francisca had a dream in which she swam Rio Nambé like some underwater bird, feathering her way with ease through its cold currents. When she awakened, a mysterious change had visited the world around her. Paralyzed in bed, she saw her room was not the same. Sun billowing in her window seemed more like liquid than light. Her cane chair wavered toward invisibility. The book on her table was translucent, as was the willowy table itself. Her room was in the river, it appeared, the universe of her dream having merged with what she witnessed here, awake.

Then slowly her alcove regathered itself, and the girl arose into her morning.

Throughout that day, while doing chores on the rancho, a tract of scratchland at the western edge of the pueblo not far from where it bordered Pojoaque, Francisca was tormented by the fear she might never be able to visit her dream place again. For though she liked working the horses and stoking the piñonwood fire in the mud oven where her mother baked their bread, nothing matched the ecstasy of that dream. But she needn't have worried. That very night she sat on one of the moonlit blades of the wooden windmill, feet dangling as she rode round and round on its spinning face in a carnival of her own devising.

Many different birds visited her dreams. Magpies that squealed like lusty cats in rough basket-nests high in their catalpa trees. Strutting crows dressed in black like debonair hangmen. Roadrunners that zigzagged the open barrens. On her ninth birthday, Francisca dreamed she spread her arms and stretched her fingers and flew above the treetops of Nambé basin. The desert wind combed her blue-black hair and made her pluming skirts flutter against her thighs. When she gazed below she saw herself asleep in her rope bed, another girl who was Francisca de Peña, she supposed, an earthbound creature for whom she felt a certain pity.

This was the dream that marked her continuous consciousness. It was so viable, so very true, that when she awoke to find herself not in the sky but on the ruddy floor, soaked in sweat, coughing and clawing at the air, flinching in her mother's arms, the girl opened her eyes awestruck to discover that her mother seemed more fantasy than her spectral flight.

Dreams flowed through her with progressive fury. Looking at another dawn over the Sangre de Cristos, or gazing toward the Jemez Mountains coppered by sundown, she dismissed the temptation to confide in anyone. Who would understand these night visions that caused her to mistrust if she ever really slept? Who would believe she sometimes knew in the morning what afternoon would bring? That this year's frijoles would grow under generous rain, while next year's crop would fail? That a cousin living near Santo Domingo was pregnant with twin girls who would survive the hour of their birth even as their mother perished? Francisca herself scarcely believed the things she saw.

All the while, the waking world of mother and father and brothers who'd been christened with good adamant names out of the Bible—Mateo, Santo, Teofilo, Pedro—moved on. Mateo, born scrawny, became a strapping buck. Santo had long sable hair and an eye for the women. Hardworking Teofilo wore a bright-red kerchief tied around his head beneath his hat. Pedro, who lived in the kitchen, grew round as an armadillo. These brothers matured, as did the ranch. More sheep and cattle in the pastures, more horses. The orchards flourished. Her father took a fall off his favorite stallion and walked forever after with a proud limp. Estrella's gray eyes got grayer, and her hair went white. Crops were sown, harvested, cellared, eaten. Seasons migrated like sandhill cranes.

While she never ventured off the place other than to make the wagon ride across the gritty, shadeless trail to La Villa Real de la Santa Fé to attend mass at San Miguel, Francisca found that she could journey across centuries and converse with people in many languages. She met saints and rogues and angels who reminded her of the brilliant painted reredos at the cathedral. She met harlots in beaverskin and virgins white as the snow-crowned Truchas. She walked beside blessed Bernardo Abeyta and caravaned with whimsical Santo Niño. She was the very penitente carved from orangewood and balsam whom they crucified as El Cristo Negro of Esquípulas. She became the stuff of myth, a question whose answer was another question. Had she not loved being awake and alive, she'd have thought how wonderful it would be to sleep and dream always. As nights glided into days, days into nights, it became harder for her to tell the difference anyway.

Francisca never married, proved herself to be alone among the de Peña children capable of running the ranch after the deaths of her parents. She outlived them all, each of those brothers with their saintly names. Under her aegis, Rancho de Peña continued to thrive. A grand hacienda was built on the rise overlooking the ranchlands, replacing the small adobe fieldhouse beside the river. Every stretch of earth was put to use. Her vines bore the richest fruits, her fields the best produce. No one had finer livestock or better-trained horses. The first guitar in Nambé pueblo was heard under the *portal* of the new hacienda, strummed by none other than Francisca herself. Dances were held, both secular and sacred, hoedown and corn dance. For a time, her world was a desert utopia.

Then the day arrived, 9 February 1880, when Francisca de Peña left her flesh behind. She was cremated—a sinful annihilation in those times, but enacted on her strict instructions—by the man to whom she'd willed the de Peña holdings, a man for years rumored to be her lover, certainly her dearest friend, and the sole person with whom she shared her *bruja*'s secret.

Juliar Montoya built Francisca's bier along the stony shoal of Rio Nambé, near the fieldhouse that fronted her favorite pasture. A snowy morning. Crows cawed overhead. Cottonwoods, some of whose recalcitrant leaves had failed to fall, rattled above as the wind gusted through. Pellets of ice hissed when they struck the fiery coals. Montoya did his work alone, watching over the fire while her legs and arms burned and curled and her beloved face flamed, blackened, collapsed, and her bones pushed forth from the searing skin that once hid her heart but did no more. Having blazed throughout the long dank day, fed with cedar branches and lengths of poplar, the fire finally smoked down to char, and Montoya broadcast with a shovel her glittering ashes in that field her feet had known so well. Blinding benevolent snow soon enough buried Francisca's remains, and as it continued to fall in thick waves it whitened the terrain, softening everything visible so that the world momentarily forgot itself. Montoya shouldered his shovel and walked back up to the main house. As long as he lived, he would never forget the sweet perfume of that funeral fire.

Journeying on in her vivid dream, Francisca kept mostly to herself. She walked barefoot the dry pebbly bed of Rio Nambé in autumn and smelled the sage that bloomed alongside it in spring. Sometimes, when the moon was new, she lay in bed beside Montoya, wrapping her arms around him after he'd fallen asleep. She admired the way he carried on the work she had begun. Itinerant workers who drifted onto the ranch were treated as confreres. A fair wage was given for a fair day's work. And Montoya, who deplored peonage—Indian slavery practiced by local friars—took in refugees even as he managed to avoid trouble with militia and traders who passed through on their way between the Taos and Chihuahua markets.

After Nambé reservation was established, the old de Peña ranch, along with others—Ortiz, Garduno, Sena, the precious ditches still bear their names today—became islanded within its borders. Of all the Tewa pueblos, Nambé would prove to be the most peaceful and the poorest. Seasons ascended over the valley and veered away. There were dry years and wet ones. The wind blew, and then came days when the air was so still fans could not push it along. There were sick animals and those it seemed nothing could kill. Violent men ranged at every periphery, and some who were less violent, and a rare few who weren't. All the while, Nambé watched the mountains abide and monumental clouds wheel above their summits.

At the center of all this passage was Francisca. Her nephews and nieces—Mateo's children; Santo's—departed the valley to seek their fortunes elsewhere, the boys having felt slighted by Montoya's inheritance which they thought might better have been their own, the girls marrying into other families in Yuma and up in Gunnison. They never accused Juliar Montoya of stinginess. He offered them a stake in the land, on the condition that they work together with him and share. None of the nephews was ever seen again, though the girls sometimes sent a letter.

Montoya married a gaunt handsome woman from Oklahoma, had children, and died one year shy of the start of the twentieth century. Francisca was saddened that on his death he didn't join her in the fieldhouse, but she understood her dream was not his. He was buried in Chimayó, three hours' walk northeast of Rancho de Peña. Every year following his death, his widow, Emily, made the Good Friday pilgrimage to the santuario there. Even in the last year of her life she dug sacred healing dirt from the posito in the mission, then anointed herself and her children with it in the hope it would cure them of illness that loomed about the valley.

Emily Montoya succumbed in 1918 to the Spanish influenza, the same plague that took all of Montoya's children but one, a kid named Gil, who had in 1895 been born with a clubfoot but was otherwise healthy, an able rider and hardworking rancher. Gil always fancied horses and kept them on the spread not only for traditional work beneath a rider or before a plow, but for breeding. He married, had two children. The elder, Carl, was his particular pride, but Delfino was well loved, too. Carl and Delfino stayed on the ranch working for their father—though Delf, never very prudent, would in later years move south to Tularosa to homestead some of the most broiling, bony, difficult acres anywhere in the desert West. As these generations went about their routines, Montoya's land changed little beyond its slow conversion from subsistence ranching of the old days to horse ranching.

Coyote fences were woven and laid up along the boundaries of their property. Paddocks were built. A new barn was erected, bigger than the last, then a newer one was raised after lightning set the other afire. Irrigation ditches were dug and redug, cleaned and recleaned. Spillways were rebuilt, sluice gates refitted. The tawny land went white in winter and greened again in spring when big

Navajo willows brightened like lime explosions among the leafing elms and box elders. Naked cuestas and hogbacks and spires out toward Chupadero were resculpted with magnificent delicacy by the slow hand of weather.

The visions that followed Francisca in her continuous dream were so richly whole as to make her unaware of time's presence. One thing she missed, however, was the raw tactility of her former waking life. She never bruised or bled now. Drought didn't make her thirsty. Winter frost failed to chill her. She walked the fields unable to feel the sharp stalks of corn or bulbs of purple garlic. Raindrops in their hurry to reach the ground passed through her body. Amazed, she would extend her arm and watch the drizzle penetrate her palm as if she were not there at all. How she wished she could feel the holy clay of Chimayó, its grainy coolness. But over time she learned not to wish for more than flight and fragrances and the remembrance of touch.

Doubt is a ghost's most dangerous adversary. Hoping she was somehow not a ghost had kept her going, but after decades gathered themselves and fell behind the arc of the new century, even Doña Francisca de Peña began to wane. Lately, daybreak exhausted her, and she crouched in shadowy corners of the crumbling fieldhouse, wondering if a dreamer could dream within her dreams other dreams. She began to venture more often into the murky world of doubt, only to return feeling worn down, bereft as some cleric who had lost his calling. She told herself that this unfinished presence, this separating spirit that seemed the furtherance of a life led, was probably some fond but spurious dream that one small part of her heart had wished into being, even though it lay as dust on the ground. Could it be that a single speck of her waking or dreaming self had simply refused to die and, as a result, was now caught in a fantasy? That she had misunderstood her death, and all this was a prophecy of a future that hadn't come to pass?

There really were signs she was wasting away. Sometimes she forgot how to ascend the veiled staircase of air. How to smell or see. Sometimes she had to work to convince herself she was the same woman, animated and full of opinions about everything, just as she always had been when this land was hers, and the name Doña Francisca of Nambé carried a weight of authority and respect throughout the valley and outlying lands.

It wasn't until this boy saw her, this boy christened Mark but nicknamed Marcos by those who worked on the horse ranch—Rancho Pajarito, they called it now—that she began to believe in herself again. She'd wandered these fields for so long that she hadn't noticed that no one noticed her after Juliar Montoya cast her ashes here, in the century before the advent of electric power and telephone lines and cellular towers, before cars ferried people in from and out to the highway where the school building had been converted into a shining sad new Indian casino down at the junction of the roads to Santa Fe, Los Alamos, Taos, and Chimayó village.

With a look of terror and skepticism tailored by reverence in his squinting eyes, Carl's son, Marcos, confirmed for her the prospect that she was there, a figure, a shape, a vision in someone else's mind, not just the spectral issue of her own weird genius. The question was, how could she express the gratitude she felt without frightening off her only witness?

A quiver of excitement stirred the air around her. Marcos, then thirteen, reminded her of her father, Trinidad: strong, rangy, carven-faced, shy yet with a stubborn cast in those midnight-blue eyes. Like her father, he bore a scar on his left forearm. Even as the boy was shocked to see her floating above the field, he wore the same determined frown of Francisca's father.

Marcos's mind was racing, What the hell?

Reaching out toward him, head tipped, she gestured, beckoning him to understand that she was the same deliberately tenacious woman as ever, possessed of the same hardness as the earth beneath them. She tried to tell him that though time had worn her down a little, and that she'd been roughened by its voluptuous desolation, she *was*—she was, she existed. How else could she extend her arm and open her fingers like this?

Marcos stared.

Heavy wind rolled slow over the desert past Tesuque, down what used to be Kit Carson Highway, past Cities of Gold casino whose name chides Coronado even as its gamblers pantomime his weakness, up the reservation road past Pojoaque cemetery where a fresh grave was decorated with pink plastic carnations and a wooden crucifix painted white. It meandered, this wind, along those same lands where Old World conquerors came, brutal Don Juan de Oñate in 1605, Don Diego de Vargas who retook the pueblos after the Indian rebellion at the end of the seventeenth century, alongside hundreds of other souls whose names were also scratched into Inscription Rock but who are now known only as icons, as words, letters, flourishes of the nearly forgotten. It meandered where explorers had worked their way into these domains and, circling as wind and humans and history will do, it blew over barrancas and came down into this valley and rushed right through her. The cottonwood leaves rustled on their numb winter limbs. This was the end of February 1981, the evening when Marcos first saw Francisca. She'd lost her sense of smell but keenly remembered the perfume of greasewood, of piñon smoke and grayblue juniper berries crushed between her fingers, the smell of rainripe droppings left by animals domestic and savage. She knew she couldn't touch the amber bark of the cottonwoods that smelled like vanilla on hot summer days, but drew in breath—air breathing air—and ran her hand over the trunk of the great tree if only to show him she could, prove to him she was more than some desert draft.

She tried to speak, a wispy *gracías,* but intuited by the way his jaw tightened and his cheekbones knobbed out, and his mouth twisted into a scowl of confusion, that he couldn't hear her. Or didn't understand. Stubborn as ever, Francisca tried to tell him stories about all the freedoms she enjoyed. Told him that, being lighter than pollen, she could balance herself on the anther of a desert hollyhock. And on the tip of her finger, at that. Told him how she could swim up the heartwood center trunk of any of these trees, counting its rings as she went, then pass the rest of the night listening to an embryo's heart beat in a hawk egg high in its branches, without ever disturbing the nesting mother.

The kid didn't move. —Christ on a crutch, he said.

She tried to tell him that on starless nights she'd retraced the same steps she'd taken over the many years, along the *portal* hung with liver-red ristras, past the room he now occupied, on whose wooden door sprays of myrtle were nailed to ward off spirits—a talisman that had no effect on her one way or the other.

Hadn't he noticed her before? the vapor breathed.

No answer.

Yes, she continued, drifting closer, flowing like sketchy mist off dry ice. She'd been here all along.

Marcos shook his head, closed his eyes and opened them looking away from the apparition. Clapping the fresh-fallen snow off the sleeves of his canvas barn jacket, he smacked his lips in disgust, hiked up the long rise to the house, ridiculing himself for being just plain out of his fricking gourd.

He thought no more about it the rest of that winter and on through the spring. There was work to do and he didn't need this crazy bullshit cramping his style. Besides, if he said anything his father would laugh him right off the ranch.

The second time Marcos caught sight of her was on a warm June night, the year after that first encounter. New moon, ebony sky, stars arrayed like pulverized crystal on black velvet. Stillness but for the genial hubbub of scuttling stone in the riverbed. The horses slept standing in their stalls. His father had asked him to check on a mare who was late to foal. Striding briskly down the cindered aisle of the wide barn, he heard nesting birds shuffling in the eaves. The mare stood in her fullness, not yet ready to drop. Nothing to do but wait, he knew. Sliding the stall door shut, he set out to kill some time by tramping over to Conchas Park to spy on the *vatos,* the lowriders from Chimayó who hung out half a mile east of Rancho Pajarito.

He walked up the pebbly road that paralleled the riverbank, listening to the voices in the water with the drowsy sense that if he were fluent in their language he might be able to understand what they uttered. His feet knew the path as he loped along, dropping his head now and again to duck some low-slung branches of scraggly riverside trees. Hands thrust deep into his pockets, he looked over at the austere creek whose pocked face dully sparkled. His jeans were loose, clenched by a rawhide belt with a worn silver buckle. His T-shirt was black.

This was his favorite dangerous game. He knew that if they caught him snooping, they would try to chase him down and beat him up. The rumor was some guy from Las Trampas who'd come down to the valley on a lark had gotten himself knifed for trying to join their party uninvited. Marcos had no rational right to be watching the *vatos,* but that was why he found them such an irresistible spectacle.

Not that they did much. Built a driftwood bonfire in their forsaken park and drank cervezas, maybe blew some horse, bragged and prattled in Spanglish. Their women—mallbang coifs teased up above their foreheads like turkey fans—sat in their sleek finned cars listening to the radio while they knocked some back, snorted and smoked, drifting through the slow ritual of a weekend bender. For his part, Marcos hid in undergrowth on the shadowy shore opposite and gazed and eavesdropped. Had the night been starless he would have shimmied out over Rio Nambé on a fallen tree trunk to sit astraddle and smoke a butt, concealing the tangerine fire in the bowl of his hand. He could while away hours here and often did.

So it was nothing unusual for him to be ambling back home late along this stark stretch of road, as he was doing on the night Marcos again glimpsed the figure in the field. Intending to check on the mare once more before going to bed, he unlatched the aluminum gates which gave a slight clatter. Glancing across the corral to the right, down at the far margin of the meadow, he saw it—or, her—an insinuation of whiteness in the window of the deserted adobe.

His shoulder quaked. He winced and the quietest cry came out of him, a muffled yelp. Whiteness first, then a kind of blue, he saw, a pallid bluish white like watered-down skim milk, indistinct, at first stationary. After several incalculable moments the light moved more quickly than he might have thought possible. How he knew the figure was a woman he would not be able to say. She glided over the ground as a skein of light illuminated from within, a demure storm cloud, away from then back toward the ruined fieldhouse. Marcos stared breathless, seized less by fear than a kind of wishful skepticism, a hope that what was happening here wasn't in fact happening. Without turning her head—for she did now have features, deep gray eyes, purling plaited hair, a magisterial, even haughty mouth, and on her face a look of abstracted curiosity—she again shifted direction to confront him, began deliberately to cross the pasture toward the oval-mouthed boy. She was as close as his trembling, outstretched palms when he stumbled back against the rattling metal paddock gate and her light frayed, faded, and vanished.

As before, Marcos told no one. After a month of walking down to that lower pasture at the same time every night to find himself saying ridiculous, insipid things like, —I'm here, or, —You can come out now, he himself began to question what he had twice seen. Even though Francisca de Peña was there, moving slowly around him, hovering before him, passing through him, she failed to make her presence known.

That mare, named Dolores, foaled finally, and her filly grew and foaled as well in the ensuing years. Having graduated from Los Alamos High, Marcos worked full-time now at the ranch. He broke new tenant horses in the day and in the evening drove to Tesuque for beer and spiced fries with friends. His bedroom wall was covered with blue and red ribbons, proving his rise through the competitive ranks as a horseman. Although a boy no more, he was unable, however, to erase from his thoughts the apparition in the field.

There had to be a logical explanation for his unworldly vision. Will-o'-the-wisp, he'd heard about such occurrences. Haze from the river. A dewcloud. Both times when he'd seen his apparition it had been the middle of the night. He had been tired, burned out. Before that last occasion he'd snuck a shot of tequila from his father's liquor case. That explained it. Still, Marcos stopped putting the better studhorses out in the lower paddocks. He didn't want to think about it anymore. Whole thing never happened. He'd long since lost interest in spying on the *vatos,* so why bother with this ghost? Kid stuff, he scolded himself. Goddamn it, grow up, man.

*O*ver in McKinley County, a young woman named Mary grew up with her sister and two brothers in a modest, tin-roofed battenboard house that overlooked dusty Gallup from the northern bluffs. Both her parents worked in town, her mother part-time at the post office and father for the utility company. Mary ran away from home when she was seventeen. Not knowing anyone beyond Gallup, adrift on a dream of making it big in Hollywood, she hitched to Albuquerque, since that's where the airport was.

Mary lived near Old Town for a while on the savings she had secretly amassed back home but, scared, couldn't bring herself to board a plane for California. For one, she had little money and didn't want to wind up on the Walk of Fame with all the other runaways, scraping a buck any way she could. Stalled and broke, she went to Santa Fe where she heard there was a waitressing job on the plaza. She enrolled in acting classes at night and found she did have a flair for improvisation and creating theater roles. The idea was that maybe after a year, two at the outside, she'd have enough money to leave New Mexico on her own terms.

Being shy, she was liked by her fellow employees and the boss but made few friends. This was fine with Mary, since friends are by definition people who know things about you. Under the assumed name of Franny Johnson—*Franny* being the character from a book by her favorite writer and *Johnson* lifted from another restaurant—she rented a small bungalow apartment in northwestern Santa Fe. At night she could hear the eighteen-wheelers headed toward Taos, or south, in the opposite direction. The eloquent music of these trucks put her in mind of a beautiful river even though the very place she'd escaped from was bisected by a highway whose perpetual traffic nearly drove her mad. Here, though poor as the proverbial church mouse, she relished her newfound independence. When she decided to grow her hair long, she did. When she decided to highlight it with streaks of orange and indigo, she did. When she got tired of all that, she dyed it back to dark blond. No one laughed at her ambition of becoming an actress because, fellow workshop hopefuls aside, no one knew.

Franny turned nineteen before finally writing her parents she was fine, not to worry. She took a bus to Denver to mail this letter, believing the postmark would help foil any attempt to track her. The ride back down the front range was strangely gloomy. She understood, gazing at the disinterested landscape out the window, just how alone she truly was. This small epiphany made her want to cling all the more to her ambition—a girlhood dream launched in darkened theaters, crystallizing when she first waited tables at Gallup's most famous hotel, El Rancho, where every star who'd ever shot a western dined back in the heyday of black-and-white Hollywood—but progress was slow. She lived a spartan life, but still the money didn't pile up the way she'd hoped. What was more, Franny had grown to enjoy the role of an incognita.

Marcos met her at the downtown restaurant where she worked the counter. He'd come to run some errands for his mother, Sarah, niggling little nothing errands she used to get him off the ranch.

—Boy's going to die a bachelor, she said at breakfast.

—I'm not a boy.

—Just my point.

Though Marcos, twenty-five now, had circled through liaisons with a couple of women he'd met on the show circuit—easy-in, easy-out affairs—he couldn't fairly contradict her. He dropped into Franny's diner because it happened to be next door to the bootery where he'd done the last of his grunts, as he called them. And, too, because he had noticed a waitress here the last time he was in town.

He ordered pecan pie and sugared coffee after coffee while watching her. Thin, even skinny, Franny moved with the fluid gestures of a dancer. Her lips were drawn into a benign pout, her nose and prominent cheeks were mildly freckled. She had rings on most of her fingers. Azure, her eyes were filled with light around the irises and rimmed by a fine line of black—eyes that reminded him of exquisite markings he'd seen on butterflies, so perfect as to seem counterfeit. Over the course of an hour he found himself infatuated.

—You keep drinking all that coffee and eating all that sugar, you'll be able to float home, she said when Marcos ordered yet another piece of pie.

He laughed. —Franny's a curious name, he said, reading her embroidered blouse.

—What name isn't?

—Marcos, for one.

—Unless you live in Paris.

—There must be plenty of Marcoses in Paris, Texas.

Small talk, but it went on for an hour beyond Franny's shift, the two having left to stroll around the plaza. Marcos surprised himself by inviting her out to Nambé, and she surprised herself by accepting. He offered Franny a ride home, and though she declined—she didn't want him to see where she lived, her room outfitted with a plywood-on-cinderblock bed, a wobbly pine table and chair, a tarnished mirror edged with masking tape, and little more—she shook his hand as if they'd been friends for years.

Next Saturday afternoon he picked her up in front of the Palace of the Governors. The day was gusty and promised rain. As they drove up out of Santa Fe valley toward the pueblolands to the north, Marcos asked Franny to tell him more about herself, where she came from, what she wanted to do one day. And Franny obliged him with all the ingenuities Mary could convene.

She felt no guilt over telling deceptive stories, having had good reason to fabricate Franny, just as her father had his for not pressing Gallup authorities to search for his runaway daughter. She'd been legally of age, almost. Let her go if that's her game, was his philosophy. He'd had enough of their battles, enough of trying to discipline his daughter. God bless and good riddance. Mary could almost hear him intoning to wife, children, any neighbor who would listen, —She had her eye on the horizon from day one, but she'll find out the hard way, and when she does, she can come limping back home to see whether the door's open or locked.

Well, she thought, he could keep his door and the prison that went with it.

—I was an only daughter, she lied to Marcos. Brought up by her mother, since her father was a career military man who spent years at a time on duty overseas. Served in the Gulf War. Her mother was some kind of mathematician at Princeton, an important one, so far as mathematicians could be important.

—They can, believe me. Marcos nodded his head toward the mountains where Los Alamos sparkled in the buttes beneath Redondo. —My mother knows a few of them up there on the Hill who've had a hand in changing the way the world works. Where's your father stationed now?

—He died.

—I'm sorry, Marcos said as they drove past Camel Rock. Out the window he could see it was storming over Quemazón and Caballo to the north. Broom rain fell at an angle from a blueblack thunderhead. —Typical New Mexico weather, clouded on one horizon and sunny on the other.

The death of her father, she did admit, seemed weirdly abstract to her, like a series of numbers and symbols in one of her mother's books, because she hardly knew the man, given his perennial absence. Marcos hadn't asked, but she told him he'd gone down in a transport somewhere in Africa. Mozambique, maybe. News about it had been suppressed from the inside so that the media wouldn't get involved. She ventured that it was likely he hadn't heard about any of this, and he agreed he had not. Franny gave a melodious downward sigh and went on to say she hadn't made up her mind what she wanted to do with her life. Growing up as she had in an academic environment, she decided to kick around some before going to college, and her mother consented.

—That's surprising.

In a cautious voice, —Not everybody knows what they want to do with the rest of their lives.

—That's not what I meant.

Mary sensed Franny had slipped so remained silent, noting for the first time Marcos's hands which lay casually atop the steering wheel as if slumbering one on the other like awkward yet comfortable creatures, callused and crosshatched with old scars and fresh nicks. Aged hands for one so young.

—I meant, isn't it unusual for a mother who's a teacher—

—Professor, she managed inconspicuously.

—not to make her daughter stay in school?

Should she say, My mother doesn't make me do anything I don't want to do? Instead she considered questioning him about Pajarito, his own apparent choice, or nonchoice, to stay home on the ranch, but again thought better of it. —My mother's unusual that way.

—You're lucky.

While Mary admired both the irony and truth of the idea, Franny said, —I guess. She then waved her hand, as if swatting away from her face something visible only to her, before continuing. So here she was in Santa Fe. Once she saved enough money, she told Marcos, she planned on traveling overseas somewhere. No maps, no destination. Patagonia, Malaysia, Timbuktu. Elsewhere, anywhere elsewhere, all the elsewheres she could find. She made no mention of the framed, autographed images of movie stars back at El Rancho that had inspired her toward Tinseltown, not Capetown, as she suffered the premonition she would come off shallow. Which naturally caused her to wonder whether it wasn't just that. Shallow, hollow. Change the subject, now. —And what about you?

Already the Jemez rain had ceased and the massive banks of clouds were silvering, while still others rearranged themselves up over Cerros del Abrigo and down along the Dome Wilderness. Even when Einstein lived in Princeton, she thought, the skies probably never put on shows like this. Should she say as much? No, be quiet.

Marcos discovered Franny hadn't ever ridden a horse only after he'd saddled a pair and brought them out into a paddock. —I've always been afraid of them, she confessed, but she was willing to learn that very day, and more or less began to do just that. She knew nothing of life on a breeding ranch, though it did remind her of some film she'd seen, Gable and Monroe? The weekend following, Marcos drove her up to a ranch in Abiquiu, to watch him and a veterinarian get a semen collection out of one of his three-year-old Arabians. Strange idea for a second date, she thought, but why not. Marcos admired how she behaved as the two of them did their violent chore, calmly observing as they shouted and shoved the struggling horse into place where he mounted an artificial mare. Once the job was done, they gathered in the small lab adjacent to the collection barn. With a pipette they dotted a specimen on a thin glass slide, turned on the phase-contrast microscope, and adjusted its focusing knob. After the vet said he was pleased by the frenzied spermatozoa he saw in the bright-green field, Marcos took a look, then turned to Franny with an open smile.

—Want to see? Progressive motility makes the world go round.

—Progressive?

—Means they're swimming forward.

—Sometimes they swim backwards?

—Like everything else on this crazy planet.

Mary was aware that her doppelgänger, Franny, was freer than she herself had ever been and seemed possessed of a bona fide boldness, an ability to embrace things around her. Mary envied this a little, though Franny was willing to share. As time passed, however, Mary became more vigilant because she understood that she and Franny were breaking a cardinal rule: Marcos was becoming Franny's friend. Not in the plan. There were no contingencies for such a development, so the closer Marcos got to Franny, the further Mary felt she must recede.

Abundant invented stories were woven by Mary into this evolving Franny, and Mary believed them even as she spun them quicker than a spider, so that remembering what she'd said at first presented her with no problem. Sometimes, in bed, listening to her sham river out the window, Mary worried she was falling for Marcos. Or that Franny was. Another voice would point out that the more of a life she built here, the more Gallup could become a faraway mirage, reflecting only itself over a domain of broken mirrors. Whenever Mary grew troubled, Franny reassured her. And when Franny became distressed, Mary would breathe slowly and deeply, as she'd taught herself to do those nights when her father came into her room, after her sister, Rose, had fallen asleep, to apologize for having smacked her over this or that quarrel.

—Let's forget about it, all right? he would whisper into the burning ear of his mute daughter, a confident hand stroking her cold forehead.

She did not want to get involved with Marcos, however sane and normal such a thing might be, but Marcos, after Franny's half dozen visits to Nambé, asked if he could kiss her.

—Maybe that's not such a great idea, she said, both charmed by his old-fashioned backwardness and perplexed by her own terror. She ran her eye down his profile as he looked away. The brown hair that spilled over the sheer straight cliff of his forehead was beautiful, she thought. His sunburned nose and long lean cheeks and brown lips drawn taut, beautiful as any she'd ever seen. She never met a more western westerner. —Look, it's not you. I'm overly wary. We'll see, all right? *All right,* echoing her father.

Marcos nodded, and Franny thanked him, though she did have to wonder why Mary was afraid of such a natural proposition. That is, until she calculated once more the fact that propositions were for mathematicians, not for impostors on the lam. Especially impostors who aspired to careers of make-believe.

*F*rancisca's mother was calling to her. She remembered not only the affectionate nickname but the timbre of that voice, the lightly trilling *para* of *esparaván,* the waveringly weak final syllable *ván* that modulated the word into a question.

—Francisca, *esparaván?*

That one voice was joined by others, voices Francisca de Peña could not so easily recognize. Women, children, men, the utterances of wind animals. These wild fugal cries came and went in waves, and the more often they disturbed the shade of her vacant fieldhouse, the more fearful she became, she who hadn't really known anything of fear for the longest time. She understood why she was afraid, and this fear of what was so obvious and necessary made her disgusted with herself, made her say, *Unspeakable,* made her say, *Execrable y no sembrado.* Yet the dying seed was sown.

The ghost Francisca spent nights and days in her adobe prison. Sometimes, nodding off toward nothingness, she found that she had unintentionally drifted through the mud walls and out into the pasture, or floated through the coyote fence toward the riverbank. She would come to as if slapped by hard cold water, dazedly reorient herself, then return to the fieldhouse more confused than ever. She'd lost almost all interest in the lives of those who came and went into and out of the hacienda. Her ability to distinguish colors and shapes was failing. What she saw was parallax and dim. She couldn't even remember her mother's name. Strella, Stella? And her father? Where was he? Who had he become?

But she did recognize the boy Marcos, and Marcos recognized her that third and final time he would ever see her, or at least know with certainty he was seeing her.

Months, superb tiny whiskers of time, had elapsed. Franny joined a regional theater company and finally confessed to Marcos her acting aspirations. After he gamely sat through a pretty long performance of one of Shakespeare's plays—he counted more people on-stage than in the audience—they kissed in the parking lot, then kissed again the next night and the next. Mary telephoned her mother to let her know she was still in Denver and all was well. She couldn't bear to hear the tearful pleas that she come home and so hung up, feeling for all the world like some thankless monster, but promising herself never to call again. Marcos's parents slowly became surrogates, flesh-and-blood variations on her imagined ideal of what parents might be in a perfect Mary world. Carl's gruff taciturnity. Sarah's ease with anyone and everything. Even the dogs sleeping on the *portal,* the doves in their cages, the horses in their pastures, seemed faultless. Rancho Pajarito carried all the weight of what home might have meant, had fate launched a kinder stork on the day of her birth.

And Marcos, the Marcos of this third encounter with Francisca de Peña, took Franny on a midnight ramble along Rio Nambé to show her a thing he used to do when he was a kid. Hand in hand they walked toward Conchas to see if the *vatos* were partying. That they weren't didn't bother her. She liked to be here with him. To feel her life being lived near his.

—Oh well, he said. —Probably isn't the kind of thing I should be admitting I used to do, anyhow. Not what somebody from Princeton would understand.

—I'm sure it was fun back then.

—Lonely rural kind of fun.

Under heavy starlight, not talking further, straying back to the house along the bank path, their thoughts wandering, they came to the horse gate, and Marcos opened it as he'd opened it a thousand times already in his life, by rote, his thoughts concentrated on the palm of his hand warmed by hers. Gate metal scraped against the earth and the chain clanged. The flume behind them was running high and the moon was just the finest sliver of white where it sat on the saddle ridge near Capulin. The aluminum latch chimed its colloquial hollow note into the cool night. Mary sensed a sudden change in Marcos and asked what was wrong. He was staring into the lower meadow.

Francisca de Peña had drifted into the field where she lay curled like a magpie nest made of long and waning sparks, or some soiled halo unevenly afloat. This light awakened and uncoiled to disclose itself and thus became more a woman than that spherical luster very near to where Marcos and Franny stood. Francisca arose to what complete luminosity and elevation were left her and spoke her own name. She uttered *de Peña,* herself calling out to herselves.

Marcos and Franny stood silent.

She spoke other names—saying, as her mother had so often said, *Esparaván*—and moved slowly closer. Moved slowly because she found that, at least by her impression, she had no other choice than to thread herself ponderous through the Nambé air. *Esparaván? Gavilán?*

Marcos asked Franny, —Are you seeing this?

She wouldn't, or couldn't, answer.

Francisca neared them and could almost taste their fear.

—Franny? Do you see this?

Together they stood as Francisca hesitated midfield. She gazed at that whisper of moon, and she admired her familiar mountains and this oddly familiar boy. And as Marcos and his unknown girl saw her fully forming, unfurling like a chrysanthemum of mist, looking much as she had when she was as alive as anyone who ever walked these lands—she who presented herself to them as a kind of soft photographic negative, clearly and with all the dignity of life—Francisca de Peña heard Franny finally say to Marcos, —Yes. Yes, I do.

PART II

CRITICAL MASS

Chimayó, New York, Gallup, Tularosa

to Nambé

1944–1996

Here sat a man whose worn leather jacket was the same shade as his drawn, haggard face. Holding a midnight-blue cap in spidery hands, he shifted his frail frame against a ditchside weeping willow whose budding leaves whispered on their swaying fronds. His wide-set eyes were jaundiced yet full of life. His dusty shoes might have been mistaken for stones had they not been attached to his long legs. It was Good Friday, 1993, and throngs of pilgrims gathered at the holy mission in Chimayó, none noticing him or the man by his side when Kip Calder gazed hard at his childhood friend and said, "I am Ariel's father, aren't I."

Should have been as simple to answer as it was fair to ask. Yet Brice McCarthy hesitated, sensing his life was somehow falling out of its precarious balance. "I answered that question over twenty-five years ago, Kip. The answer is the same now as it was then. I wish you'd believed me. You might have spared yourself a lot of useless pain. Assuming you have suffered because of it."

"Assuming I have suffered . . ."

"You were wrong not to believe me."

"It's true," he said, which again disarmed his friend. "But does she know about me? is what I'm asking. Does she know who her father was—is, I mean."

She did not. She had grown up in the dark, kept there as much by

Kip as Brice and her mother, Jessica Rankin, the woman both men had loved. Wasn't it time to tell Ariel of her tangled heritage?

After securing Brice's pledge, Kip pulled a bound ledgerbook from a leather satchel that lay beside him on the grass. "Something I'd like for Ariel to have, if you might see fit to give it to her," and handed it to him, along with a tattered envelope. Brice placed them on his lap as the sun lowered itself slowly behind the tawny notch and hills that rimmed this valley, one hard ray illuminating his friend's drawn face. He asked, as delicately as he could, about his failing health.

War, Kip said, was the cause. He'd been poisoned by yellow rain—poor man's atom bomb, they called it—that the Communists had dropped over the mountains of Laos. Not unlike the black rain that drizzled on Hiroshima in the aftermath of the bomb their own fathers helped create. "It comes in other colors: blue rain, red rain, white rain, black rain, too, a colorful rainbow of venom. . . . You begin to bleed, from your nose and mouth and ears. You cry blood. And I'm one of the lucky ones because I didn't get that big a dose of it." Kip described how after the fall of Saigon he stayed behind illegally to help Hmong refugees flee the Pathet Lao by escaping into northern Thailand. Far up in the highlands, he was visiting a thatched encampment filled with poor farmers and their children when the attack came. Aerial poisoning by choppers. He'd been a peripheral victim and wounded ever since.

Brice said, "I always thought it would be Los Alamos that got us. You remember where we used to play when we were kids? I wonder about some of those canyons, what they buried down there before they knew more about radiation."

"I'm probably sick from that war, too. Who knows. Maybe I'm just worn out and it has nothing to do with rain of any color, just the marathoner coming to his wire a little earlier than others. Strange race where you lose by coming in first."

As the afternoon drew down, these two men who'd been estranged for half their lives told each other about what they had done, where they'd been, what they believed. They talked about

Hill people, as Los Alamos natives called themselves, and others they'd known from college days in New York. With every passing story, the natural rhythms of friendship reemerged, the way a wilted flower pulled from the garden and tossed onto the compost heap will sometimes take root and rebloom.

Brice nodded toward the ledger, though he had already guessed what Kip was passing along to Ariel. His father's Los Alamos notebook. Kip claimed not to have read the thing, saying he couldn't decipher the physics and theoretical stuff—Ariel might not either. But interspersed with the math and science were personal diaries and some ink drawings that would give her the chance to know her third grandfather a little.

"Your father was a good man."

"Both our fathers were."

"Hard for kids to know things like that at the time."

"Hard for us, anyway."

In the envelope was a key to the storage locker where Kip had stowed his parents' possessions after the accident that took their lives. He'd kept up with the bills, he said, but had no idea what was in there anymore. "Anything she wants is hers."

Such were Kip's feeble, freighting gifts that day, offered in the shade of twelve leafing cottonwoods and that willow behind El Santuario de Chimayó. Then the dying wanderer and the family man, who shared so much and terribly little, parted company. Kip, who had refused Brice's offer of help, walked away from the day sicker in spirit than he had expected. Brice felt oddly elated. Years of guilty feelings were about to be lifted off his shoulders by finally confessing to his—their—daughter. He bore his promise to tell Ariel the truth about her paternity like some charmed silver milagro such as those the pilgrims wear for good luck. So he mused as he caught his flight back east.

While Brice would soon enough honor his commitment, others of Kip's hopes would not be fulfilled. Most prominent among these was that he succumb swiftly to his lymphoma, as his illness had been

diagnosed by a Taos doctor. That whatever blossomed so badly inside
him might cause his unholy soul to rise into an awaiting purgatory,
where it might lodge with the souls of all the men he killed in Vietnam and of those who had participated in the preparation of his
own long death by inhalation of trichothecene mycotoxin in Laos.
Though he didn't die promptly in the aftermath of his reunion with
Brice, he did make a covenant with himself not to seek medical help.
Not to go back home to the Hill where he might still know a few people in the frayed contrail of his warred-out life. Vietnam and Laos,
Hiroshima and Nagasaki—enough was enough. But this wish he
himself would also inadvertently dash.

Midnight after Easter. Kip found himself alone, still in the village
of Chimayó, having spent Saturday and through the night into Sunday with straggling believers, some high on the spirit of the Lord,
others on wine or weed, whatever was passed around. He had wandered through Resurrection Day listening to mariachi hymns and
prayers at the Stations of the Cross, as the crowd in this place of
miracles dwindled.

Time had come for him to leave. But Kip had nowhere to go. The
week before, he'd given away his few possessions and quit the single-
occupancy motel where he'd been living in Rancho de Taos. He'd
told Brice he lived in Chimayó, an innocent ruse to keep him, his
wife, Jessica, and Ariel, too, in the dark regarding his true whereabouts. His longing to see his daughter was perfectly matched by the
strong desire not to. Vanity, was it? Pride? Simple fear, maybe. The
misgivings and conflicted wishes ran deeper within him than he had
the power to fathom.

He owned what was on his back and even that seemed a heavy
burden. Absurd, he thought, to realize he'd made no plan beyond
this encounter. Had he believed he would simply atomize once his
desire had been met? He found a bottle of water one of the walkers
had left behind and drank it. He slept in the park behind the church,
using his leather satchel as a pillow.

Two, three hours before sunrise he began walking in the natural direction his feet carried him, along the crumbly macadam shoulder of the road to Pojoaque. Wanting to avoid anyone else who might be traveling this way, he traipsed along like some fugitive unworthy of pursuit, a hundred paces out in the desert. Putting one foot in front of the other, he paralleled the road, more or less, out of sight and half out of his mind, pushing blindly along toward the finger mesa where he and Brice had been born.

He walked across pueblolands. He crossed wide seco arroyos and breaches in the earth. He climbed with difficulty small hills, grabbing at juniper or outcroppings of stone to hoist himself up over ridges. Lights of distant villages glowed like hallowed clouds, as if their dreaming residents were spinning out auras high over their beds. His head ached and leaden legs pained him. His guts swelled against his ribs and his straining lungs were like two antique bellows whose leather had dried to dust, and now merely whistled and wheezed. His heavy heartbeat made a shushing in his ears that reminded him of an Indonesian sea coruscating over a beach. For a while he crawled. Lay on his side, breathing. Crawled some more. Tried to breathe.

He must have slept if only because he sort of woke up, finding himself curled like some shoveled snake under the wooden porch of a faded turquoise trailer house, the Nambé Smoke Shop, then set out again, more slowly, stumblingly than before, not seeing those few who saw him but left him alone, assuming he was stoned or mad or both. The day passed—rising, nooning, setting—with a weird density and quickness that proposed it never happened. Wind kicked up through that afternoon, chasing the last winter leaves from their branches, driving tumbleweeds across the scape, sequining Kip with elm pennies, catkins, and twigs that caught in his hair and clothes. He'd lost his satchel somewhere along the way.

Next morning, a wan milky sun lifted over the Sangres. Kip might have reached the intersection where the highway connected with the road to Los Alamos had he not instead fallen asleep in somebody's horse stalls in Nambé. Blood, dried to an evocative blotch at the corner of his mouth, caused the woman who found him lying there in hay and dung to cry out.

The few women in the world who might have cared about Kip would have screamed with her had they seen him so annihilated. Instead, two thousand miles away, a serene Ariel Rankin set out for her morning walk from the East Village through Union Square to work. In Chelsea, her mother, Jessica, sat beside a window, thinking about her husband's momentous call from New Mexico, pondering the best way to admit to Ariel what they'd kept hidden for so many years. And many more thousands of miles away, Kip's Vietnamese wife, who had been east of Haiphong just long enough to help get citizenship for her boys, was asleep in Hanoi.

Marcos's mother, Sarah, who came upon this sick vagrant, was neither serene nor meditative nor dreaming, much as she wished she were. She leaned close to his face, presuming he was dead, but saw the pulse in his neck and heard his breathing. He opened his eyes, and again she screamed. Apologizing in a language that seemed like English but was more a dialect of delirium, Kip tried to crawl onto his hands and knees. "What's the matter?" she asked, but he looked at her as if to say he had no idea. They worked together to get him to his provisional feet. Despite his continued efforts to avoid remedy—Kip mouthed apology after apology for trespassing, then collapsed again under himself, knees buckling—he had wandered into a place of refuge. Sarah sturdied him along the barn road to the ranch house, his arm over her shoulder and hers around his back, his slim ribs reminding her of the tines of a pitchfork.

Spent, starving, sore as hell, Kip was possessed of sufficient presence of mind—or a professional spook's habit—to give, when asked in the kitchen where Sarah led him, a name that was both false and yet his own. "William," he said, offering his given name, eyes darting about as he thanked her son for the fresh change of clothes. He demurred at Sarah Montoya's proposal that when he was feeling a bit better, she and Marcos might drive him up to the Hill so that a doctor could look him over at the convalescent center where she worked. He was much obliged to her, he said, and to her husband, Carl Montoya, who sat there straight and tall as winter yucca. He thanked them for offering to put him up—"In a bed, not the barn," said Carl—but would probably pass on the opportunity of visiting the clinic overlooking Acid Canyon, one of the very ravines he and Brice roved back in the fifties, rowdy boys with bottle rockets and homemade wire squirrel traps and a talent for hiding in the caves of North Mesa beyond.

"We'll see how you feel about things tomorrow," said Sarah, looking at his ochred eyes. "Step at a time."

Carl rose from the table. "Meantime, you're alive, so get yourself a bath, for all our damn sakes," he said, with a caballero nonchalance that disconcerted even the wary Calder, whose cup of black darjeeling had begun to bring him around. "See you later. Marcos?"

"Down in a minute."

Kip liked the casual rhythms of the Montoya family and wondered what ironic angel bothered to direct him here. He glanced at his scratched hands and broken fingernails, still filthy though he had washed them. Must stink like a bosque skunk.

"Where you from, Bill?" Marcos sat down, displaying, like his father, an indifference toward the stranger's dishevelment, and asking his question while he read yesterday's *Albuquerque Journal*.

"Originally?"

"Is there any other place a guy can come from but originally?"

"Marcos," Sarah warned from the adjacent pantry.

"That's a pretty good question," Kip answered with a skewed but sincere smile that had the effect of making him look more unwell.

"See?" he told his mother, hoping to hide the fact he didn't quite know what to make of this William. "No offense."

"None taken. Besides, I'm the one who should apologize for crashing your morning. I'll get out of your way as soon as I can."

"You haven't crashed anything and there's no rush."

Marcos studied the stranger's glazed, meaning-filled eyes before returning to his coffee and rustling the paper as if to brush away the need for further talk. Poor dude. Doesn't need to be pushed to get where he's plainly going.

The front-page article was illustrated with murky colored photographs of walkers on the road to Chimayó. They estimated thirty thousand made the pilgrimage to the santuario during Holy Week, from as far away as Grants, Belen, El Rito. A few faithful had even walked from distant Alamogordo, down in the Tularosa basin where Marcos's uncle Delfino lived. Marcos wondered, Don't these people have work to do? and meant to mention this, but Sarah was speaking. More questions.

"You have family around here, William? Is there somebody you'd like me to call?"

"Nobody, no."

"You were over at Chimayó for the services? Lot of people from out of town this time of the year."

"So I saw."

"I was there. Walk every year. I'm not much of a Catholic, but I always feel better for having done it."

Marcos said, "Look, Chimayó was a holy place for the Indians long before Santo Niño knew his halo from a hole in the ground," watching Kip tentatively eat a biscuit, noticing he was missing part of the little finger on his left hand. Old warhorse, he'd clearly seen his share.

"There must be somebody somewhere who's looking for you?" she pressed.

Kip resisted, feigning an amateurish amnesia, shrugging his shoulders and moving his head slowly from left to right. Sarah missed this small spectacle, but Marcos didn't. "He's not sure, I don't think."

"Let William speak for himself."

Marcos quietly got up to leave. Time to help Carl exercise the horses anyway.

"Thanks again," Kip said.

"No problem."

Kip passed the rest of that day sleeping in a guest-room bed, dressed in a pair of Carl's pajamas, having vomited breakfast on his wet legs and feet as he showered in a bath whose walls were lined with festive Mexican tilework. That evening he managed to sit at dinner beneath a hammered-tin chandelier with the Montoya family. He succeeded in keeping himself out of their conversation both as topic and as participant. Sarah tried to engage him once or twice, asking could he use another helping of posole, had he gotten some rest? She mentioned again that she wanted him to consider letting a Los Alamos doctor look him over.

Once more Kip refused, but though he'd begun to contemplate his escape, he started seriously to doubt whether it would be possible. "I'm really feeling much better now," he said, settling on his face as healthy and robust a look as he could manage in the hope it would camouflage his dishonesty.

It didn't. His eyes were tainted as trophy ivory, his face pleated with threadlike wrinkles, his tongue blanched. Kip looked worse after cleaning himself up and napping all day than he had when Sarah first stumbled upon him. He offered to help clear the dishes, but Carl said he had it under control, take it easy. Excusing himself, Kip returned to his room. Alone, he could smell his illness, taste its rot, like an animal licking a festered wound. He removed one shoe, undid a button of his shirt before collapsing onto the bed. All he really wanted was to descend into sleep, and if that sleep were to broaden into the deepest possible sleep, so be it. He whispered into the moist pillow as he writhed.

"Ariel," softly, trying to conjure his daughter's face.

As he drifted away in his skiff of suffering, he could have sworn she was standing beside him here, smiling a prayerful smile while chanting the disannulling ritual *"Los Días de los Muertos"* . . . dreaming in words . . . *"y difuntos y sin espíritu y triste y profundo desolado"* . . . whispering . . . *"y en las altas horas de la noche"* . . . words he heard in Chimayó these past days. Words he'd known since childhood when he listened, hand cupped to his ear at a wall in the old Sundt house where he grew up, as his mother prayed those nights when his physicist father worked late at the lab. Ariel, he thought, and as he looked for her in the swimming imagery of this sea of pain it was as if his mortal soul were being drawn to float free of the bonds of this burning earth and quaking body.

*K*ip's daughter would always remember with crisp clarity the day she was brought in on the secret.

"Ariel," Brice began. "When my father passed away, and your mother and I went out to New Mexico for the funeral? I wonder if you remember what you said when we got back home."

Sitting in her favorite old stuffed chenille chair as sunlight played across the threadbare kilim rug, Ariel confessed she wasn't sure, why? Her wavy chestnut hair, like that of a younger Jessica Rankin, pirouetted in nine directions, and her prominent cheeks were flushed from the April breezes and the hasty walk to Chelsea that weekend morning. When her mother phoned, a tone of urgency edged her voice and Ariel threw on a mishmash of clothes. Secondhand pink cardigan sweater, camouflage cargo pants, a pair of rubber clogs. Truth to tell, she believed she was being summoned to learn that her grandmother McCarthy had died.

"You made a beautiful welcome-home sign and said something I'll never forget. You told me that since I didn't have a father anymore, you'd be my father from then on. It was one of the kindest things anybody ever said to me."

Ariel watched Jessica's hand move across the sofa to take her husband's. Averting her eyes downward, she noticed her mismatched socks. Black and blue. Almost laughed, but the mood in the room did not encourage laughter.

Jessica said, "You know how much we've always loved you."

"I love you, too. Is somebody dying?"

"You remember us telling you about our friend Kip Calder?" Brice's barrister voice descended toward meekness, as if some sorcerer had turned down the volume on the room itself.

"The one who was killed in Vietnam?"

"Well, no, he wasn't killed."

"I remember you talking about him."

Jessica said, "We've tried to figure out how to tell you this for years and years. But there's no way to say it, other than that I was in love with him back in college. He was your father's best friend and we all loved each other—"

"Pretty sixties." Ariel tried to smile, hoping this wasn't going to be what it clearly might.

"He's your natural father. Your biological father."

"What?" She could feel her pulse rise. They sat not looking at one another. Finally Ariel asked, quietly, "You're sure?"

"We're sure," Brice said, watching her with a regard akin to terror. What a lovely young woman she was, with her dark eyes, her eloquent unspeaking lips, her long fingers weaving and unweaving themselves like warp and woof working invisible thread. How rarely over the years had he thought of her as a stepchild. Even now, in this stunningly awkward moment, it seemed inconceivable she wasn't of his flesh. He wondered if telling the truth was everything it was cracked up to be.

"He ran off to the war, disappeared on all of us. In some ways even on himself. Brice and I fell in love after you were born."

"Why are you making this up?"

"Kip is your blood father," Brice said with a finality that sank the room into deepest silence.

"Well." Ariel sighed, staring out at the seminary across the street. The window was open and wind stirred the tulip trees and ailanthus. Some nesting sparrows squabbled. The bell on the knife sharpener's cart rang. "Look, if you held off telling me because you were worried I wouldn't love you anymore, or love you as much, that wasn't a good reason. Or if you thought I couldn't deal with it—"

"There were a thousand reasons."

Jessica added, "None of them good, in retrospect."

"I understand, I think," Ariel said, numb, still disbelieving. "We can handle this, definitely."

As best they could manage, her parents elaborated about Kip. About life a lifetime ago. About how, after his folks had died, he'd volunteered for service at just the same time Brice was becoming more active in the antiwar movement at Columbia—intimates since youth diverging at the crossroads—and had then gone the crazy extra mile into Thailand and Laos. How he'd slipped over the bamboo fence, become an invisible member of a covert paramilitary group known as the Ravens, working with anti-Communist Hmong in the jungle mountains of Long Tieng. About how he'd slipped forever into his own distant abyss, having left behind his pregnant girlfriend. And how Jessica had fallen in love with Brice, and Brice with Jess, who had never withdrawn from the memory of Kip, but had made the decision to move forward into her life.

"Why now?"

Brice told her about meeting with Kip in Chimayó. "He didn't ask for much, just that we tell you about him and give you these," handing her the ledger and envelope.

"Didn't ask for much," she echoed, holding the artifacts in limp hands. Everything was as if in a grainy black-and-white film, at a remove from itself, like life remembered rather than life being lived. "He didn't ask for much, is that what he said?"

"Does it matter?"

She set the ledger, bound in black pebbly cloth, and the soiled envelope on the floor beside her chair. "No, I suppose it doesn't. I never interested him, so why should he suddenly interest me?"

"Because he's not well," Brice said.

"No one is," she responded, though with a voice she recognized as insincerely cold.

Jessica came over to Ariel and lay her hand on her daughter's shoulder. "I hope you can forgive us for not telling you before."

"We'll get through it. He doesn't really exist, does he, at least not in our lives."

Fathering her father. Momming her mother. She could do that, could begin right now by urging them to believe she was fine, better than fine. All shall be well, she found herself thinking, even as she drifted into a temporary parallel universe, not wanting to admit such a cataclysm was happening to her. But look, it was. Ariel shook her head, snapping to. She must have begun to cry given how damp Brice's handkerchief felt in her hand and how worried Jessica's face looked as she helped her daughter drink from this glass of water. She told them she was sorry to be abrupt but she needed to get some air.

"You want one of us to walk with you?"

"I'd rather be by myself for a while."

"You'll be all right?"

Ariel kissed them and left. Ledger under arm and envelope stuck without ceremony in the back pocket of her pants, she walked and walked as one can only in New York, in rich silence framed by squealing brakes, talking pedestrians, nearby sirens, the subway rumbling belowfoot, every kind of noise. She was weeping and not weeping, blindly finding her way along. No matter what, she had to acknowledge that the magical ordinariness of her life had been blown to bits. She bought cigarettes at a kiosk, though she rarely smoked, and kept walking in a daze until she found herself by the boat basin in Central Park. A flash of light reflected off a white toy schooner, a model whose sails had caught a gust that knocked it flat on the surface of the brown pool where it began to swamp. Two small boys, its landlocked captains, argued over what to do. She watched this sinking as if it were the most interesting event she'd ever seen. Sitting on the concrete lip of the basin, she thought of how her past was similarly humbled now, like a silly play boat succumbing to brackish water and fickle wind.

Who did she think she had been up until now? Brice once said, punning on her name, —You're a view from above. An airy spirit.

But from this new vantage, what kind of view had that been, and how free a spirit was she?

Never having had reason to believe otherwise, she'd presumed for all the world that she knew herself, insofar as anybody could know such a thing. Absurd hubris, but the idea had endured through two dozen years. All that was undone by this news. Busted, shattered, despite her assurances otherwise to her parents. Still, lighting yet another cigarette, Ariel remembered fondly the visceral sense of being a little girl sure about this or that. Of knowing she'd been born not far from this very spot. That every night at eight her father would read her to sleep. That her mother would walk her to school until she was old enough to get there by herself. Trusting the basics, the building blocks.

Most of what she'd always believed remained true, though, did it not? The problem was degrees of familiarity fading toward the unknowable. Brice's mother, the religious one in the family, once told her that her name was also that of a desert city in the Book of Isaiah. How could she save the person Ariel from the fate of her namesake city, destroyed millennia ago? Architects know better than to build on uncertain bedrock, but Ariel lacked an architect's skills, never having faced the need before. One clear memory could prove that much—the memory of a sharply determined city kid on an innocent afternoon in deep December, asked along with the other children in her grade-school class to make a faithful rendering of the buildings outside their bedroom windows. She could recall her excitement on that darkening day which threatened the first snowfall of the season, and the glorious dread her teacher stirred in her beating heart with that word *faithful*.

She pictured herself setting out pencils and smoothing flat the sheet of heavy paper on her homework table. Her cat, a Russian blue named Buddha, arched his back on the windowsill, then chattered at the wretched pigeons huddled together, shivering in their shabby feathers on a ledge across the street. She pictured her young face, tongue caught at the corner of her mouth, as she began her drawing of ornate granite pediments, eyes glancing up, focusing, down, refocusing. She couldn't resist adding one of those poor birds, beak tucked into its breast against the storm. Knowing her teacher would disapprove, she remembered adding another, a companion. Then others, pigeons with impromptu feathers and plump breasts, stroked with her quickening pencil. The building started to disappear beneath its growing menagerie of pigeons, but the birds were there, weren't they, clinging to the narrow ledge, part of the personality of the facade? This was faith, wasn't it? A faithful interpretation of the building out her window.

Ironic that just this year she'd had that drawing framed as a reminder of unassuming rebelliousness. Whenever she looked at it hung on her adult wall, she could clearly hear the teacher's chiding voice—she'd been right to assume it wouldn't meet with approval—dismissing the girl's shy if precocious contention that birds gave the sketch relative scale.

What exquisite dissidence, she thought. A quality her parents had always cultivated rather than censured. Something precious she wanted never to lose. Something more useful now than ever.

She resurrected with equal ease Brice's own rebellious nature. For one, his refusal to celebrate Christmas.

—Look at this, calling her over to that same childhood window. —Look at them down there dragging home their dead Christmas trees. It's delusional.

—Delusional, Ariel mugged.

—You know why Santa's suit is red? Because the Coca-Cola advertising department decided sixty, seventy years ago that red matched the color of their product logo during holiday ad campaigns.

Another myth smashed to smithereens. She nodded.

—Isn't a pine tree better off in the woods than propped up in somebody's apartment and gaudied with mountains of tinsel and goofy ornaments?

She didn't disagree then or even lately, nor did she complain about working side by side with her parents in the soup kitchens over the holidays. Charity volunteering was still trademark Ariel come December. A familiar way of shirking society even as she contributed to its unfortunates.

Not a bad life. She remembered her beloved little Buddha, as alleywise as any cat from the animal shelter over in Kip's Bay. Remembered her bedroom wall shelved with books, many of them twice read, thrice—some children's books but mostly history and science, novels and poetry, biographies of Mary Shelley and Madame Curie and Harry Truman (whom her grandfather once met). As the older Ariel gazed back at herself, she framed what she saw much the same way she'd framed that drawing of transgressive birds. With an eye toward making the past inspire the present.

Brice had never been less than a complete father. How could she even consider another? Those Christmas revelers bearing trees years ago down the snowy streets were gone, never to be seen again. Her foundling cat lay buried under a stone cairn in the yard of their upstate farmhouse. Some things you didn't miss, others you would always miss. Either way, your story went on with or without your consent. As an only child, hadn't she always been furnished with a generous private imagination and felt sufficiently nourished by her books, her drawings and penciled stories, her friendship with her parents, that she rarely if ever perceived her life as defective in any way? Damned if it was any different now.

The boys had left and taken their toy boat with them. She awakened as if from a dream. The evening breeze was scented with new flowers and, she could swear, the bay brine of tidal rivers. She carried Kip's ledger and envelope back to her East Village apartment and found a box in which to store them. Tying the bundle with dental floss—wasteful, but she had no string in the house and was driven by a deeper urgency to finish its entombment than she cared to contemplate—she placed it behind an obsolete encyclopedia on the top shelf of her tallest bookcase. She burned a votive candle and sat cross-legged on the floor. When the flame guttered, she swore off thinking about faith, fathers, and the risky weight of unknown ancestries.

Every curve, every rise and dip of earth out in the pueblolands of Pojoaque and San Ildefonso, every flat and vista returned like an old confrere to feverish Kip Calder, who rode with Sarah and Marcos in the Jeep while some country singer on the radio carried on about love lost and love regained. He winced at the music but was mesmerized by the careening world beyond the windows.

If visual memories could be judged with the exactitude of musical perfect pitch, Kip's recall of the various shades of sand and brush as he squinted over his right shoulder toward Black Mesa was so clear that he could name the notes with his back turned to the piano. Sarah noticed that the man who sat beside her seemed to anticipate where to look and when. She was intrigued that he'd begun to stare out toward the north after they passed Arroyo San Antonia, and let out an involuntary moan when this butte, known to San Ildefonsoans as Tunyo, the Orphan Mesa, came into view. As sacred as it was starkly conspicuous on the wind-flattened plain, Black Mesa— the mesa of the abandoned—was a landmark that had fascinated Kip as a boy. His father told him a giant named Savayo once lived there and was set on devouring all the children of San Ildefonso pueblo until a local cacique slaughtered him in an explosion of flaming blood and lava. He wanted to tell Sarah the story but couldn't, of course, and still hide from her his intimacy with the area. Besides, he figured that she, who wasn't that much older than he was, already knew the legend from her own father.

When they descended toward Otowi and the greener river-fed lands clotted with cottonwoods, he flinched at the grandeur of the brown Rio Grande rolling between its silty banks. And as they left the river to begin their ascent to the crescent plateaus of Los Alamos,

Kip studied the shadows up in the columnar cliffs on whose mesas Anasazi men and women, a thousand years deader than he himself was presently to be, had crouched to look out over this fossil-dust floor.

Kip was shivering. Yellow pine and mean-ass purple spidery ocotillos and weatherworn cliff dwellings covered with petroglyphs superimposed themselves on his eye and memory. His teeth chattered like a shaken sack of dice.

Ki-pki-pkip.

Marcos took off his jacket and gentled the garment over the man's shoulders. Sure hoped he would make it.

Ki-pki-pkip-ki.

Everything in the world was conflicting, yet everything was in harmony. The beauty of this difficult place was inspiring, as was the curious sweetness of his approaching doom. He felt Sarah taking him in, peripherally observing him, and sensed that she did so not out of idle curiosity but true humane concern.

Ki-pki-pkip. . . .

Which had the odd effect of making him more wary. Were he to perish, Kip was persuaded that the way to do so had been shown him long ago by the spiritual man he'd mentioned in his letter to Ariel—would she ever read those words?—a fellow pilot named Wagner who had simply etherized into the mystery of absence. Captured by the Pathet Lao, he'd been taken into the darkness of Nowheresville for, as they said back in those days, *reeducation.* Wagner was educated beyond any such punishments, so they probably offed him, as well they should have, given how dangerous was his enthusiasm. What a terrorful, punishing fate he must have met—though Kip never knew for sure—far from home, at the hands of an avenging military. At least Kip found himself among strangers who were friendly and didn't mind that he hated this kitschy cortege music on the radio. Some song about an achy breaky heart. With two bony fingers he reached to turn it off.

Calder was being driven to his birthplace to die, on the same road

he had taken when he left the Hill years ago, paradox of paradoxes—
though there was no other road into or out of the place, not really.
This was okay, he thought.

"This is all right," he said aloud.

"What, William?"

"He said he's all right," ventured Marcos.

Was as it should be. He was becoming marl, and just as eroded as
these pale canyon walls.

"We're almost there."

Yes oh yes, all of it interlocking, Los Alamos the nucleus and Kip
one of its elliptical charged particles, circling and circling it, himself
a small systemic domino effect, his own cells metastasizing, ingest-
ing other cells of his within the tiny heavy-water basin he'd become,
mercuried and mercurial, inside and out.

So why did Kip suddenly feel his former ambivalence about ever
seeing Ariel now tip toward a desire to survive long enough to meet
her? She who had every right never to do more than curse him from a
great remove. His daughter with that awful name Ariel, that atro-
cious boy's name, or else a sprite's, an angel's—but a name unfit for
sprites and angels, too. Something imported from Shakespeare because, years ago, it was said that Robert Oppenheimer loved *The
Tempest,* written within a year or so of the Spaniards' founding of
Santa Fe—the oldest capital in North America—a fact that would
have intrigued a man obsessed by connectivity. 1609 was it? Oppie
had thought of Los Alamos as being similar to Prospero's island, beyond the natural conditions of the world, a sorcerer's lab where
alchemical experiments were the daily mortal magic. Where politics of good and evil were manifestly understood. Where positives
and negatives, contemplated as physics systems, made themselves
known in the most thoroughly vicious manner. Where a person could
see what was happening in the valley below the mesa and make a
precise if blunt choice regarding matters moral and immoral.

Time passed in rich anonymity, cruelly blank dullness. The re-
membrances triggered by seeing all those burdened geographies of

his childhood began to evaporate. Sarah was speaking. She was telling Kip that she'd prefer to take him to the hospital instead of the convalescent center, but he refused, cleaving to his suicide covenant.

"I can't make you, but if you change your mind—"

"No hospital," he said as they pulled into the parking lot of the center. He shook his head, hoping perhaps to dislodge Ariel and the atom bomb from his thoughts. His legs gave way under his feathery weight when he stepped out of the Jeep. My god, how fucking sick he felt. He was borne aloft by many hands. He heard as if from a great distance worried voices before he blacked out.

Time seemed to fold like batter before Kip sensed hard light pouring down through a window, falling across his blanketed body, illuminating the room itself where other men seemed to be in beds, too. Old geezers and a thin fellow who was young but wore the same pall as the rest. A symphony of coughs punctuated by an occasional groan. Kip couldn't for the life of him remember how he got here.

He was offered an intravenous drip but turned it down, if only to test his rights. Within the same hour he relented because he was too parched to hold out any longer. He was not the courageous philosopher his venerable friend Wagner had proved to be, so he signed a document agreeing to the drip feed. They sponge-bathed him, got him into a quieter room. Lying in his new bed, dressed in a generic polyester gown and pajama bottoms of no known color, Kip remembered who he was. The unworthy beneficiary of Sarah Montoya who'd probably pulled strings to get him admitted, a poor and worthless wastrel.

Phrases floated of their own accord across his dreaming mind. The term *mad pact* was involuntarily happening within him. *Mutual assured destruction pact* in Pentagonese, the lingua franca of the fighting man's command. It was something resurrected from the Cold War, the aftermath of the nuclear one his father helped brainstorm— *that* was a real honey, too, was it not, as wars and brainstorms go? Well, it was not. Yet this *mad-pact-brainstorming* Kip was suffering in his sweaty bedclothes vivid visions of somber conspicuous beauty. White phosphorous haze billowing up from the Rousseau jungles where they dumped it to mark Charlie targets for big Thunderchiefs and Phantoms. Boiling Day-Glo tangerine clouds edged in black, belying the deaths that had gone down beneath them. Some of those deaths, brought on by Kip himself in river crannies and realms so green they made you weep for joy, he remembered far too well. Deaths of boys who were bonemeal now and relegated to the same history heap as Hirohito and hell's own Hitler himself. Sure, he was mixing up his wars. But at the end of the day weren't they all the same? Was it possible only war and worms were immortal? Kip was not thinking clearly but he couldn't stop his mind from marching on. His old visions named their own time and place to race across the petrochemical skies of his consciousness, and there was little—no, there was nothing—he could do about it.

How did Sarah Montoya divine this particular abyss into which her salvage, her guest, her appalling acquaintance who was now at least temporarily her patient, stared, with eyes closed and voice muttering? Because she had seen variations on the theme before in these rooms scented by pungent soaps and decaying unopened roses. After all, many brave children from the Hill served in the conflicts that followed the one that brought Los Alamos into being. These people had traditionally been patriots. From Tech 18 geniuses to dirtpoor youths from the pueblos who fought before they had the right to vote. Many landed here, crippled, disabled, on their last legs—Hill people soon to be laid beneath the hill.

She discovered documents not terribly well hidden in Kip's shoe and clothing. William Calder, the license read. She asked Carl, down at Rancho Pajarito that night, if he knew any Calders. He mulled it over before saying he recalled somebody up at the lab was named Calder, but never knew the man. So, was this William fellow going to make it? her husband asked.

Had Kip not rebounded, they would have been forced to arrange his transfer to the hospital, which he'd have tried though surely failed to spurn. Since he'd been born at the first hospital erected in Los Alamos, fate would thus have brought him full circle. But his road curved elsewhere.

Too weak to do much more than swear his strength was returning, Kip spent the next weeks strolling his I.V. tree up the corridors and down, with a brave smile on his unshaven face. On good days he did what he could to pay, as it were, his way. He encouraged an old fellow from Guachupangue, one Alvas Trujillo, to play cards—he, Kip, who'd never much liked games—speaking with him in more than passingly competent Spanish until the viejito's emphysema worsened. Kip gathered, even before the doctor ordered him to be moved, that the tubes expediting oxygen to his nostrils were insufficient life support to keep him alive and the ambulance that might have taken Kip over to Los Alamos Community took Trujillo instead. And he engaged others in various states of decline—the overdose patient here; the head-injury patient there; the forlorn smiling little woman who clutched to her chest an exhausted Teddy bear in one hand and a Porky Pig in the other. The center managed several dozen residents, with a bed or two to spare. He asked Sarah if he could sweep the floors, or mop, or help out in the kitchen.

"Get better, we'll square things some other day," she told him, an arrangement that made Kip more restless than becalmed, as his continued impostoring began to weigh on him. Sarah was so straight, he so crooked. More than once he contemplated slipping out one night and running away from the Hill, presumably this time forever. But he knew it was a coward's game, so stayed put.

Weeks ran into months. Some days were better than others. He and Sarah managed to make light of his unevenness after their own fashion. Mornings, she came into the room, brushed the curtain aside, and asked, "How's the weather, my friend?" Depending on how he felt, Kip would reply, "Overcast with possible showers," or "Sunny and continued warm." If he didn't have a sense of how the day was going to go, he might say, "Barometer's broken."

The Montoyas continued to be charitable. Carl dropped in to visit once a week and Marcos came by from time to time with his friend Franny and talked about horses—his Western Pleasure stud, a new yearling filly. Kind of them, but it begged the question, Who should care about Kip Calder? He had led a life of not much trusting people, and now he was doing just that with Sarah—trusting her. Had he really agreed to undergo the procedure, the chemotherapy, and see what happened? They'd done blood work, taken the scans, discovered the tumor. Hard to believe she'd managed to win such concessions from him. Suicide was no longer in the cards.

Meanwhile, the Ariel question came to temporary closure. She hadn't come to find him. All for the best. He now wanted to get well in order not to see but evade her. Of late, not a night passed during which he failed to castigate himself for having invited Brice to Chimayó to set the record straight. History is meant to be elusive, unfinished and unfinishable. By trying to tame his past he only unleashed more of the present. He certainly wouldn't blame Ariel if she trashed his pathetic tokens and told Brice and Jess that it was all too late.

Finish this chemo, put on a few pounds, get his strength back, and split. He could get a cash job somewhere and send the money to Sarah. Alone again, nameless. It was a pretty dream, but he knew he wasn't employable. Knew his running days were over. Knew his avenues of escape had closed.

Beyond his window the skies continually changed from azure to white to pink to amethyst to amber to mauve. Summer walked by, fall behind it, and then it snowed outside, and the snow draped itself in the boughs of ponderosas on the bluffs of Acid Canyon and set white hats on the strawberry pots on the patio, itself covered in powder. The flowering fruit trees then blossomed, and patients planted seeds and seedlings in the raised beds—homely snapdragons and ugly petunias—which they could access from their wheelchairs and walkers. Cassin finches returned to the bird feeders, and still he was not dead. Indeed, Kip, having balded last autumn at the behest of chemicals and then, over winter and into this spring, regrown a head of hair in their aftermath, was more alive than Sarah had ever seen him. He pushed patients' wheelchairs, even bounced around atop large red exercise-therapy balls with other convalescents, rocking and rolling to Menudo on the loudspeaker. He watched *I Love Lucy* dubbed into Spanish on the television with a fellow who looked for all the world like a very old baby in a robe printed with foxhunting scenes. Kip was coming along so nicely that the resident nurse allowed him to take over feeding the tropical fish in the saltwater aquarium—a red-eye tetra and Indian dwarf botia, an exotic silvery bichir that he contemplated for hours on end. When Sarah inquired, the doctors agreed that all indications were his cancer was in remission. The question was what to *do* with him. Once more, he had nowhere to go and soon would have nowhere to stay, either.

Kip faced a new dilemma brought about by, of all things, his improving health. One question formulated deep in the night when he couldn't sleep any better than other insomniacs who resided at the center was whether or not he should allow himself to continue with the broadening respect he felt toward Sarah Montoya. Where did she think he ought to go? What should he do? Could he tell her that the drifting, seesaw fantasy of reuniting with or running from his abandoned daughter made him feel more alone than ever? Could he try to tell her who he was? Did he even know anymore?

As it happened, he needn't have worried about some of what he wanted to confide to her. Having slowly turned it over in her mind as Kip processed through his recovery, Sarah remembered the name suddenly, an unusual joining of Anglo and Hispanic, not unlike her own. Emma Inez, she thought as she walked from Juniper across the long grass lawn toward Fuller Lodge, where, in a cluster of small rooms on the top floor, she meant to look it up in the records of the Historical Museum. All of it came back to her as she stood on the grounds of that most recognizable landmark in town, where the Manhattan Project physicists had argued theory, schedule, strategy, and everything else under the sun about their atomic gadget during colloquia in the greatroom, held before the massive tuffstone fireplace where burning logs big as men cast an amicable glow over the proceedings. A butterfly wafted by Sarah like some sentient rusted leaf as she recalled hearing how this Emma Inez and her husband had been killed in a car crash—something to do with a trip back east, in the late sixties, to visit their boy at college in New York. That boy, nicknamed Kip was he not, would be this very same William Calder, her charge now. The wind, still invested with winter, ruffled her navy blue wool coat fronted with bone buttons as she turned back toward where she'd parked near the movie theater. She walked with her arms crossed, deep in thought.

The day on which she intended to confront him as to why he would want to remain anonymous in this place where he had been born and raised, and from which he'd gone on to be a local but unknown hero in Asia, was the same day Kip decided to attempt his revelations to Sarah in his own roundabout way. Not finding him in his room, she was told that he was out back of the infirmary, where she came upon him raking stones and troweling the flower bed in which columbines and lavender would soon be blooming.

She wished him good morning, and he her. "Have a moment?" she asked and Kip, face pinkened by the morning light and his exertions, answered by saying he'd been wanting to discuss a couple of things with her if she had the time. He rose stiffly and sat on one of the rocks that served as perimeter for the garden. Sarah sat beside him.

"At the risk of sounding like an ingrate, I hope you don't mind my saying I don't understand why I'm alive."

"You let us help you is why."

"I appreciate that. But what I mean is, I'm left with the question, What for?"

"You're obviously meant to be alive or else you wouldn't be."

"It wasn't what I wanted at the time, but whether I wanted it or not, I'm here thanks to you."

"Thank you back."

"Why thank me?"

She shrugged a shoulder. "Because you lose most of your people in a place like this. Sometimes they go in a matter of days or weeks, other times they're among the living dead for years. Dignity and comfort are just about all we can offer. What I'm saying is, I appreciate your recuperation."

Kip quietly said, "Dying's easy compared to living. Don't get me wrong. Like I say, I'm grateful. But if I don't do something that makes up for it somehow, don't use this spare chance, what's the point? The world doesn't need another air waster."

"I'm not all that romantic or religious but you'll forgive me for saying there's some purpose to everything. Living on a ranch, I see it every day. Ecosystems—you're still part of one, like it or not."

She wondered how to broach her question. As she opened her mouth to speak—ask him directly; he was a direct man, she'd come to believe, despite the fact his mind sometimes cruised in ellipses—Kip asked her something instead, out of the blue.

Did she know that the Spaniards, who'd had difficulty pronouncing the Tewa language, had renamed Nambé after Francis of Assisi, feeling a greater affinity toward him than any crazy local bird spirit—*k'untsire*—for whom the pueblo people cast cornmeal heavenward during ceremonies that the colonialist padres frowned upon as fetishist?

"You've been reading," she said.

"Somebody left a book behind."

"Well Saint Francis, I know, is the patron saint of the poor and crippled," Sarah said, wondering where this new exchange was leading.

"I like Francis, but *k'untsire* and the idea that we should act with goodwill and generosity toward the gods—those things are even better. Fact they need our goodwill keeps the gods in their place."

"It's good if you think gods need to be put in their place."

"Oh, they do," Kip nodded.

"Saint Francis fed the birds but he always knew that it was the birds who were letting him feed them. It was their gift to him, not the other way around. Kind of the same thing."

Kip said, "A little different, I think, but I get your drift."

"Would you rather be Saint Francis or the birds?"

"Either way."

Now Kip was getting lost.

"You know what the word *Nambé* means in Tewa, too, then?"

"Something to do with circling," said Kip.

They watched a hummingbird, a rufous, at the plastic feeder, both of them quiet in the warming light.

"You're from around here, aren't you."

"*Nambé* means 'roundish earth' or 'circle of earth,' doesn't it? And the pueblo is protected by some kind of water dragon."

"People used to call you Kip, didn't they."

He paused to look down at his hands, which silently clapped, palms touching, fingers splayed. His profile was sharp, forehead smoother than riverstone though finely lined; his jaw and nose were so clearly defined as to seem drawn in ink.

"This book said that the Nambé Indians buried the water dragon when they built their dam up in the Sangre foothills by the falls."

Her turn to nod. A long silence before Kip spoke again.

"I used to go hunting down in the box canyons around here when I was young. Jackrabbits mostly. I remember being haunted by this strange feeling that they could sense me taking aim at them. They couldn't see me, couldn't smell me. But they knew. You could see them square themselves in the crosshairs of the rifle scope. Like they knew they were about to take the bullet and just like that be gone. Well, that's how I'm feeling. Squared up in the crosshairs. Maybe I always felt this way but never admitted it to myself."

"I'm sorry, Kip. Kip's the name, right?"

"People used to call me all kinds of stuff," he said. "But I haven't lied to you, if that's what you're implying."

Sarah didn't flinch. Again out of the blue, Kip asked, "What happens when you spend your life running away from home and then life forces you to go back, but there's no one waiting for you?"

"If Saint Francis is your patron saint, and I think he is, you find out that other people are willing to make their home yours," she said, causing him to look at her with the first wholehearted smile Sarah had ever seen on his face. Their dialogue did not come to an end before Kip confessed what had brought him to Chimayó a year earlier, and what had driven him across the desert into her life and the lives of her family.

*I*n the weeks after she learned about Kip Calder, Ariel kept to her routine. Mornings, she strode up Broadway, passing through Union Square with its statues of Washington on horseback and Gandhi carrying his humble staff. She walked with shoulder bags full of manuscripts—a studious burro with panniers, she liked to joke—crosstown to the West Thirties. At the publishing house where she worked she'd recently been promoted from editorial assistant to assistant editor, a titular hopscotch that brought her little more money but twice the work. Which she didn't mind. She felt lucky to have a window in the cluttered niche that served as her office and everyone else's file closet. From it she could see other glass and steel buildings, like a colossal forest of quartz crystals, when glancing up from the page at hand. If her budget allowed, she ate lunch at a soba restaurant with other women from the office. An apple and yogurt on solo days. Evenings, she retraced her steps, stopping by a favorite bookstore to browse the new-arrivals table. Some nights she went out with friends, but often she settled in with the book of the moment or her journal, which she filled with word sketches, ideas toward a narrative of her own.

Ariel's friendship with her parents continued uninterrupted, almost as if nothing had happened. She looked forward as much as ever to Sunday night dinners with them in Chelsea. She and Jessica cooked ratatouille or pasta primavera while Brice uncorked wine and parodied the news in preposterous Elizabethan doggerel. This prime minister was a whoreson dog. That defense contractor a boodle of lily-livered knaves.

So yes, she not only went on loving the father she knew, but went on liking him as one of her two oldest pals. She admired him as ever for his outmoded lefty politics, his amused cynicism about how readily his generation had sold out, cashed in, traded tie-dyes for pinstripes. All those doves become bulls and bears. All those dreamy hippies now weighing their retirement options. A defense attorney, Brice was committed to representing idealists, pacifists, protestors in need of legal help. Ethical remained the word for him, Ariel believed. For both her parents, despite their one grand mistruth, now expunged from the record.

This routine was toppled one night as she stood in the stacks of the Strand. She was poring over a volume of Stieglitz nudes of the youthful Georgia O'Keeffe. Torsos, thighs, breasts, those sinuous hands and sharp black eyes of the painter were caught in silverprints cropped so tightly that they seemed about to burst from the page. Absorbed by these images, Ariel didn't hear him the first time he said, "She looks like you, her face, that is . . ."—David Moore's gawky pickup line they would both laugh about later.

Over the months that followed, it would occur to Jessica that her daughter was ironically behaving like some jilted lover on the rebound, an impression she didn't share with Ariel at the time. To every other watching eye she was simply a young woman who had fallen in love with someone who seemed equally in love with her. They went to the Cloisters, strolled hand in hand through the knot gardens adjacent, and kissed beneath the flowering trees. They admired the unicorn in captivity, woven into voluminous tapestry, and looked at the griffin and kissed some more, and at the gargoyles and kissed again. And like the espaliered quinces trained by the monastery gardeners to grow in intertwining patterns, they lay in each other's arms on Ariel's bed. She had never explored a man's body with such abandon. From her mouth came words and from her throat noises she'd never uttered before. Outrageously, she painted his initials on her forehead with her menstrual blood. What began in bed might end up on the floor or in another room, she couldn't remember how.

They boarded the Circle Line like a couple of giddy tourists and rode the boat around the island. They went out dancing at night, throwing their arms over their heads and whooping under strobe lights that illuminated others crowded against them on all sides as the sound system blew bass beats that walloped their very bones. After David proposed they visit the botanic gardens—calling her Friday afternoon at work, while fellow commodities brokers shouted strings of numbers in the background—Ariel made lunch for them the next morning, and off they went to Park Slope. Another Saturday, after a softball game in Sheep Meadow, they walked up to Columbia where Ariel showed him her old dorm window. At the Chelsea flea market they discovered two treasures, a church-shaped birdhouse and an ornate bamboo birdcage whose door was broken. Ariel bought David the birdhouse, joking that he could use a little religion, and he got her the cage, saying it would serve as a symbol their love should always be free.

A year to the day after their first encounter, he showed up at her door holding aloft a cardboard box with airholes in its side, and in his other hand a bottle of champagne. "Happy anniversary," he said, as Ariel peeked inside and saw two brown-and-white zebra finches. "Songbirds for your empty pagoda."

It was a sweet gesture, she knew, but one that had the weird effect of making her feel wary. Notwithstanding her unease, she smiled and thanked him, uncorked the champagne after fixing the door with wire and settling the finches in their new home. Then, as ever, though serenaded from behind the bamboo spindles instead of by the usual music of the city, they took each other to bed, and her faint sense of odd misgiving vanished.

That Ariel didn't get pregnant, with all the love they made that second spring into summer and autumn and during the holidays beyond, was something of a miracle. Their craving for each other, having bordered on the obsessive, slowly calmed. But even when the affair waned toward more tepid registers, they sometimes left themselves open to the possibility of an accident. None chanced to happen. Which was fine, especially with David, who'd made it clear—despite his having forgotten the birdcage was meant to be left empty, its door broken—that family life was not for him.

So how much more miraculous was it that now, with three years gone by and their surfeit passion not extinguished but oddly abstracted, Ariel faced this improbable crisis of motherhood? No, absolutely not. It wouldn't be fair to either of them. So she felt when she first suspected something was wrong. She'd missed her period and blamed it on nerves, the moon, anything that came to mind. But her nausea, though mild, elicited real fear. A home pregnancy test showed positive. But that couldn't be right. She tried another company's product which gave her the same reading. When her gynecologist confirmed the earlier results, the news put Ariel back onto the sidewalks of Gramercy Park, in a haze matched only by the stifling late July morning itself.

When had it happened? She remembered as she walked around the gated gardens. After the worst argument they'd ever had, over whether to go to this party or that, something of no inherent consequence, which ended with apologetic sex, in the midnight wake of which he'd quietly left. They'd patched up their problem over the phone, but David called less often than ever in the weeks that followed. There was no denying they'd hit a bleak stretch. That what had arisen with such unexpected passion, then floated along for unquestioning years, now seemed to be dwindling with equally unexpected quickness.

Whether because of this downward spiral or independent of it, Ariel found herself ambling through midsummer days with a wintry heart. Even before she learned that she was pregnant, a disconnectedness settled over her. No manuscript stirred her lately. Her

once-treasured morning walk seemed longer than ever. Her note-
books slept in the desk. Sunday dinners in Chelsea became a bit of a
drudge. The phone seldom rang, maybe because she failed to return
most calls left on her machine. She allowed herself to be dragged out
to dinner by two girlfriends who showed up unannounced, then
coaxed on to see some action movie with futuristic gunships flying
through exploding air and fiery fusillades ad infinitum. Yet compan-
ionship and entertainment didn't provide even a temporary cure.
Grateful though she was for her friends' concern, she couldn't wait to
get back home and lock the door. It was as if some emotional law of
thermodynamics were dispelling her will to feel. Aware this was
gnawing at the edges of everything she'd ever loved, she nevertheless
seemed unable to stop it. What was wrong?

The possible answer occurred to her that day of confirmation. She
left Gramercy, pace quickening all the way. Having climbed the steps
of her walk-up two at a time, she turned the key in the lock with a
quaking hand. She pulled a chair into her book closet and climbed
up to retrieve the dusty box in which Kip's banished gifts had lan-
guished for these past three years.

Her old Dodge Dart was parked on the street a block away. She
carried the finches in their cage down the hall and gave them to her
surprised, elated neighbor who had always coveted the little birds.
She threw together some clothes, locked her windows and doors,
and left for the funky, cherished family farmhouse upstate. It was the
only place in the world where Ariel could truly be by herself. And as
the Palisades loomed north above the Hudson while she drove across
the George Washington Bridge, she thought if ever solitude might
serve her well it was now. Hadn't her childhood hero Thoreau, that
other David, chosen seclusion over social engagement? What about
solitary Emily Dickinson, loner Coleridge?

Wind on her face felt good. The long slow burn of delaying the inevitable had flared into a wildfire of wanting to know who Kip was.
Banishment tripped toward an embrace of needing to fill in the vast

rift of willful ignorance. David himself had long ago urged her to do this. "You're never going to be a whole person until you meet him," he'd argued.

"My wholeness or lack of it has nothing to do with Kip Calder," was her response. She could almost hear the faltering in her voice from this present vantage.

"You know how when somebody loses a leg, they say they still have feeling in it? Whether you want to admit it or not, you must have feelings for him."

"I never had the leg to begin with, and I don't see the point of trying to walk on it now."

She remembered his shrug. "My analogy may be off," he persisted, "but I still think you need to connect with the man, if only once."

Why hadn't she listened? she thought as she turned off the quickway and drove through broad hilly farmlands muggy with summer steam. Would that he were always so insightful. The David who had suggested she meet her birth father was the best David, a man she realized she lost months ago. If only it were that David rather than this disaffected one whom she would have to face in her present predicament. She who didn't feel she had anything to say to anyone. Who wrote that to achieve greatness all one had to do was learn to sit in a room and be quiet? Some French philosopher who wouldn't want his name invoked.

Maybe the bias wasn't so aberrant. Perhaps the most gregarious among us are quietly dying to be left alone. So she thought as she pulled into the dirt drive that led to the isolated white clapboard farmhouse, set in the middle of green grass edged by daisy fleabane and wild basil, by ferns and the sheltering forest beyond. She cut the engine, climbed out, walked down to the pond ringed by cattails and the bald stalks of irises she'd planted with her own hands long ago, now spent. Shedding her clothes and shoes, she walked into the water which received her in all its own fecundity as the maple and

ash trees and black cherries waved, in greeting or farewell or merely
because the wind rustled their branches. Yes, the time had come to
address Kip Calder.

*T*he Carpenter household of Mary's youth was not locally famous
for its sanity. To wit, people never asked her father why so many years
after the war a black flag still hung in all seasons from the pole in
front of his house. They didn't ask because they knew why it was
there. Black flag of remembrance, to honor those missing in action
and prisoners of war. Mary's mother often wished Russell would
make the gesture of removing it, if only because she believed he
might find it therapeutic. The countries themselves had reached
diplomatic and economic accords, and Vietnam, she'd heard on the
news, had allowed American officials to help identify what servicemen's remains could be found and repatriated, though those remains
were but corpseless dogtags in some instances. She dared not suggest that if these countries, which had so hated each other that
they'd decided to go to war in the first place, could now see their way
clear to making peace, wouldn't Russell be smart to try to do the
same? He'd tell her she didn't know what she was talking about. Tell
her she didn't know what it was like to lose three brothers in the
same year in the same war. Perry at Khe Sahn. Nick somewhere
north that spring, as their parents had been informed, succumbing
by all accounts courageously under monsoon rains in a filthy prison.
Clifford who had come home in body only.

Russell himself had been a frustrated 4-F patriot grounded at
home because some military doctor pronounced him unfit for duty
on account of his arrhythmia. —Irregular heartbeat, for godsakes.
It's what's in a man's heart makes him a good soldier, not whether it
beats like some freaking clock. You want a clock? Go to a clock-
maker. Yet given his brothers' fates, the wonder was why Russ still re-
gretted that he never got the chance to fight.

Perry—Bravo Company, 3rd Reconnaissance Battalion—was among the first to go down in the stunning barrage of shelling that caught the marines off guard in an infamous moment of bad timing, February 1968. Overseeing the building of bunkers out of sandbags for recon, he took some searing shrapnel along with half of his men who didn't return home alive, either. Perry at least had some story attached to his death. The words *Khe Sahn* were, like the term *Tet Offensive*, recognizable to many condolent neighbors, who learned them from battlefield reports that flooded family rooms in endless nightly cathode streams the first months of that pivotal, luckless year.

Nick's death was probably worse, as deaths went. Slower, and frustratingly mysterious. Nick had no such story. His remains were not released, and the intelligence regarding his demise from *natural causes while held as prisoner of war* was sketchy. Not having an official story was like not having lived or died.

Unlike Perry and mad Cliff, poor Nick was never repatriated, and this bothered Mary's father more than anything under God's sun. Russell loved his brothers, however conjecturally and distantly and even hatefully, and so, as Russ answered whenever he was asked, he would continue to display that POW/MIA flag against the day when the government—theirs, ours, anybody's—could attach a believable story to the capture, internment, and death of his middle brother. Their mother and father had died without knowing. It seemed a reasonable goal.

Russell and Rebecca Carpenter's children grew up with the flag flying beside their front door, and to them it was as much a part of the architecture of the house as its windows, battenboard facades, and tin roof. Mary's uncles were still, in different ways, missing in action, was what it meant. Over in the cemetery, two had their names, dates, and *In Memoriam* carved into marble tablets, but only one was there in the ground. Since neither Mary nor her siblings could remember which of their dad's brothers had been killed in action and which died a prisoner of war, Veterans Day was always a kind of roulette game. When the kids were made to dress up and go to the cemetery to lay at each grave an annual wreath of red carnations, they would whisper, —Which grave's got the maggot food, which one's empty? To Mary and Jimmy, and to the twins, Johnny and Rose, those chiseled names were as interchangeable as bicycle tires, though they'd heard narrated their uncles' battle fates on many occasions. The children knew, as did their mother, never to betray their perplexity nor raise the matter of the black flag in their father's presence. Perry and Nick were grudgingly sacred.

Russell's esteem, what some might call his obsession, was, as the Carpenter kids got older, an unwelcome theme at school. Wisecracks were made about Jimmy and Johnny's nutzo pop who was stuck in the past. —Get over yourself. The Civil War is *done* already, Battle of the Bulge is so yesterday. Dead as croak. One Halloween, a local prankster from Washington Elementary took it upon himself to steal the flag, which Russell replaced within the week.

During dinner once, after Jimmy had taken a ribbing at school about the flag, he tested his adolescent grit against his father's mettle, saying as nonchalantly as he could manage, —Hey, I heard something good today.

The family continued eating.

—What's that? his mother asked.

—I heard that people think we're pirates.

—Really? asked Johnny.

—You heard me.

—I don't get it, said Johnny.

—Me neither, Rose added.

—Hey, Dad?

—What.

—Why do you think people would say something like that?

—People say crazy things all the time and only crazy people listen to them.

They ate.

—Pirates. Jimmy shook his head dramatically. —It must be that pirate flag that gives them the idea.

Russell's hand swiped the boy's cheek so fast, so hard, that the pain spread across his face before Jimmy even knew what had happened. Reddening, he scraped his chair back violently and fled the table.

—Jim, you stop right there, his father said.

—Let him go, his mother breathed.

The boy halted.

—He didn't mean anything.

Jimmy's father rose from the table and with a hooking finger motioned his son to follow. When they returned to the room, Russ, like some prison guard, followed his elder son whose chin was as if attached to his chest, eyes downcast, shoulders narrowed, hands shoved deep into his trouser pockets. No one asked any questions, though the quietest was Mary who understood better than most her father's will to punish.

His ire would have been funny had it not been ugly. A stern disciplinarian, Russ fancied marine protocol and order, however ad-libbed, and brought them to bear on his household. Later that night, Jim and his brother and sisters would agree in secret that their mean friends might not be so far off the mark. Maybe it made sense to disparage the pirate flag and Russell Carpenter who waved it in everybody's face because he was jealous his brothers were dead or deranged heroes, while he was just a living grunt stuck in a low-end job at Continental Divide Electric, dangling from the transmission grid, stringing 230-kilovolt line thirty feet above the ground. Not even high enough that if he fell it would necessarily kill him.

For somebody whose life was electricity he seemed, at least in the eyes of his daughter Mary, unenlightened. No, worse. Utterly lost in the dark.

Kip settled in at Nambé with greater ease than he or the Montoyas might have imagined. Through that first summer and into autumn, he learned his way around by watching and helping out whenever the chance arose. He took his time, which, as Sarah said, was the right time for him to take. Carl offered wages on top of room and board, but Kip told him to keep his money. All of it was Montoya charity as far as he was concerned. When he got enough strength back so he could pull weight to merit a wage, the money would go straight to the convalescent center.

Friday evenings, Marcos and Franny brought him along to the highwayside Roadrunner Café in Pojoaque pueblo. He was treated to quesadillas and even drank a beer with Marcos's friends, bemused if bemusing in the role of raconteur. Tales of Laos captivated his small, fascinated audience—*Lales of Taos,* he said after indulging in the cerveza. Hootch narratives. Stories of crashing, surviving, being caught in crossfire as he and his copilot were choppered out in a blizzard of tracer bursts. Describing Mekong refugee camps as running sewers—*running sores,* as the beer would have it—into which he ferried grateful Hmong families. The beauty and industry of subjugated Meo farmers who reinvented themselves as fierce mountain warriors and whose losses were far worse than ours after Saigon fell. The troupe of monkeys that befriended the CIA and Ravens, attended their dinners like invited guests, sat along the runway watching FAC planes ascend into morning mists for another day of reconnaissance along the Nam Nhiep, or up near Ban Ban, or down the Nam Sane, which the men naturally dubbed the *Non Sane.*

He had many weaknesses, as he would have been first to admit, but in spite of every effort to push her out of mind, his greatest remained Ariel. She circled him, influencing his tides of thought, even as she began to seem imaginary rather than the only flesh relative he had left on earth. Because he knew Ariel would never have anything to do with him, or because he couldn't help himself, he found he was drawn to Franny Johnson. In Franny he divined a similar yet different kinship. He had no idea what all this meant but felt somehow paternal toward her from the first time they met, at the convalescent center. She herself recognized a conversant hiddenness in Kip's eyes, the eyes of a fellow runner. When Franny shook his parchment-dry hand the day they were introduced, she saw in those ancient eyes something difficult to define.

For one worn down by life, Kip had seemed unwontedly spirited when Franny asked him about his past. Presaging their Roadrunner evenings, he told her and Marcos he had been everywhere they could find on a map. Forty days in God's dark desert and then some. He cobbled together a mosaic, one she hoped was true if only because someone should live such an audacious life.

Nor did he concoct a boring spreadsheet of triumphs. Rather, the reverse. He'd failed once as a cowboy in Arizona and again in Argentina. Been a failure as a stevedore on a rustbucket registered in Holland and chartered up beyond Yankutat Bay, where retirees cruised to see whales and polar bears and vast chunks of million-year-old ice sliding off floes into the cold black Alaskan water.

That was only the geographic As. Bangkok, Beirut briefly. Camotlán de Milleflores, never making money at any turn. He was once so poor he drove stolen cars from the States to Mexico, where they were sold then repurchased for cash under the table, driven back, and finally resold to the border dealerships from which they originated. He never ran drugs, never ran guns. In the course of his turbulent journey he gave away everything he ever owned.

"Really?" she asked.

"Sure really. I don't own one damn thing."

"I mean, really did you drive stolen cars across the border?"

He shrugged. "Despicable episode. Better to fail at the worst legit job than succeed at stupidity like that."

He had once given up everything—whatever *everything* meant—to go follow the dream of living alone in a stone cottage in Newfoundland. Worked as a lighthouse keeper on a rock island.

"Two months out, one week ashore."

"Why'd you leave?"

"I got bored with the company I was keeping."

All three smiled, though Franny sensed at the time that William's anecdotes were as fragile as his health. Still, she couldn't be sure. Her perception of this man as a fellow counterfeit acquired its own dubiety, since the stories he so freely reeled off seemed just too far outside the realm of possibility to be falsehoods.

Now he lived at Rancho Pajarito. Ailing William had meta-morphosed into Kip the late-blooming ranch hand, frail but sailing forward. A phoenix, Sarah dubbed him. Anything but counterfeit, he was yet mysterious to Franny. Not given to *chisme,* she was no meddler but had watched him closely these past months. And this presumptive, damaged father figure likewise watched her, whose countenance bore the intangible marks of a classified past, like en-crypted stigmata invisible to anyone who didn't bear similar wounds.

Vernal equinox. Kip walked up the slow rise, returning from the barn, long arms swinging at his sides, dressed in worn denim pants and a holey jacket inherited from Marcos. Headed toward the pad-docks in the opposite direction, Franny strolled beside an unshorn saffron hedge twittering with small birds. Each had been much on the other's mind these days but when they collided, knocking heads, both were so caught up in thoughts having nothing to do with the other that they hardly recognized who stood before them.

In Franny's face Kip mistook the prospect of Ariel. In Kip's, Franny saw a shocked confusion that anticipated how Marcos would look today when, or if, he learned the truth about her past, her vari-ant selves.

"My god, sorry, I wasn't paying attention," she exhaled. "You all right?"

Drawing up hard, he grasped her forearms as much to capture his own balance as to help her keep hers. She looked like she'd seen a hallucination see another hallucination.

"All I can say is, you're as hardheaded as I am," and he gamely laughed.

Rubbing his temple, he thought, What a curious girl. Weathered but pristine as some of those children he'd seen back in his cloying war. She had on a jean skirt and floppy wool sweater whose sleeves came down past the tips of her fingers; her plum hair was in disarray, not unlike his own grayed brown. Franny reached out and touched his face, searching for a bruise or cut, then straightened his hair. Thirty years ago he might have fallen in love on the spot.

Hearing that word *Franny* while peering into his wizened but piercing eyes, she wondered, wouldn't this cockamamie old Kip be her perfect confessor? She knew Marcos liked him—had begun to adore him, in fact, as had Carl and Sarah. By working to the very edge of his reserves, he'd become a part of the ranch itself. And Kip seemed to value the Montoyas in ways she felt she didn't dare, given the big lie that hovered behind her relationship with them. Maybe she and Kip were meant literally to bump into each other. Maybe he could hear her out first, before Marcos.

The Mary within hesitated, but Franny said, "Hard heads hide soft hearts. Isn't that the saying?"

A shadow ascended across her face, and Kip was reminded of *melárchico* children, who were sad because they'd lost someone precious whom they were deeply attached to. Maybe this was what he'd noticed in Franny before, the abandoned *melárchico* look. In the olden days, kind strangers were supposed to tie red ribbons on their wrists in the hope this would cure them. He remembered that it was Brice McCarthy's mother who had taught him the word back in school, telling him that it wasn't just boys and girls who became *melárchico;* a pet bird or family cat could be so upset when its mistress or master died that it would no longer sing songs or play with a ball of string.

"I'm not much for sayings. My mother used to swear *There is none that doeth good, no not one,* when she was in a bad mood. Book of Common Prayer. I remember that expression because I never agreed with it."

"That's surprising."

"Why?"

"Because you're worldly wise and it seems like the kind of proverb somebody who's been around the block would go along with."

"Well, Franny. I think it's more a worldly weary than worldly wise kind of saying."

"I'm not sure I agree with it, either."

"My mother had a lot of wisdom in her. She sometimes hated her circumstances, is all."

"Your father working at Los Alamos and everything, you mean."

Kip said, "You're looking for Marcos, I bet."

"I was."

"He'll be happy to see you. Got to go," Kip smiled and began to walk away.

"Can I ask a question?"

He stopped, turned around, saying nothing.

Hesitant, unsure of herself, she nonetheless took the leap of faith. "Remember how your name was William when I first met you?"

Kip's premonitory sense about moments such as this kicked into overdrive. She was going to offer him a confidence he might not want to know. He could feel it.

"What if I told you my real name wasn't Franny?"

"Lot of people have nicknames." What bogus ingenuousness.

"—wasn't Franny but something completely different, then what would you think."

The weather in his mind clouding up, Kip squinted, staring beyond her.

"Like if I made that name up for really good reasons but my name was something else."

"Franny's a fine name," he said lamely, leaning away, somewhat feigning physical distress. What was it about Franny that both drew him to her yet made him want to retreat? She was speaking.

"That's not what I mean."

"Franny—"

"My name's Mary."

Kip said nothing.

"Mary from Gallup, New Mexico, not Princeton, New Jersey."

A heavy interior squall was settling in. How many times had he done the same thing, invented a past to scuttle a future? Like when he lived in Costa Rica under the crazy pseudonym Brice McCarthy, for no other reason than to walk a mile in another man's name.

"Mary's a good name and Gallup is a good place," he said, one eye closed because the sun was in it.

"Gallup's anything but a good place."

"Marcos doesn't know about this—"

"No."

"Why are you telling me?"

"I'm not sure, and that's the truth," recognizing that today was not going to be the day she set everything straight with Marcos after all. "Because I trust you."

"Why trust me?"

"I'm not sure about that, either."

Kip's faint smile was intended to camouflage his dread. He wanted to engage her, wanted to help somehow, but the miserable failure of a father within him was afraid.

"Well, thanks for listening," she finished, wondering whether she'd gone too far.

"But I didn't hear you out at all, Mary."

"Franny—better call me Franny until I sort things through."

"Franny. Sorry."

"We sure seem to be apologizing to each other a lot today. You're busy, I should let you get back to what you were doing."

"I was just going to—I'm not busy. Tell me about your name."

"Maybe we can talk another time."

"Now is fine."

She looked pale, confused. "Hey, Kip."

"Yes."

"Remember up at the Hill that time when you offered to teach me some phrases in Vietnamese? Are you still willing?"

"I know just enough to get you into trouble and not enough to get you out. But sure, if you want."

"That'd be great," she said.

He watched her make her way down the leaf-cluttered path to the paddock, studied her dappled by ten thousand quivering shadows cast by elms and box elders. For her part, caught between the faded urge to speak with Marcos about how she'd run away from home and assumed this new identity, and her unanticipated confessions to Kip, Franny was seized by a twinge of guilt. She'd talked about her problems without showing the least concern over his. How pale and preoccupied he'd looked. Hatless under the Chimayó sun, working outside as he did, he should be burned not bleached. Gone was his berry-brown complexion of those first painful months on the Hill. Funny what a blend of strength and fragility Kip was. She turned back to find him. He had disappeared, though. She would have called out, but she didn't know what more to say. He might return to where she stood—hovering between her two lives, two lies—and he might smile that knowing, unassuming smile of his. Maybe it wasn't fair of her to expect him to do more than cope with his own quandaries.

A silver bracelet that Marcos had given her flashed in the sun as she drew her hand across her forehead. She had driven out to Nambé on an impulse to fess up, so Marcos hadn't been expecting her. Kip, who'd vanished into the violet shadows of the *portal,* was the only one who knew she was here. Wind chimes hanging from the low eaves made their uncanny music as she looked around. She could retreat to her car, parked beside the adobe archway on the far side of the hacienda, without being seen. Who would be any the wiser if she simply fled? So she fled, and as she did the realization she could just keep driving west until she reached California hovered before her like a beacon. By the time she crested the knoll overlooking Santa Fe, however, the idea dimmed, then departed.

*T*he procession of vehicles behind the waxed hearse rolled through Carrizozo. Headlights shone pale and bleak beneath the early afternoon swelter of sun. In her wooden coffin lay Agnes Montoya. Delfino, now her widower but only the day before yesterday her husband of forty-nine years, refused to be chauffeured in a black town car from the mortuary. Instead, he'd driven his Ford pickup with his nephew, Marcos, riding shotgun.

Agnes would not have been surprised at his bullheaded behavior. She'd have been touched, though, that rather than wearing one of his usual turquoise bolo ties he'd dug out the only necktie he owned, which Marcos had knotted for him back at the bungalow. Agnes would have loved to see her man dressed proud like this, and had she made it to their golden anniversary it might have happened. As it was, one would have to go back and look at wedding photos from 'thirty-nine to see Delfino similarly decked out.

A few members of her family were here from Oklahoma, and on Delfino's side people were down from Nambé. All were sad but not shocked. Once Agnes had been diagnosed in Las Cruces and it was understood that the growth was inoperable, her dying had moved swiftly.

A brother of hers—John Bryant, his name had been—who'd come with her to this valley toward the end of the Depression, was buried not far north, at White Oaks Cemetery, fenced by wrought iron and cradled by forested mountains. It was her wish, fulfilled now, if she couldn't be buried at Dripping Spring, the homestead she and Delfino had settled years before, that she be laid to rest beside this brother. Dust blew as the minister read. 1926–1988. A few people succinctly spoke of her qualities and virtues. The ceremony was, again according to her wish, brief. Afterward, they entouraged back through Carrizozo and on toward Tularosa, as the massive skies spun toward eventide and a first planet brazenly flickered in the still-pale blue behind them on the horizon. After the mortuary people took their leave, with gravity and antique courtesies, Agnes's families drove down to Alamogordo to have a smorgasbord dinner at the Holiday Inn. Delfino was lost in an understandable daze, but spoke with Marcos, red in the face not from grief but flourishing anger.

—Her tumor was their tumor, Delfino said.

Marcos did not question his uncle. Tacitly he agreed, shaking his head while choking on a deviled egg. Muzak, strangely soothing, underscored the quiet conversing among these two families, who did not know each other well.

—They'll be hearing from me, Delfino assured his nephew.

—What are you going to tell them? he asked, daring to look at his uncle who had shed, by now, black tie and jacket, leaving buttoned his weskit from another era, of purple, orange, and gold paisley, white shirtsleeves rolled up, the grief only enhanced in his profile.

Marcos didn't inquire who *they* were. He'd known for years who they were and happened to agree that Delfino and Agnes had been evicted, defrauded, gypped, swindled, deceived, fucked up and down by the amorphous, considerable *them*.

—These people murdered my wife and to add insult to injury they murdered her after they'd already killed her. How many times is a soul supposed to die?

His nephew sat still.

—First they made it so she couldn't have a baby, with all their radiation drifting over the mountain. Then they made it so the only thing that could grow inside her was cancer.

Marcos placed a tentative hand on his uncle's shoulder.

—I hope they're happy.

Astounding, thought Marcos, that the tune "Raindrops Keep Falling on My Head" should be piped through the sound system as his uncle spoke, but there it was. He watched Delfino lay his fork on the plate of uneaten food. *But that doesn't mean my eyes will soon be turning red*—

—As if Communist socialism ever stood a snowball's chance.

Sarah Montoya had been eavesdropping on her brother-in-law while she engaged with others in the funeral party. —Delfino, I'm sure you're right, but don't you think Agnes would want us to leave them out of the discussion on this day of all days? Her voice was demure, even tranquil, and her hand found Delfino's where it lay like some wounded animal on the white tablecloth.

—I'm sorry, he nodded.

—No need for apology. I just want you to be all right.

He lifted a piece of bread to his mouth but couldn't eat it so put it down again beside his plate before telling Marcos, quietly, —Fact is, they probably are. Happy about it, I mean—proud of themselves.

—How could anybody be proud of pushing folks off their land and then slowly depriving them of life?

—That's how it works. That's how it was. And the more they do nothing, more they just keep good and tight-lipped and leave us dangling, the more all that's left of us die off. One day it'll come to pass that nothing will have happened. I'll be with Agnes. The Onsruds'll be gone, like the Harmans, the Wards, the Stearns, the McDonalds, everybody. Every one of the other ranchers down here'll be dead and gone and that'll mean they were right and we weren't. Why wouldn't they be proud of being right?

Sarah overheard, despite his whispering. —Maybe you'd like some coffee, Delf.

—He's okay, Marcos said, and rose, after his uncle did, to follow him to the men's room where the widower wept quietly in one of the stalls. Marcos washed his face and dried it with a paper towel. He left the echoing room, then waited outside in the corridor for some while before his uncle emerged, stonefaced, to take his nephew by the elbow and ask him to accompany him to the parking lot. Would he mind making the necessary excuses for an old man who had to get back home, and who truly appreciated everybody's concern and the effort they'd all gone to, coming from such distances to be with Agnes today?

The air outside was sere and smarting with gypsum sand carried on the breeze from the white dunes west of town, past the gargantuan air force base. —Tell Sarah and your father I'm fine, just tired is all. Need to be by myself.

Marcos asked if he might drive Delfino up the road to Tularosa. His uncle was grateful but climbed into the pickup with no further comment, turned over the engine, and pulled out onto the highway that bisected Alamogordo, paralleling the old El Paso–to–White Oaks railroad line, which had, before drought settled in a century before, falsely promised this catastrophic basin fruits and wealth beyond dreaming.

When he got home, the widower folded his necktie into a kind of crunched coil, like some burned and flattened sidewinder, then placed it ceremoniously in Agnes's rags drawer. He changed out of his suit into a flannel workshirt and khaki trousers, then set himself the task of laundering his wife's clothing—her seersucker robe, her cotton nightshirts, her thin white ankle socks. He had it in mind that on the following morning he would bundle everything up and take it to the Salvation Army in El Paso.

Others would be wearing Agnes's wardrobe by next week, in Juárez and Carlsbad and even Galveston. They would never have heard of Agnes Montoya, a ranching wife who'd poured every energy of her youth into homesteading a few hundred acres of wickedly thorny land up by Dripping Spring on this side of the San Andres. Some woman visiting her sister down in El Paso would score Agnes's favorite dress at the thrift shop, a dark-blue polka-dotted rayon number with a scalloped hem. She'd drive back to Truth or Consequences feeling extravagant as the wind ruffled its sleeves. Others would carry away her stuff, too, unaware that in the early forties their original owner had helped build a house, dig its cistern, erect the windmill, herd cattle, and break wild cayuses at her husband's side. None who wore Agnes's jewelry, slacks, coats would ever know how deep had been her grief that she and Delfino never had children. Nor how devastated she'd felt when, in 1944, the army evicted them from their ranch, promising that they could return once the war was over. And how angry over the passing years this wife and her husband had grown, after the government tested its plutonium device just beyond the mountain, on McDonald's spread, and then other gadgets, rockets, bombers, no one knew altogether just what, on their own usurped land. A girl who wore her shawl to a Halloween party up in Galisteo would never be able to imagine how Agnes and Delfino had lived out their marginal lives in exile. Nor would the welfare woman who fancied the pair of red lizard-skin shoes, which she would pass on to her daughter years later, ever know how much Agnes used to love those chukkas, as she called them, which she always wore with such pleasure on birthdays in their little nothing house in Tularosa.

Sure, she and Delfino wrote dozens of letters, to presidents and senators, representatives, secretaries and undersecretaries of the Department of Defense, a variety of officials in the army and the air force, and White Sands Proving Grounds folks, who were often sympathetic and always unhelpful. They penned articles for the *Lincoln County News,* sent letters to editors of distant newspapers. They organized meetings, coffees, discussion groups, even drear socials with the other 150 or so families similarly evicted. They waited. Received their disgraceful if not illegal settlement back in 'seventy-five, along with the others—a sum that failed by many millions to compensate for total ranch values. Ground out more petitions and got back polite letters of nonresponse. Endured the repeated defeat of congressional proposals to establish a commission charged with evaluating claims submitted by those "displaced from their land and livelihood." Saw the lives of others caught in the same plight vanish.

And Agnes, whose clothes would be floated to the seven winds, had watched Delfino's life and her own fade as surely as things left too long in the sun.

—He said he needed to go be alone, Marcos told his father and mother when he returned to the dining room.

—Should we check on him? Sarah asked Carl.

—No, I know my brother. Best leave him to his grief. We'll look in on him tomorrow before we drive back home.

Some days after Agnes was laid to rest—days after Sarah, Carl, and Marcos dropped by with a box of doughnuts before heading back to Nambé, days after his trip down to El Paso, and days subsequent to the departure of everybody who'd turned up for her funeral—Delfino sat himself down to write another letter. Agnes, he believed, would have approved. Giving up had not been in her glossary. He had never yet spent one red penny of the settlement check they'd awarded him. That word *awarded* had stuck in his craw when one of their public-relations people had called to let them know that the check was being sent via certified mail. The money sat like so much rotten dross in a bank account in Carrizozo, and even when he and Agnes had fallen on the hardest of financial times they never once considered withdrawing it. He would give it all back with interest—so he'd written them before and wrote them now. But what was more, if Delfino died doing so, he was going to get his goddamn ranch back.

A chorus of pond frogs under racing stars. The rising moon like a decayed tooth sunk in the tender flesh of a melon cloud. The plaintive veery in the oak tree. This sagging porch she'd paced over many extinct summers. They all offered their stability to unstable Ariel who, though sitting on her favorite Adirondack chair, felt as if in a free fall. Given the day's disclosure, she had to ask herself questions she'd never needed to consider before. What would it be like having someone in your life day and night, dawn to dusk to dawn? Someone who has every right to rely on your love, solace, thoughts, values, support, understanding, sustenance?

She drank from a fresh glass of shameful, ridiculous gin and would have scowled had her face not been numbed under its influence. A bat dropped through the silent air, out over the unmown grass studded with wild strawberry and devil's paintbrush, and she half envied the gnat that was targeted in its orbit. Ariel had always come to the family farmhouse to consider important matters, away from the din of Manhattan. Never, though, did she have weightier business to consider than tonight.

With hasty scissors she cut through the floss and, like some latter-day Pandora, opened the box on her lap. Taking a deep breath, she opened the ledger at random and found a photograph taped to the page, a black-and-white faded toward pale butterscotch. The snapshot had scalloped margins that dated it to the fifties or early sixties. Two boys standing side by side, arms thrown casually over each other's shoulders. The kid on the left was unmistakably Brice, with his earnest, squinched eyes and broad smile; the other, with a distracted cast and wide forehead wrinkled under the open sun, looked uncannily like Ariel herself. *McCarthy and me, Four Corners area, 19-whatevereth.* At second glance she could see behind them the needly throne of volcanic rock rising over a thousand feet above an otherwise flat desert floor. Altogether unreal, the boys standing before that mythic monument carved by fire and rain. Even more unreal was that Brice looked as if he were there at Shiprock with Ariel, the two of them like brother and sister, a decade before she was even born. If any questions lingered about her parentage, this image dispelled them.

Flipping back through the ambered leaves, she encountered equations, beautiful if incomprehensible strings of numbers framed by detailed marginalia, drawings of plants and animals, butterflies and reptiles, themselves annotated in a tiny hand beneath the pen and inks with notes such as *P. douglasii, short horned lizard drawn 6.7.49 in alpine tundra Mt. Taylor brick-red with brown blotches and orange chin, big lizard syntypes collected by a David Douglas, no relation to namesake working with Bradbury.*

Musing through the notebook, Ariel admired its purple, blue, and black inks, its meticulous script. Here was a palimpsest of physics, facts, educated guesses, not to mention deep regrets from days as distant as the stars burning above in the present night. Flickering suns, fiery nuclear reactions chained to their positions in the sky, any one of which—all of which, really—might have burned out millennia ago, and who'd be the wiser?

Page after page was saturated with pyramiding blocks of theory—
frustrating if not unnerving—punctuated where her eye might rest
on something at least half recognizable, such as *RaLa core* or *beta-
tron pulse* or *U235*, which she remembered from chemistry class and
the table of elements that had hung on the wall at school. She
turned the pages from left to right, as if reading Japanese, since
what could it matter which way she traveled through this gnarly
thicket of science.

What caught her fingers from pitching forward—or backward, as
it were—was the sporadic island of English. Her grandfather making
the occasional observation for his private keeping, all these years
later reluctantly read by someone he'd never known. *Emma tonight
at Norris's shindig radiant in that new organza, a terrible splurge for her
birthday but worth every penny.* And on another page, *Sick with flu
these last four days, Kip down with same grippe, played pinochle with
him, he won every time.* And another, *McCarthys over to dinner last
night, roast of lamb with mint sauce, Mrs. McC. ate only yams, testing
vegetarianism and why not, more lamb for me this morning, Brice turning into an awful swell kid and I hope he has positive influence on the
Kipper.*

Thoughts such as these, the unadorned flow of people living their
lives as simply as the top security and sequestration of Los Alamos
would allow. The diary of this scientist, yes, and a deadly brilliant
one at that, but withal a person who married a girl from a family on
the outskirts of Havana—did this account in part for Ariel's black
irises and olive skin? she wondered, as a thrill ran through her at the
probability—who bore him one son, the orphaned and orphaning
Kip. The diarist meticulously kept what were surely prohibited, possibly treasonous records, from prebomb 1944 through the middle sixties, of his activities at the Los Alamos Research Laboratory, his
specific work on the Project, his initial patriotism, subsequent growing doubts, and final dire misgivings about the results of his labors.

There were other darker elucidations in the book, and Ariel cast an eye over them as if over the history they encapsulated. How could she not shudder at the agony of

> *. . . At least the murderer knows the horror of the knife driven into his victim's heart, can try like Macbeth's wife to wash that blood off stained hands, but how do I help sharpen these ten trillion knives to rain on the heads of victims I will never know, never meet, never bury with my hands—how in hell do I go about mourning them? No hagas mal que bien no esperes, Emma says—Don't wrong others and expect kindness in return. Maybe that's why my boy doesn't like it here. Nothing I do makes him want to stay home. His eye is constantly looking away from mine. Nobody's said anything to us about it but Emmy and I think everybody on the Hill knows what's happening. They feel sorry but I just feel discouraged. Last week the MPs found him down in Bandelier, hiding in one of the Indian caves. Even camping in a cold cave is better, by his lights, than sleeping here under the same roof as his dad and mom. Is this what I've done? Our only child. Brought this on all of us—Kip, too?*

Eyes welling, she clutched the ledger against her chest. It reeked richly of must, familiar, smelling like the rain-damp hay she and Brice used to spread as mulch over grass seed whenever one of those crazy apple trees toppled under a killing frost and had to be yanked out by its roots in spring, chopped up, and run through the chipper. She knew with the precision of a child's memory where each tree used to stand, the ones she climbed when she was a kid, fell from, breaking her arm once, her wrist another time. She remembered her horse, Maxwell, on whose broad back she loved to fly through the summer woods, until he ran her beneath a low branch that dropped her to the ground, dislocating her shoulder and fracturing ribs. Life measured by broken bones. Remembered, too, how Buddha often acrobated the branches, bringing home once a fledgling wren from a nest he raided, not because he wanted to eat the poor beast—she shouted at him, *You're overfed as it is, you murderer*—but because, as her father tried to explain while she cradled its gangly fluid corpse in her hands, —Ariel, cats kill birds. It's in their blood. It seems cruel. But it's natural, part of life.

And what about people? What's in *their* blood? she'd wondered as she dug an afternoon grave for the tiny wren.

She could resolve, now, what had been posed those many years ago down in the field beyond the porch where she sat on this different but oddly similar evening: Kip was in her blood. And in the wake of her initial shock at learning those three years ago that he was her father, she had come to a quick judgment that beyond the shared genetics, the mutual biology, Kip should not be pertinent to her life. But he was. He was.

Yet if Kip's was a runner's blood, so might hers be. That would certainly explain why she had run—or if not exactly run, then walked deliberately—away from him when given the chance to encounter the man. Or had her refusal to deal with it been more a case of the ostrich burying its head in the sand? The ostrich that sometimes suffocates in the same sand that was meant to protect it from harm. Daughterhood, she thought, scrunching at the page before her, lit by a citronella candle that was supposed to discourage mosquitoes but didn't. Who in their right mind would put a contentedly unaware nonentity through it? How could anybody feel compelled to drag serene nothingness from the void into the harshness of the baby cradle and not expect a great deal of justified crying and crapping? She shook her head. One problem at a time, she thought.

Reading deeper into the book she uncovered Kip's hidden design, the text within a text he intended for her to find. *Dear Ariel*, his letter began where the elder Calder's writings left off, abruptly, after a diary entry for 1968 alluding to an imminent trip to New York, where his and Emma Inez's son was drifting and ruckusing his way through Columbia. Ariel wondered whether Brice's eyes had passed over these words but sensed not. Given he hadn't mentioned any letter from Kip back when he presented her with his confession and this battered inheritance, he probably didn't know that her other father had written his own thoughts in an addendum.

Dear Ariel, she read,

There was a man I met and knew for a while many years ago who believed in every religion and religious book, read the Bible and was versed in it, and who loved above everything else to quote from Proverbs. I don't know whether or not you are a religious person, but I liked this man, and in time I came to like some of his quotes. One in particular comes to mind now, which went, No one who conceals transgressions will prosper, but one who confesses and forsakes them will obtain mercy. I apologize for this terrible beginning to what must be a terrible letter to read (one you may never read but that I need to write), but I wanted to say that the proverb promises, in exchange for setting things right, nothing more than clemency, maybe a kind of pity, in the best sense. I hope that you will find it in your heart to feel mercy for me even though you don't owe me mercy or anything else. There is nothing more I could wish for, however, than clemency, mercy, whatever the right word would be. If you can't give it, you can't, and you would certainly be within your rights not to. Love is out of the question, I realize. You don't know me and logically you cannot love what you don't know. What's more, I'm not sure love would even be appropriate to the circumstances. Understanding may be the best I can hope for, and at least a chance to end my concealment, because the time has come for me to give that up for the rotten burden it always was. If you can find enough patience to hear me out, my ghost will be grateful.

Eyes going out of focus, Ariel whispered that last clause, *my ghost will be grateful.* Her voice, and she heard it, strained not to be taut with rebuke. What was to rebuke? Here was a man trying to articulate what must have been inarticulable, as he set pen to a notebook that his own father had begun. Two ghosts speaking to her from the portal of one book would be overwhelming in any circumstances, but in her current state of mind the whole thing seemed altogether unearthly.

Written in different inks, apparently at different times and in different places, this letter unfurled over some dozen pages. Kip plainly had started his letter, then started it again and again. His addendum constituted a mess of addenda. The document attached to Calder senior's might be deemed a father's final failure to communicate with his daughter or, inversely, his most faithful possible account of the bewilderment he felt. And what had Kip made of his own father's confessions of remorse, his feelings of accountability, the growing perplexities that had been terminated when the physicist and his wife were killed on their way to visit a son who himself was about to spin off the planet? She lifted the glass to her lips and drained it down, shuddering at its bitter juniper bite.

I will probably be dead by the time you read this, and good riddance. Your parents, among the best friends I ever had when we were all younger than you are now, will have told you about our friendship, about how your mother and I were together and in love, and how I went off to serve in Ca Mau, a dump way to the south of Saigon, then went underground in Laos, trying in that same gesture to find and lose myself. I got the latter done, but now failingly work at the former. Better never to lose yourself. Saves the trouble of having to go on a hunt. They'll have told you that Jess was pregnant with you and that I didn't trust her, or Brice, and believed you were not my child. I've had years to concoct every kind of rationale for my abandonment of you, Jess, Brice, the world I knew, choosing instead to marry mistrust and return to a war that I barely believed in anymore either, but that in my callous juvenile stupidity seemed more reasonable to me—can you imagine?

Reasonable! An idea that only someone who'd reached real depths of unreason could muster. But yes, more reasonable at the time, than

*shouldering what could have been the authentic mission. I failed
you, failed myself, failed everyone. There is no defense.*

*One gift you can give yourself, if you have the patience to listen
to someone you have every right to ignore, would be to cut your
mother and father, Jessica and Brice, all the slack you can manage.
None of this is their fault, just as none of it is yours. Where does the
fault lie, other than with me? I have been all over the world, running and now walking, slowing down as I've come to the place
where I begin to see that it lies nowhere, maybe. If I'm nowhere and
the fault lies with me, then the fault lies nowhere. You'll agree
there's a logic, a complementum as your grandfather's sometime colleague Niels Bohr used to put it, to such a lie of reasoning.*

And as tears streamed down Ariel's cheeks, she wondered whether
he meant to misspell that word *line.*

*I*n her role as incognita, Franny Johnson was freed of the awkward
truths most lovers must face about their romantic pasts. She could
make hers up as she went along, and so she did. Her powers of invention surprised her at times. Although she'd never really had a
boyfriend before, she conceived of several. The relationships were
nothing serious, she assured Marcos. Sergio had been an exchange
student back in Princeton, from northern Italy, near Milan. He'd
hoped to become a diplomat one day. After he went back home, he
wrote her a nice letter inviting her to join him in Venice, but she
never did, and that was that. Then there was a graduate student, a
research assistant who was her mother's acolyte. His name was—
Peter, Peter Cummington. Came from a good family, blue-blooded
rather than red-blooded. Tall, slender, memorable for his cable-knit
sweaters and tortoiseshell glasses but little else. No chemistry, a total
fizz. The sound of his wingtip shoes clomping down the corridor
of the mathematics building still made her shudder. The last was

Sebastian, before she swore off men altogether and prepared herself for a life of celibacy. Sebastian was clever but conceited, handsome in a vain sort of way. The last time she saw him—well, never mind.

All of this would have been a perfect backstory for Audrey Hepburn in the film *Love in the Afternoon,* had Marcos resembled the game if aging Gary Cooper, which he didn't. But for all its fraudulence, her Billy Wilder–worthy performances did project curious truths—among them her desire to make her man covetous—and through the course of her fictions, Franny watched a most unexpected thing develop. A love affair. One that deepened from ideas to words, from words to acts, on the very stage they themselves walked.

Yet Mary lingered, enigma that she was, in the wings. That day on which she had begun but failed to reveal herself to Kip receded into the past. Honoring her silence, he never broached the matter again. And honoring his, she willfully neglected it, a path abandoned at least temporarily for fear of finding out what lay at its end. One question she neglected to ask herself was whether Marcos would not have been just as happy to know the real Mary as the fabricated Franny. Mary tried to bring this to Franny's attention, and while the question never quite formulated itself, it nagged at her in subtle and unsubtle ways. She dropped a bowl of black bean soup at work for no reason. She lost the key to her house so many times that she finally hid it as a matter of course under the doormat, and even then it disappeared. When driving out to Pajarito, she forgot her license— her only remaining piece of material evidence that Franny Johnson didn't truly exist—hidden in the medicine cabinet.

The whole damn mess was nearly brought to an abrupt end on the feast day of San Felipe de Nerí, Mary's twenty-first birthday. It was a Saturday morning bright and blue as her eyes, and Franny's day, as she'd foreseen it, was going to be spent at home, alone, maybe reading, maybe just sleeping. When Marcos turned up at her door unannounced—she had at last, though reluctantly, divulged where she lived—and told her that Sarah, Carl, and Kip had come along with him "to go to the celebration for San Franny and San Felipe," she recoiled imperceptibly. Which is to say, a smile spread across her face and she waved toward those waiting for her in the Jeep, while her heart sank paradoxically at the prospect of spending this birthday with people she treasured.

"You okay?" Marcos asked.

"Just surprised, is all."

"That's the idea."

Two hours later, at the fiesta in Old Town Albuquerque, she saw one of her brothers across a crowded concession area billowing with violet smoke. She gasped. Instinctively glancing back toward where her own party had been absorbed into the crowd, she locked eyes with Kip. He'd noticed her blanching and half smiled at her—what else could he do?—before turning to see what she was looking at. No one stood out, nothing unusual seemed to be going on. Confused, he raised his eyebrows and shrugged, as if to ask, What's wrong? Do you need help? Marcos walked up to her meantime.

"What have you been up to?" she asked, grateful for the reprieve from having to answer Kip.

"I found a birthday present at one of the booths."

"Being here with you guys is gift enough."

"Hardly." Holding up a small brown paper bag, Marcos added, "Besides, it's a done deal. I'll give it to you later."

She thanked him with a kiss on the cheek and said, "Speaking of which, it's getting kind of late don't you think?"

"We only got here an hour ago."

"Maybe we should have lunch. I know a place near Placitas."

"Well, it's your day. Let me go find Carl and Sarah."

Kip stood standing, as they say. Franny glanced again in the direction of her brother John, who had vanished into the ranging crowd of fiestagoers. Then she turned back to Kip.

"What are you looking for?"

"Nothing, why?" she lied, then changed the subject. "I don't know about you, but I'm not that used to people caring whether it's my birthday or not. Haven't celebrated mine in years." No sooner had her wistful remark slipped out than she asked herself, Why do I keep revealing myself to this man?

"You're too young not to celebrate birthdays."

She scumbled the moment, saying, "When's your birthday, Kip?"

"I don't have one."

"They just dropped you here from another universe."

"How did you know?"

"Really. When were you born?"

"Post-Christmas, nineteen forty-four. Between the Savior's birth and the atom bomb. Rude syzygy."

Where were the Montoyas? She had to get out of here. "What?"

"When the planets align. Causes strange things to happen."

Franny felt compelled to pat Kip gently on the back. A gesture of affection. Of unmeditated fellowship. She was surprised by how thin he remained, yet how sturdy and solid he'd grown.

"Come on, Mary. What were you looking at before?"

"I told you not to call me that."

"No one heard but you."

"I thought I saw somebody I knew."

"Your worst enemy or just a stray demon? You didn't look too happy about whoever it was."

"It's not that. Just somebody I haven't seen in a long time."

"None of my business."

"Doesn't matter," she said. "I was wrong, anyway."

She put her hands in her pockets and stared at the pavement.

Kip said, "You know, if you ever need to talk to me some more about what you brought up a couple months back, I can be a pretty good listener. Not judgmental. Can't afford to be."

"You have kids?"

He shook his head.

"That's too bad. You'd have made a good father."

"I doubt that very much."

"Well, I don't," and glanced up suddenly mindful that there was every chance her own father was somewhere in this throng.

Positioning herself subtly behind Kip, she searched the torrent of faces—so many cultures mixed in among them, people democratized by where they lived and the blue jeans they, like Franny, wore— and located her oldest brother, Jimmy, as well as her sister, Rose, who stood watching the electric band Cinco de Mayo with their mother and, yes, Russell Carpenter, her detested father. As fortune would have it, their backs were turned to Kip and Franny. They seemed to be enjoying themselves, swaying to the distorted music. Her father had put on weight since she last laid eyes on him, while her mother looked to be diminished by half. Jimmy wore a smartly pressed khaki uniform and a Stetson and had his arm around a young woman whom she didn't recognize. Had he gotten married? Was he in the service, after all those years of screaming, unpatriotic skirmishes with dear old Dad? Rose had grown her hair long, as had her twin brother, John, who now joined the group. Kind of a surprise given how strict Russell had always been about such life-and-death matters as personal grooming. Maybe he was slipping, losing sway over the lot of them. She'd like to think her departure had to do with this subversion, but was startled from such musings when her sister, who'd been talking animatedly with John, turned around and seemed to look directly at her.

She had to escape, right away, and without creating a scene. Still, she gazed for one clipped instant at her mother with whom Rose was now speaking excitedly, and saw how these few years had reduced her, pulled her unkindly toward the ground, wrenched down the corners of her mouth, a mouth that once had been as full and young as Mary's own. Stung a little by guilt and overwhelmed by frantic fear, she asked Kip if he didn't mind walking her back to the Jeep. She wasn't feeling well, all of a sudden. He took her arm and the two of them threaded their way to the parking lot. Having noticed everything, Kip said nothing. Carl was asleep in the front seat, and within minutes they were joined by Marcos and Sarah, whose arms were full of gifts.

On the drive to Placitas, Franny sat in the back between Marcos and Kip, whose cooperative silence extended to his making no mention of Franny's abrupt recovery. "Hey, who is Felipe de Nerí, anyway?" she asked, using all the acting skills available to her.

Nobody knew, except Carl, who said, "Just another Italian saint from a thousand years ago. Dime a dozen."

"He should know. They were friends back then."

Nodding toward Marcos, Sarah asked Franny, "This is the kind of man you go around with?"

"You're his mother," she laughed.

"That's right, Franny. You tell her," Carl said, mock-serious.

Franny bundled up the vision of her Gallup family as if into a little crumpled ball that she then threw, mentally, out the window, but couldn't help wondering if any of them remembered that today was her birthday. Of course they did, she assured herself. But why care?

After a celebratory dinner that night at Rancho Pajarito, after opening her presents and blowing out the candles on a cake, she lay in bed with Marcos, her back turned to her lover. The silver necklace he'd given her felt unfamiliar against her flesh, but she was grateful and was sure she'd grow accustomed to its weight there. His callused but supple hand moved from her neck down the small of her back to rest on her hip. She whispered his name as his fingers waterfalled over onto the flat of her stomach and caressed her, nuancing themselves into her gently under the sheet, across her warming skin.

This was where she belonged, she thought. Not on the stage, not on the screen, but in this small home constituted by Marcos's hands and arms. Yet as she listened to his deepening breath after they made love, that thought was superseded by others. Wasn't it true that she'd fallen in love with the Montoyas as a whole, their son bridging her from her old, garbled world to one intimate, ordinary in ways she'd always dreamed a family could be? And wasn't it also the truth that the other evening, when she and Marcos saw a flick in Santa Fe, she caught herself critiquing the actors' gestures, voicings, timing, the interplay of music and lighting? Neither was it some grand classic of world cinema—just another love story set against impending war.

But every error was her mistake, every tiny triumph as if her own. She had traveled a nervy, dire road fleeing Gallup and the father she saw in Albuquerque today, to embrace a mawkish dream of dramatic make-believe. So what meant more? This real story she was living—a good story, with a promising premise and kindly dramatis personae—or some unknown fantasy drama with high potential for disillusionment and disaster?

Head aswirl, as the last fire of the season burned down to orange piñon coals, balmy and sweet smoking ash in the corner hearth of the bedroom, she whispered to him, knowing he was asleep, "I made all that up about those other guys. I never had any lover but you."

Then she, too, fell asleep, having wrapped up the day in a ribbon of truth.

By the end of the letter, Ariel's fingers were frozen. On a close warm moonful summer night, at that. Yet another gin, whose ice melted in the glass, stood on the wide arm of the Adirondack chair. Shouldn't be drinking like this. Look what it's done to Grandmother McCarthy. She took another gulp, saying aloud to the fireflies, "Stop," though she didn't heed her own advice, deciding instead this might be the perfect night to get stinking plastered.

No one who conceals transgressions will prosper, that passage quoted by Kip's friend, from the Bible—she'd heard it before. Granna, of course. Gin on the rocks and the Holy Scripture had always been her twin stalwarts, no matter how much Brice complained about having to run their gauntlet his whole life. Still, Ariel recalled how Granna's ginny interpretations of the Bible were something to hear that first time she flew by herself out to Los Alamos for a visit. Face blossoming and eyes weepy with conviction and liquor, Brice's mother happily clarified for her son's receptive daughter any textual questions the young lady might have about the Pauline epistles. Lecturing away, she stared at the adobe walls of her kitchen, walls white as the clay pipe she puffed. Ariel listened amazed, then was amazed the more by the woman's brusque switch from one subject to another in the anemic air of that mesa where she lived, having stayed on long after her only son left. From her beloved Saint Paul's—Kiplike?—wanderings and his awful crucifixion spiked head-down to a wooden cross, to other scandalous matters such as why the devil Ariel's parents hadn't given her a brother or sister, Granna progressed like a grand peremptory army of one.

—Your father says he's an atheist but you know he isn't.

—He thinks of God in his own way.

—No offense, Ariel, but why didn't they? Have other children, that is.

What *did* Granna see on the wall there? Ariel'd wondered. It was as if she were reading its blank page as she drew deep on her pipe and blew out a cloud that spread over its surface, like airy fingers deciphering braille.

—Maybe one of me was more than enough, the young woman said, looking at her own fingers splayed on the pearlescent kitchen table, then glancing up to marvel at the polished silver knobs of the vintage McCarthy stove. Her grandmother's kitchen was cluttered, much like Aunt Bonnie's—Granna had provided Brice with a sibling—with a lifetime of human accumulation. Tins of Jackson of Piccadilly tea and of Fauchon Bourbon's Préparation Aromatisée stood behind glass in canisters sent from New York, part of her son's annual Thanksgiving parcel. Colanders, birds' nests, herb wreaths. Granna liked things that came from places she might never visit— such as the postcard her son had mailed from Prague—and from people she'd never see in this world again—roses, now dried and dangling upside down, had been a gift from her late husband on some long-ago birthday. Her place was full of stuff but spotless. Immaculate as the Conception, pristine as her glass of Tanqueray. A long minute passed, measured by a ticktocking clock, while Ariel watched her grandmother frown at the wall calendar. What a magnificent, eccentric woman, she thought as she waited in the densely metered quiet for what would come next.

Finally Brice's mother said with assurance, though perhaps without clear context, —Well, as the Good Book has it, *His mercy is for those who fear Him from generation to generation.* You could have used a sister.

—Probably.

—Girls need sisters so they can have someone to talk to when, you know, things happen.

—What things?

—Things that make you unhappy, her grandmother said. And then she drifted away again into other worlds, musing on the fig tree under which Adam wept, or Augustine's lust, and how that reminded her of the hike she and Brice's father once made up the notch at San Agustin Pass. Which was where, her granddaughter surmised, Brice was conceived.

It occurred to Ariel, sitting on this summer porch, that right now she could use, as much as some sister, a good dose of Granna's fearsome faith. Not to mention her talent for chasing hunches in circles, like a dog its own sometimes catchable tail.

Where had Ariel's own thoughts now veered if not into mad cyclings, like the Milky Way, which while wheeling out of control cast light on so much? Here at the farm, the kitchen walls were also white. Plaster laced with cowhair rather than the pure adobe of New Mexico, true, but she liked the idea of connection between this house and Granna's. Anything that proposed continuity, cohesion. Ariel could see by the citronella's flame that the siding could use some fresh paint. Maybe once she got things straightened out she'd do the job herself. Scraping, sanding, brushing the rows of parallel clapboard—tasks that smacked of normalcy and healing. A project Granna would find worthy.

After another trip inside to refill her glass, she returned to the porch. With David having agreed to drive up late after work, and given the magnitude of the news she had to tell him, getting smashed was not, perhaps, the best idea. Good thing she phoned him before cracking open the liquor cabinet. "Go *away*," she shouted, addressing not so much her predicament as the doggerel music that would not dislodge its looping track from her head. What mad genius ever thought to rhyme *lettuce* with *upset us*? Some jingle she must have heard on David's television, since she didn't own one, hadn't grown up with one—a childhood abnormality that once made her weird in the eyes of telesaturated kids at school. At recess, on the paved playground, they discussed shows about cookie monsters and ranch tycoons. Smiling, she'd nod if asked, Didn't this or that episode sound great? Probably yes, but it was a world she didn't know, which always left her a bit the outsider. She wondered what books Kip had read. And which, if any, had sent him into rapturous joy, or plunged him into doubt. His letter was more than articulate. It seemed inspired by the eloquence of knowing loss.

So Ariel thought, as vertigo voices singing *Special orders don't upset us* carried on and on and she gazed beyond the yard, past the pond, and into the woods where white birches stood out like skinny ghosts, down where she often gathered mushrooms, having learned as a girl to distinguish the edible ones from the poisonous. And oh, she thought, before passing out in the hard chair, if only everything were as simple to sort as boletes from morels, morels from ringstalks, ringstalks from . . .

She jolted upright on hearing David's car coming up the dirt road through the woods that surrounded the farm. Stiff and aching, Ariel felt the undeniable here-and-now upon her. The ledger had fallen from her lap and she grasped for it, clutched it again, oddly felt that without it she might float away. Parenthood, she thought, remembering what was inside her, the fetus, embryo, zygote. The idea of an idea. Like parentheses around a vital aside. Parents, parentheses.

Must be after midnight. Some of the stars seemed to be making lateral curlicuing movements, as if astronomical baton twirlers up there had fallen out of formation but kept their figure-eights going.

She listened as wind moved gently around the house. Sounds carried here as if they made themselves up out of nothing.

The low grind of the engine climbing the hill, and the flash of headlamp light across the barrier of trees. Crunch of stone in the short curved driveway. She didn't move but heard David open and then slam shut the door of the car on the opposite side of the house. She tensed, willing the batoning stars to cease whirling, willing Mrs. McCarthy back into her kitchen those couple thousand miles away, willing herself to get undrunk and face David.

She rose unsteadily to her feet, hearing him call her name, which echoed in the shallow valley.

"Back here," she answered.

"Sorry I'm so late."

David kissed her upturned face, Ariel kissing the air as she half turned away.

"Sorry for the short notice," she said. "You want a drink, something to eat?"

"I had dinner in the city before coming up, but some scotch would be good."

He knew where the liquor cabinet was, knew where everything was in this house. He and Ariel had spent many days and nights here together, sometimes visiting her parents, often by themselves. As he poured his drink he hesitated, lingering a moment in the pantry to listen to the voluminous silence of the place, a stillness that always soothed and frightened him. How could the world tolerate such a quiet corner as this? Life prefers clamor. If only to prove it is living. Carrying his glass back to the porch, he dreaded whatever he was about to hear. Ariel had never phoned him out of the blue like this with such an adamant request.

"Is it something we could put off until the weekend?" he had asked. "I've got to be at work early tomorrow."

"It's nothing we should put off."

She'd sounded grim. So he'd agreed, telling her he would cancel a morning meeting that, in any event, was not on his schedule. Now he sat beside her and, assuring himself there was nothing to worry about in the long run, took a breath of night air and a taste of his scotch.

Ariel wasted no time with preliminaries. "I'm pregnant."

After a moment he said, "You're joking, right?"

"Do I look like I'm joking?"

"You look like you've been drinking."

"I'm not joking. I've been drinking. I'm pregnant."

It occurred to him that he had expected much worse, somehow, though he'd not construed the precise possibilities, or at least never anticipated this one. Without thinking, he said, "I'm really sorry."

"What's to be sorry about?"

How hateful the assumption that funded his automatic response, even though his instinct wasn't so different from her own. When he continued, not missing a beat, saying, "Look, it's my responsibility to pay," she passingly wondered whether David hadn't been through this before.

"Pay what?"

"You have to suffer through the procedure, so I should cover the cost."

"That's very generous of you, but who said I'm getting an abortion?"

Here, then, was that worse crisis he had forecast. "But Ariel, in all the time I've known you, you've never once expressed any interest in having children."

She couldn't contradict him.

"What's this?" he asked, pointing with his scotch at the ledger cradled in her arms. "Is it what I think it is?"

Ariel nodded in the flickering light. Poor David—couldn't blame him for wanting to change the subject.

"No wonder you're so upset," he tried, reaching over to take her hand, which was very cold, though she pressed his in return.

"There's a letter from Kip Calder inside."

"We can't have a baby, Ariel. We've been struggling as it is."

"You're probably going to think I'm out of my mind, but I've decided that I made a mistake, a bad one, when I didn't go out to New Mexico to find my father after I first learned about him."

"I remember being an advocate of that idea when you told me."

"You were. I should have listened to you."

He resisted the easy comeback, that she should listen to him now regarding this new issue. Instead he stood, took the Calder ledger from Ariel's other hand and set it on the wide arm of the chair, then drew her up from where she sat and gathered her unsteadily against him. How familiar she felt, her body banking into his, holding him close, her face burrowed into the crook of his shoulder. "I'm sorry you're having a hard time," he said, but she neither responded nor resisted when he walked her upstairs, saying that she needed sleep, they would figure it all out in the morning. She said nothing, since there was nothing else she could think to say, except that an abortion was temporarily not a possibility, however much he clearly assumed it was a probability. Let the world go away for a few hours, she dizzily thought.

When she awoke, the sun was pointing gentle light into the room where they lay in bed, its warmth baking her pained eyes and her pounding temples as she ascended like some poor bat startled from its daytime lair into flying blind at noon. However burdened by bad sleep and a blameworthy conscience, she understood that her failure to tell David what she really thought—that they'd reached the end of their road together—offered her a fresh chance at imagining why her parents had themselves failed for so many years to tell her about Kip. When it came to furnishing the facts and acknowledging the truth, however hurtful, and hurtful to whomever, be it the teller or the one told, she had not measured up any better than they.

Feeling her way to the staircase, palms flattened against the night's damp cool in the walls, she stopped and laid her cheek against the plaster, as if to cool her mind as well.

David slept on while she withdrew downstairs, semidrunk still, clasping the smooth oak handrail with both hands. How she wished she could cry. Wasn't that what one ought to do? She paused at the newel, breathed through pursed lips. No tears, just thinnest breath. As if her grandmother McCarthy were beside her, she thought she heard that familiar raspy voice whisper, *Hair of the dog ad majorem Dei gloriam,* which didn't make her laugh.

Instead she found her way to the kitchen sink, whispering a matin prayer of sorts. She drank tap water from the bowl of her cupped hands. Coughed and shivered but still found no tears to shed over the twin misery and abundance that faltered inside her. Without a thought, she ducked her head under the faucet and allowed the water, now running much colder from deep in the well, to flow over the back of her neck. A thin thread trickled over her shoulders and along the furrow of her spine, coursing like a glass snake down her thigh and calf to the kitchen floor of wide hemlock planks, where it pooled, a trembling mirror reflecting the morning sun. When she glanced down, through the thin fabric of her slip, she sensed her breasts and flat belly had, even if imperceptibly, ripened with this pregnancy. Was that possible?

Her sunlit body seemed suddenly like a candled egg. She closed the faucet, sank to her knees, sat back against the cabinet door. Supporting her downcast head on fisted hands, she stared at the sun's tiny face dancing on the puddle of water. She noted its purling eye but wasn't sure, in that moment, whether it was withering from view because she was crying or because the miniature sea had merely cast her back upon herself, as a wave might a broken bit of coral.

When David joined her an hour later, the spirit of nostalgia had vanished. She was down by the pond drinking her cup of coffee, sitting cross-legged on the grass, watching a whitetail dragonfly flit among the asters. As he approached, he could see her body's profile through the sheer beige of her shift and recognized that these might be among their final minutes together. Whereas he'd always respected, even revered, the deep solidity, the centeredness and strengths of Ariel in times past, this morning he found himself resenting them. Shouldn't one as exposed as she was, there in the bowl

of wildflowers and deep calm water, seem vulnerable? Seem disarmed and defenseless in the face of nature, somehow? Not Ariel, at
least not here and now. On the contrary, she seemed impregnable.
Irony of ironies. He sat beside her, irritated that they had to argue
over the indisputable fact they weren't going through with this baby
stuff. "You must feel awful."

"I feel fine," she rused.

"I meant, having overdone it with the gin."

She nodded, not looking at him, not truly looking at anything.

"We can't have a child, Ariel, and you know it."

"You don't need to worry," she said, quietly. "I'm freeing you of all
responsibility."

"What's that supposed to mean?"

"Just what I said. You don't want to deal with it and I'm not going
to make you."

"Great. Perfect."

"In fact, why don't I just free you of me altogether?"

"Even better." Such stoniness surprised him, but his mind, too,
was made up. They stood and walked back to the house. A quarter
hour later, before throwing himself into the car and backing crazily,
furiously, out of the driveway, he taunted, "What's going on here is a
delayed reaction to what started when you learned about your biological father."

"Maybe so, probably not."

"You're finally angry about having been lied to your whole life by
your parents."

"They have nothing to do with this."

"Transference is what it is. You're displacing hostility—"

"David, don't play psychologist with me. I don't feel hostile toward
you. I don't feel much of anything, if you want to know."

"This is destructive behavior. You're not mother material."

Not unfair, but as Ariel sat once more in the Adirondack chair to
stare at the prolific bed of orange tiger lilies her parents had planted

in honor of her junior high graduation, she thought of chain reactions. First her nucleus had been split by one father's merging with another. Then she'd become the hapless next split atom. Then the private tissue of her own ovum, like some puzzling nuclear core, had been halved by the saturation of sperm protons. Ariel could almost hear Jessica, who scolded her whenever she thought with her mind absent her heart.

And now David was gone. His last words hadn't been amiable. He told her he didn't "get them" anymore. That he couldn't love somebody who didn't know who she was or had been or was becoming. That he couldn't see their having a baby together, not when they hardly had each other, or themselves. They'd been a couple once, but coupledom seemed to be a thing of the past.

"Coupledom?" she'd groaned, the hangover she'd earned having abruptly arrived.

Ariel had developed a private face, one at times as difficult to read as any of her more abstruse books. And that was the face she'd worn as the discussion ended, though David would have a few words to add before slamming shut his car door and raising pebbles and dust as he backed out of the drive with his bare foot pressed hard against the accelerator pedal. He knew he was leaving behind drawers of clothing in the armoire in their shared bedroom, and downstairs in the mudroom snowshoes, his hiking boots, camping paraphernalia, the sleeping bag in which he and Ariel had spent nights together during chilly autumns just before hunting season, when the stars were at their thickest and in the mornings wild turkeys would drift through the fallen leaves, pecking and scratching their way along, clucking and foraging. Ariel watched all this, eyes bloodshot, in a state of suspended disbelief.

She asked for it and got it. Maybe he was right, maybe wrong. Maybe she didn't know what she was talking about.

One thing was certain. The person she needed to tell about this pregnancy was none other than Kip Calder, since he was the only

one who could give her the straight dope on what it felt like to abandon your child even before that child was born.

The house and surrounding woods were silent again. She dressed
and walked to a place where she used to love to hide as a girl. Lying
on the long, warm lichened capstones of the barn wall, past the
apple orchard, she sweated out the toxins in air laden with midday
light. She tried to get her beating mind to think slowly, carefully. A
voice that mingled with her own, her mother's, and even that of
Granna asked, Was she sure she should go to New Mexico and raise
dust that had settled so long ago? Told her Kip was most probably
dead by now, that she'd blown it by being so damn diffident in the
first place. Declared that if there was any chance she might go ahead
and have this baby, she'd have to lay off drinking. Poor thing was
probably wretched in there, adrift in a gin cauldron. *Poor thing*—
listen to her. Best she not begin thinking that way.

Having barely slept the night before, she nodded off in the sun,
hands folded on her chest, and was awakened, startled, hours later
by her cat Buddha, who nuzzled her cheek and then bounded down
off the wall into the underbrush of blackberries. Buddha boy? How
she used to love watching him stalk chipmunks and mice and butterflies and then stretch out to sleep on this bluestone garden wall,
smiling his gray, unperturbable smile.

"Buddy?"

Sitting up, coming back to consciousness, she remembered he
was long dead and buried. Maybe a spider had brushed against her. A
fieldmouse.

"Permission to go crazy?" she asked herself, climbing the knoll to
the house. "Permission granted," she answered.

She knew what lay ahead, at least in the proximate sense, at least
insofar as what she herself could do about matters. There was no real
choice. No number of hours or days spent sitting around in this
farmhouse was going to resolve or mend the fractured thing she'd
both been given and become. She telephoned her parents the next

morning and told them she was going to New Mexico to find out what happened to Kip Calder. She phoned work and with apologies said she needed to take an emergency leave of absence. Family crisis. She packed a few clothes in the car, locked up the house. The dormant village of Callicoon was where the bridge crossed the Delaware from New York State over into Pennsylvania. Long ago, she'd waded halfway across with Brice in the shallow, stone-bottomed upper reaches of that river, and even now she could recall how heavy her tennis shoes were, cold and hefty in the swift flat water, and how frightened she'd felt being so far from the riverbank where her mother sat, but also how unwilling she'd been to let her father see her fear. A big brown trout had broken the surface twenty feet out toward the deeper channel and she'd screamed with excitement. To be in the river and see the fish emerge from its waters into her airy world for that briefest instant seemed terrifying, wonderful. But now she crossed the Delaware in her car and, without consulting a map—she didn't have one and didn't really want one—drove beyond Callicoon into Wayne County and through a hamlet prayerfully called Galilee which led her through Rileyville and on through townships with names like Dyberry and Canaan, knowing at a minimum she was headed in the right direction. She knew, too, that though this was not a dream, her truly going to Chimayó to look for Kip was nonetheless tinged by the surreal.

*W*as it the brilliant physicist John von Neumann who once told his brilliant colleague Richard Feynman that cultivating the concept of social irresponsibility was the first step toward becoming a happy man, or was it Feynman who said it to von Neumann—the godfather of radar, game theory, nuclear deterrence, artificial intelligence, and the superbomb, to name just a few of his progeny? Kip knew it was one or the other. Both had worked on the Hill. Each had tried to use his genius to build, as the phrase goes, the future.

But which had proved himself to be more irresponsible? Feynman in that he enjoyed playing the bongos and cracking wild jokes? Von Neumann who indulged himself in the obsessive habit, to the chagrin of Los Alamos secretaries, of peeking up women's skirts? And how did one go about defining responsibility, anyway?

Kip remembered that both had been, yes, brilliant, and both also barbarian in their different ways. Too, he recalled one evening back at the convalescent center—not far from where Feynman and von Neumann dwelled during their days at the lab—when he and his fellow patients congregated in the rec room to watch satellite television after downing cranberry juice and angel food cake in celebration of some birthday. The resident patients chortled and coughed warmly through an episode of *The Simpsons*, a cartoon Kip found neither humorous nor entertaining. Yet he was the only one in that bedeviled audience to laugh, laugh hard and long, when Homer Simpson averred in a philosophical moment, "Trying is the first step toward failure." Another brilliant barbarism, in its way.

Kip now stood before the fieldhouse, which itself stood at the northwest margin of the lower pasture at Pajarito, and these few thoughts more or less stood there with him—them—as he looked at this old ruined bastion from an earlier century, erected a short reach from Rio Nambé, which he could hear scuttling along unseen on the other side of a coyote fence overhung with vines. He had gotten it into his head he was going to restore this fallen-down place and make it his home so long as he stayed with the Montoyas.

Having been here for a couple years, he'd become an honorary Montoya. Hard to fathom. The bridges he'd burned over the course of his life had never been rebuilt, not even the one he'd attempted pallidly to extend toward his daughter. The fires had burned hot and thoroughly, and none so much as smoldered now or allowed reaccess to any place he'd ever called home. Whereas home had always been an idea to inhabit, a truant hunch, a somewhere other, now the idea had morphed. Nambé, for Kip, was as close to a real home as he could imagine.

But more and more he didn't like living in undeserved comfort at the far end of the *portal,* in a nice room he knew the Montoyas might otherwise use to put up clients or visiting family. He had no use for its antique mirrors, its radio, its photographs of show horses, or even for the almond-scented soap that Sarah set out for him in his bathroom. Further, he believed he still had no talent for society, didn't know how to be near people. Even charitable people like the Montoyas. The fieldhouse suited him, too, because it was set at a remove from all but brat horses and punk ponies they let into the adjacent pasture.

This was a Wagner move, he supposed. Distancing himself from the living while paradoxically embracing the idea of life. Yet Kip figured that when he left Nambé one day, as surely he would, the fieldhouse restoration might be some kind of legacy. And while he remained here it could be—another truth and another paradox—his reason not to leave. He would, of course, continue with his chores. He'd fully adapted to, even cherished, his role as an assistant and felt his strength growing whenever he raked the reddish cinder-dust scoria aisleway that ran down the center of the barn ("It's an art, man," Marcos explained, "like zen gardening"), or washing down a horse with chlorhexadine scrub mixed with shampoo, rinsing it with warm water, spraying it with lanolin, then walking it back to its stall. He learned how to clean tack and restitch saddles. He helped, when and as he could, with feeding, watering, rotating broodmares into and out of the several pastures. These tasks had become his bread and butter. The fieldhouse would be caviar.

Marcos, with whom he'd first shared his idea, was enthusiastic and volunteered to help in his spare time. So did Franny, or Mary, whoever she was—Marcos still didn't know and Kip would never snitch on her. He knew what it was like to be assumed and unassuming. He remembered von Neumann's sly riposte to Oppenheimer's famous words quoted from the *Bhagavad Gita* after the Trinity implosion was heard around the world on July 16, 1945. Oppie had intoned, "Now I am become Death, the destroyer of worlds," but von Neumann upped him one with, "Some people confess guilt to claim credit for the sin."

Why was all this circulating through Kip's psyche now? Because he still couldn't shake the idea of her, no matter how pathetic it was to be thinking about it three years after the fact, as if he'd just posed the problem to Brice the week before. Because increasingly he thought of his letter to Ariel as a travesty, a confession of the kind von Neumann had accused Oppenheimer of making. Unsubtly pressing Ariel and her parents for credit where none was due. Perjuring himself by asking a daughter to know who her real father was, when indeed—in deeds—he certainly was not. Hiding from Ariel even after he'd clumsily invited her to search him out, since hadn't that been the deeper, even deepest, motive behind his meeting with Brice in Chimayó? To give him that diary he himself could barely read? Not to forget his own maudlin letter. Even carrying on thinking about it was preposterous. Why not just get over it. Understand she has not come and won't.

Kip was hotly aware of his sins, his false claims and bad credits. Maybe if he built something tangible with his hands, with what was left of his physical self, it would help offset a little of what he'd ruined. He had divulged some of these thoughts to Sarah that morning up at Los Alamos, and she had attempted to reassure him that we all share such imperfections. Well and good, he'd thought then. But now he told himself, Don't fuck up, Kip. Make something right. Even if it's only a bustdown clay hovel, it's better than the bustdown clay mongrel who stands before it. This place at least once served a worthy purpose. Who knows? Restoring it might teach you a thing or two about yourself.

So he thought as he traipsed through the tall cheatgrass and rye, peering through the fieldhouse windows into its dark interior and imagining how once this place had been a habitat where people slept, woke, loved, argued, thought, lived. They'd probably planted these sweet grasses that brushed against his hands, and which flourished like all thirsty desert plants do near running water. He remembered it was called cheatgrass because Europeans had introduced it in Nambé for stock feed. Well, at least Kip was native rather than cheat, even though the cheatgrass thrived better than he ever would.

Sarah said she would speak with Carl about the proposition.

"He have any experience building?" Carl wondered.

"You know sure as day he's too proud to say he'll do something he can't," kneeling beside her husband in one of the stalls, where he was wrapping a filly's leg with supportive bandages. "He seems to know something about everything, and I doubt he'd make the offer if he wasn't equal to the task."

"People do things all the time they're not qualified to do. Kip isn't that kind, though, I'll admit."

"Listen, the fieldhouse is such a wreck nobody could do but make it better. I'm more worried about whether he's up to it physically than whether the place could tolerate an attempted restoration."

"Hand me that standing wrap." Carl Montoya did not look at his wife but concentrated instead on the tender fetlock of this four-year-old, whom he considered way too wild for all the training they'd put her through. "I got to tell this gal's owners we can't board their crazy horse anymore." Carl chewed his words like a cheroot, with amiable disgust, as he rose to look the bay in her wet velvety black eye. "You're an ugly hag of a nag," he told the ribboned show horse with a smile. "Too smart for your own good. Handgalloped me right into the rail today."

"Look, it might give Kip a sense of purpose. My worry is he's started thinking he's underfoot."

"Who says he isn't?"

"That's nice. Look, I took responsibility for him, and I want to do the best I can by the poor guy."

Carl placed his palm gently on the filly's roan teacup muzzle, then ran his hand up her smooth jaw to her throatlatch. "She took responsibility, and when are *you* gonna learn not to run me into the fence, jerk?" he said, his voice purring, as the horse nodded and sputtered appeasement.

"Come on, Carl."

Her husband turned his squint on her. "I don't know why you bother to ask, being as you intend to let him go ahead no matter what I say."

"It's your decision."

"I like old Kip, too, and if rebuilding that fieldhouse is what he wants to do, let him go ahead so long as he can keep up with his load down here. Anyways, he's like you. He'll go ahead even if I don't want him to. I lost control of this place a long time ago."

"You're an ugly nag yourself, you know."

He chuffed at the compliment, said he had work to do, and went on about his business.

Sarah found Kip already down at the fieldhouse that morning, himself chuffing and soughing like confused wind as he shoveled the thin loam that had drifted into what used to be the entryway to this lowly morada-style structure.

"Montoya said it's fine, so all's well."

Kip looked around and smiled, then went back to scraping off decades of pale soil as if he'd only been born to the task.

"By the way, he asked if you'd ever done this kind of work before."

Kip pulled himself up straight, hand over hand, using the shovel for support, then crooked up one shoulder.

"I guess that means yes?"

"I'll do it right."

Men, thought Sarah Montoya. Jesus God save us from men, and left for the Hill.

*W*ith no map to guide her, Ariel contented herself with a westward drive weighted by a gentle southward drift. Perhaps nervousness made her a wilier, more savoring observer, causing her to notice with fresh eyes such everyday things as a pink dawn or fiery clementine sunset. Or maybe fatigue had somewhat stripped her down, giving the world clearer access to her consciousness. Either way, she bristled with acumen. The fine hairs on her arm tingled in the freeway wind like needles when she cocked her bare elbow out the open window. A cardinal that bounded through a bank of rhododendrons on the shore of the Kanawha near Charleston, West Virginia, displayed the purest, brightest red Ariel had ever seen. As she drove past miles of voracious steel furnaces in Tennessee, smelting coal and iron ore filled the sky with symphonic clouds. Oil refineries in East Texas tasted savory, like burnt molasses on her tongue. For one who felt as if her life had tumbled into a darkening pit, the world beyond the windshield seemed anything but a dreary catacombs.

Still, these moments of intense witnessing were counterpointed by equally strong waves of anxiety. Panic came over her whenever she thought of the evolving life in her belly and about whether she should, in fact, get an abortion in New Mexico, where few knew her and no one need ever know it happened. Grief over the irreparable rift with David, no matter how inevitable it had been. Fear regarding how very unlikely it was, over three years after Brice and Kip had their brief reunion, that she would discover anything in Chimayó or Los Alamos but a gravestone. All these crosscutting thoughts and the mapless journey itself made every waking instant as brash as a slap in the face. And now, having driven up against the border that separated New from old Mexico, and dry brown Texas from both, she recognized that the time had come to give up edgy dead reckoning for a slightly more composed approach.

El Paso. A banquette table at yet another diner. She spread the brand-new map of New Mexico before her, as if to lay a grid of rationality over her darting mind. Setting down her coffee cup on Carlsbad Caverns, Ariel traced the final miles of her trip with her forefinger. Las Cruces she would hit first, following the blue ink of the Rio Grande. Up past a settlement called Radium Springs. Past the town of Truth or Consequences, above Caballo Reservoir. All the while skirting the desolate stretch of desert east of her chosen route, aptly colored on the map in pewter, also aptly shaped like a blunt-nosed bullet casing—White Sands, the missile range wreathed along its westernmost edge by the San Andres Mountains and marked at the eastern frontier by that place with the comely name Alamogordo. Around Alamogordo there were hamlets with equally evocative names like Sunspot and Cloudcroft, Weed and Bent. The outline of a plane, indicating an airport in Alamogordo, brought to mind the *Enola Gay*, that unhappy bomber, presently housed in a Smithsonian warehouse, which had been repatriated on a nearby Roswell runway after its deadly flight over Hiroshima. Now here it was again, circling back into her own life.

Christ, she was way overweary. Nevertheless, here she was, her father's daughter. Or fathers'. Or rather, grandfathers' granddaughter. That protracted desolation on the printed map, White Sands, its barrenness plain to see, lay beneath her fingers on the pleated page. When her three eggs scrambled were set before her, yellow rice and refried beans with them, she shook a heavy dusting of salt and pepper from shakers shaped like chili peppers, then drizzled a river of Tabasco over the food. She ate hungrily, and as she did she followed the line of highway farther north, having left the map where it was, like a place mat. Long stretches of Route 25 were townless. Jornada del Muerto, Bosque del Apache, Sierra Ladrones. From the journey of death to the thieves' mountains she traced her course like Coronado before her until it reached Albuquerque. After that came Santa Fe, then left to Los Alamos or right to Chimayó, heaven only knew which.

Glancing around, she pulled her wallet from her backpack and counted four hundred in twenties. It would have to last a while. She extracted the ledger and looked again at the photo of the youthful Kip and Brice. She had this and Kip Calder's name but not much more to work with when asking around. What it was. She left a generous tip for the waitress who wore a memorable vintage pair of crimson lizard pumps.

Through bony splendor she drove, through massive upheavings that resembled stone skirts blown high skyward from the recumbent desert with its flora here and there. Most of the traffic was high in the sky, aircraft with military markings or no markings at all, in a multitude of shapes—now stout, now trim as a firepin—and never silver like the *Enolas* of old but matte black. Her map, embellished by Tabasco stains, fluttered beside her, applauding as she whisked along the straight road through these arid ranges and flat arbitrating plains. Isolated towns whose names she recognized from her map reading hugged either side of the highway—parched low buildings with a sporadic general store ascending to a second tier. Dogs napped in their blue shade. Once in a while she saw a person walking dreamily along.

Darkness had fallen by the time she finally made Albuquerque and pressed on through Santa Fe. Ariel decided she would crash at the next motel on the road and face what she had to face in morning light. A blinking neon sign read *Vaca cy,* and she entered another exhausted room, this one different from the others with its hopeful framed print of pastel pueblo people, an Indian family gazing out from a butte, the father shielding his eyes from the sun, cliché squaw beside him, children gathered around her clutching at the beaded hem of her deerskin dress. The bedspread, curtains, and couch fabrics bore matching prints of someone's idea of Anasazi geometrics. The carpet was gray, the windows unopenable. Curled on her side beneath the covers, she quickly fell asleep.

Somewhere between postmidnight and predawn. The weird sense of waking up not knowing where she was. And the weirder one of then realizing. Morning sickness forced her out of bed and across the cement rug into the blindingly bright bath. As she knelt over the toilet bowl, naked but for her black sweatshirt with the stenciled legend *Leave Me Alone* on the back, Ariel thought how wonderful religion must sometimes be for those who have faith. Believing in Christ would certainly make abortion a moot point. Believing might offer other strengths, too, that she sure could use right about now. Christ had never walked with her as a child, though. And he sure as hell wasn't here in the bathroom of the Cities of Gold Casino motel.

Grandmother McCarthy would bemoan her son's lack of religion all over again, and probably in stronger language than ever, when she learned that her granddaughter had come, unannounced, unanticipated, in search of a father who wasn't her son. Brice and Jessica's God-free household did have something to do with her present malaise, no getting around it. But in fairness she had to admit that even if they'd been married ministers she'd likely have fallen from the faith. Born apostate? More like a blind spot, a missing strand of DNA.

—Charity's church enough, Brice always said, and Ariel as always listened. —Most of these pious lambs who flock to houses of worship are either sheep getting sheared or, often as not, wolves in sheep's clothes doing a bit of fleecing themselves.

Pretty harsh. Still, she never felt more alone. And as such, she wished she knew how to pray. Whom to pray to. Eyes closed, she even tried. *Dear God, Ariel here, asking your help. You probably already know that I'm Ariel. You probably already know everything. Well, of course you do. What I wanted to ask is . . . Maybe never mind. I'm sorry. Amen.*

No better than usual, she thought, washing her face. Once you come up against omniscience, any presumption of dialogue collapses.

Poor believing Granna had tried to teach her years before. Having admonished Ariel that it was bad luck to bow in prayer at the end of a bed, the woman had knelt with her, elbow to elbow, during one of the girl's half dozen previous solo trips to Los Alamos. Ariel could even now see that bed covered with its white *broderie de Marseilles* wedding quilt patterned with laurel and mockingbirds, an antique older than Brice's mother's mother, from whom she had inherited it. Ariel could still hear Granna saying, in a voice frighteningly gentle, —Dear Lord Savior, in Jesus' name I beseech thee, come unto this young girl and show her, Lord, how to address thee, in God's name, and how to beseech thy grace and comfort . . . and on and on, until Ariel thought how Granna's prayer was lasting for many more minutes than she would have imagined necessary for God to make contact with them had he so desired. But then, how was anybody, God included, supposed to hear Granna's whispering so softly that even she who was on bended knee right next to her had to strain to understand? The prayer lesson might have seemed a consummate failure had her grandmother not declared it quite successful.

Now things weren't so pure as that beautiful quilt. Granna's prayerful clarity held no sway over this ungentle night. Now everything in Ariel's surround seemed struck by discord, disorder, and dislocation.

Back in bed, she pulled the ledger onto her lap and opened it to that page on which her grandfather questioned why his son kept running away. Outside, in the distance, the familiar sound of a siren disrupted Kip's father's written voice and harkened her back to New York and the day of her revelation. How curious that a moment so consequential could already be hazing over in memory. Was this a mind protecting itself, detraumatizing the pain by making its own personal history murky? She felt mildly comforted, as the siren faded into the distance, by a growing belief that this new truth was the right one.

"Ariel Calder," she tried it out loud. The old Ariel truths were frauds, sort of, but she decided not to dismiss them. She made a decision, a cutting off of all other possibilities, which was after all what the word *decision* meant. She wouldn't banish the old truths, however crippled they were, because they still were truths. They might be contradictory, but both old and new truths were irrefutable.

She flipped the wall switch beside the bed to extinguish the lights, tried to sleep, but couldn't. The hard fact that she was in Pojoaque, seven thousand–plus feet above sea level, two thousand miles or so from the farmhouse, and possibly near the man who'd given her life, sat like a stone in her gut.

Ariel had daydreamed her way west. She opened her eyes into the pulsating darkness, closed them to some pretense of sleep, but still reveries came in evolving bundles. They came in color; they came in shades of gold. They streamed, or swelled. She reached for the lamp toggle and pushed. She dialed David in New York and when he answered, she said, "I'm really sorry about what's happened and I don't blame you for any of it." He hung up. Quivering, after listening to the dial tone for some seconds, she replaced the handset on the bedside table and turned on the television, of all things, for distraction. A game show, *Jeopardy!* Just perfect, she thought. Jeopardy before and jeopardy behind. She pulled the sheets over her head.

Before she finally fell asleep again, one of the things her grandfather McCarthy used to tell her came to mind. When one person does a foolish thing, it's foolish. When two people do a foolish thing, it's still foolish. When three do a foolish thing, it is foolish.

A lifetime before Ariel wended her way north between the Rio Grande and the Jornada del Muerto, just east of the Oscura Mountains, which ranged out the passenger window of her car, a dusty and limping jackbottom had stood staring down the length of dry ditch into which it had stumbled, appearing for all the world to be the foreigner it was there. A salamander and Delfino Montoya watched this forlorn ass, which shook its loaflong head with the magnificent obtuseness and ponderousness available to this singular beast and no other, or so it would have seemed on that overwarm midday. The salamander had stretched itself under the sun on the far side of this same acequia, and for his part Delfino sat on the tan grass some hundred feet back behind his bungalow, under a shattered, shedding cottonwood, leaning against the hard trunk of the tree, his feet splayed before him like unearthed roots. What sweltering shade this cottonwood cast, Delfino occupied. The heavy sun produced dark pockets in every hollow, chink, and cove in view, whether natural or fashioned by the hands of those few people who had bothered to try to make a go of it in this tough valley.

At hand, on the scrabbly dirt floor beneath the shade tree, were a pencil and a paper tablet on which Delfino had tried without success to shape his ideas, his profound resentments, into words. Instead, now, he stared at this wild mule that had wandered off the cantankerous plain, maybe thirsty or out to pillage somebody's garden. It scowled with a forager's dullish eye and gave short shrift to the salamander's sharper gaze, as well as Delfino's own, as it hobbled and slumped toward both in search of a way to higher ground. Delfino, without moving, looked about for a stone to throw at it. The jackbottom did not take this in, nor did the salamander bestir itself. In the distance a freight train ran across the valley floor and a delicate clattering along the tracks could be heard. A dog barked, then another barked back without enthusiasm into the dead hot breath of the desert day. The ass continued to gimp along the trench, raising trivial puffs of dust with each fall of its dull grayblue hooves.

Finding no pebble within reach, Delfino chucked his pencil stub at the beast. Neither the jackbottom nor the long-tailed salamander noticed, nor for that matter did Delfino know what possessed him to throw his pencil at the trapped animal. The pencil, which he'd sharpened with his pocketknife, lay on the bottom of the waterditch in the dust, bright yellow against dun brown, and the jack trod on it without ado and without knowing it had done so.

No damn pencil was doing him any good anyhow, and so what did it matter, Delfino reasoned.

Then he thought, There you are, Montoya. There you are, old man. You're no smarter than that goddamn jackybottom stuck in that gully. No wonder you're throwing things at it. You're no better than some thickhead jack yourself.

The salamander had meanwhile disappeared.

When the jack passed directly in front of Delfino, like some four-footed storm cloud before a frowning moon, it paused and turned its massive laggard head in the seated man's direction, taking him in where he still sat, unmoving. A marginal breeze stirred the paper beside Delfino, and the jackbottom—not ten feet from the man who watched him under this heavy weather of pale blue and fierce sun—bared its yellowed tombstone teeth in a nasty smile of feigned threat, very feigned, very exhausted, and eccentrically pacific.

—You numbskull tub of shit, Delfino said.

It breathed dryly. The ribs on its sides stood up in the day like long curved mummified barrel bands stretching its speckled and putrid and dust-shellacked hide. Cataracts made its eyes, each the size of a rotted-to-black patio tomato, evocatively clouded. Delfino clapped his hands, but the jackbottom did not flinch. He clapped a couple of times more, harder, and the animal only continued to look at him.

—You deaf? he shouted at the ass, which then turned its large head to study the rock where the salamander had been lounging not three minutes before. —Well, are you?

Agnes had come out from the back of the bungalow, having heard her husband shouting these words. —What's that you're saying?

—Look at this, Delfino said, climbing to his feet and slapping the dirt off the butt of his work trousers.

—What happened?

—Must've wandered off the valley and got himself stuck in the trough, I guess.

—Poor thing. Let's get some rope.

—All right, Delfino said, and he crossed to the small shed he'd built in their yard and fetched down a length of white rope that hung in a coil on a nail.

Together, Agnes and Delfino got the rope around the animal's neck and led the docile, cooperative beast a quarter mile down the acequia, to a place where they could walk it up an angled ledge. From there they doubled back across a couple of fields and roads to their bungalow where they kept it tethered in their backyard for the following month. They fed and watered the animal until it seemed strong enough that they felt comfortable about loading it into a borrowed horse trailer and driving it back to the edge of White Sands Range. There they parked, opened the swinging trailer doors, backed it down the clamorous metal ramp, and released it to the parched wilds where it had been conceived and had survived without incident before wandering down into Tularosa proper and getting itself gnarl-kneed, stuck, and salvaged.

The jackbottom stood in the morning, still homely but fatter, kind of weirdly lilac in the dawn light.

—Go on, get, said Delfino.

Agnes watched. She resisted the reluctance she was beginning to feel about returning it to the wasteland, though this had been her idea all along. It was Agnes who'd said that day the month before, —We'll nurse him back to health, then we'll take him where he belongs.

—Go on now, Delfino shouted again. —Maybe it'd be easier for all of us if you let me just shoot him, he joked, turning to Agnes for some counsel as to their next move.

Agnes didn't dignify his humor with any response. She struck the side of the horse trailer with her open palm, shouting, —Go on, now, get.

None of the three of them moved. The jackbottom stood facing the Montoyas, favoring its right foreleg to elicit sympathy.

—Maybe we ought to take him back home, Delfino said.

—He *is* home.

The ass looked at her, glaucous and unhearing and stubborn with all the stubbornness that inhabits the innermost heart of every beast, whether sentient or idiot, and with the basic recalcitrance it had regained precisely because she and this man had succored it. The ass looked her in the eye and defied her. Surely she was not going to abandon it here in the middle of nowhere? The beast, in all its fear and audacity, even showed its benefactors those squarish rows of agate teeth once more, combining a sneer with a primordial grin.

Agnes waved her arms and beseeched, —Go on, *go*. Yet the jack merely ventured forward a bit, limpingly—both surly and pleading— confused maybe by how alien a human voice sounded in the void of the desert. Unfamiliar, small. Agnes quietly said, —Damn.

Had his wife decided she couldn't go through with her plan to reintroduce the derelict jackbottom to its habitat, Delfino wouldn't have argued. But she surprised him that day, just as she surprised him other days. She turned her back on the jacky, climbed into the driver's side of the pickup, started the engine. Delfino got aboard, saying nothing, and they drove away in a mayhem of dust. Sunlight made her face glow as might an angel's, he remembered thinking as he looked across at his wife, then in the rearview mirror at the lone powder-cloaked figure of the doubly lost bray standing along the dirt track flanked by ocotillos.

That was back in 'seventy-seven. They'd received right around that time a note from some man in the Ford administration—or was it Carter's?—who said he passed their letter and their problem along to another department. Maybe the State Department or Defense, who could recall? Not that it mattered much anyway, since that was the last they heard of it. Delfino, who now sat alone in their bungalow, remembered that odd morning and his reluctant friendship with the lost jackbottom and the glowing face of his aging wife.

As Agnes had followed through with her conception of the right and proper response to finding some abstracted savage mule in the acequia, and as Agnes had so resolutely left it there on the valley floor to fend for itself, so Delfino resolved to try one last time, with pencil and paper, yes, but also with his hands and his feet, to bring to pass what he'd told his wife he someday wanted to do, told her more than once, told her often, told her ad nauseam. One or two things to do, then in he would go. After that, it wouldn't matter.

This was a story Delfino Montoya would soon tell his brother and sister-in-law's salvage, that fellow Sarah kept mentioning whenever they spoke on the phone. Fellow with the peculiar name, Kip. It would thereafter become one of Calder's favorite stories because he felt a deep empathy for that jackbottom and wondered whether their fates might not one day be the same.

During Kip's year up at the convalescent center he met a man named Clifford who was afflicted with mild dementia. Kip had befriended Clifford as much as anyone could befriend such a man. He enjoyed listening to Clifford's stories about his hometown of Gallup, which he memorably said wasn't a kindly place for folks whose minds were like shafts of grain, because the wind galed hard through town. Wind in the form of cars. Threw and blew. Tornado alley of a different stamp. The united flakes of America coasting west and east on their way to this shining sea or that.

Ever since Kip had returned to Rancho Pajarito, he'd been wondering whether or not he ought to ask Franny Johnson if she happened to know this Clifford. Not that he was of her generation—not hardly—but Gallup was the kind of town where people knew one another, despite old Route 66 running through its dusty heart. Or maybe it was precisely *because* Route 66 ran through it that the town hung together. Somebody had to know somebody.

Kip first met Clifford down on one knee in a corridor, very absorbed with trying over and again to pick up a black scuff mark off the green linoleum floor.

"What're you doing there?" Kip asked, neutral, hands in his pockets.

"Can you help me get this thing up, sir?"

Clifford hadn't looked at his interlocutor, but continued with his repeated gesture of plucking at the smudge.

Kip kneeled down beside the man. "Let me give it a try."

"Thanks," Clifford said, dramatically moving away to give Kip room enough to address the task.

Startled by Clifford's quickness, Kip looked levelly at him and saw that he was staring at the scuff mark in a state of combined horror and fascination. Reaching down with his thumb and forefinger, Kip then made a display of trying to lift the black mark from the floor.

"What do you think?" Clifford asked.

"Not sure."

After several further attempts, Kip glanced once more at Clifford, who was now staring saucer-eyed and with smiling panic at him. "Too heavy for you, too, huh?" said Clifford, and Kip rose slowly to his feet, even as did Clifford, and replied, "Too heavy for both of us."

Clifford walked away with perfect outward ease, giving the impression that all was right with the world, and all ends had been met, loose or otherwise. Kip admired that, envied that, though he did feel the need to remove his shoe and erase the scuff mark with a back-and-forth of his sock. He would think of this incident any number of times before he later entered some realm of true dementia himself. He would remember Clifford with respect, yes, but he would also recall the compassionate Kip Calder of that particular moment—a Kip he was proud of. He who was proud of so little.

That small incident came to mind this morning, some days after Carl Montoya had given his approval for the fieldhouse project, because Franny had the day off from the restaurant and had come down to see if she could help him. As she walked across the lea toward the grove of nineteenth-century cottonwoods whose branches extended over the casita like maternal wardens in gestures of embrace, she thought of that night when she and Marcos had seen something inexplicable down here. Hadn't crossed her mind in the longest time. Everything seemed simpler back then, freer, more promising. Even a ghost wasn't outside the realm of possibility.

"Kip?"

"In here."

His fieldhouse was low to the ground and cast, as did he, scant shade. Its adobe was discolored and had partly fallen off in chunks around the corner bases of the walls. Unlike the adobe of the main house in the upper park, this place had not been repaired for years.

Tin gutters had let some rainwater off the flat roof, but not enough, and so the round vigas that supported it sagged. Many of the old latillas that had originally been laid in a herringbone pattern from viga to viga had rotted into wood dust and fallen in. Kip and Franny stood side by side looking up at the sky through the ceiling, like a pair of celebrants gazing into sacred sunlight from the depths of a kiva.

"Kind of a mess," she said.

"I've seen worse," he replied, and they went on with their appraisal of where to begin in earnest. The windows were square and meager, a traditional design of pintle casement meant to hoard heat in winter and ward off the merciless sun of long summers. Earthen floors in what had once been a kitchen, bedroom, and sitting room, fitted with a corner bell-shaped fogón blackened by piñon smoke, were in pretty good repair, except where holes in the roof had let the weather trespass. Other than a rusted spring mattress, a rickety table, and a few other broken chattels, the fieldhouse was empty. A wooden horse, grayer than time itself and probably used for lasso practice, was the biggest prize. Kip and Franny set it up by the front door, a guardian god.

No one had lived within these thick mudded walls for a century, or longer than that, really—since before the days of statehood. The last inhabitant had been some Hispanic gentlewoman, one Francisca de something or other, whose name showed up in the deed, but about whom little was known. And yes, the place was rumored—beyond Marcos's sightings, which he'd still discussed with none but Franny—to be haunted. A couple of boys from the other side of Rio Nambé had told a patrolman they'd seen the ghost of a woman in Carlos Montoya's pasture. That was a decade ago. Poker-faced, the patrolman had taken notes with the eraser end of his pencil and never reported the claim.

Now, using trowels like archaeologists, Kip and Franny began to remove deteriorated adobe from the south side of the house, their backs to the sun, the grainy chipping music of their work such an ancient percussive sound, the air dry around them as they labored together. Franny noticed Kip seemed resurrected incrementally, not unlike the adobe he'd become obsessed with fixing, and though she still felt shy around him, she said as much.

He hummed a sort of thank you, audible over the several soft noises of the wind in the higher branches, the nearby shushing river, and their own scrapers. Then he surprised her by asking when she planned on telling Marcos her real name.

"I sort of hoped we could forget about that."

Kip just kept working at the lower section of a wall where water had capillaried up to rot it away into nothing more than semi-hardened mud.

"It didn't seem like you wanted to hear," she added.

"Sure I do. Why don't you tell me what you were going to tell me?"

She fell quiet while Kip waited, not glancing over at her but hearing her breath pass in and out.

Franny Johnson had very much remained Franny Johnson, while Mary had begun to protest less often her own chosen hiddenness. But lately matters had gotten more tangled, not less, in her head, thanks to her unwonted growing affection for Marcos, for all the Montoyas. Pulling her past and present into harmony, coming to some kind of truer truth, had thus become matters of some urgency.

As before, Kip seemed her ideal confessor, because like her he was someone assembled from fragments, a patchwork person. Franny empathized with this trait. She trusted him and what he might say to her more than she trusted her own meandering thoughts. She was awed by what appeared to be Kip's real freedom from the small fears that dictated other people's lives. On all this, Franny and Mary agreed—a curious interior colloquy that didn't feel strange, since she wasn't some split personality. More that the person she was accustomed to being differed from her earlier single self.

Look. Kip was here. The time had presented itself for her to try again to speak. "Can I ask you to keep it—"

"A secret?"

"*Secret* seems kind of a strong word. I meant, just keep it to yourself for a while. Do you mind?"

"If you don't, I don't."

"I suppose I *should* mind, is what you're saying. But I've got to talk to somebody or I'm going to burst."

Kip suggested, "One question first."

"Yes?"

"Wouldn't it be better if Marcos heard whatever it is you've got to say?"

"What if he doesn't understand?"

"Shouldn't understanding be *his* problem? Yours is simply to offer him the truth."

"I can't right now. I wish I could."

Kip thought, What would a good father advise? "Say whatever you want to say. Nothing leaves this place. Fair enough?"

"Thanks," Mary whispered, suddenly grave and compressed into the small sovereign world they inhabited together under these trees and beside this house. She told Kip she was a runaway, and why she had run. She told him her father had raged at his kids from as far back as she could remember, about anything and everything. Told him how the man's outbursts had come in clusters, like storm cells moving over the family landscape. How, after upbraidings and tongue lashings and shoving and screaming, periods of calm would settle in, not unlike a hangover following a binge. The physical stuff was what had finally pushed her over the edge, she said. Her father had constructed a spanking paddle from a thin flat plank of oak in which he'd drilled half-inch holes that made for a sharper, more succinct blow. The backs of her legs would sometimes bear his appliance's marks—a polka-dot patterning of welts—and as often as not she'd be grounded, so no one could see the bruises. Badges of honor, she came to think of them. Like those of Saint Catherine on her beautiful wheel of fire, or Ingrid Bergman as Joan of Arc at the stake. Even early Bogart hoodlums never treated anyone like her father did her.

Cagney had at least been a gangster. And Mary? She was Cool Hand
Luke unwilling to play the Audrey Hepburn part in *Wait Until Dark*,
except she wasn't blind and intended to escape with her eyes wide
open.

Kip stopped working and listened intently to Mary. Before she
finished, she began to cry. It had been years since he tenderly embraced anyone, but he held this Mary Franny Johnson against himself and felt the warmth of her tears on his shoulder, through the
thin cotton of his shirt and the even thinner fabric of his skin. She
was asking him what she should do. Tell Marcos and risk the possibility that he and his family would never want to have anything to
do with her again? Go back to Gallup and face her parents, who
might tell her to leave or, worse, to stay? Head back to Albuquerque
and catch that plane to Los Angeles the way she had originally
planned, back before everything got derailed because she had no
money and no connections? Or just remain in this present abeyance, this limbo, living a daily lie that more and more was overtaking
her, like a shadow rushing ahead of the very body that cast it in the
first place?

"Back up," Kip said. "What was that about Los Angeles?"

She told him of her aspirations. *Sea of Grass*. Hepburn, Tracy. *The
Desert Song*. *Sundown* with Gene Tierney. Susan Hayward, Louise
Brooks, even Mae West. Burt Lancaster in *Hallelujah Trail* and
Robert Taylor when he filmed *Ambush*. They'd come to Gallup to
shoot their films at Acoma or in Zuni pueblo. Ronald Reagan and
Larraine Day in *The Bad Man*. William Holden when they did *Streets
of Laredo*. And at night, in the nondescript house on Jefferson, up
on the heights above Gallup and its famous route, where the song
told you to *get your kicks*, there Mary would listen instead to freight
trains that ran day and night through the center of town, and hear
the wind gusting as it carried along hopeful chirruping birds past
the fenced yard up toward the pink mesa, which embraced them
in its large silence, as did the sky, clouds within silent clouds, and
always more silent sky beyond. And she would dream herself

into those films, which were far more real than any life she was living.

"Everything that had any chance of surviving seemed to pass right through Gallup. Movie stars, trains and cars, truck drivers. Only the dogs stuck around. And the pawnbrokers, forever and a day the pawnbrokers. Gallup's heaven for pawns and for the broke. It's not a place to live, it's a place to leave. And that's what I did."

While he couldn't follow many of her movie references, Kip heard things he understood.

"You know the joke about Gallup being well named?"

Yeah, gallop. He knew that one.

One of her father's chronic taunts had been, —If you don't like living under this roof, you can hit any road you want so long as it doesn't bring you back. Do you hear me?

She did, and after years of cycling through the same pattern of mutiny, terror, anger, guilt, meekness, stoicism, and then back to mutiny, she'd eventually called his bluff. The golden lights of sprawling Albuquerque, as she crested the ridge that night after finally making her move, leaving behind family and the waitressing job at El Rancho and every bad memory she had of home, had seemed miraculous at the time. "Like my future was lying there in front of me, this glittering gold magic carpet, with Sandia backlit by a big fat full moon. It was some kind of fine vision."

Mary smirked. She told Kip she'd ended up in Santa Fe because it offered her a brilliant opportunity to wait tables for better pay than in Albuquerque, which in turn paid better than Gallup. Her plan had been to save some money, take the bus down to the airport, and persevere west. But none of it happened. The hopeless dream was fading, as well it might or even should.

"Not so hopeless. You have a hell of a flair for invention. Aren't you more or less writing, directing, and acting a role every waking minute?"

"I never thought of it that way."

One confession deserved another, so Kip told Mary a few things about himself. That he considered himself no better than a living, unmoored Gallup. That he'd messed up more often than not. That somewhere out there another daughter had been left by an unworthy father to find her own way—nothing he was pleased about. Indeed, it was the greatest shame on his head, had shadowed him for a quarter century.

"Is that why you were such a globe-trotter, because you were running away from her?"

Kip shook his head. "Pitiful, isn't it. Running from somebody who not only wasn't chasing me but didn't even know I existed."

"I'm sure she'd love you if she met you."

"She never will, though."

"So long as you're both still alive, there's always hope."

He turned the focus back to Mary, saying, "Look. You're brave enough to share your problems with me. Why not trust Marcos to the same end? Promise me you'll at least think about it."

At breakfast the next morning he sat with the Montoyas. Spoons in cups, the spring of the toaster, the creaking of a cane chair as one or another shifted weight. Their familiar voices riffing over the purr of the refrigerator compressor in the kitchen. Kip thought of these as fundamentally the music of family. A place at the table was set for Franny, who often spent the night with Marcos when she didn't have to work a late shift in Santa Fe or attend rehearsal. Kip sometimes wondered if he would be so tolerant about his child shacking up like this, not merely right before his eyes but coolly, calmly. Marcos and Franny sometimes came to breakfast dressed for their different days but bouqueted by the love they'd shared an hour before. This morning, however, she entered alone.

"What's Marcos up to?" he asked her, not knowing why, other than that he wanted maybe to underscore the last point he made after trading revelations the day before.

"Up to what he's usually up to, right?" she asked Carl, who nodded. Of course he was, thought Kip. Marcos was an unfailingly consistent man, not unlike his folks. Reliable, tried, true. Traits both he and Mary, in different ways, emulated yet resisted. When Carl rose from the table, Kip knew he would, too. Would walk with him through the kitchen, out the door, and into their workday. Marcos would already be out dragging the arena with a round harrow pulled by a small tractor to prep it for the morning's free-lungeing and sweating the horses. Kip wouldn't need to ask which of those horses to let out first, or which paddock to put them in. Wouldn't need Marcos's help washing down any of their boarders. He had become integrated into Rancho Pajarito, despite his habit of behaving otherwise. That knowledge—brought on by the clink of a spoon in a cup, the most paltry sign of household commonplace—would follow him throughout his day and into the late afternoon down at the fieldhouse.

What Kip did before he left with Carl, though, was ask Franny, seemingly out of nowhere, if she'd ever met a guy named Clifford.

"Why do you ask?" her breath coming short.

"No reason."

"There're a lot of Cliffords in the world."

"This guy's last name is Carpenter."

Franny blanched as she said, somewhat sternly, "Don't know him, Kip."

"Well, you'd like him if you did. Has some cobwebs in the attic if you know what I mean, but then we all do. Me especially."

Sarah asked her, once Kip left, "What was that about?"

"I haven't the vaguest."

"You've been helping him down at the fieldhouse. He seem okay to you?"

"Right as right."

"He's a complicated character, but we love him."

Franny sat unstirring, thinking how funny it was that people referred to themselves as characters, as if the world really were a stage.

"That Clifford Carpenter he was asking you about has been up at the convalescent center quite a long time, poor dog. Disconnected from everything and everyone. War vet. Just as sweet as can be. One of those people who make you remember that there but for the grace of God go you."

"Do you think it'd be so bad. Being totally out of it, I mean? Sometimes I wonder if it wouldn't be blissful."

"Who ever said bliss was the be-all?"

"He and Kip were friends?"

"Kip was always gentle with him, very kind—brotherly almost. Not that Clifford even knew who he was from day to day."

Franny rose from the table. "Got to get to work myself."

"I ought to take Kip up to visit Clifford sometime. You'd be welcome to join us."

"Maybe sometime. If you think it'd be a good thing."

How much smaller could the world get? What she wouldn't give to visit him, but she couldn't. One thing was sure—Franny was beginning more and more to ruin Mary's life.

Good Friday or bad, which would it be? Ariel drove east up out of Pojoaque through Nambé pueblo, toward Chimayó. Thank god it's Friday. Name of a bar? She hadn't had a drop since a week ago tonight. The gin debauch at the farm. Was she taking care of herself or of this other she hosted? Forget about that, keep moving forward.

She drove past corrals where chestnut horses and paints stood. A big cat lay dreaming in the purple shade of the overlook mission, El Sagrado Corazón. A goat wearing Moses' beard and Lucifer's horns crossed the road and a midnight-blue magpie strutted along its shoulder. Sometimes a brilliant field of green grass came into view but most of the scape was variant browns—tawnies, powders, hazels, beiges, tans. She saw no people anywhere as the road left all dwellings behind.

The turnoff to Chimayó. Before her, behind, and also to either side was a sweeping magnificent emptiness. Brittle thumbs of terra firma reaching upward. A formation that resembled a flock of nuns.

Sandy flats stretched between blackgreen globes of piñon and juniper billeted along arroyos and over the jagged flats in all directions. Masses of clouds heaped themselves with mythic luxuriance on the mountains, which they mimicked with such perfect, dwarfing authority as to make Ariel, their witness, disbelieve her ability to distinguish the one from the other.

And speaking of witnesses, she thought, he's seen all this. Seen it, breathed it. She rolled down the windows and her hair swarmed her head. All those days and nights since she'd left the farmhouse began to feel right suddenly, even righteous. Home for her could surely be here as much as back there. It was reshaping itself into a larger idea than she'd conceived before this moment. She wanted to find him. Said aloud, "I'm here." As she drove up the final ridge along the western slope of Chimayó valley, then began her descent toward the village, Ariel sensed, spiritedly if wrongly, that she was about to realize this fresh, expectant hope.

The plaza of El Potrero was quiet, empty. El Santuario de Chimayó, humble in the morning sunlight, stood before her looking for all the world like a thing built by creatures from one of her childhood fairybooks, so phantasmagoric were its adobe towers and rounded mud walls. She'd not guessed wrong. This was precisely where she should be right now.

The sudden calm, the peacefulness of the place, brought the gravity of what she faced into focus. Thus assured, Ariel climbed out of her dusty car, with ledger and photograph like bell and candle in hand, and entered the santuario, passing under its modest zaguán and through the walled cemetery courtyard that fronted it. The darkness within the church was cool, dank, and smelled of many thousands of scented candles. Without quite knowing what she was doing, or what it might mean, Ariel tucked a dollar in the painted wooden box just inside the nave, took a votive candle and lit it using the matchbook that was also set there on the little table. Alone, she walked up the central aisle margined by wooden pews as if drawn, like an acolyte, toward the reredos with its painted images of Christ,

Mary, the saints. She marveled at the radiant, untutored architecture in gilts and greens, reds and blacks, behind the altar rail. Pigeons cooed, echoing in the rafters, a familiar sound made mysterious by this holy room so far from the city that accompanied their song back east. Halfway down the aisle, she glanced up over her left shoulder and caught sight of where they lived, in a crawl space that gave onto a mullioned window whose glass was broken.

She stood breathing the heavy, drowningly rich scent of burned wax. This was, she thought, ancient air. Her knees buckled beneath the weight of some fine ecstasy.

Still alone in the hushed room, she came to. Finding herself on the hard floor, she realized she'd fainted or gone into some sort of fugue, or dream, or she didn't know quite what, though the duration of it must have been brief, since everything around her seemed the same as it had been before. Kip's ledger lay splayed beside her and looked like a fallen bird. Feeling dizzy but also, as on the road, alert beyond alertness, she gathered up the book and the guttering, smoking, but still burning candle and pulled herself onto a rugged wooden pew to collect herself.

Time passed. She climbed again to her feet and walked the rest of the short distance to the altar.

Unbelieving, she knelt at the altar rail and attempted, for a quick instant, a prayer. Mindful as ever she didn't know how to pray, she asked simply, *Help me.* To her left was a low portal that led to another chamber. She ducked as she made her way through this passage into the sacristy. She'd never seen anything like it.

Hung with crutches and baby shoes, with rosaries and homemade placards of gratitude, with framed photographs of the sick who'd been healed, the sinful who'd been saved, the young who once were crippled or mute or deaf or blinded but now could walk, speak, hear, behold, this narrow, long room was a documentary shrine to belief. Gaudy, it was nevertheless blessed; brazen, it was subtly enchanted.

On her right was a small anteroom in whose center was a hole carved in the earthen floor, which made her think of Gaia, of Mother

Earth's navel. Entering this claustrophobic alcove, she knelt, remembering what Brice had told her about the posito and its curative dirt. Astounding to think they'd both been here, Kip and Brice, back when they were boys, her two fathers. She gathered up a handful of sacred soil from the shallow hole that centered the chamber, lifted her palm to her nose, and inhaled deeply. She put her tongue on the consecrated loam. It tasted, well, spiritual.

Ridiculous, she thought, and then just as quickly responded, Ariel, don't ridicule what you haven't understood. She walked the length of the sacristy to lunge, like a swimmer reentering the world of air after diving into a deep pond, from the darkness of the church into the irreverent light of the plaza.

She passed the trickling acequia that coursed out in front of the santuario, and entered the church gift shop where she showed a woman behind the cash register her photograph of Kip and Brice. Had she heard of a man named Kip Calder? Nothing. Then over to the Potrero Trading Post whose front was decorated with ristras and a defunct Sinclair gas pump beside the screen door.

Ariel suspected that the man behind the counter had never seen the face in the photo he held before his eyes, though his hesitation suggested otherwise. Raymond Bal was his name, and what she didn't know about this dark-eyed thin serious man was that his tardiness had to do with his being a thoughtful person who—having lived his whole life in Chimayó and having been asked similar questions over the years by other pilgrims come here in search of the miraculous—wanted merely to give her an honest answer.

When he said, unexpectedly, "I did, maybe," she nearly dropped the ledger.

"Where? When?"

His Anglo wife had written a book about the history of Chimayó. Indeed, other friends and relatives of Raymond Bal had written books about the place, its penitentes, its curing dirt that made this the Lourdes of New Mexico, the center of annual treks on foot across miles in drenching rain or under heavy sun on Good Fridays.

But Raymond knew he couldn't answer this weary young woman's questions with any accuracy. "I don't know, I'm sorry."

"But you said—"

"Where's he from?"

"Los Alamos."

"A lot of people from the Hill come through here. What's his name?"

"William Calder. His nickname was—is, Kip."

"Don't know that name, Calder. What about the other one?"

"McCarthy."

"I really couldn't say if I've seen him, either of them, I'm just sorry. I don't know how to help you."

The more Raymond thought about it, the less sure he felt about giving her any hope. The fact was, though he didn't remember it, he had seen Brice three years earlier, back in 'ninety-three, when the man dropped in here to find Jessica and Ariel herself presents. Brice had bought them each Peruvian burial dolls. Odd gifts, he had thought. Nonindigenous and morbid, perhaps, but pretty with their serene cloth faces, legs and arms made of sticks, and clothing of woven, handpainted fabrics. Raymond had told Brice they brought good fortune, and so he had taken them home after meeting with Kip and presented them to Jess and Ariel along with bags of sacred soil, tierra bendita. Both wife and daughter were delighted. Ariel's was a late birthday present, as she turned twenty-four that year, three years past the deadline that Jessica and Brice had set for themselves to share the secret about Kip with their mutual daughter, having agreed that her twenty-first would be the right time. For his part, Kip had been inside the Potrero Trading Post, too, that Easter. Bought a Popsicle. At the time Raymond thought how sick the poor fellow looked and how he hoped the healing posito dirt would help him, though he doubted it could.

With Kip's eyes, Ariel stared at this man who pointed at one of the faces in the image. "That one must be your father."

"He is," she said, adding quietly, "I've never met him."

Discouraged but not defeated, Ariel picked a few postcards from the carousel, colorful depictions of the santuario, and rummaged a couple of dollars from her pocket. Raymond refused the money and wished her luck. As she left the small shop, she failed to observe, on a lower shelf in the display case, the few Peruvian burial dolls that were still in stock, lying together on their backs gathering Potrero dust. She walked into the dense sunlight that warmed the upper plaza and made the chrome fenders of parked cars glint like cruel smiles.

Hazarding the appearance of one who had at least mildly lost her mind, she passed the rest of that day showing the snapshot to others around the village. No one recognized their faces. Up where the road to Taos wishboned, a woman in the weavers' shop remarked, with a kindly inflection that could have been misconstrued as optimism but wasn't, that unless Ariel happened upon someone who'd been a childhood friend, she probably wasn't going to succeed in finding this boy all these years later.

Kip's daughter looked down at the rough plank floors of the weaving shop. The close smell of wool hung in this room filled with ponchos, blankets, sweaters.

"You need find somebody who know the name. This photo not help you too good. People get look different when they older. I know too well."

That was fair. More than fair—a courtesy.

As afternoon shadows began to engulf the valley, Ariel sat in the deepening silence of her car, having tucked the image back into the Calder notebook. How could she have failed to foresee the weaver's obvious point? Should she merely write it off to inexperience, fallibility, blindness, or had she come all this distance *not* to find Kip Calder but merely to weigh in with the apparent effort so she could feel she had completed the circle he'd begun here, in Chimayó? Pretty damn long distance to travel with the underlying goal of not arriving somewhere. She frowned, turned the car around in the stony lot, got onto the paved road, and headed back toward Pojoaque and

Los Alamos, whose towers shimmered way off to the west under the dusking sun.

She suddenly realized she hadn't been to the Hill—*Los álamos,* that home of poplars—for how long? Had unconsciously boycotted the place since Brice came home with his news of Kip. And hadn't been here even for a couple of years before that. What did she think, her grandmother was going to live forever? Life proposed changes, constants, and the uneasy middles between. While her pursuit of Kip seemed doomed to failure, at least it could prompt a reunion with this woman she loved. It was always worth running the gauntlet of mixed feelings she had about the nuclear lab in order to visit Granna. She knew about the research that proceeded down at the ends of these numerous service roads she saw on her way up the mesa, disappearing behind chain-link fences with official signs that read *No Trespassing Danger Live Explosives.* Yet most everyone she loved best in this world either came from here or had some hand in building it.

She guessed her way to Pear Street, parked beside the cottage, and rested her head against the steering wheel for a moment before gathering herself to start up the walk. Lights burned welcomingly in the windows of the house. She knocked on the door. Brice's mother in her arms seemed thinner than ever—ethereal, somehow. Ariel apologized for not phoning ahead to let her know she was coming, but Granna would have none of it.

"This is your house," she said, and once inside, Ariel knew she was right. For the first time in days a sudden ordinary calm settled over her. As if she'd been delivered onto solid ground from a world that was wildly whirling. "What brings you to New Mexico?"

"Everything and nothing."

"Well, that's exact if vague."

"You look radiant as ever."

"Mountain air and faith—you know me."

"Doesn't get better than that, does it?" She smiled, noticing her grandmother had let her off the hook.

"Have you eaten?"

"I'm famished."

"Well, let's do something about it."

Ariel sat with her kin for several hours, catching her up on news from back east, though leaving out for the time being all the most salient points.

Next morning the air in Los Alamos was pristine, washed by light Saturday winds. Ariel, having slept, was greeted in her grandmother McCarthy's kitchen by the welcome sight of milk, peaches, and cereal. Granna's question from the night before was on the table, too, as if it had been set there with the checkered napkin and white bowl. As difficult to answer as it was reasonable to ask. What, then, had brought her to New Mexico?

Even as Ariel formed the first words of some obfuscation, the truth overwhelmed them. "You must know who Kip Calder is."

"I know who he was."

"Was?"

"What mother wouldn't know who her son's best friend growing up was. Why do you ask?"

Ariel paused. So many questions begged to be asked, but she held back lest they come flying in chaotic multitudes. Nor was it her place to be the one to reveal that Brice, her son, was not after all the father of her granddaughter. Or was it? God bless the child, there were no maps for this part of the journey, either.

"When was the last time you saw him?"

"Kip Calder, heavens. Maybe thirty years ago."

"That long?" Her heart sank.

"Brice fell out of touch with him. They were born the same day, Brice and Kip, did you know? I was always of two minds about Kip, couldn't ever figure the boy out. He was a good student, very smart, smarter than most. Troubled kid, though, always getting your father into trouble. They ran away once, hot-wired a neighbor's car and took a joyride almost to Wyoming, until they finally crashed it. Kip was pretty badly injured if I remember right."

"My father never told me that one."

"No, I suppose he didn't."

Ariel lightly laughed.

"I heard Kip died in Vietnam."

"Not true," Ariel said.

"You're sure?"

"Didn't Brice tell you he saw Kip when he was here a few years ago?"

"Maybe so, could be. Did you know your grandfather died thirteen years ago?"

Ariel nodded, worried by this unexpected cognitive slippage, as she poured orange juice into, of all things, a *Deep Space Nine* glass. She had to remember that conversation with Granna was an up-and-down business, moving with no warning from sheer lucidity to consummate forgetfulness. Those prune-headed space barkeeps, what were they called? Ferengi? She poured juice into her grandmother's glass. Odo, shape shifter. All of it ripped off from the Greeks and Shakespeare. Shylock, Proteus. This was David's fault. Now look who was cognitively slipping.

"He was a good Christian, your grandfather. I'm sure he's in Heaven waiting for all of us."

"So how have you been feeling, Granna?" changing the subject away from both Brice's father and her own.

"Have you seen Bonnie Jean yet?"

"Don't forget, I just got here last night. We'll call her after breakfast, would that be good?"

"If you like, dear. We'll do whatever you want to do, since you're my unexpected guest and wonderful granddaughter."

Ariel immediately rose from her chair, went over to this splendid old woman, and, leaning down, gave her such a strong embrace that Granna whimpered slightly.

"I'm sorry," releasing her, taken aback by the vigor of her own affection.

"Not to worry. I don't break that easy."

Which caused Ariel momentarily to consider discussing her pregnancy with Granna. Who could be wiser, more forgiving, understanding? Although she would have but one position regarding the
abortion idea.

"Do you believe in Christ yet, Ariel?" Her cataracted eyes were
full of rich earnestness.

"Since last night?" Ariel managed.

These tangents were as angular as ever.

"Since anytime you allowed him into your heart," she said with ut-
most quiet vigor.

"I'm trying." Her unwed pregnancy as a possible subject slipped
back into the realm of impossibility.

"You don't have to try. Don't have to do anything. You allow him in,
he comes in. You believe, he saves you. Done, finished. Praise, hallelujah. Your grandfather died these thirteen years ago and I certainly
didn't want to live thirteen years longer than he did—"

"But if you hadn't, we wouldn't be here together."

Mrs. McCarthy paused. "True. But Ariel, I'm thinking of John,
chapter six, verse seventy or thereabouts. *Jesus answered them, Have I
not chosen you twelve, and one of you is a devil? He spake of Judas Is-
cariot . . . for he it was that should betray him, being one of the twelve.*
Jesus knew thirteen was the traitor's number, a number fit for a devil.
Did you ever notice that there are twelve months?"

"I, of course—" Ariel marveled at how Granna's freewheeling
mind might carry them anywhere.

"Not thirteen months, twelve. Thirteen's too many. Twelve signs
of the zodiac, twelve tones in the musical scale. Twelfth night at
Epiphany, twelve tribes of Israel, twelve gates of Heaven, twelve
steps to sobriety. Thirteen worries me."

If she knew the Bible, Ariel might have been able to say something apropos to interrupt this tumultuous flow. Instead, she said,
"I'm surprised numerology fits in with your belief in Christianity and
everything. You sure you're not just a touch pagan, Granna?"

"You sound like your father." She got up, opened the cabinet, retrieved her bottle of Tanqueray, waved it at Ariel who said, "No, well, why not, yes, okay, a little," remembering she was here to find Kip, not Christ.

Let gin be wine, let pipe serve as censer. They sipped their spiked juice and wandered—as each was eminently capable of doing—from idea to idea.

"Schiller knew all about it, but then Schiller knew everything there was to know about everything."

"Knew about what?"

"Eleven's the number of sin. Thirteen's the witches' number. But heavenly Jerusalem has twelve golden gates."

While they didn't get drunk, they didn't stay sober, either. Ariel weighed the reality anchor, as it were, and coursed along on a stream of affectionate ideas with her charmed wacko grandmother. Kip, Brice, Jessica, and everyone else in the world was asided, set as if on a nearby riverbank, while this two-paddle floating opera of straddling generations drifted by, free and unmoored for a few hours.

*T*his used to be his secret boyhood sanctuary, Marcos told Kip. He and his younger sister, Elena, nicknamed Lanie during her brief life, were inseparable best friends. But Lanie refused to ride down in the lower pasture with him, much less stalk around the tumbledown fieldhouse waging gun battles with driftwood sticks culled from the rio flatbanks. She took no end of ribbing from her brother about her unfounded fears, yet always maintained a good distance between herself and the adobe. Carl and Sarah never bothered her about it, but Uncle Delfino once told the children it was an ominous place—

—What's *ominous?*

—Means *scary,* Marcos chimed.

—a scary place, Delfino continued. —Because the last person who lived there was an ogre who had powers—*Itoayemu,* they called this ogre—

—What's *ogre?*

—Means *very scary.*

—and at night, when no one was out and about except for Santo Niño, not a chap to trifle with, either, this ogre would lumber around dragging his hairy foot behind him, like this—

And Uncle Delfino gimped in circles, snorting and huffing.

—making curses on little children's heads, especially children who hadn't behaved themselves during the day.

—That's enough now, Sarah interrupted. —No limping ogre with evil powers ever lived in that old fieldhouse, Lanie, unless maybe your uncle used to live down there. But you two should stay out of there anyway.

—How come? asked Marcos, his voice back then still soprano.

—Because it's not safe.

—Not safe, you say? Delfino asked, his eyes rounded and the ravines at the corners of his lips deepening into an ironic frown. —You hear that, kids? Their uncle couldn't help himself, —You children had better listen to your mother. *Itoayemu.*

Marcos remained unconvinced. For months he assured his sister there was nothing to be afraid of, that he would protect her from any evil, that he'd hung garlic on the plank doors and painted them blue to ward off spirits. Elena's fear was stronger than Marcos's promises, however, and though she rode with him bareback on un-broken horses far out into the adjacent plains where scorpions and yappy coyotes lived, she would not accompany him to the fieldhouse. She'd steal corn from pueblo gardens with him for the heck of it, but wouldn't go down to the adobe. She would swim right under Nambé Falls flashing like blue tinsel in the tumbling mist. She would even play stupid games with Marcos—she who hated games because she didn't like losing and didn't enjoy winning—because she infinitely preferred games to visiting the fieldhouse.

—You're being silly, he'd chide, as they played poor-man's golf.

—Not as silly as you, she'd respond, smacking the rawhide ball with a putter carved from a fallen fence post.

As it turned out, the old adobe would become the one place in all
Nambé where anyone's seclusion could be assured, since no one entered it after Lanie drowned in a heavy spring runoff flood that came
flying unexpectedly down the creek. Marcos discovered his lifeless
sister, wet, muddy, as gangly as a newborn foal dropped from a mare
that hadn't yet tongued its eyes open. The flood had caught her in its
furious arms upstream, near the mother ditch where the girl had
been mucking about by herself. Churning detritus in its gray maw,
its gorged water carried her in a roar of plunging stones and tires and
tin cans and tangled branches torn from riverside willows. Swept
into the murderous brown clot, she was delivered right beside the
very fieldhouse she so preposterously shunned.

With Elena gone, the Montoya family changed forever. Sarah was
for years unspeakably defeated, to be resurrected only by the slowly
evolving idea that she could help Lanie by helping others. Carl and
Marcos were stupefied, voiceless, and threw their grief into daily
work. Though Delfino assured young Marcos he made up that
Itoayemu ogre story, nothing could persuade the boy to enter the
fieldhouse again, however much he once delighted in its intoxicating
gloom and mystery.

Marcos shared these stories with Kip while they worked on the
restoration, and Kip listened quietly as he sawed fresh latillas from
cedar saplings and then later slung on scratch-coat mud—clay, sand,
straw—after they'd scraped the wall's eroded surfaces. When Marcos, during a break, surprised himself by telling Kip about the ghost
who lived here, and how he'd come to believe she was the legendary
Francisca de Peña, daughter of the ranch's first settler, Kip suggested
that if there had been some kind of spell on the place, wasn't it about
time to break it? "Set the poor spirit free, so to say. At least make it a
place for the living as well as the dead."

"I suppose you're right," said Marcos.

"I believe you, by the way."

"About the ghost?"

"Why not."

At times like this, when Marcos opened himself up to Kip, the older man found himself growing impatient with Mary's ongoing fraud. He sympathized with her but having himself been down duplicitous roads over the years, having failed people, some of them very badly, Kip hated to watch this probable disaster unfold before him. What was more, he saw himself being drawn into new duplicity and increasingly didn't like it. Proverbial rock and hard place, though. He wished them both impossible happiness. Or was that the prerogative only of parents, such a wish?

Either way, as Kip toiled down here, he found he was able to take some measure of where he was in relation to where he had been. In his mind he walked from the adobe in lines that radiated from it like rays of the *zia*. If he began his march at the new front door, headed straight across the porchstone—now scrubbed and reset—due east, he would walk parallel to Rio Nambé and up into the foothills until he reached Trampas, where the trout ran in the cold mountain streams of his boyhood. Were he to walk in the opposite direction, his feet would carry him across Pojoaque reservation land to San Ildefonso pueblo. He'd ford the Rio Grande in his mind and climb into the canyons below the Los Alamos mesas of the Jemez. To his right was Tesuque pueblo, and beyond that Santa Fe. And over his left shoulder was the wide shallow creek and the main settlement of Nambé, population three hundred, give or take. Then desert, more desert.

Kip found that he could spend many hours on end working, half haloed under the wooden beam collar of the doorjamb, and make these treks in his imagination. Sometimes one of the bad-tempered or maladied horses would wander across the fenced meadow and eye him, this thin figure, then wander off again to browse the orchard grass while breezes curled around the wet-limed walls, jostling shutters and making the rusty hinges on the set of pedimented doors sing like stuttering crickets.

Alone one morning, a Friday in August, he drew with a stick *Elena* in the soft adobe mud. And beside it, *Ariel*. He looked at the two words and, again shepherding thoughts that were outside his unfatherly rights, wished both of them peace. Peace beyond all understanding, as Wagner had sometimes said, in the Buddhist blessing. Then, before Marcos happened to come down with Franny, or Sarah, or Carl, or anyone else, he smoothed the names over with the palm of his hand.

*Y*ears ago a woman with straight silver hair, framing a sunned oval face and spacious cobalt eyes, walked into a room to find her husband, his head bowed as if in prayer, illuminated by lamplight, studying a piece of literature. Peering over his shoulder, she read aloud, —"Hot deals on cool stuff." The man pretended to ignore her, as now he recalled. Thinking back, he only wished he could hear her clear, strong voice once more. He would give a year off whatever was left of his life to relive just one such typical, even banal exchange as they had that evening.

—Agnes, he complained.

—"Factory closeout blowout sale of a lifetime"?

—Please, I'm reading.

—So you are, she needled Delfino, who shuffled the catalog then concentrated again on studying this gaudy illustrated page, which offered a free quiver with every purchase of a smooth-shooting, one-cam, superstrike Bear bow. —What cool stuff have we here?

—Nothing, some guns and bows.

—Why you reading about guns and bows?

He refused to respond. She walked away, then returned and asked the question again.

—History, all right? It interests me.

This was dusk, after dinner. Was before bed, when they used to sit together in the bungalow's small living room. The early eighties, a time when their valley world had gone from reticent to terribly reticent. When neighbors didn't need to speak with one another about what might be going on down at the base, or why Roswell, over to the east of the mountains, had become the capital of night sightings of the inexplicable. This was dusk, when their windows and doors were left open from May through September, and sometimes of a summer night they could hear other aging couples arguing, or a baby screeching, or young marrieds coupling, or some cat in heat mewling, or a bitch dog barking in the distance under the sumptuous diffusion of stars. When, in their hearts, they knew that the outside world had forgotten them and they remembered themselves only upon hearing—whether by design or mistake—other Tularosans, people or beasts.

Delfino recollected her pressing further the next day, catching him again hunched over the catalog. —You never showed this much interest in the history of guns and knives and combat gear before. He remembered her returning to stand behind him, quoting in a voice honeyed with soft sarcasm, —"Government surplus bargains. Veteran used gear that's ready to serve you for mere dimes on the dollar." Question is, are you ready to serve time for spending those dimes?

Look here now, he was reading a mail-order catalog, was all. Not against the law. A warehouse-overstock clearance pamphlet he'd received from an outfit with a post-office box up in Montana, for sportsmen who fancied owning, say, this night-vision monocular scope with infrared illumination, these cotton duck overalls in camouflage print, these thirty-round magazine sets for the carbines Delfino never really wanted or needed before, as such, but that had begun to enter his imagination as something he might not be averse to owning. If only for their collector's value, he might rationalize.

—"Bowie knife prices slashed to the bone"? That's clever, Agnes harried further, knowing him better than anybody and maybe sensing what really interested him here.

Delfino deflected her, —I always carried a Bowie knife when I was a boy. We all did. Carl, Daddy, even Kayley.

—Your mother never carried a damn Bowie knife.

—Course she did. Sometimes.

Agnes said nothing by way of response, which registered more loudly than if she had thundered her distaste for the things offered in the catalog.

Delfino finished, —No crime against reading.

—Reading's not the crime that worries me.

As if it were only yesterday, not over a decade ago, Delfino could remember her final parry, her parting gibe, reading over his shoulder once more, —"Conceal yourself in the bush of these unused old French military BVDs." These guys are comic geniuses.

Delfino chuckled.

—That's what you need, old man. Vichy underwear.

—Lord, he said, and stuck the catalog in his documents drawer in the kitchen. He was tired, was going to bed.

But he couldn't disagree with her, even as he meditated on how these obsolete weapons presented no problem for one who desired to remilitarize them. Sure, it'd be easier to go down to the gun store and acquire something licensed, Delfino reasoned that night as he drifted off to sleep. Yet there stirred in him an unnameable attraction, an instinct that using period pieces from the war that ruined his simple life would equate fighting might with right.

Agnes let the matter rest. She'd made her opinion known. This was her marginal form of protest, not that she truly protested her husband's idea, which grew in his heart like some sedulous cancer. She did not ask to look more closely at the catalog, knowing even more pernicious armaments were displayed in its colorful pages. She respected how hard Delfino worked every day to contain his perennial anger, and believed he would never, without her blessing, maybe even her collaboration, pursue his dream of retaking his ranch from the government that had stolen it from them.

She and her husband were equally part of each other, had grown into each other through their marriage. Were like a unique organism melded by time, love, trust. Agnes didn't give his catalog much further thought after that evening. Nor, however, was she shocked when he indulged himself in the purchase of a night-vision monoscope.

He insisted, —Just for the hey of it.

—Did I ask? she answered.

The Montoyas of downstate had been through many trials and disappointments over their decades together, but their setbacks were rarely visited on one by the other. If Delfino became possessed of some curious desire, Agnes might tease a little, needle him, even complain some, but she seldom denied him. And if Agnes liked wearing her stupid red shoes on her birthday, well then, have at it, live it up. After they lost Dripping Spring, and after they learned that the lease forced on them during the war was to be extended, then regrettably extended again, and then again, little rehabilitations such as some unnecessary nightscope were just that—compensatory gestures against the larger depression that hovered near them at all times.

They found they lacked some essential talent for giving up hope of returning to their vacated land. This was true of most of the families that had been similarly evicted from the Jornada and Tularosa flats on either side of Mockingbird Gap back in 'forty-four. The Trinity bomb worked; the war was won. But the lease and lockout continued. Some clung to a fading belief they'd be allowed to return and, as they waited, slowly lost the strength needed to move along and set up some kind of substitute life elsewhere. Like blue moons, the waxing of any confidence in reaching a fair settlement with the government became rarer and rarer. Alamogordo prospered as the military base grew. Rockets populated their skies at unexpected, odd moments in the day, and during the night they might be awakened by roaring overhead as stealthy mechanisms broke sound barriers, racing through darknesses hundreds of miles long in matters of seconds, more or less out of the world's purview.

Delf watched sometimes, sitting with his nightscope on his quarter acre under the same cover of gloom that the military types used to hide their triumphs and sporadic instances of nonachievement. The crashed turboprop. The lost payload. He watched the night tinted green in the monocular glare and waited to see what might pass through its rounded field of reduced heaven.

More often than not he would come to bed at two in the morning, three, four, slipping in beside his Agnes, having seen nothing but yellowish stars in green fields of vacuumous infinity. Yet once in a while he did spot things up there, fast batlike machines moving high and silent, or on occasion so low to the valley floor he doubted the rationality of the person or being who dared pilot with such absurd abandon. On those nights he would awaken Agnes and tell her what he'd seen. They'd talk for a while, fall asleep. There was no need the next morning to report anything to the local newspaper. Everyone hereabout knew of White Sands and its titanium hawks, its black airships, the so-called secrets being developed on their old lands and tested over their contemporary shelters, some of which were just flearotten trailers and withering adobes and pressure-cooker bungalows. In any desert, hermetism is possible, but secrets are hard to keep.

Growing up on a working ranch, Delfino, like Carl, had learned to be a jack of many trades. Trades of the hand, labor accomplished on your feet, not your derriere. As such, he never had much trouble finding work during the long personal drought that settled over him after their eviction. In a land so terribly unpopulous, where one acre per head was compulsory for the cattleman who wanted to keep a viable herd, the multitude of skills that came to be required of Delfino in order to scrape together a living was noteworthy. Clerk at the Satellite Inn, cook at Sí Señor, picker in the pecan groves. At the time when he ordered his monoscope and began his nightwatches, he was working as a roofer and, most weekends, doubling as a driver for the bus company that ferried souls from Alamogordo to Las Cruces or El Paso and back. Agnes worked part-time for the forest service, at Three Rivers, a petroglyph field twenty miles north of Tularosa.

Tres Ritos was their second-favorite place in all the world. From its black lava heights they could see—looking out over the seeming infinity of desert flats, fenced only by the San Andres at the western edge of this panorama—the bluish alley, a tantalizing tiny hint of what had been their home. They loved few things better than to hike up through impromptu channels of talus, the tough crescendo of rocky slope, until they reached a summit where they might open a knapsack and have their lunch of tomato sandwiches, cucumber salad, and apricots, joined only by the ghosts of Shanta Indians, of Pat Coghlan, Judge Albert Fall, and the misnamed Thomas Fortune Ryan who, like so many, had attempted and failed over the years to tame this basin.

For Agnes and Delfino, sitting on these buffblack stones carved by people long since gone to earth meant something inexpressibly life-allowing. They had their favorite glyphs and visited them like old friends. The kachina with the lightning bolt striking its head or, as Agnes liked to believe, emanating from it. The flock of thunderbirds. The coiled snake. Flute players, deer, rain shaped like combs. A weatherworn open-air museum on whose sculptures they sat gazing toward the vanishing point of the Burrito Range, the Organs—at the foot of whose massive rock pipes the dunes of White Sands glittered bright as a blizzard—and Old Baldy, looming like a shaved head above the timberline. At the center of this overwhelming cosmos were shadows where slopes converged into a level alcove. It was there that their ranch house probably remained, their earth tank and windmill, maybe, and some belongings they left behind on the assumption they'd return sooner rather than later—certainly sooner than never. Even seeing Dripping Spring from such a distance made them feel connected.

Their lives came into scale here. She liked telling hikers who asked her when she was on duty, —Yes, there are over five thousand petroglyphs here, thought to have been inscribed by the Jornada branch of the Mogollon culture around nine hundred to fourteen hundred A.D., and if you climb high enough you'll see the white dunes that have been there for two hundred and fifty million years. A quarter billion years, just imagine, she'd say with equal wonderment each time. For Agnes—who loved these numbers, as they made her feel small, innocent, somehow safe—this was a place where you learned to know yourself and those around you.

One thing she didn't know, however, was that Delfino, in a rare moment of acting behind his wife's back, had ordered several vintage rifles from that catalog she'd long since forgotten about. Rifles and quite a few rounds of ammunition. Moreover, he took great care to hide them from Agnes. She died without ever discovering them.

Now they looked both pathetic and arrogant on the oilcloth where Delfino laid them out the evening before he left for Nambé. He was reminded of the excitement he had felt on Christmas Eves, when his mother, Kayley, made her kids set out their nightshirts and turn back their beds all neat and nice before they were allowed to join the adults in the casa greatroom, where a fire crackled in the hearth that was taller than either young Delf or Carlos, raggedy punks with bowl haircuts. Christmas nog, chocolate fudge squares, snow on the ocotillos that made them look like anorexic Jack Frosts. A profound feeling of order settled over those bygone Navidad nights, and Delfino, impressed by the chimera of such a memory, now felt that youthful sense of promise again, however disparate might be the image of his bed and nightclothes and presents under the tree—the lovely lost past—with these shotguns, rifles, rounds, and five-gallon plastic water canisters beside them. He had paint and boards for the signs he would make, and lengths of barbed wire rolled and stored in a canvas satchel. Dried food was packed in saddle bags. Bedroll, binoculars, of course the nightscope. To hell with sunscreen, he thought with a laugh—he couldn't get any more burned than he already was. While the authorities and news media would no doubt declare him criminal, berserk, an extremist—if they bothered with him at all—he was in truth none of those. Rather, a ticked-off romantic. Dreamy maverick. Or else just a guy who got it into his head he wanted to go home. Even if he were able to think through all the probable *tragic consequences,* as they would phrase it on the radio, he could never talk himself out of it now. Deeper forces were at work.

The wall clock read four. Meticulously, upon finishing setting out his desert gear in the garage, he shaved and showered, then packed a couple of clean shirts and climbed into the truck. He'd always loved the heavens on clear nights such as this, loved how unquestionably the Milky Way traversed the sky and earned its name. Driving, terribly awake, toward Carrizozo, he listened to the wind pummel the hood and windscreen of the pickup.

First he would have to visit what was left of his family. Carl, Sarah, Marcos. He didn't want to be remembered as anything other than a gentleman by those who loved him. He would meet Marcos's friend Franny and wish her every advantage in the world. He was curious about this man whom Sarah had mentioned so often, the veteran who fixed up the fieldhouse. And he wanted to visit the place of his birth and childhood, if only to make some kind of peace with it and pay respect at gravesides.

He felt very light of heart, standing under the first pinks and sundry blues and the fluorescence of the gas station as he filled the tank, and when he got back into the cab and made toward Bingham and San Antonio, past the malpais with its whiskery cacti flickering in the dawn rising behind him, he felt voluptuously at peace, more so than in any recent year.

He'd be there by late afternoon, poking along, taking in the familiar geography as he went. Somewhere down the road he'd phone his brother, and if he couldn't reach him at the stables he would call Sarah at the convalescent center, to say he hoped they wouldn't mind that on the spur of the moment he decided to take them up on their standing invitation. Then, after visiting his first home, he'd return to his true home once and for all.

*I*n Zuni, dreamers are said to accompany their dreams outside their dreaming bodies. Some Zuni believe that the dreamer's breath leaves the body to accompany the dream, like a sigh chaperoning another sigh, as together dream and breath move away from the sleeper to experience the fantastic narrative world beyond. Others believe that the mind, not the breath, goes forth from the sleeping person to become the dream's wandering mate. Both are valid—*sa tse'makwi allu'a,* the dreamer's mind leaving its flesh to range the darkness of night, and *an pinanne allu'a,* wherein this dangerous privilege is performed by the dreamer's spiritual "air." Either way, Zuni traditions about death and dying, about concepts regarding the loss of rational mind, are inevitably nourished whenever the sleeping person begins to dream.

Mary knew that night was the most fearsome time in Zuni. She knew this not because Zuni pueblo stretched like a dream of unruined land south of Gallup, but because the thing she remembered best about her uncle Clifford was his obsessive love of Zuni culture, Zuni spiritual beliefs, anything from the four-cornered world of Zuni. Like any novice who manages to teach himself about another culture, he reveled in it and talked about it to anyone who would listen. After the war tore part of his mind away, what he understood about Zuni and retained in his fragmented memory—that Kachina Village was where the dead lived, witches among them carrying on the matriarchy, for instance—he shared excitedly with his brother Russell's kids, before he was shipped off to the ward.

—Listen up, you might learn something, he said with winning enthusiasm. He hinted that by telling them about Zuni, he was guiding them into a secret society. That each bit of lore he offered was, as the Zuni themselves would say, precious *mi'le,* and would serve them well in their lives in unexpected ways.

His nephews, naturally, laughed behind his back, but Mary sensed that there was maybe something true and valuable in all this Zuni stuff their nutty uncle was telling them, something not to be forgotten or taken for granted. She was reminded of this when she awakened from a dream about a witch in the form of a dripping doll who was pursuing her into a field of sharp-leaved cornstalks, until finally she could run no more. When she looked down, she saw that her legs had grown into a single limb rooted in the soil, and realized that the witch who was chasing her was none other than Mary herself. Or else a nameless girl who looked like Mary. She woke in terror, remembering the two theories of how a person dreamed.

Had her breath or her mind left her body when she had this nightmare? She might have insisted both had wandered into that field of razory corn with her dreaming self. However freaky, her nightmare came as no surprise. Chasing herself into a cornfield where she took root—wasn't this the most thinly veiled dream she ever had?

Rising in the dark, she made her way across the room to the kitchenette where, still half asleep, she lit the gas burner for tea. The circle of flame put her in mind of a wreath shimmering on the stovetop, the wreath in turn becoming a fiery martyr's crown. But who was the martyr if not Marcos? Not a good thing. Not what she wanted.

Water from the faucet half filled the saucepan; Franny owned no kettle. After placing the pan on the burner, she glanced down at her body, her breasts, the tuft of hair where her thighs met, her naked feet, and wondered why anybody would bother to make love with such flesh. But he did, sweetly, just as she adored his strong body. He'd been over earlier this evening, after dinner in town. They had undressed each other and, kissing, collapsed onto the braided rug. Marcos skinned his knees in the precious tumult, and afterward rolled off onto his side, both of them laughing until tears came to their eyes.

That was when he said, "Franny, let's do it, move in with me at Nambé."

"You're such a wonderful man, Marcos," was her answer.

She sat facing him in the shadowy room and combed his hair with her fingers.

"Franny?"

Running her hand down his stubbly cheek, over his shoulder, as he lay there propped on one elbow, she said, "I do love you. But I'm not sure about moving in together."

Plain words plainly said though not plainly explained. Marcos put on his clothes and went home. Afterward, the trucks that passed along Saint Francis sounded to her not like the flow of a beautiful river but rather like what they were—filthy eighteen-wheelers, moving metal junkyards driven by undreaming men on stimulants who transported goods from one place to another. Nothing like a nightmare to wake you up to reality.

Franny drank her tea as she got dressed. She didn't know where she was headed, but knew she wasn't going back to sleep. Something essential in her waking dreams had cracked. Albuquerque had not led to any movie studio or screen. Santa Fe, by the same token, was drawing her on to Nambé, farther than ever from the dream in those photographs on the walls of El Rancho. She was being pulled into a lasting relationship, a mooning girl destined to become some ranch wife instead of a celebrated actress. Go figure. She now walked vaguely toward the plaza, trying her best to think, alone under a blithe ceiling of stars, a charlatan in love with Marcos Montoya despite her own wary distancing. The weight of her falsehoods, lies lying on more lies, freighted each step she took. She'd arrived at this crossroads because at so many earlier crossroads she'd made choices. Good ones, bad ones. Did the word *coincidence* rightfully belong in the language?

Well, Kip was coincidence. Accepting Marcos's invitation to visit Rancho Pajarito, in a moment of unguarded enthusiasm, didn't mean she'd signed on to meet Kip Calder who seemed to see through her as if she were a pane of glass. Kip, who not only appeared to understand her mess but was caught in his own. And it was just that, a fucking mess, she freely conceded, seated on a bench in the plaza, shivering some. Just as hypochondriacs do get sick sometimes, and paranoiacs do have enemies, some coincidences are simply in the cards. How absurd was it, for instance, that her drama class had staged a closed reading of *The Tempest*, with her in the role of Miranda, only a few weeks before Kip told her he had a daughter named Ariel? Not very. Not at the end of the day. What was crazy was that the young guy who'd played Ariel was a truly gifted actor who would never go to Hollywood in a thousand years for a million bucks. She admired him but found his unjaded purity, in a backwater night-class acting school in Santa Fe, a bit sublime. Sublime as in loony.

Several people passed her. A couple, probably a little drunk, spiraled by, their laughing voices punctuating the echoing quiet along the Governors' Palace arcade. None noticed this lone figure across the street facing them, hands nestled under opposite arms. They had, however, broken across the meander of her thoughts and—again, chance provoking fate—brought her to a decision. As if in a more benign dream, Mary walked back home. For one who had risen after a nightmare, dressed, and fled, she hadn't gone very far. But in another sense she had traveled light-years. During what remained of the night she slept more peacefully than she had in months.

Come morning, she phoned in sick to work. Small white lie. Then she drove out to Pajarito and found Marcos. The chronological ordering of truths might not have come out quite as Mary would have wished, but her doppelgänger was doing the best she could, given the knot she'd tied them both up in.

"I didn't give you a straightforward answer to your question last night," she began.

"No, you didn't."

"If you're still willing to consider me living with you, I'd like to accept."

"You would?"

"Yes," and they embraced—*an pinanne allu'a*—sending forth her breath with this waking dream.

It would remain for Mary to persuade him to leave Nambé and move west to a place where they might both tackle the world from a greater vantage, and for Franny to be exposed and then retire to some kindly Kachina Village where witches would not torment her.

*A*ccompanied by the younger of her sons, Bonnie Jean met Ariel at the emergency room. Aunt and niece had never been much closer than were Bonnie Jean and her somewhat estranged brother, Brice, but they kissed each other on the cheek in the hospital foyer. Bonnie stood in her daisy-print housedress, looking dazed and hapless. Her wispy browngray hair was bobby-pinned arbitrarily to her head, her drawn face was bleached by worry, and her bloodshot eyes conveyed that she, usually stalwart to a fault, had been weeping. She blinked as if, roused from a long nap, she discovered herself in a place where she had never been before. "Do they know what happened?"

"A mild stroke is what they're saying," answered Ariel, herself ashen. "They've got her stabilized, said they'll know more over the next few hours. She's going to be all right. She's tough."

"Too tough for her own good."

"Well, she does things her way, if that's what you mean."

Bonnie Jean said to no one in particular, "I warned her. This was inevitable, smoking that pipe of hers like some merchant marine and drinking like a sailor. Eventually catches up with you."

Sam adjusted his oversize stovepipe jeans on his narrow waist and nodded mute greetings to this cousin, who was more than a decade his senior. His basketball jersey was either half tucked in or purposely left half untucked, she couldn't tell which.

Mountaintop hip-hop, thought Ariel. "I sure hope my showing up unexpected didn't cause this to happen."

"Of course not."

"She was pretty wound up this morning."

"How so?"

"We'd finished breakfast, and she was talking about, about the number thirteen—"

"Her latest fixation."

"—and Christ and your father."

"Her other two."

"She was really lucid, but all over the place—"

"Was she drinking?"

"—then she suddenly got the strangest look on her face, and put her hands up in front of her, and I thought . . . well, I didn't know what to think. Then she blacked out. That's when I called Emergency and rode over in the ambulance with her. I would have phoned sooner, just it all happened so fast."

"No need to explain, Ariel. If you hadn't been there, who knows what would've happened. She was drinking?"

"Not much."

Bonnie Jean smirked, raised her eyebrows.

Sam and Ariel sat in the waiting room while Bonnie conferred with the doctor and paid a visit to her mother in intensive care. Wearing rumpled black drawstring pants and the same black tank T-shirt she'd slept in, Ariel knotted her untied tennis shoes, conscious she was being watched. What a morning, what a life. At least it looked like Granna was going to pull through, poor angel. "You've grown a lot since I saw you last, Sam. How old are you now?"

"Me? Fifteen, almost."

"Really," she said, affecting a diplomatic distance and feigning surprise. "That's getting there," her voice cascading into deeper registers, elderly-aunt sounds, she supposed, to ward off his unequivocal gaze at her bralessness.

"Getting where?"

"You know what I mean. Older."

"We're all getting there."

Ariel thought, Shut up, Sam. She rose and walked to the bank of tinted windows, which afforded a mesmerizing view of gnarly ponderosa pines in nearby yards and, beyond, forests, more forests rising above Los Alamos into the Jemez Mountains. She'd driven up there with Granna once, through Douglas firs and lodgepole pines, dizzy from the switchbacks and altitude—nine thousand feet, almost ten—and made it to Valle Caldera at the summit. She remembered being dumbstruck by that vast grassy crater, the product of an eruption some million years ago, whose lava had brought this finger mesa into being—this place where Sam had been born, Bonnie Jean, Brice and Kip, and the atom bomb itself, a pale imitation of such an instance of natural apocalyptics, so dwarfing of human time. Ariel imagined the magma scorching the volcano's flanks, the enormity of the event as the mountain collapsed, having thrown its very core up into the sky. One surely could have seen its rosy orange blast from the darkness of space. Granna's God would have seen it and called it good. Let there be light, she thought, unconscious of her right hand that lay flattened against her belly. Now, pregnant Ariel stood here too. Funny, the idea had the momentary weight of epiphany. What could it possibly mean that after she turned her back on the mountain and made her way toward Sam, a nurse crossed her path wearing a plastic name tag that read *Faith*?

That evening, after a second visit to the hospital, Ariel had dinner with her relatives. Bonnie Jean's husband, Charlie, barbecued whatever he could find in the freezer while Bonnie threw together the rest of their impromptu meal. Ariel sat on the patio and held, as best she could, a conversation with her uncle. Not the brightest light bulb, especially in this cerebral county of nuclear physicists and high-tech engineers, Charlie nevertheless possessed what her grandmother would call a sweet spirit. Potted geraniums and petunias stood at every extremity of the modest backyard, and though she loathed geraniums and petunias, Ariel complimented him on them. Long day. Keep the peace.

"It'd give Bonnie a boost to know you like them. Some are as old as the Hill itself, swear to you. They're her pride and joy," he somewhat mournfully smiled and sat down at the pebbled green-glass table with his niece, who was sipping a lemonade from concentrate. "She says you'll be staying a while."

One was perennial, the other annual. Not as old as the Hill.

"I'd like to stick around until Granna's better. But only if it isn't an imposition."

"Not hardly. You're family."

"It's good news they say she's going to be okay."

"Myself, I'm more scared of hospitals than sickness itself."

"She seems in good hands."

"Never liked hospitals," Charlie concluded.

Amid the mayhem, Ariel tried phoning her parents a few times but never reached them. Well aware of Bonnie's long-standing animosity toward Brice, she nonetheless thought it odd that her aunt hadn't mentioned his name all day. She decided, however, to cut the woman some slack, distraught as she was beyond distraction. Bonnie's first thought would be not of her brother but her mother, who lay in the hospital, frightened surely, sedated, attached to a cardiac monitor.

Bonnie Jean clearly still considered Brice the boy who'd left the Hill for the big city back east, the man who'd disenfranchised his family and the community that had given him so much. If it was true that one could never go home again, Ariel thought, maybe it was because the people left behind never discarded their sense of having been abandoned. She wasn't surprised when Bonnie, after thanking her for complimenting the flower garden, finally mentioned her brother by vaguely dismissing the need to telephone him that night. Why not wait a day or two, until they really knew something concrete about their mother's affliction? No need to bother Brice until they had some specifics.

"We have specifics to tell him now, Aunt Bonnie."

"Not really. We don't have a prognosis."

"Very mild stroke. A little rest and she'll be back home better than ever."

"This will put the kibosh on her smoking and drinking, anyway."

"If you don't mind, I think I'll call him tonight. He'll want to know."

"You go ahead, Ariel," said Charlie, not looking at his wife. "And tell your father everything's under control."

The three of them ate, Sam having rambled off with friends to play WarZone 2100, a video game they considered ultracool for Hill kids to access, given its premise of rebuilding life after global nuclear devastation. Ariel asked after Sam's older brother, Charlie junior, who was rock climbing up in Eldorado Springs, having grown up in a hurry since his cousin saw him last. Conversation ran calmly at variance with the day. They sat, each abstracted.

"These pork chops are perfect," said Ariel, filling a lull.

Bonnie Jean agreed with her niece.

"You're not eating very much," Charlie noticed.

"I guess I'm not that hungry." Soft warm air rose from the canyon below. Religious music downloaded at random from a satellite piped through the television in a room off the patio. John Tavener's *The Protecting Veil,* with its cadences of Russian Orthodox chant. "Granna would like this," she said.

"Poor thing," Bonnie whispered, then pulled herself together, moved the subject away from her mother.

So then. What was Ariel up to in New Mexico? Did Bonnie Jean know a man named Kip? Kip Calder, *know* him? No offense to Charlie here but there was a time in her life when she thought she was in love with Kip Calder, believed that he and she might even get married one day. He was a little too much like Brice, though. Always running, always skipping out on family and home. Well, at least he served his country when the time came. Like Dad did with his work here in Los Alamos. And served, she'd heard rumor say, with distinction. Again, no offense but he'd been an extremely handsome young man, just a little touched is all, but then who isn't? Kip Calder. The last time Brice was here, he'd mentioned something about Kip.

"Did they ever have their reunion?" she asked, leaving Ariel in a perfect limbo between telling and denying her one truth that might lead to others she hadn't the strength this night to address.

Scents of concession food wafted on azure smoke. Toasted corncobs in blackened husks and hot salted piñole nuts. An aroma of burned coffee mingled with the smell of sausages stewed in jalepeños on a Bunsen burner stove. Cactus candy, used clothes, mildewed books. Under a wide sky, people pawed through piles of stuff, bartered, hustled, peeled off bills and placed them in hands. Beyond that ridge was the opera house, standing empty today but only last week filled with an audience come to hear Stravinsky's *The Rake's Progress.* Sets now struck, orchestra and singers all gone home, and the aria

> *They go a-riding.*
> *Whom do they meet?*
>
> *Three scarecrows*
> *And a pair of feet . . .*

carried off by desert breezes.

What remained were businessfolk and bargain hunters. Old hippies, road people. Honest antiquers and hucksters who'd given up dealing pot for the purity of caravaning the Southwest from fair to fair, selling nothing new under the sun, their wares spread out on blankets or under the tarpaulin shade of stalls. Here was a rarity, a bull-pizzle walking stick. There were Hopi moccasins, Navajo squash blossoms. Mickey Mouse memorabilia, a portrait of Elvis on black velvet. Bulovas from the forties, when somebody's young daddy had fallen charging the beach at Normandy, his watch just like this one, still ticking on a lifeless seawashed wrist.

And here was Kip communing with these artifacts and feeling somewhat artifactual himself, wandering the rows of merchandisers, gazing at their recycled arcana, their fur hats that wouldn't fit any head, their sheep bells from Pakistan, their scratchy vinyls of John Denver and The Doors. Franny and Marcos followed, holding hands, poking through the relics, too. Kip bought a kerosene lamp for three dollars. He haggled down the price of a green rain slicker. Marcos got Franny a nice old piece of goldblack-veined turquoise mounted on a silver bracelet. They ate fresh tortillas and Marcos gnawed on carne seca—venison or beef, he couldn't tell which, really, so spiced was the shredded meat that stuck in his teeth. Kip found a sheepskin rug that would go beside the bed he and Marcos had welded back together earlier that same morning, as well as some army blankets, chairs, and a chest of drawers. Things to outfit the fieldhouse. And Franny bought Kip a battered painting from Mexico, on a warped piece of tin, for him to hang in his sitting room. A saint spearing a dragon.

"Housewarming present," she said, handing it to him with the warmest smile Kip had yet seen on her face, as they drove back to Pajarito in the pickup with their finds. "I thought he kind of resembled you. The saint, I mean."

Next day, Marcos helped Kip carry these new furnishings down through the lower pasture. Moving out of the main house, the man found himself in a bittersweet mood. These had been some of the best months of his life, his mind never so unclouded. Superstitious in his way, Kip worried that now that he had nearly completed the task he'd set himself, his usefulness here was concluded and the old demons that had been kept in abeyance might move into the fieldhouse with him. Too, he wondered what living apart from the Montoyas would be like. Of course, he'd still take his meals with them and continue working for Carl. But this sworn outsider had grown used to being near the others. His natural will to run away from everyone and everything had unusually slackened as he'd matured, like some grafted limb, into the Montoya family tree. Damn strange sensation.

The camaraderie of working with the others would be lost as well. Through spring and into August, everyone at Pajarito had managed to help. What Kip didn't know how to do, Carl did; what Carl didn't know, Marcos did; what Marcos didn't, Sarah or Franny did. Even the structure itself, after a fashion, informed its restorers how to renew it. Sun-dried bricks of strawstrewn mud had been replaced here and there, covered with adobe and lime set coats. Window openings had been fitted with fresh glass, their facings and lintels painted tomato red because that was the paint color Carl happened to have in a can left over from another project. There were some touches still to add, but the project was winding down. Marcos had found shutters in a storage room and, after stowing the new furniture and other gear, he and Kip sat down to scrape off the old blue paint together in cottonwood shade, alone for the first time since Franny had moved in.

"So when are you two getting married?" Kip asked with a sly grin.

That was unexpected, but Marcos, being a horseman, knew how to respond to unexpected moves. "Franny's keeping her apartment for a while, you know."

"Is that a good thing or bad?"

"Tell me, Kip. Have you ever been married?"

"I suppose you could say I have."

"How can you suppose you've been married? It's like being alive or dead. You're either married or not."

"You're forgetting about comas and trial separations."

Smart-aleck duffer. Marcos waited for more.

"I'm married to someone I'll never see again. That's all."

"Because you don't want to or because she doesn't?"

"Because because."

"You must have had a bad falling-out."

"No, just two people worlds apart not meant to be together. I don't know if she'd even recognize me. We didn't get married for love, anyway. It had to do with American citizenship for her children."

Letting that one go, Marcos asked, "Have you ever been in love?"

"I had my chance once, when I was about your age."

"And?"

"And I missed it."

Marcos wanted to ask but sensed from Kip's voice, its hushed depth, that this was another subject best left alone. "Sorry things didn't work out for you."

"Things worked out like they were supposed to. They always do."

"Always?"

"Always. It's inevitable."

Time passed as the dirt beneath their bench became slowly cluttered with blue chips of old paint, which now looked for all the world like a pile of dusty once-iridescent butterflies. Kip tucked a fresh piece of sandpaper into the block, tightened the wing nuts, and began stroking the scraped wood.

"You and Franny seem perfect for each other."

"You think?"

Kip hummed, his mind moving away from the subject he'd come close to broaching. He wished to keep his promise to Mary but hoped somehow to inspire Marcos in the direction of discovering a path into her truer life. Franny hadn't been fabricated for no good reason, nor was Mary's apparent love for Marcos without foundation. Any former professional spook would know that secrets were sometimes founded on principle. But still, he wondered how much longer Mary was going to hold out. A prop plane passed overhead and Kip glanced up to watch it surrey across the sky. Cessna. He'd flown one of them years ago, taken his Vietnamese stepsons up for a whirl. He remembered their gaping mouths and excited chatter. Nice kids, but he'd known them no better than he knew most anybody else. Everything but this given moment seemed so far away, so long ago.

For his part, Marcos had a question for his friend here on the bench mottled by sun moving past its zenith. "You mind me asking how you lost it?"

"Lost what?" jolted from his darkening reverie.

Marcos nodded toward where Kip's hands worked at the wood laid across his lap.

"What, my virginity?" Kip quipped, hoping to lighten his sinking mood.

"That'd be an interesting story, but I mean your left hand. I always wanted to ask why you're missing part of that finger."

"The rest of it's in Laos somewhere."

"The war?"

"I lost a lot more important things than my finger there, but that's another story."

"Your war stories are interesting."

"Hand me that, would you?"

"I like hearing them, I'm not sure why."

"Because, thank god, you've never been and don't face having to go."

Marcos handed him a wire brush that lay on the ground. "War."

Kip ignored the word, tried to. Crazy, wasn't it, that such a complicated enterprise of mass destruction was summed up in a small burst of air across the lips. *War.*

"I would think the most important thing not to lose in a war is your life. At least you came home with that."

"Nobody comes home from a war with anything other than his country's victory or its surrender. Everything else in a war is lost, no matter which side you fought on, and don't let any fool tell you otherwise. All my fingers are gone. They just look like they're here."

Marcos said, "Well, they say you can't be a good carpenter and have all ten fingers."

"You don't mean to offend me so I won't take it that way. I wasn't a good soldier. I didn't belong in Vietnam so I connived my way to Laos, but I didn't belong in Laos, either. In retrospect I'm proud I wasn't that good a soldier. I tried to be, just wasn't. I still have the middle finger left, and that's the one I raise to salute our fine Indochinese war and all valiant, important, and necessary wars waged from now until kingdom come. Maybe we ought to call it a day with these shutters. I'm sure Carl needs some help."

"Yeah, got a couple more horses to work. Guess I'll get to it," Marcos said, wanting to apologize for having touched a nerve but understanding that he could not.

When Marcos stood up, covered with fine sky-blue paint from his scraping and sanding, Kip was reminded of Krishna, the blue Hindu boy god. His earlier fondness returned immediately, not that it had ever left. Shouldn't have been so short with him, but what's family for if not to work out your hardest ideas on?

*T*he season of largesse, of things and stuff, continued that evening when Delfino, who'd arrived before sundown, brought out a present for his brother's family, as he always did when he visited them. In years past, Delfino's *visit gifts*, as they were called, had been magnificently ordinary (a cropper's spade) or funny (a whirligig of a gunslinger bowing to a barmaid) or just plain odd (a glassed display case of rattlesnake tails mounted with pins). This evening's present was a nineteenth-century photograph of some people formally gathered around a mule, taken just a few miles, Delfino believed, from Dripping Spring.

Sarah held it up to the light and thanked him, saying, "Why, that's just beautiful."

"Wonder how old it is?" Carl said.

"If anybody ought to know it'd be you, Methuselah."

"Very funny."

Fraternal banter.

"Look," said Marcos. "Somebody wrote *1890* on the back."

"Well, then, not quite as old as Carl," said Delfino.

"Go ahead, ruin your presentation of the visit gift, see if I care." They chided each other with relaxed, toothy smiles.

"What you think they're doing?"

"Mule beauty contest," said Carl.

"Carl," said Sarah.

"Damn handsome mule," said Marcos.

"Always thought you were a sheep fancier," said Carl.

"Carl," said Sarah.

The mule did, however, have a fuzzy white muzzle and the soulful eyes of a sage, standing there untethered. Sarah held the print closer and asked, "Are those some kind of headsets the children are putting up to their ears?"

Delfino smiled. "You're getting warmer."

The glass-plate photo showed thin boys in light-gray shirts, probably the only shirts they owned at the time, some with broad suspenders. All wore baggy pantaloons and boots that resembled leather puddles in the dust. On the beast's back was a black contraption, squarish and somewhat sinister-looking. Seven boys held to their ears the ends of thick wires that were connected to the saddled box, while another loitered under the sun without a hat, leaning on what appeared to be a crutch, waiting his turn to listen. The majordomo and his wife stood solemn at either edge of the frame, he frowning under his bowler, she with hands on the sturdiest of hips. Not a living tree in sight, only scrabble wilderness rock. Behind them was a log structure that might have been a ranch house or the office of a mining company.

"What do you think they were listening to?"

"John Philip Sousa was around back then—maybe it was 'Stars and Stripes Forever.'"

"Probably a jingle for Coke."

"Marcos."

"The real thing."

"I doubt those kids had the faintest idea what they were hearing. Look at their faces."

Kip studied the sepia wasteland scene of adults and children listening to a scratchy black disk—Chincester, Bell, and Tainter wax-board going around at seventy-eight or thereabouts—and spoke for the first time. "Must have been the absolute strangest thing that ever happened to any of them."

"Depends on how long they lived after eighteen ninety," said Sarah.

Kip agreed, "Model T, the Wright brothers. It did all happen pretty fast."

"Not to mention discovering the atom."

"Men on the moon in less than a hundred years," said Marcos, and Franny added, "Don't forget about the Internet."

"Christ save us," said Delfino, suddenly realizing his gift didn't mean quite what he had intended.

"Christ-dot-com, you mean."

Sure, the image alluded to Dripping Spring, the old ranch and old dream, and as such it was a memento of his strong fondness for the place. But now he recognized it also marked the nanosecond when technology had first come to the desert, and with that the irreversible wave of scientific systems under which he himself had faded, as much a memento from yesteryear as those folks gathered around a mule with a gramophone strapped to its sagging back.

For dinner they ate cayenne chicken and grilled squash from the kitchen garden. The small dining room was redolent with food and wine.

"What brings you to Nambé?" Carl asked his brother.

"Felt like it."

"Come on. Nothing gets you here unless something's up."

"I felt like seeing you. No crime in that."

"Nothing doing, Hoss."

"This is their old game," Sarah told Franny and Kip. "Carl still doesn't get why his brother left Nambé for downstate back when they were Marcos's age."

"Younger than Marcos," said Carl.

"Wanted to breathe some fresh air is why."

"Nambé air is a hell of a lot fresher than Tularosa basin."

"Not to my nose."

"This," Sarah continued, "is where I stop listening."

"I always told you you ought to get your nose examined."

"And you ought to have yours looked at by a vet."

"I don't need a vet to tell me horse shit smells better than cow shit."

"See what I mean?" said Sarah.

Turning to Kip, who was seated across the table in his best linen shirt, the visitor changed the subject, not to mention the spirit of the conversation. "My sister-in-law here tells me you come from Los Alamos."

"Born and raised, but I haven't lived there since I was a kid."

"Not my favorite place on earth, forgive me, Sarah."

"If you're referring to the Project, it's not my favorite place, either," Kip said, seeing in Delfino's half smiling eyes the look of one of those overwhelmed boys hearing music from a gramophone for the first time. He believed he saw fear there, apprehension about some unexplored future. He knew the demeanor. A blasphemy of calm. Had seen this sanguine look before on the faces of soldiers who knew they were about to lose their lives on the field of battle.

Kip glanced around the table to see if anyone else picked up on it. None had, and none—aside from Sarah, who'd surely seen it in the eyes of her patients on the Hill—would or could. Some things you can learn only from experience. Kip, who'd flown, then run, then walked, then literally crawled away from his inescapable war, now saw it sitting at the pleasant August evening table in the form of Delfino Montoya and wondered what lay behind it. He could feel one of his old episodes coming on, a slippage, gnawing like flame at his edges, but he didn't want to be backdrafted into some drastic scenario. Delfino was saying something directly to him, yet he couldn't hear. Then, as if Kip managed to grasp the delicate, broken quadrant of his mind and lift it clear of that growing flame, he forced himself back into the present.

The man across the table was saying, "Lots of great people come from not so great places—you all right?" to which Kip answered, "Of course, thanks," which in turn led Delfino to begin considering what had already traversed his thoughts over these past months, and even during the long morning stretch of his drive.

And that was this. Were he to tell his brother what he was going to do next week, Carl would talk him out of it. That's goddamn lunatic crap, he'd calmly shout. Sarah would agree with Carl, if not in those precise terms, Marcos with Sarah, and Delfino would be left either to capitulate to their collective wisdom or to march forth onto White Sands range not just alone but more than alone, pushing on against the best wishes of what family he had left on earth.

But what about this Kip Calder? He was the victim of Vietnam, not War Two, granted, but of war nevertheless. Maybe, Delfino mused, Kip would be kind enough to hold his last will and testament for him, and the letters he'd written, see to it that Sarah execute his wishes if indeed he didn't come back out of Dripping Spring in one piece, which he figured reasonably he might not. Maybe this remnant of one war would be chivalrous toward the remnant of another. Kindness of strangers—wasn't unheard-of. In fact, it seemed the best way for Delfino to proceed. He saw in Kip's eyes the depths of a man who'd borne burdens in the past and might be equal to a burdensome charity case now. The Montoyas had taken him in when he was down and out. Perhaps he'd indulge an old man a similar favor.

After dinner, as always, the brothers sat on the *portal* and smoked beneath the stars that framed the serrate silhouette of the eastern mountains beyond Nambé pueblo. Kip sat with them. They prattled on wonderfully about people Kip didn't know and never would. He was reminded of nights he'd passed aboard ships, sitting on an idle deck under luminous constellations and a half moon that itself looked like a sail on some floating skiff. Ships above, ships below. Here the veranda rocked because of the wine Kip sipped and because the slippage was still there, nearby, he could feel it. Yet the moment seemed rich with chance, though he couldn't say why, just as any sailor's starry moment of reflection before dawn brought its endless struggles and possible storms. Kip thought of his wife. What he'd told Marcos was true. He would probably never see her again. Hadn't he eaten cayenne chicken with her once in Hanoi? And her boys—the elder in San Diego now, the younger in Port Arthur,

Texas—prospering immigrant youths who'd always been grateful if perfectly withdrawn. What would he tell them had he one last chance? What would he say to his distant wife? To Jessica? And Ariel?

Kip rose from the creaky rawhide chair and shook hands good-night. He said, "My pleasure," to Delfino who asked if he might come to the fieldhouse in the morning and have a look-see at the restoration.

"I thought about fixing it up myself way back when, before I left Rancho Pajarito instead for other terrain," Delfino continued, then abruptly grew as pensive and mute as this fellow Calder who left the Montoya brothers to walk under the Dippers great and lesser toward the lower pasture, thinking, Sometimes there's just nothing you can say.

*A*riel woke up wired. Wired and disconcerted. Her week on the long road, culminating in that Friday reality-check reckoning in Chimayó, had finally weighed in on her. Having tossed, turned, remembered where she was and why, she pulled back the sheets and tiptoed—though there was no reason to do so, since the house was empty—into Granna's kitchen. Sitting at the table with a glass of milk, she thought about how much Granna wanted to join her husband. After Ariel said goodnight, the woman's parting words, garbled by drugs and the stroke, were, "Maybe a gaw nigh in Heaven."

"It's always a good night in Heaven, right, Granna?"

"You come too when's your time, awrigh?"

"I'll do my best. Meanwhile, get some sleep. Heaven's not ready for you yet."

She thought about how much her grandfather McCarthy had liked to sit at this very table with her, drinking warm milk to soothe his ulcer. He loved physics and a good conundrum, those two things maybe more than anything else besides Granna. Work and wife made sense, but his devotion to riddles was a character quirk, no doubt about it.

The old man was a master of *conundra,* as he liked incorrectly to call them, penumbras of cognition. Trick questions he collected. Ariel remembered how much he delighted in posing even simple classic riddles like, —What's black and white and red all over? in his crumbly dry voice, then awaiting her response.

If his granddaughter guessed, —Newspaper, he would say, —Sunburned zebra.

If she guessed, —Sunburned zebra, he'd say, —Communist Manifesto.

If she tried another tack and guessed, —Ovaltine in a red cup, he'd say, —Not bad. But not right, either.

He loved answering one conundrum with another's solution.

—The more you take the more you leave behind, what's that?

Ariel considered the problem for a minute, but it wasn't a difficult one. She answered, —Footsteps?

—No, he said. Try again.

—Breaths, breathing.

—Closer.

—Come on, Grampa. Footsteps was the right answer.

—The correct answer was wedding rings. Here's another. What single word has the most letters in it?

She knew this, knew the answer was post office, but said, —The alphabet.

Naturally, calmly, swiftly, he said, —That's correct, by god.

It was two words, but so is post office. —Hey, Grampa, what can fill a room but doesn't take up any room?

—Light.

—Nope. Light takes up room.

—Darkness.

—Naw, come on. Darkness takes up room.

—Air?

—No. Air takes up room, too. You're not trying very hard.

—I give up.

—Silence! she shouted.

—One could make the case that silence is spatial, you know.

These games endured through their brief years as granddaughter and grandpa, on the telephone, in letters, in person. She rose to every occasion and he marveled at her mind, telling his son once, —Do whatever you can to nurture this girl's imagination and nothing to hurt it. She's special.

Brice concurred, saying he was doing his best.

—Why is Grampa's eye so milky, like there's a cloud in it? she asked Jessica after the McCarthys made one of their rare visits to New York, some seven months before he died. No conundrum; Ariel's forehead was furrowed, her arms were crossed, her black shoes were locked side by side. At times such as this, she looked mature well beyond her baker's dozen years. Her mother explained that this was something that happened to certain people when they got older.

—It's called a cataract.

When Ariel looked the word up in the dictionary, she found that it came from a much older term for *waterfall,* for *abrupt,* for *floodgate,* and for *striking down.* She remembered those backgrounding words when her conundrumming pal was gone. As she wept in her bedroom, she thought how abrupt death can be in striking us down, how those who are left behind are flooded in tears. A heart attack seemed so unfair, she believed, to come to a man who had such a good heart.

During that last visit to the city, he asked her the queerest question. She recalled it because it was his final riddle.

—Here's one for you, he said with a wink. They were sitting side by side on a bench in Washington Square, feeding the squirrels. —When a man gets hit by a train, is it the engine or the caboose that kills him?

Her grandmother, flanking Ariel opposite, overheard this. —Don't be morbid.

—It's not morbid, Granna. Don't sweat it.

—You heard her, he gently laughed. —Don't sweat it.

—Ariel, we should be getting back to the apartment so your grandfather can rest.

—I'm not tired. Ariel, which is it?

But he did look tired, drawn, even emaciated.

—Let me think, she said, staring into his ivoried eyes.

They left the park soon after, and though she had several more days in which to do so, she never concocted an answer. Then he died and with him went the secret to his last conundrum.

It occurred to Ariel now, as she finished her glass of milk, that she never figured out whether it was a true riddle or instead an instance of his losing hold on lucidity, a prophetic, enigmatic protest against the rushing onset of his impending death. Either way, she knew the answer, suddenly. Too easy, too obvious, and that's why she hadn't put it together. Neither the engine nor the caboose killed the man. The man killed himself by walking out onto the tracks in the first place. How she wished she could give him her response. It might have earned her one of his cherished smiles.

Here at the table she had to ask herself, how had she wound up walking these metaphoric tracks, aware the train must eventually bear down on her, if only to keep another's schedule? And how would her finding Kip Calder, an iota of whose body had combined with Jessica's to make her own, offer an answer to any conundrum, posed or not?

Because of Kip's early abandonment, her first moments on earth—even before she was born—had been fraught with puzzlements. Her maternal grandparents, now long deceased, had come east from Ohio for the big event, though they hadn't been happy about the situation surrounding it. They'd had good reason to be unnerved, if only because their daughter hadn't bothered to marry Ariel's father. Brice McCarthy and Jessica Rankin were admittedly unconventional and, as Ariel would also come to learn, were indeed still virgins—with each other, that is—odd as it might seem, given they'd come of age in the era of free love. But however unconsummated, their love had never been in question.

—William is what we've settled on, Brice told Jessica's dad, answering his question about what the child was going to be named if it turned out to be a boy.

Innocently or fake innocently, Jim Rankin asked, —Is that your father's name, then, or this other fellow's?

—It's her father's, sort of—

—I'm her father and my name isn't William.

—I mean the baby's father.

Awkward beyond all measure.

—But I thought you didn't know whether it was going to be a boy or a girl.

Very Abbott and Costello, thought Brice, who then shifted the geography beneath the subject, just as he'd do later in life as the lawyer he would become, saying, —Well, it hardly matters, since I know the baby will be a girl and we've decided on Ariel for the name.

—What kind of name is Ariel?

—It's out of Shakespeare, and the Bible.

—William's a better name.

—For a playwright.

The name game, straight out of *The Naughty Nineties*. At that point Brice must have wondered whether he and Jessica really should have pressed ahead with his pretending to be her husband, Ariel's father, that whole bit. Which pretense would have been less eccentric, which more tenable? Didn't matter. This was the way they'd chosen to go, the honest way. Only later would their veracity evolve into a much more powerful mistruth, or dual truth, thus positing the oldest riddle of them all. What in heaven's name is the truth?

Jessica's parents received the news of her pregnancy complete with an accurate description of her romance with Kip and a firm recommendation that if peace were to be kept in the family there should be no insults, no sarcasms, no denunciations. If they wanted to be supportive, she'd welcome their support. If they couldn't in good conscience support what she was doing, she would respect that. Her parents hadn't the least interest in arguments or anger. Brice's parents, on the other hand, were never given the details about their granddaughter's knotty parentage, a decision their son took early on to avoid the inevitable *Bible beltings,* as he termed his mother's peppery sermons. Over time, the decision to curate a half-truth—Ariel became, after all, legally his daughter—ossified into whole truth. The McCarthys asked, once, why the girl had her mother's surname rather than her father's. But as she was born of sixties parents, the countercultural thing to do was just that. Ariel Rankin was her name, for better or for worse.

And what kind of a name was Kip? Sounded like an acronym. Keep Isolation Pure. Kismet Isn't Practical. Karma Is Pain.

Word games. She'd come an awfully long way to sit at a kitchen table in Los Alamos and think up Sunday morning acronyms, reminisce about games with her grandfather and idiosyncrasies surrounding her birth. What about Granna and Kip? The now. She had to reach her parents this morning. She wanted to phone David again, but had less to say to him than ever, and besides, she couldn't take his rejection of her again. Having left no messages on her machine, he'd become a complete absence. Except for the pain that more or less replaced him.

Maybe ought to give herself a break, she could almost hear her grandfather's advice. Her life had been largely floated on words. Airy, eerie, weirdie. On her name she'd heard every pun in the book. Time to forget conundra and homonyms and get some breakfast going, head over to the hospital. Ask around about Kip Calder. Make discreet inquiries about where one might have a procedure done to abort an early-term. Above all, stay off the train tracks.

*B*oth men were up with the magpies. Each saw the sun cut sickles of light into ten thousand dense cloud waves that rose like white vulcan smoke on fenders edged purple as locoweed, datura in the shadows. They met, as if on some kind of businessmen's schedule, in the kitchen of the hacienda. Kip hand-ground coffee beans while Delfino put up water in the kettle on the big black Wolf stove. One asked the other if he'd slept well. Yes, and you? He did, though the drive doesn't get any goddamn shorter. Which led them to Tularosa and the Jornada del Muerto, a province of New Mexico Kip knew better than Delfino might have expected.

"My father worked at the lab during the Manhattan Project. He was down there the day they detonated the first A-bomb."

"Trinity?"

"He saw the whole thing from Compañia Hill."

"July 'forty-four. I should know, I was there, too."

This surprised Kip, who looked carefully at the man in the room with him, a handsome cayuse in his seventies, strong, lean, weathered as any who lived his life under a desert sun, with a prominent browned nose narrow as a ruler, a taut wide mouth, high Hispanic cheekbones, and furrowed cheeks. With black eyes, and tall—easily as tall as Kip himself—Delfino cut quite a figure. The younger of them sensed that while they were of distinct generations, their very different lives had ruined them in ways that had the odd result of breaking down their differences. Embracing them both, time and fate had brought them here, and though Kip knew nothing of Delfino's plan, he did sense something was at work. This notion blew through him like light. "Nobody told me you'd worked on the Project."

"I didn't. More like the Project worked on me."

"Meaning?"

"Long story," Delfino said. "But no, I had nothing to do with the bomb, other than being pushed out of its way."

"Better out of its way than in it."

How was it possible that in half a century, Delfino Montoya had never quite thought of it in those precise terms? "You're right. But that's not how I saw it back then, and it still isn't."

"How do you see it?"

Innocent enough question, though Montoya frowned—not at Kip but some specter over and behind his shoulder.

"I was in Tularosa, just east of the mountains behind where they lit their candle that morning. It'd been a rainy night and we were asleep in a rented shack the government had put me and my wife up in. The ground shook, knocked us both right out of bed onto the floor. Don't remember hearing any sound, really, but there must have been some kind of rumbling, had to have been. The light was brighter than staring at a thousand halogens. Brighter than I can tell you. We ran outside and looked due west and there it was, this huge gray rope of smoke coming straight up over Mockingbird Gap with a boiling mushroom cloud on top. Deathly, filthy, ugly. Ugliest, ghastliest thing I ever seen."

"That's just the opposite of how my dad told it."

Delfino drew a palm across his mouth and down his chin, then dropped his hand into his pocket. "Go on."

"He never said it was beautiful, but he remembered being awed and flabbergasted that it'd worked. He changed his mind later, as time went on and the war was over and instead of building down the Project they went on to hydrogen and thermonukes. He had a hand in the Nevada tests but eventually withdrew himself and moved over to theoretical work."

"He still on the Hill, your father?"

"He's been dead for going on thirty years."

"Sorry."

"I'm sorry he had a hand in causing you whatever trouble you're talking about. I know he'd apologize if he were still around. He used to be proud of his role in the Manhattan Project. Then one day he just wasn't."

"What changed his mind?"

"Winning that war was what mattered to the Hill, and nothing got in the way. Among the victims who survived Hiroshima were people like my father. Alcoholism, depression, suicides hit more than one Hill family after the great victory. Not that my father went that way, he didn't. But privately he renounced the whole business, mostly the tactics of deployment."

"Japan was a ruthless enemy that might have won. That's what they always said."

"Little girls in their school uniforms going to class that morning? Their *mama-sans* washing the breakfast dishes before going to market? Soldiers, sure. They're supposed to kill each other's asses. But more often than not, civilian deaths outweigh military ones, certainly in modern war. Soldiers should slay each other by definition, not shoot civvy fish in the barrel. I don't see why generals and career men shouldn't be the ones forced to step into the fray, instead of conscripted privates. But that's war for you. Chop down the innocent. Even Darwin would have been ashamed of the formula."

Delfino held his tongue, thinking, Here's a like-minded man if ever I met one. "You were going to show me the fieldhouse."

Coffee cups in hand, they walked past the horno, down to the path that flanked Rio Nambé and the lower corral.

"Will you look at that," Delfino exclaimed sincerely at the sight of the adobe, now pale pink in the sunrisen light. "You really have done a job of it. I don't think it ever looked so sharp, even back in the old days."

The house did look good, Kip saw. *Relevant* was the word that came into mind. It sat low, clean, modest under the massive trees. "Had a lot of help."

"That's not what Sarah says."

They went inside. "Sarah exaggerates. Marcos and Franny did most of the work. Carl, too."

The men looked the place over, each noticing, though never commenting, that the other seemed oddly distanced from what was being admired. Each had his strong connection to these walls, but more than that, an ineffable harmony flowed between them. They heard it, saw it in each other's eyes. Something shared beyond personal histories around the Jornada and its Trinity grounds, the commonality of nearing demise. Each was mortal and had lived beyond what he expected or even wanted. This passed between Kip and Delfino, unspoken. Not even wholly formulated in either's thoughts.

"When we were young, Carl and me, we always heard this adobe was haunted, but I never saw nothing."

"Don't look at me," Kip smiled.

"Well?"

"No such thing as ghosts, just dead people and ones that are alive. I might have thought there were ghosts once, but I don't anymore. Came too close to being one myself."

"I'd like to think there's a ghost here. I always used to tell Marcos and his sister—"

"Lanie."

"—that spirits haunted the place. Their eyes would get this round. I used to enjoy that. Hell, I sure wouldn't want to be a ghost."

"How's that?"

"Hard enough to get people to believe in you as it is."

Kip laughed. "I was a ghost once, come to think of it. A spook, at any rate, during Nam. You're right, it wasn't much good."

Couple of old fucks talking about war, death, and ghosts on a beautiful morning like this, thought Kip. Boys of winter.

As they pushed back outdoors, Montoya said again how much he admired the restoration and then, without so much as considering further any possible consequences, he launched straight into his request. "I know you don't really know me, and I don't know you, and I know I ought to be thanking you for putting this place down here back together—"

"No," Kip said. "I'm the one who owes your family the thanks, not the other way."

"—but I have a favor to ask."

"Name it, you got it."

"You might want to hear me out before you go agreeing to anything."

Kip did hear him out, as they sat together on that same wooden bench where he and Marcos had worked and talked not long before, and where Franny had told him all about Mary. He learned of

Delfino's plan to go back to his homestead at Dripping Spring, out on the military's most restricted badlands. He wasn't going to live forever. Time had come. Kip didn't agree or disagree, but understood the bias. "You ever fished salmon?" Delfino asked.

"In Alaska, once."

"You ever heard the word *anadromous*?"

"No."

"My wife, Agnes, liked collecting words like that. Most of them I forget now, but anadromous stuck."

"So what's it mean?"

"You know how salmon are born in fresh water then migrate out to live in the saltwater ocean, then come back to spawn in the same river they were born in, then die there, just where they started? That's anadromous."

"And that's what you want to do."

"Well, I don't know as I intend to die out there, but I got to force it to some conclusion. If I lived ten lifetimes I know that the bullycrats and burrocrats at the other end of my letters and calls won't ever bother with me, and I'm damned if I'm going down dead silent."

Kip agreed to all that Delfino asked of him. He half wished he could mount some reasonable argument against the juggernaut Montoya proposed to bring upon himself, but honestly could not. When all was said and done, wasn't Kip himself anadromous? He was. And had every intention of helping this fellow migrant.

"Chim ó," was what she called him, using her rudimentary Vietnamese, just a few words really, a couple of phrases she now knew, thanks to Kip. *Chimayó* without an assenting *aye*.

"Meaning?"

"Ask Kip."

"Come on, Franny."

"*Gian.*"

Marcos genially frowned.

"*Chim ó* means buzzard. *Gian* is cockroach."

"*Gian* yourself."

The name calling, all in jest, was her comeback to Marcos's allegation that she'd been spending more time with Kip than with him, and that maybe there was reason to be suspicious. "And now you want to meet his friend," he said. "What's next? A formal announcement?"

"Jealousy becomes you."

"And English suits you better than Kipamese."

Franny smiled, disparaged him in Vietnamese once more, then repeated what she'd originally said, that she didn't want to go to the Hill without Marcos coming along. Los Alamos—*cao nguyên* was Kip's closest analogue—had entered their conversation because Sarah persuaded her to join them at the center to visit Clifford Carpenter and afterward have lunch. Kip's convalescent friend had asked for him and, as Sarah said, "Given he doesn't seem to remember the names of people he's known there for years, can't even recall what he does from hour to hour, Kip must have made quite an impression on him."

"Seems to be a trait of his," said Franny, who was moved to go visit her uncle out of a combination of curiosity, confidence that he wouldn't recognize her anyway, and unwonted homesickness—or if not that, the desire to fill some void she herself could neither admit to nor understand.

Marcos proposed that on their way up they take a couple of hours and hike the Indian ruins of Tsankawi. He'd loved the mesa since he was a kid and wanted to share it with her. Not often having witnessed this side of Marcos, in which he waxed nostalgic about his childhood—his telling her about spying on the *vatos* being an earlier instance—she wanted to know more. Besides, they too rarely got to be by themselves, all joking about Kip aside. It might give her the opening she'd been looking for to broach her idea about California. Why not? *"Xin mời anh đi."*

"Meaning?"

"Meaning, All right, cowboy. Well, sort of."

"No Vietnamese spoken there, though. Promise."

"I promise nothing."

Marcos waited until she finally said, "Okay, I promise."

Copper out the windshield, sun reflecting in clay and stone and stems, off rabbit brush and seared saltbush. Light the hue of dying golden asters hovered in the white tuffstone of the canyon heights as they drove across the Rio Grande. Like one on sudden furlough who wanted to kick up heels for the simple joy of it, Franny said she'd like to wade in the river, whose water ranged from Navajo tea brown to sedimentary red to sheep-shit obsidian. Marcos said, "Let's do Tsankawi first, then the convalescent center, and if you still want to wade at Otowi on the way home, you got it," which seemed fair to Franny.

She felt oddly free this morning, liberated from past or pasts. Maybe it was delusional, definitely ironic, but who cared? There was something positive in the idea of seeing poor Uncle Clifford, not that she could do a thing to help him. She trusted Kip not to breathe a word about Gallup, but she knew more clearly than ever that he was right about what she had to do. Maybe, just maybe, the visit would help her to confess her duplicity, her many lies, to Marcos. Meanwhile, she would inhale this mountain air deep into herself and set the world aside for the day.

They took the road toward White Rock, soon pulled over and parked on the shoulder. An open solitude settled heavily over the vista as they hiked in the warming breeze down a rocky gulleywash trail. Having made their way through the sparse piñon and juniper woods, they began their ascent up the ancient trail worn deep into the stone by women and men whose dwellings in the southern cliffs came into view. Franny followed Marcos along this sunken path, one foot directly in front of the other as if on a recessed tightrope, climbing the pumice rim well below the flat summit, snaking their way mutely, beholding the vast widening valley as raptors dark as the smoke-charred ceilings of the ruins circled on updrafts. A mountain bluebird toppled by in a tumult of azurine. Red ants charted courses across the winding, rising trail. Crickets chirruped in shady spots. To the left were holes chiseled into the cliffs, handholds and toeholds for accessing the table mesa where, Marcos told Franny, the community of Tsankawi thrived in its three-storied pueblos a millennium or so ago.

"How're you doing?" he asked.

"My god, it's just too much."

"Should we go back?" turning like some awkward dancer, feet caught in the stone furrows. He'd forgotten what an arduous trek this was, a difficult hike even for him now that he was no longer climbing with the pliant legs of a boy.

"No, I mean this is unbelievable," she answered, gazing out at the long horizons that spread below. "Imagine them in the winter after a snowstorm, huddled in these cliffs with only fire and each other to keep them warm. Reminds me of when I was young and saw Red Rocks for the first time."

"Red Rocks outside Gallup?"

"Yes—no."

"The ones near Denver?"

"What?"

"Which Red Rocks? I've been both places."

"You misunderstood but it doesn't matter," she tried, her flight into the past brought to earth by Marcos's innocent question, itself prompted by her own slipup. He let it go, unaware he'd touched on a place even more protected than these rimrock steeps. The guise, though—was it beginning to collapse of its own accord?

After a rugged hour, they made it to the southeastern face of Tsankawi and sat with legs dangling over a five-hundred-foot plunge. The world lay literally at their feet. Marcos named from north to south the faraway summits of the Sangres. "Jicarilla, Sheepshead, then Truchas and Sierra Mosca, West Pecos Baldy and Capulin," between which lay Nambé, due east. She listened intently to these beautiful names, leaning into Marcos, her arm over his shoulder as if to protect him from herself. Given the stark transcendence of this place and his deep love for it, Franny began to lose her nerve about discussing a future for them elsewhere. She never felt so alone with Marcos before, and though she liked the abundance of this world of his, its natural dignity, she had to wonder how and if she could ever fit into it. Still, she had to try to say something.

"You remember when I came out to Pajarito that first time and you were asking me about my plans for the future?"

"Sure."

"How I said that once I saved enough money, I wanted to go overseas, just anywhere far away? Timbuktu, I think I said."

"I remember. You bought tickets without telling me?"

She smiled. "No. Besides, I don't think I care about flying around the world anymore."

"Why bother when you're sitting on top of it right here?"

"That's something I wanted to talk to you about."

"Sitting on top of the world?"

"You know how devoted I am to my acting."

"Why shouldn't you be? You're good."

"Well, I was talking with the director of the company and he said the only way for me to get ahead, really excel, is to go out to the Coast."

"Coast."

"You know, West Coast."

"Hollywood."

"That's where all the real actors are, the dedicated ones. There and New York. Why swim in a small pond when there's a great big world out there just waiting?"

"So we'll go to California, if that would help you."

"Marcos, you'll meet more powerful people in your field, too," Franny said, her heart leaping, hardly believing her ears.

She needn't have doubted, since Marcos went on to say that while it wouldn't be easy, he could hire some outside help to keep the stables going for a month, maybe more. The regionals had taken him all over the West, but he'd never been to California. Would they need to be out there longer than that?

"Probably, well, I'm not sure." Insane of her to ask such a thing of him. What was she going to do? "Thank you, Marcos," she said, hiding her profound disappointment.

"For what?"

"For being such a good man." Kissing him, she noticed out of the corner of her eye a pottery shard—there were many along the path—and pulled away to pick it up. Simple black design on an ivory field, last touched, probably, by one who had used it for carrying water up to the pueblo from a nearby canyon.

"Here," and gave it to him. "For good luck and protection always."

In the aftermath of Tsankawi and the feelings it stirred in Franny and Marcos, who made love in one of the cliff houses at the eastern-most brim of the trail, the drive to the convalescent center was marked by streaming stillness. Marcos drove with one hand, the other resting in Franny's. He sensed something had changed between them, but not knowing what it possibly could be, kept the intuition to himself. They parked on the perimeter of Acid Rock and were greeted by Sarah, who took them to the glassed atrium where Kip and Clifford sat together, talking, pointing at exotics in the new aquarium.

"Clifford?"

He turned his face toward the three who stood there, his eyes not leaving the world of the saltwater tank, and in particular a small spotted blue shark that cruised it with undulating authority.

"Clifford, I'd like to introduce you to my son, Marcos, and his friend Franny Johnson."

"Good to know you," Clifford said, his eyes darting from the aquarium to the others and quickly back.

"Hello, Clifford," Marcos said, stepping forward and taking his hand, gently shaking it.

"Oh, yes, hello."

Now Clifford did look at Marcos, who smiled at him. Clifford peeked over at Kip as if to ask whether he was supposed to return the smile. Kip nodded and the man smiled back at Marcos.

"Clifford." Sarah spoke a bit more loudly than necessary, given he wasn't hard of hearing but simply unpunctual in the way he responded. "This is Franny."

She put on the strongest smile she could manage, while gazing at her father's brother from a depth of grief she had never anticipated. "Hello there," she said, stretching her hand toward this frail man whom she'd known from her early childhood, the perennial bachelor, the crazy uncle who'd been touched even before he went crazy.

"Hello," Clifford answered, shaking her hand.

Kip watched Franny even as Clifford found it impossible either to stop looking into her eyes or release her hand.

"Hello," he said again.

"Hello," she answered this time, very tenderly attempting to free herself from his grasp.

"Mary, what took you so long?" he asked.

She looked at Kip, then at Sarah and Marcos.

"I'm sorry?" she asked, with a broad smile.

"Mary. You're my niece, aren't you?"

Removing her hand she stood up straight, turning to Sarah. "Does this happen? What should I do?"

"Just go along with him," Sarah said. "No harm."

"Yes, Clifford, if you say so."

"Why'd you take so long?"

Clearing her throat, reaching behind her for Marcos's hand, she said, "Take so long?"

"You've come to get me out of here, haven't you? We can go back home now, can't we?"

"Not today, Clifford," Sarah said.

"Why not?" he asked Sarah, never taking his eyes off the younger woman, whose cheeks now flushed crimson.

"Because Mary's not ready to take you home today," said Kip, intervening at last, gently touching Clifford's forearm.

"What about tonight?"

Sarah said, "You don't like it here anymore?"

"I do, I do," answered Clifford, concentrating now on Sarah. "I just thought my niece had come to take me back to Gallup."

Marcos tried to help. "She's not from Gallup, Clifford."

"I think you're confusing me with somebody else." Horrible.

"No." Clifford shook his head, solid and swift, back and forth, gazing at the linoleum. "No, no."

"Maybe Cliff and I should take a walk," said Kip.

Clifford looked at Kip, still shaking his head.

"Let's do it, pal," Kip finished, standing, urging Clifford to his feet. And as if nothing unusual had happened, they walked down the corridor that led away from the atrium.

"Sorry, Franny," Sarah apologized. "I never saw him act like that before."

"It's all right," she said. "I understand."

They had lunch at a restaurant near the Norris Bradbury Museum, Sarah's treat, and though Kip had planned on joining them, he stayed behind at the center and ate with the patients instead. They talked about Tsankawi, about the incident with Clifford, about evening plans, as families do, but even the vigilant Franny failed to notice Sarah's eyes on her. Having long since accepted Franny into her life, much as she embraced Kip, Sarah suspected that the day was coming when she'd have to ask Franny—much as she had challenged Kip—to reveal a little more about herself. Yes, Clifford was mentally out of it, but where in fact was Franny's mother, Mrs. Johnson? Why all the delays that Franny had alluded to in her coming west to meet Marcos and the Montoya family in Nambé, where her daughter had been living? On holidays, when she didn't phone her mother or get any calls from Princeton, Marcos must have asked himself these same questions, but looked blindly beyond whatever she might be harboring. Sarah inferred that day a different history might range behind this business of Franny's mother. Franny disguised her secrets well, but after Clifford's peculiar onslaught, Sarah sensed some fabrication subtly betraying itself. She didn't know what, but the stitching showed, the persona's mask had fallen a tad askew.

After lunch, the couple headed home. On the way they stopped at Otowi, the sacred place—according to San Ildefonso belief—where the Rio Grande speaks. With pants rolled up to their knees, they waded along the narrow silty shore, listening to the river burble and chatter and sough.

"What do the Indians believe it's saying?"

"Whatever you think it says," he answered.

As Franny understood it, the river spoke of continuity. Itself a continuity, it spoke of cycles, flooding forward to the Gulf of Mexico, some of it evaporating and rising, condensing into a cloud, precipitating, becoming part of the water table, reentering the river, circling around again. An autobiographical river. Was she, too, condemned to travel in circles?

That night, as Franny lay close to Marcos, her legs aching from the climb, her mind aswarm with images of the day—evocative cliffs and provocative Clifford—she broke her pledge to Marcos and exhausted her skimpy knowledge of Vietnamese by whispering in his ear, *"Tôi mệt, tôi may mán. Tôi ân hân."*

"You promised," Marcos whispered back. "No more Kipamese." A quarter of an hour later he softly asked, "Okay, what does it mean?"

"It means, Thank you for today."

"That isn't what it means."

"How do you know?"

"I could tell it meant something else."

"Tôi mệt means I'm tired. *Tôi may mán* means I'm grateful."

"Wasn't there something more?"

"Now you speak Vietnamese, too?"

"You never know."

Franny fell asleep before interpreting *Tôi ân hân* for Marcos, who drifted away into sleep himself and would not remember to ask again the following morning. I'm sorry.

*L*ike entering a time capsule. Viewed by flashlight until Ariel found the string connected to a bulb. The room was small, twelve by twelve. Flavor of mold in the air. Shapes under sheets. She pulled one back, as might an investigator, to identify what was beneath. A wingback chair from midcentury, its brocade as bright as on an up-holsterer's bolt. She ran her hand over its cushion. Under another sheet was a wardrobe, inside which were suits of clothes. Nothing elaborate, nothing Madison Avenue, but the gabardines and lush flannels of the day. Some camisoles. Undraping one more, she found a bookcase, the stacking kind that lawyers used to have in their of-fices. She'd always wanted one. But thought, More fitting to give it to Brice. Heaven knows, he might even remember seeing it in the Calder house when he was a boy.

Though these several things were hers, bequested by Kip, she looked at them only for a matter of minutes before resheeting every-thing, pulling the light string again, and locking the door of the stor-age room.

"We sent him letters from time to time, you know, telling him that he might just want to let us go through it for him, update the inven-tory, since he said he didn't have one. Probably what he's got in there isn't worth a tenth of what he's been paying in storage over all these years."

"Well," said Ariel, signing the registry. "He did what he thought was best, undoubtedly."

"People're funny about their stuff. Some of them take better care of what they got in storage than themselves."

"I'm sure you're right."

"You're right I'm right."

"Well, thanks," turning to leave.

"Miss Rankin?"

"Yes?"

"Will you be closing the account, then? Disposing of the articles?"

"No, I don't think so."

"All right, then."

Ariel understood. "I'm sorry." She reached into her wallet for a check. "God, there must be a three-year outstanding bill for the storage fees. How much do I owe you?"

"No," the woman waved her off. "Everything's paid up, as ever. Never missed a rental payment yet. That's why we keep it in such good order. Those sheets in there, I laid them on the furniture myself."

"That was nice of you."

"They was old sheets, anyway."

"What you said about the storage rent's being up to date, you mean to say it was paid long in advance?"

"No, once a year, every year. Like clockwork, last week of December. If everybody was as responsible as Mr. Calder, this world would be a better place."

How could she not have thought of it before? "You must know where he's living, then."

"Even if I did, I wouldn't be able to say."

"I'm his daughter, as I told you. I have the key only because he passed it along to me."

"Don't take me wrong, but if he passed it on to you, don't you know his whereabouts? If he's your father."

"I've lost track of him. That's why I ask."

The woman considered this for a moment. "He was living in Rancho de Taos for some while, but left there."

"Does he pay in person?"

"By post."

"What's the return address?"

"He doesn't give one anymore, I'm afraid."

"Is there a home address on the checks?"

"Certified bank check, anonymous as it gets."

Ariel frowned.

"Like I say, I think he's throwing away good money keeping all that in there. We're in business to make a living, of course. But it seems a shame to see somebody wasting forty dollars a month for no good reason."

"I agree, but he must have some attachment to it or else he'd have let it go. It's my responsibility now."

"What happens when I get the payment from him?"

"If there's really no return address on the envelope, then hold the money. If there is, send it back to him."

"And tell him what?"

"Tell him Ariel has come to claim him."

A dozen red roses, stems rubber-banded, wrapped in a pretty cone of plain white paper. Another dozen, and a few others. Five bouquets altogether for Delfino, who, having paid more for these roses than all the other flowers he'd bought in his entire life, carried them into the cemetery near Chimayó, where he laid them, pausing on a knee at each of the weathered headstones of his mother, Kayley McDougal Montoya, and Gil Montoya, his father, and at the resting places of his grandmother Emily Montoya, and Juliar Montoya, 1839–1899, his grandfather these almost hundred years deceased, the man who'd inherited Pajarito from the de Peñas of Nambé. In Agnes's honor, he set the last bouquet beside a grave whose headstone was so worn that the name and dates had been erased. The dead don't mind sharing.

Late that afternoon he returned from Chimayó in high spirits about his visit to Rancho Pajarito. Marcos had grown into a fine young man. Carl could be proud. Sarah was as good a woman as ever walked the earth. Delfino himself, however much he admired Pajarito and all Carl and Sarah had done with the place, felt that he, too, had gotten it right years ago when he chose to set out on his own into the world. One could make the case his life hadn't unfolded quite the way he envisioned, but Agnes and he had experienced much

happiness withal. He wouldn't trade one moment with her for anything, though he would forever regret that she and he had only so
briefly shared the home they'd built together in the shadow of the
Oscuras. Could have been better, could have been much worse. The
roses were laid on the graves, the world spun on like an oblivious
toy top.

That second evening at dinner, Delfino's sister-in-law broached a
subject she'd brought up before. That he consider moving back to
Nambé. While he figured Sarah would suggest this—why should he
go on living alone in Tularosa when he could be among people who
loved him?—he hadn't prepared any viable response.

"Christ knows," his brother grumbled, "you might even make
yourself useful for a change."

"I don't want to be useful any more than you do."

"Don't worry, I'm not. Ask Marcos."

"He's not, Uncle Delf. Kip and I could use some more muscle
around here," Marcos said, knowing he often wound up the fall guy
in these verbal jousts between the Montoya brothers. He was game,
though, why not?

"You be the brawn, I'll be the brains," Carl went on.

"This dump's headed into the ditch with that kind of setup."

"You're too weak to even steer it into the ditch. Marcos, never
mind. Bad idea."

"That's enough," said Sarah. "I'm serious."

"Sarah's serious, watch out," Carl said.

"I know she's serious, you know why? Because she's the only real
brains over here."

"If that's the case, why did I go and marry your brother?"

They laughed, Kip along with them, and Franny, though both saw
this was family banter, intimate and breakneck, and knew to stay
clear.

"Because you were too smart to marry a dusty desert mule like
Delf here, is why. Like that self-portrait photograph he brought."

"She just likes older men," said Delfino.

"Shit. Mature, more like," said Carl.

"Very old men," Delfino said.

"Refined."

"Legend in his own mind."

"A seasoned stud."

"Broke-down plow horse."

"Wild bronco."

"Sodbust jenny."

"What does Franny think?"

"Jesus, don't drag her into this," Marcos grinned.

"Gelding. Glue base."

"That's enough already," Sarah said. "Really, Delf. Don't say no without giving it some thought."

Carl reversed course, abruptly becoming tranquil, pensive. "So what was on your agenda today, Montoya? Saw your truck was gone the afternoon."

This was how it was done, by hard turns. Delfino immediately joined his brother's solemnity. "I went over to visit Kayley and Daddy. Been a while since I was there. Quite a few fresh stones."

"That's what happens in graveyards."

Was this why skulls smiled? Kip wondered.

"You'll know soon enough," Delfino couldn't resist. "Laid some fresh flowers for the grandparents, too. Hard to imagine Juliar's been dead almost a century."

"If Marcos here has children who have children, I wonder if they'll bother to lay fresh-cut flowers at our graves."

"Plastic ones, more like," Marcos said, "or virtual," trying to joust, to keep up with the other Montoya men, though the mention of his great-grandfather stirred a memory of his youthful sightings of what he still believed was a ghost from Juliar's day, the woman rumored to have built this ranch.

"Better plastic than nothing. Or virtual, whatever that is."

As the evening drew on, conversation flowed with great affable angularity, while Marcos withdrew into his thoughts, recalling that apparition and wondering whether, if he ever had a son or daughter, he or she would walk that same river road and see her in the cotton-wood field. Ghosts were, he'd decided, for children. Adults with heads screwed on straight couldn't see them—at least he hadn't been able to, he who had seen her easily enough when he was younger. Maybe ghosts are attracted to children, since what they must really wish for is to be as wildly alive as youngsters. Maybe it was the wine, or the visit to Tsankawi, or that look Kip was giving him from beyond some pale himself, but Marcos had the strangest thought. This nonexistent child of his, would it understand what was happening when it was still in the womb? Comprehend through some process of human biology—the same process of information coding that told its small body to develop five fingers on each hand—what its life might be like? Was a fetus like a prebirth ghost? Could it predream? Sarah once told him that she'd held a radio up to her belly when she was pregnant with him and he'd responded with a vigorous dance recital. Brahms, Chubby Checker, it didn't matter. After that she'd often let the unborn Marcos listen to music, he and she playing together that way, across the distance of her taut skin. How had he known the Twist? When he kicked and punched and pushed, what had he, the unnamed Marcos, believed he was seeing through his closed eyes in that amniotic cosmos?

God, it was getting late. For all of them. From cemetery to womb and back to the life that lay between. Marcos took Franny's hand and said goodnight. Sarah hoped everybody would sleep well. Carl yawned and went to bed. Delfino and Kip sat at the table alone, washed by silence, saying nothing yet somehow everything.

Kip awoke the next day with a preposterous idea, almost absurd in its simplicity. He was going to accompany Delfino Montoya back to Tularosa, and with Delfino he was going to ride on horseback across the basin and help him expropriate from the government his spread, or whatever might be left of it, at Dripping Spring. Delfino had never killed a man. Kip had. Not that Montoya intended to kill or even hurt anybody, but chances were pretty good that the military

range security guys would enjoin him with force. If things got violent, wouldn't it be better for someone with blood on his hands to
stain them again, leaving innocence to the innocent? Kip believed
that if there was a hell, he was probably going there. He was sure,
with the bold unexpected surety of dawning insight, that this was
why he'd survived everything—Los Alamos, Southeast Asia, the wide
wild world—to arrive in Nambé: to serve out a final role as the
younger brother Delfino needed. In a way, to subvert Big Brother.
Not Carl, but the fatherland in one of its more miserable guises.

Two Wagnerisms combined to bring Kip to this decision. The
first was *Um einen Gegenstand zu kennen, muss ich zwar nicht seine
externen—aber ich muss alle seine internen Eigenschaften kennen.* As
with Kip's couple dozen phrases memorized in Lao and Vietnamese
back during lulls in the war, words learned in the interest of killing
time rather than Pathet Lao soldiers, this German fragment had no
adjuncts in his memory. It was a stand-alone, just as Kip himself had
so often been, and as he wanted Delfino not to be. He knew what
the passage meant but couldn't recall who had written or said it. *In
order to know an object, I must know not its external but all its internal
qualities.*

He fired up his small gas stove, put on the coffeepot. He lit a rare
cigarette. He sat at his new-old table on his new-old chair and ate
one of the oatmeal cookies that Sarah had given him, wrapped in a
napkin, after dinner last night. The second Wagnerism was even
simpler than the first. It came in the form of a Sufi precept—the pri-
mary of Sufi truths, in fact. All souls are in exile from their maker and
are born longing to return and lose themselves in that birthsoul, despite how nourished or confused they may be by mortal attractions.
Wagner had cherished the Sufi journey of souls back to the locus of
beginnings more than any other idea in any other religion.

Standing over the slim dead body of a Vietcong insurgent deep in-
country near Ban Pak Mène, in the last year of the war, Wagner had
asked Kip if he ever noticed how the dying tend to curl themselves
into the fetal position. As if in preparation to be reborn. No, Kip

never noticed before Wagner drew it to his attention that faraway Laotian afternoon, amid the greens and reds, on one of their few personal sorties undertaken on foot from Luang Prabang rather than in the air.

—It's all about pilgrimage, man, Wagner remarked. —We just think we're walking forward. What we're really doing is walking back to where we started every time we take a step. Like with everything fucking else, Einstein had it right. Light bends, time bends. Check it out. I'm staring at the back of my head, no matter where I look. So are you.

Coffee always smelled like life, preamble to the day. Was it any wonder everybody was addicted to it? Kip thought, stubbing out the half-smoked cigarette on the bottom of his shoe and dropping the butt into his pants cuff. How would he tell Delfino of his intention to join him? After all, hadn't he already promised that he'd pass along to the family news of this gambit?

—You've been to Wat Xieng Khwan, near Vientiane. We were there together, remember that big Buddha statue thirty feet tall with the four arms made it look like a spider? Four heads facing every direction at the same time, with six Buddhas in lotus position on the heads of the four Buddhas, and more stone Buddhas atop those, and all surrounded by more Buddhas, a hundred stone Buddhas. . . . Wagner was coming in loud and clear this morning—less, it seemed, from within Kip's head than from some distance without. Kip asked him, Is it a good idea for me to go to Dripping Spring with Delfino Montoya? Isn't it a way of looking at World War Two from its altruistic, damnable birth down in the Jornada by staring dead straight into the teeth of Vietnam, finally? None of what Kip was proposing to do was any harder than learning to ride a bike, or jumping like some tiger through a ring of fire. The more difficult part would be to convince Delfino to allow him, an outsider and the son of one of the minds that had consigned the older man to a life of exile, to participate, however lamely, in his act of retribution.

Delfino was down in the barn with Carl and Marcos. They were saddling a new horse, of the kind Marcos called a *no-history*—not a *puke,* just unknown to them. And it looked as if Delfino got to be the one to give her a go.

"Might just be a dullard," Marcos encouraged him.

"Or else the horse from Hades," Carl muttered. "You sure you want to try her out? Marcos here's young enough that broke bones don't matter to him."

"Kip, you're just in time to watch Delfino break his neck."

"That's too bad," Kip said.

"I ain't breaking anything but this horse."

Delfino was up on her, this green, unbroken stick, and she did herself and him proud, loping around the ring like a natural. When Delfino circled her around to the post-and-rail where they leaned, scrutinizing the performance, Kip asked, "Mind if I have a go?" Marcos looked more concerned than Kip might have liked. "I'm no horseman like Delfino, but I know how to hang on."

Having leapt down, Delfino handed Kip the reins, saying, "Seems a talented horse."

Carl said, "Talented enough this morning. Just don't want to see Kip hurt himself."

"I rode a lot as a kid."

"Baby hair don't know and gray hair don't remember."

Kip shoved his boot into the stirrup, grabbed the horn, and lifted himself into the saddle, just momentarily catching his knee on the cantle. The horse appeared not to understand she had a rider aboard. Gently reining her away into a slow walk around the ring, Kip maintained the illusion of not being there. He made no audible sound. Several laps tracking left, several right. He never pushed her beyond a walk, nor did he relinquish control. Kept his back straight, pushed his heels down and legs forward, sat deep, hands quiet and low—two parts of the same beating heart, as he remembered his father telling him when he first learned how to do this, so many years ago.

Then it was as if the horse, too, remembered something, changed her mind. Rearing her head, tipping it to the side, she looked this rider in the eye before lighting out at a sudden full zigzag gallop, stopping abruptly to tack, lurch, halt. Kip was first thrown back, nearly losing the reins, then pitched forward. The onlookers began shouting and waving their hands, though Kip couldn't hear or see them. The corral fence loomed and he prepared himself for a rude launching, but as suddenly as she'd gone mad on him, the horse calmed down.

"What the hell was that?" Marcos said.

Kip shrugged.

"Held his own, didn't he," Carl laughed, holding the reins as Kip climbed down.

Not a bad showing, which was all Kip had hoped to accomplish. Delfino couldn't reasonably reject his new friend and self-appointed conscript on the ground he couldn't ride—that was the point. Marcos clapped him on the shoulder with more exuberance than was necessary, yet with an affection that Kip realized, to his slight chagrin, he was going to miss. The inveterate veteran outcast riding a crazy horse around a corral before an audience of friends? Of his own volition, even at his insistence? Wagner would never have believed it possible. Nor Brice, the other of Kip's twin towers, or towering twins, both rising—Brice and Wagner, antiwar hero and sainted soldier—to greet him on this same resolving if raveling day. He thanked them for the spin, excused himself, and retreated to the fieldhouse, more or less to hide from all that was incoming—clairvoyant bombardment as he, always the covert warrior, saw it. His mind was made up about Dripping Spring, however. It was the necessary end to all his wars, personal and public.

He was suddenly exhausted. Maybe the gray-hair gibe hadn't been so far off the mark. His mind was troubling him, but then his mind had been troubling him, tiring him, more and more these past days. They say this happens to people—they keep it together until some dream is attained, then promptly fall apart. He lay down on his unmade bed and slept with the sun on his face, fitful, dreaming.

The next living voice he heard asked, "Kip?" and he opened his eyes to catch Franny looking at him with concern. "Are you all right?"

Still dressed in shirt, pants, boots, Kip blinked and pushed himself up onto one elbow.

"You were crying out. I heard you all the way from the far end of the paddock. I thought you were dying or something."

He was speechless.

"That must've been some kind of nightmare you were having," she said, sitting beside him on his bed.

"Daymare," he managed, squinting in the noon light. His pulse was quickened by these shifts of consciousness, and a kind of drear disgust hovered over him like a surreal smog. As one who felt he'd achieved what Oppenheimer once termed "profound serenity through discipline"—the discipline of renunciation, no hatreds, no ambitions for self, no desires other than to vanish into the ether—he was astonished by his dream. The world was drawing him back into its current, and his expressive unconscious exhibited good evidence as to why it had become preferable for him to be out of rather than in the flow.

"What made you so afraid?"

Kip lay back on his pillow soaked with sweat.

"I don't know," he lied.

"Marcos told me you were in the ring this morning. I didn't know you could ride."

The image of a dignified woman atop a funeral pyre was as if seared onto the back of his lids. Her eyes were wide open, and she looked knowingly at him. He must have been floating above her as the smoke drifted upward, just like it did during second passes in Laos, flying low over fast terrain to lay down white phosphorus in places where the living would soon be dead.

"I can almost do anything, Mary. Emphasis on almost."

"Don't call me that."

"Call you by your right name, you mean?"

Franny stood up. She was wearing a loose white dress that in this limewashed, sundrenched chamber gave her the appearance of a statue draped in finely hewn, supple marble. "I'm just trying to be nice, Kip. You've already made your opinion known about what I'm doing. Besides, you promised."

"I remember my dream now."

The statue remained standing, unmoving, listening to Kip as he concocted a dream in which three people—Franny, Marcos, and Mary—who had all been good friends were told by the doctor they couldn't see one another anymore because each had a disease that, though not threatening to his or her own health, would be fatal to the other two.

"That's no nightmare. You're making it up." Franny had never been cross with Kip before, but his fake, even preachy dream distressed her. She'd built him up in her mind as a kind of guru, with earned convictions and a light, disinterested touch. Why was he pressing her? Of course, the problem he raised was as real as the dream he used to pose it was sham. "I'll leave you to your fictions," was about as disparaging a remark as she could manage.

"Thanks for troubling yourself, really. I'm fine now."

She turned to go, to flee this reminder—the last Kip would ever furnish on the subject—but couldn't escape his final observation. "I had a friend back in Laos, very religious person, for a killer. He slaughtered the enemy without fussing, was a deadeye with any weapon you put in his hands. Still, this guy never met a spiritual creed he didn't like. Philosopher. He had a saying I was thinking about earlier this morning. The only way to know somebody is from the inside out, not the other way around."

"You can't be a murderer and a religious man at the same time."

"Most murderers think they're God. And God has blood on his hands, too, don't forget."

"Well, none of this has anything to do with me."

"You're right. I apologize."

"What you mean is, Marcos doesn't know me."

"That's what I mean."

Franny's white dress swung luminous in the doorway, and once she had gone, Kip listened to the birds chattering and scolding one another in the high branches.

What right do I have? he thought. What right in the world.

*H*er left side was partially paralyzed, though her fingers moved at the doctor's command and her thin wrist rose with difficulty but nonetheless rose. She could feel the hands that held her own, and pleased everyone with her ready half smiles. The stroke had mildly slurred her speech—she didn't feel much like speaking those first days, anyway—but her physician believed she had every chance of regaining full articulation. She fought sadness and fear as best she could. She prayed, though her prayers, begun with energy and commitment, would trail away before she got to a proper Amen. She tired, slept, awakened refreshed, then tired again.

Once they moved her out of intensive care and into her own room, she brightened up altogether. Fewer external stimuli, no moaning beyond the drawn curtain. Less frightening equipment, just intravenous and a catheter. Her cheeks blushed with new color when she found she could clasp a rubber ball. Bonnie Jean and Ariel worked out an alternating routine—Ariel in the morning, Bonnie the afternoon, either or both in the evening—so she was never alone during visiting hours. Daughter watched television with her, soap operas and talk shows. Granddaughter arranged orchids in a round glass bowl of water and set them on her windowsill. Granna saw that the mountains were upside down in the globular vase.

"Refrac . . . shion," she said slowly, appreciatively.

Ariel chose books to read to her from Granna's shelves. She

brought a Bible to the hospital, and other volumes that appeared to have been left purposely within reach of her reading chair in the cottage living room.

"Wall Whitmah," the patient requested, impatient with her diffident tongue. Then tried again a bit harder, straining and succeeding with, "Walt Whitman or . . . or Eh . . . merson."

Ariel read from an essay by the latter. " 'My book should smell of pines and resound with the hum of insects. The swallow over my window should interweave that thread or straw he carries in his bill into my web also. We pass for what we are.' "

She lifted her fingers then her braceleted wrist and quaking arm off the bedsheets and said the words *Self* and *Reliance* separately, enunciating each with painstaking care. Nodding, Ariel continued as the woman lay her hand on her chest with deliberate heedfulness, as if she were holding some gossamer string connected to life itself.

Sooner than any of them might have expected, the doctors advised Bonnie Jean that her mother had made wonderful progress and needed to begin physical and speech therapy. The prognosis for a complete recovery was entirely positive. Plans were made to transfer her to a convalescent facility where she could recuperate. Under cloudless blue skies and a white sun that made her blink and brought to her lips another partly lopsided smile, she was moved in an ambulette van. Her daughter decorated her new room with metallic balloons emblazoned with the words *Get Well Soon* and a huge—Bonnie might have thought a little overhuge—arrangement of gladiolas from Brice and Jessica. Explaining to her mother that no, this wasn't a nursing home, Bonnie Jean assured her she was going to be here for only a month, or six weeks at the most, and then it would be back to Pear Street. Ariel added that her departure would be not in a wheelchair but on her own two feet.

"That sounds good, doesn't it?"

"Yeh," gazing as it were into Ariel's very soul.

And into her soul, that very evening at Granna's house, Ariel herself began, in the wake of this aberration from her purpose here, to address anew her own quixotic quest. She'd finally reached Brice the day after his mother's hospitalization and told him everything, reassuring him there was no immediate need to fly out. She felt a twinge of guilty selfishness about wanting her parents to stay away from Los Alamos for the time being. That and a sense of disgraceful collusion with her aunt, whose sibling rivalry with Brice she found distasteful. But Ariel desperately desired to have a week or two to finish what she'd begun, removed from Jessica and her father. She saw this with cold clarity, and the idea caused a shiver to run through her. Be that as it may, when Brice agreed that Ariel and her aunt could handle matters until Granna settled into this convalescent center, whereafter he'd come assist with whatever there was to shoulder, Ariel exonerated herself from further worry. There was the question, also, of when or if Brice intended to tell his mother and sister about Kip Calder's true relationship with Ariel herself. For the moment, she let it pass. Family dynamics. As always, the indelicate balance.

Afternoons, she continued looking for Kip. She drove to Rancho de Taos and asked around until she found the funky motel where he had lived till three years before. The proprietor remembered him well. Bright man, kind of sickly, kept to himself a lot.

"Left his room way nicer than he found it. Fact, it's almost like it was when he took off. I don't let people in there unless I'm full up and have to. Best apartment in the joint."

Ariel asked if she could have a peek.

"Vacant right now, I don't mind," she was told.

Its walls could not have been whiter, nor the room more simple, spartan. Its warm wooden floor was sanded and varnished like some pauper ballroom's. For a vagrant, a wanderer, he surely had a refined ascetic sense of what home, if only a plain room, should be. Like some monastic cell, but purer yet. She left, reminded of how she had felt once when she visited Arrowhead, up in Massachusetts, the austere house where Melville had written his great novel. Kip was no novelist, but she could imagine his mind swimming through kindred dark waters. And what shores had Melville beached on if not the most desperate and melancholy, convinced of his failure even as he merely triumphed?

Feeling conflicted—as she knew it was not her place to divulge her parents' long-held secret to Brice's mother and sister—she decided to go ahead and put up a few tentative posters in places Bonnie and her husband wouldn't likely see them. Bowling alley, a couple bars—certainly no churches, and nowhere near the center. Had to do something; even half-measures were better than none.

Missing
William "Kip" Calder
Born Los Alamos 1944, Viet Vet
Any Information Leading
To His Whereabouts Appreciated
Please Contact . . .

appended with Ariel's name and the Pear Street number. Up they went, handmade things, foolish and hopeless. Muddy way-outdated photograph and no reward. Notices for stray dogs were more assured of success.

She contacted Social Security but got nowhere: Privacy Act, and besides, she didn't have his number. Went through every local phone book in the state, looking up Calder in the central library. She even encountered a few, but ran up a telephone bill without result. Hesitant, she finally called the police to inquire if there was any William Calder in their records. Brice could have told her how unhelpful she'd find them. A visit to the morgue was equally in vain.

Illumination came slowly to Ariel, but come it did.

Kip Calder was gone, extinct, vanished, never to return. It had to be so. The conscientious thing for her to do was abandon her search. Pathetic, the forsaken child hunting for the wayward father. One of the oldest, most hackneyed tales in the book. Kip as grail, as end of the rainbow, as Wiles's solution to Fermat's Last Theorem. No, no. She would see her grandmother through her crisis, and then would get back to New York and start over. As for the pregnancy, she hated to admit it, but maybe David was right that she wasn't mother material and an abortion was the only wise choice. All else was leading to nothing but a botch. Damned if Emerson hadn't nailed it. Self-reliance was our beginning and our end. You had only yourself to work with. Others might show kindness toward you along the path, or meanness. But only your feet walked that path, only yours chose the course at every crossroads. Platitudes, surely. But it seemed to Ariel tonight that these carried the weight of truth. Every cliché was once a revolutionary concept.

*F*rom the vantage of a few winding miles up the dry riverbed of Rio Nambé, they could see the big satellite dishes far off in the western distance catching and reflecting sunlight from their safeguarded perches on Mesita del Buey and Frijoles. The three men of three generations sat down to rest on the bank, and Marcos smoked slowly and tossed egg-shaped stones into the current, which ran meager even in the deepest channels, threading its way down to Pojoaque. They'd talked about this and that on their walk, some about good old days, some about bad ones. Turned out Delfino had noticed a newspaper article Kip clipped a few weeks ago, a lengthy obituary of Kenneth Bainbridge, gone to his maker in July. Why had Kip scissored that particular column from the paper? he asked, sensing that through Bainbridge their paths converged once again.

"My father knew him a little," said Kip. "You probably met him yourself."

"Not personally, but he had his impact on my life."

"All our lives. Not only did he build that first cyclotron at Harvard that they moved up to the Hill when they were just getting started, but he was there at the end."

"Top of command down at Trinity—oversaw the building of the tower, positioning of the device, that first explosion. They say if it'd hangfired, he'd have been the one to go out there to see what went wrong."

"You wish it'd hangfired."

Delfino said, "Let's get this straight. I didn't want us to lose the war. In my small way, I was trying to help us win. All I'm saying is, they could've done their work, then kept their word. What good's a homeland if you got no home? When it comes to nukes, the brass has always had a hard time keeping its word about anything. Pretty weird getting screwed by the government when all's you're doing is acting like a patriot."

Kip saw the half-smoked cigarette in his trouser cuff. Marcos offered him a fresh one but he declined, relighting the fag.

They had their way of making you feel you were the one who was nuts, and even if you were, a little, they rendered the definition of nuts obsolete, passé. Delfino had seen so-called UFOs, but knew they'd been launched from quite close quarters and so never for a moment bought into extraterrestrials. Spacemen were for the birds, even if they did exist.

"Look here, a lot of things exist that shouldn't." It didn't matter a good goddamn, Delfino continued, whether we were or weren't being observed by intelligences from other solar systems. They were out there, most likely. So? What he had learned during his years of research sickened him, earned him the badge in his heart of the disgusted, the abused, the ruined.

Kip sat listening, empathizing more than Delfino might have thought. A pragmatist, he knew that when things went wrong one needn't point one's finger to the heavens at either God or green men.

In 1951, Delfino went on, the Atomic Energy Commission established three-point-nine rads as the max threshold for troop exposure to ionizing radiation. Seven miles from ground zero was set as the safety distance for nuclear tests in Nevada. A year later, eight volunteer officers were hunkered down in shallow trenches, flanked by cactuses and nothing else, at a distance of just two thousand yards out, to play a part in Shot Simon. A dozen others were located at twenty-five hundred yards for Shot Badger, and other officers beheld Shot Nancy from the same distance. These shots were umbrellaed under the dumbshit code name Upshot-Knothole, or as one clever serviceman renamed it, *Up Your Nuthole.* The officers were exposed to at least a hundred rads on deton. Some were temporarily blinded. All were burned, leaving them with skin ulcers that looked like silvery purple worms wandering a scrapheap of shriveled beets. The men underwent physical and psychological exams before and after the guinea-pig tests, but none was given any intelligible consent form to sign off on. Other troops were ordered into combat attack mode. They ran with bayonets toward ground zero, shouting and crying as the earth rolled under their feet in waves, like some dirt ocean heading for shore. They returned to camp bleeding from noses, eyes, ears, and muted mouths. As for the phantom enemy who was supposed to be frightened by all this, he heard none of their shouting that day because he had no ears. He didn't see their bayonets because he had no eyes.

"Ever since they thought up nukes, they been moving people around like chess pieces, packing some of us off to get us out from underfoot, sending others to slaughter. Worse damn invention in the history of man."

Marcos continued to toss stones. Kip sat at a kind of weird attention, hands spread on thighs, spine erect. Whenever the bomb came up in conversation or in the news, Kip's thoughts usually torqued in different directions, either ricocheting away or mothing to the flame. Born during Christmas season, he might as well have been born on Christmas Island, or Eniwetok, Yucca Flat, or Bikini—the bomb had stalked him for half a century, ruined his father's life, poisoned the lives of so many people he encountered over the years. And here was Delfino now, another casualty category altogether, asking Kip whether being the son of one of the physicists who invented the gadget haunted him.

"My whole life. But it haunts every single person in the world, whether they ever think about it or not. At the end of the day I'm afraid it'll take us all out."

"Holocaust?"

"It'd be a total statistical anomaly if it didn't happen. The ratio of warheads to maniacs with access is too high to avoid it. Could be the next generation, the one after, but it's a total probability. Kubrick got it right all the way back in the early sixties—"

"Who's that?"

"Film director. *Dr. Strangelove.*"

"Never saw it."

"Slim Pickens riding an A-bomb like one of Saint John's horses, waving his cowboy hat and hollering all the way down to the target— probably the most perfect image of human lunacy any movie director ever shot. But my point is that when it does happen, it'll be because somebody screwed up, somebody had too much scotch—"

"Vodka, more like," said Marcos.

"—somebody keystroked in the wrong numbers, overrode failsafes by mistake. Kind of makes all your stories about atomic veterans even sadder than they already are. Why kill rats in the lab when your field research already shows you know how to kill rats? It's less clinical than flat-out homicidal."

Delfino thought about that for a moment, then stood up and brushed the sand and dust off the back of his trousers. The others got up, too. Their shadows stretched long behind them in the creek bed as they walked back toward Pajarito.

His stay in Nambé was nearing an end. Most of what he came here to accomplish had been accomplished, and what few things he hadn't been sure about seemed clear now. He wished he could tell his brother what he was going to do but knew Carl would repeat it to Sarah, and Sarah would move heaven and earth to dissuade him. Probably ought to be dissuaded, he thought, but he didn't want to be. Kip had proven to be the unexpected catalyst. He'd inadvertently made the concept seem real, as if it had hardness to it, body to match soul.

Souls, bodies, laws, earth. Delfino pondered what to do about Kip's proposal he accompany him into the basin. Wasn't a question of whether he'd earned his saddle. He had earned his berth, such as it was, in this highly promising disaster in the making. Nor was Delfino's hesitation prompted by the fact that he didn't really know Kip, and that sharing a potentially suicidal experience with someone you didn't know might be an even greater madness. None of this bothered Delfino, nor even did the realization that Kip's joining him would mean Kip couldn't fulfill his promise to tell the family what was going on, give them the documents Delfino had entrusted to him. No, what troubled Delfino was Agnes. Would she be looking on, thinking, Who is this other man? Would Kip somehow dilute what was to be, finally, a spiritual experience? Delfino mulled this as the three of them made their way back down the riverbed. It didn't occur to any of them, as each trod his own thoughtful path, that they constituted the river that ran here today. None recognized at that moment, though they would understand it later, that they were able to march along, to think, to worry, to struggle, only because they *were* Rio Nambé in this fleeting instance. They were water and clay, the difficult thinking, meandering, willful kind, and they flowed back toward their sources.

*T*he solitariness of Granna's sainthood was confirmed by how rarely her phone rang. If not Bonnie Jean, the caller was either Brice or someone soliciting for a magazine subscription or new, lower long-distance rates. Hearing Charlie on the other end was unexpected, then, but what he asked was more surprising yet because the issue he raised was so conspicuous, so indisputable, so obvious, that it should never have escaped Ariel's attention in the first place.

Embarrassing—how could she have posted those signs inquiring after the lost Kip and really have believed her aunt, uncle, cousin, grandmother—*someone* in the family—wouldn't become aware of her search? She'd come close that night in White Rock to confessing why she was here. Close wasn't disclosure, however. What a mare's nest.

"Sam told me," Charlie said. "What's this all about, Ariel?"

Was his voice quivering? What was the protocol?

"I guess those posters are a little confusing, Uncle Charles." She who never addressed him by his proper name.

"You're right about that."

"Does Aunt Bonnie know?"

"I told Sam to keep his mouth shut. Apparently she hasn't seen anything. But my question is, again, what's going on?"

Just say it. "Brice is my stepfather."

"I don't understand."

"Brice isn't my birth father. Kip is."

A silence, then, "How come you never told us?"

Protocol, once more, decorum. How crazy was it that these conventions, meant to sustain social order, as often as not skewed things between people? Again, though, Ariel had always imagined this revelation to be Brice's sole prerogative and she'd followed his continued silence in the matter with what now appeared to her to be an unmanageable devotion. The truth was out now. She realized, for better or worse, it was as much her truth as anyone else's. Speak, say something. "I only found out myself a few years ago."

"So you're telling me Kip Calder's your father?"

"Biologically, is all."

"Is all?"

Charlie had other questions but ceased asking. Perhaps Bonnie Jean hadn't been so wrong about Brice all these years. Obviously he did have a screw loose in the ethics department. "Sam and I can only play dumb for so long, and Bonnie's bound to find out sometime. Why not tell her, Ariel? She'd appreciate the gesture, and besides, your aunt loves you a little more than I think you give her credit for."

Everything had become about articulation, had it not. Ariel'd never heard her uncle speak more thoughtfully, cogently. She agreed to his gentle request. "She's probably over at the center, isn't she."

"Where else?"

"I'm going now," Ariel said.

"Just tell her, that's all."

"Thanks, Uncle Charles."

"Please. *Charlie.*"

"Thanks, Uncle Charlie."

During the drive over, Ariel composed her words to Bonnie Jean but found herself much more concerned with how her grandmother would react—presuming, that is, she should be apprised at all. Why hadn't she gone around and taken down those stupid posters after she decided to abandon the hunt? The apostate at work again? Backsliding away from her firm decision because some hope of finding him still lived in her? It was true, regarding matters still living, that she hadn't taken any steps to arrange the abortion, either. What was she doing?

She'd closely followed her grandmother McCarthy's recovery, its daily routines and subtle victories. With Ariel at her side, the woman now pushed her walker down the center's linoleum corridors, greeting those she had gotten to know a little, and then out into the stone-enclosed garden, where she might sit and proselytize for Christ, preacher to the choir. She glowed with renewed life. Ariel had splurged on a silk robe for her, bright blue with white piping to match her blue leather slippers. Bonnie did her hair and painted her nails. Her appetite, never ravenous, grew day by day. Applesauce and rice pudding had graduated to gravied chicken with hot biscuits. She could read for herself but still loved to hear Ariel's voice, so feigned eye strain—they both knew it was a ruse—to prompt her granddaughter, whose delivery was as impassioned as if she'd written the words herself. Oddly, Granna had not mentioned Brice in all this time. Had she forgotten him in some neuropathway fracture? She'd initially struggled in speech therapy with simple words like *fish* and *foot* while recognizing, uttering, and defining with marvelous ease more abstruse terms—*neuropathway*, for instance, and *fracture*. Had his name fallen between synaptic cracks?

Ariel wondered, as she got out of her car and walked toward the twin glass doors of the convalescent center, if she hadn't embarked upon failing her stepfather in much the same way he'd failed her. *Stepfather*—she'd never thought of Brice in that sense before, the cool, distancing legality of the word. What was its etymology if not *one-step-removed father*? She decided that the term was, in her case, grossly inappropriate. Lawful, but false. She'd never use it again. But how would she react when Bonnie insisted that it was the "only possible term," as soon she undoubtedly would do? Could she really respond, "Terms are what criminals headed to prison get, and Brice is no criminal"—as she would?

Yes, but not before Sam greeted her in the visitors' lounge of the center, wearing his uniform, Bulls jersey and camouflage army surplus cargoes, with the new addition of a tiny silver nose ring. She began to compliment the jewelry by way of making some gesture toward the boy, but Sam beat her counterfeit compliment to the draw, blurting, "Why look for some guy you don't know?"

"It's a little more complicated than that."

"How so?"

"Listen, Sam. Where's your mother?"

"With Grandma."

"In her room?"

"No, down in the solarum."

Ariel's instinct to say *solarium* was subsumed by the absolute need to unburden herself, come clean about Kip with those here who did love her and were presences, rather than an absence, in her life.

As she began walking side by side down the corridor with her cousin—who'd asked, "So what's with this Kip guy, anyhow?"—Ariel pressed ahead with an explanation, as if to rehearse her words for Bonnie. They passed the nurses' station, passed some patients' rooms. And they passed the office of Sarah Montoya, who was seated with the family of a dying invalid, citing, as she had done quite often in these past couple of years, the case of a veteran she'd encountered at death's verge and who, despite every indication he would never pull through, was now living strong in his remission and had become nothing less than a member of her own family.

"Hope isn't the worst risk you can take," she said. "Without really meaning to, my friend Kip has taught me that—"

"Kip is my—" Ariel said, then stopped, having heard this echo quietly resound from the open doorway beside her. She glanced in at the woman seated behind a table within, and the woman, who'd heard that echo, too, looked up at the convergingly hopeful face of a youthful female Kip Calder, and recognized instantly who she was.

Knowing she'd misheard, sure of it, Ariel took her cousin by the arm and proceeded, shaking her head. Sarah Montoya apologized to the family seated there, rose from her chair, promising she'd be right back. Ariel and Sam were nearly at the solarium doors when Sarah caught up to them, calling, "Ariel Calder?"

If Ariel had been miles underwater, she might not have moved so slowly turning to face the woman who had spoken her name, the name that might have been hers had everyone's life been lived just somewhat differently.

Ariel Calder. Stepfather. Invented words, inaccurate but tenable, too.

"Yes," she breathed.

"My name is Sarah Montoya, and I know a man who'd be very happy to meet you."

Ariel's face drained white. She reached for Sam's bony shoulder, but missed, and would have fallen to the floor had her cousin and Sarah not caught her in their collective arms.

So much was happening at the same time.

For Jessica, as always, the rising moon upstate meant blue shadows cast by the apple trees in the scraggly orchard, and the last brave fireflies of the season twirling slowly upward in search of mates, so slowly in the nocturnal warmth that you could easily palm one and place it in a hollyhock blossom and imprison it there by sealing the petals shut with a toothpick. The hollyhock would then come alive with eerie light. If you caught another firefly, and another, and detained them in hollyhock flowers, you'd soon have a miraculous twinkling hedge of hollyhocks, the sight of which you would never forget.

It was the full moon, and Jessica, who hadn't played this rather pitiless game for many years, stood out under its barren amber in the field above the orchard, beside the old creamery, neither quite laughing nor crying. She'd learned the hollyhock trick from Ariel, who had learned it in turn from the boys at the bottom of the road, down at the dairy farm. Those boys had all of them grown up now, just like Ariel, and were gone, as was Ariel. Wasn't it one of the laws of nature that everything runs down, moves away from its source? Was that Isaac Newton? Ariel would know. Jessica herself had once known, but memory runs down more precipitously than other things in nature. Law of forgetfulness.

She lay on the pond dock. Its grayed planks were still warm from the long day. Pressure-treated wood—it started out slime green but forgot its color. There you go. She could smell the algae carpet on the water's stagnant surface, green foam teeming with photosynthetic life. The wise trout swam in the cold depths. The stand of cattails stirred, though there was no wind. A frog gulped. A thrush called, another replied. Jessica looked at the first stars, thinking, Families are supposed to last. Memories go, minds go, but family is family. What on earth remained with Ariel gone? Neither Jessica nor her husband, however much they loved their daughter, could have suspected how central she was to their ecology, their balance and sanity. Kip wouldn't try to turn her against them, would he? Probably not, but the abruptness of Ariel's departure, combined with her rare uncommunicativeness, did leave Jessica open to all kinds of bleak thoughts.

Her husband remained, though he'd drifted these last few weeks in the absence of his version of a norm. More white hair, she could have sworn, at his temples and filigreed on his forearms. An extra punitive glass or three of wine at dinner. His distracted morning face, new dark rings under his eyes, drinking coffee after intermittent sleep.

Jessica had come to the farm alone. She needed time away from the city. The only problem was this. The house was as if haunted by Ariel, her recent presence reflected in every room. This half-read book left on the kitchen bench. That pair of sunglasses in the pantry—had she forgotten to take them?

The man in the moon regarded Jessica with the same poker-faced insouciance he showed toward all who ever stared at that unblinking eye. Sure, he was aloof and self-composed, but he had no answers. Having revisited that not completely uncruel game with the fireflies and hollyhocks, Ariel's mother had released them before coming down to the dock, flicking toothpicks here and there as she demystified the garden, robbed it of its faux Japanese lanterns. As for the man in the moon, he could take a flying leap.

Should she go to New Mexico to help Ariel? The idea seemed as threadbare as the cotton dress she wore in this drowning light. What else was left her? To wait and worry?

Her daughter, at that very moment, two time zones removed from Jess's early glowing evening, was bringing Sarah Montoya into Granna's room, where the elderly woman lay on her bed asleep in the dying afternoon. Whispering so as not to wake her, Bonnie rose from her bedside chair and told Mrs. Montoya how glad she was to see her again. They had met once before, Bonnie recalled, when Mother was admitted, though she didn't quite understand what all the fuss was about just now, as Sarah and Ariel quietly spoke of connections about to be made. Something was wrong. Ariel and Kip Calder? What was this all about? And what did it have to do with Mrs. Montoya? When Bonnie asked if they should wake Granna to let her know her granddaughter was off to Nambé, Ariel said not to disturb her—she'd be back soon. Bonnie looked at Sam, who was staring at Ariel wondering whether he had ever been alone in the same room with four women before.

Inside the farmhouse, walking its pearlescent rooms, Jessica thought about what life might have been like if Kip had come back between tours of duty and believed, as he should have, that Ariel was his daughter. What kind of father would Kip have made? How differently would Ariel have turned out? What would it have been like to be friends with Brice, to watch him marry another woman, maybe have five kids instead of just the one, who wasn't his own flesh and blood. They had made their rounds from doctor to doctor and finally discovered it was not Brice but Jessica who was barren. Harsh word, good for what it meant. She remembered Brice's using a male word for it, *impotent,* just as bad, and remembered shouting, "Barren, the word is *barren,* unless you mean *incompetent.*" That wasn't their best week together, yet, like the week itself, the crisis passed.

Jessica telephoned Brice to say goodnight and soon fell asleep not in her bed but Ariel's. Her last image of the day was neither of daughter nor husband but rather of a young man she'd known back in the sixties who'd been terribly sure of himself. A man with long fluent hands, beautiful in his pleasures as well as his anger, eloquent in his lovemaking and in his words, softly telling her that he and she had been more than intimate that summer night in June.

—You're going to have a child now.

She could hear his voice all these years later.

—I don't get pregnant, she'd whispered back.

—Wait and see.

Long time ago. All the more incomprehensible that Kip would not believe his own prophecy. Would become so different and damaged a Kip that the falsehoods he concocted about Brice and Jessica were more real to him than his own true knowledge.

During his third tour in Laos, by then having abandoned America altogether, Kip told Wagner about his possible clairvoyance that one time, and Wagner said, —Everybody knows when they've made more than love. I remember being conceived.

—Get out of here, Kip smirked.

—You get out. Everybody remembers the moment of conception.

Kip was sitting not quite out of the rain. The Laotian morning was young. A few nodding Hmong, some Kmhmu guerrillas, and a couple specters in from Vientiane smoking expensive Camels, sat listening in a leaking thatched hootch by the muddy runway at Long Tieng.

—Let me try it from the opposite angle, Kippy. Do you think that when you die you'll experience that moment of transition in all its glory or inglory, pain or magnificence?

Kip didn't feel like being an amicable bodhisattva so didn't reply.

Wagner looked around at the others gathered among his miserable audience. —Well? What do you say? You there.

A Hmong nodded.

—He agrees with me.

—He doesn't understand you, said Kip.

—You're wrong. He understands me better than you do.

Kip shrugged. —That's not saying much.

—Wrong again, I think. Do you understand my question?

The Hmong nodded again, quietly.

—I think his answer is yes. Do you believe you'll comprehend the moment of your death?

—Yeah, the man answered.

Wagner paused, then glanced at the CIA cats. —And do you remember the moment you were conceived?

They looked at one another and dragged on their cigarettes.

—What about you? to the Hmong.

The Hmong again nodded.

—I'm telling you he doesn't understand you, Wagner.

—He does, and I think you do, too.

Jess remembered Kip's writing her about that episode. Ariel had already been born and had forgotten, in Jessica's estimation, the moment of her conception, if she ever perceived it in the first place. However, Kip hadn't been long deterred by his initial doubts. By the time he penned his letter, which he sent through a friend down in Thailand toward the end of everything, months before the People's Army declared victory and not all that long before he and Wagner went far beyond bamboo, giving up everything to live with the Lao along the Mekong's lackadaisical waters, Kip had come around to believing in Wagner's doctrine of instant consciousness.

She never mentioned the letter to Brice. Things had been tough enough without the inevitable commentary Kip's absurd ideas would have provoked. War *is* madness, Brice would say. Kip is war. War is madness. Kip is mad.

He had no better explanation for his friend's psychological catastrophe than this old-hat Aristotelian model. So Jessica—who herself had nothing to offer by way of understanding Kip—hid the letter, saving it for many years until she finally lost track of it. Proving once more the law of loss.

Kip was flying through Ariel's thoughts, too, now that she'd accepted Sarah Montoya's offer to drive her to Nambé. Her only hesitation was whether it might be better if Sarah let Kip know his daughter was in Los Alamos, anxious to see him. At least that way he wouldn't be taken completely by surprise, would have time to do whatever it was people did in such circumstances—even if it was as negligible as putting on fresh clothes, combing his hair, pondering what first words might be appropriate.

One of Ariel's grandfather's conundrums came to mind:

The part of a raven not in the sky,
That swims in the river
And yet remains dry.
Who am I?

That was one that stumped her when she was young. Now it seemed both obvious and apropos, as Ariel was to encounter both Raven and shadow, no longer acting some heedless role in a word game. Easy though it had been to imagine she'd be tense if this moment ever came to pass, Ariel never dreamed she'd be so short of breath, so terrified. Her mouth was drier than that conundrum shadow. Why wait?

"I've come a long way to meet him, Mrs. Montoya—"

"Sarah. Let's go, then. You can stay at Pajarito tonight if you like, and if not, my son can bring you back to the Hill."

Ariel took Bonnie Jean aside to say she couldn't explain everything right now, but would later. Then she kissed Granna on the forehead and left. As they passed the rusting guard tower where, back when Kip and Brice were boys, all who entered or left Los Alamos had to produce a security pass, Ariel asked Sarah to tell her about Kip, what he was like, how his health was, whether he ever mentioned her.

"He's given up hope of ever seeing you. Doesn't talk much about it, but not because he doesn't care. He's no complainer. Private man, fragile and tough at the same time, not somebody who tolerates prying. But I've found if I show I'm curious and bide my time, he tends to open up."

"That sounds like advice."

"I guess. Although with you, who knows? He'll probably act very different."

"Not knowing him, I won't be able to tell one way or the other."

Sarah said, "It's uncanny how much you two look alike."

They traced the switchbacks hugging the canyon cliffs. Ariel's ears popped. Yawn, take a deep breath, calm yourself.

At the same time, two others traveled an anxious road, past thirteen cornfields and lands rich with alfalfa and pecans. Down through Sabinal hamlet they drove, through sweet cedar thickets, with the Ladrón and Gallinas and Dátil looming against the horizon, mountains named for robbers and chickens and dates. Then on into Bernardo, where the junction would take them on a final leg past desert willows and wild verbena, through arid country the Rio Grande could not water. Flaming sunset behind them. Nambé behind, too. Delfino wondered aloud if it was fair to have left Marcos shouldering the burden of letting the others know what they'd set out to do. But fairness, it struck Kip, hadn't ever been part of the equation with regard to Dripping Spring, or Long Tieng, for that matter.

"I'd hate to think I was a burden to Marcos."

"How's that?"

"Hitching the boy to my war."

Kip said, "Marcos is solid, like all you Montoyas. He wouldn't have agreed if he didn't think it was fair or right. He's up to handling rough problems."

Delfino grabbed a glance at Kip, then turned his gaze back to the road, over the steering wheel. "You mentioned something like that yesterday. He have problems besides this load we dropped on him?"

Franny was too much to broach, Kip thought. "Point is, he'll do everything right."

Delfino had been gone only a few days but his bungalow, framed in the truck headlights, had already taken on the weary air of abandonment. The brown siding and gray windows reminded him of a dead sparrow, its feathers tawny and its eye blank. Never saw his false home looking so wretched. They went in through a side door.

"I never was much of a housekeeper."

"Me either."

"Come on, you had that fieldhouse looking sharper than I've ever seen it."

"I did it for Sarah. Left to my own devices, I doubt I'd have the place looking that good."

Kip wondered why he just lied to Delfino. He'd been questioning all the way down why he had begun to fabricate a little of this and that about his past. Embellishments more than lies, but not his usual truths, the truths that Wagner had sworn would always set him free.

Kip had insisted, for instance, when Delfino came to the field-house to fetch him earlier that day, that he'd slept like a log. Why bother with such baloney when he damn well hadn't slept at all but instead spent his final night in Nambé sick as a dog, and haunted by the foreboding that Ariel was somewhere nearby?

Wagner had instructed him to feel such things in his bones, but Kip was never able to until he lost that segment of his finger. It didn't even happen in a combat situation, but while helping a crew chief load a rocket on his Birddog.

—You heard of ghost limbs? his guru once asked. —People who reach out to shake someone's hand with an arm they lost years ago? Well, now you've got a ghost limb, my man. Use it to good purpose.

Just as some people predict the weather by what they feel in their joints, Kip, under Wagner's outrageous tutelage, studied his hands for meaning in the world. His missing finger segment often told him more than he wished to know, especially when the flashbacks came, forcing him to relive radical scenes of war, his own lifelong war. He learned to anticipate these nightmares, learned how to handle them. But what he never learned to handle was the inarguable fact that his deeper Vietnam, his saddest Laos, was nothing if not his irremediable abandonment of Ariel. What he'd done to himself, he forgave himself. But Ariel—he had to admit that he had never learned self-charity when it came to her. God knows he'd tried. Tried hard, tried often. He'd made his gesture to contact Brice, meet with the man. Nothing had come of it, not even what would've been the easiest closure—death in the desert, or in the Montoyas' barn, or up at Los Alamos. Three years had passed and the gambit failed. There was only this left to do now. Nambé was over; Los Alamos was over.

And it was of Los Alamos that Brice too thought at that moment, looking down into the city street. Brice who, having gotten off the phone with his wife, was compelled to get out into the night. His shirt was untucked, his khakis rumpled, and he wore no socks with his shoes. He didn't care what he looked like. The air outside was dense and rubbery. His head ached all of a sudden. He decided to walk a few blocks to a bar. A drink, a pointless conversation with some fellow seated next to him. He walked uncertainly among Friday night couples back to the apartment, legs heavy—heart, too.

His sister heard the answering machine engage. In the few meager moments that lapsed as his message unreeled, she tried to decide whether to leave her news about Ariel—Charlie and Sam having, despite their assurances of secrecy, filled her in. Maybe it would be better for him to hear it on tape, impersonal and chaste. That way he'd have time, she thought, to process his humiliation, yes, before getting back to her. She prepared her abbreviated speech, awaiting the tone, but started when Brice interrupted his own recorded voice, saying, "Hello, hang on."

"Brice, it's Bonnie Jean."

"What's happened?"

"Why do you always think something's happened when I call?"

"Because you don't call unless something's happened."

Bonnie cut loose not just with her news from New Mexico but her opinion that his having kept Ariel's real paternity a dirty secret all these years was beneath comment.

"Then why are you commenting?" he asked. Brice's face felt as if it were on fire. Who on earth did this woman think she was? Arbiter of all things ethical, maven of morality? Come on, already. He should simply hang up on her, grab a cab straight to LaGuardia, catch the next flight out. Barely containing his sarcasm, he apologized for not having exposed what he considered a personal matter between himself and his most immediate family. He was sorry she didn't deem him to be a worthy brother. "We obviously can't talk about this now," he finished.

Bonnie was left speechless. Meeting silence with silence, her brother lowered the receiver onto the cradle. To knock one's head repeatedly against a wall was a sure symptom of chronic stress. Brice remembered this factual detail from a civil lawsuit as he leaned against the prewar plaster and brought his head to its cool surface, withdrew it, struck himself again, pulled back, struck once more.

Kip's head, too, was aching. He ranged unsteadily out into Delfino's yard in the early darkness of the Tularosa basin while his host prepared a cupboard feast of canned lima beans and corn potpourri, tortillas furnished with sardines and mustard. At the western edge of the yard loomed a grand cottonwood, fluted like a misplaced Doric column attired in shaggy bark, overhanging the mother ditch—the main artery—of this community. A trickle of muddy water scudded down the acequia. Kip could hear but not see the little flow.

He sat himself down, thinking, What brand of crazy bastard are you? Thinking this because he'd had a new idea. Bark clawed through his damp shirt. His feet were a long way from his head. The darkness curled. His stomach churned as in years past, gurgled like some small choking creature stuck inside him. He massaged the trapped beast with frightened probing fingers. It was as if he could feel the resurgent cancer, a meaty sponge or coral reef of flesh in his gut, wet yet firm, pliable, as he imagined, and he knew this was it. He knew his having hidden from Sarah the new acidic ache in his belly probably amounted to a prideful death sentence. She'd have helped him, might even have been able to save him one more time, but Kip didn't want to return to the Hill. Souring body and undimmed pride made for the worst combination, he thought, while quietly vomiting under Delfino's tree. Oh well, yes, he'd been through this onerous drill a few times down at Pajarito recently, mornings and evenings behind the fieldhouse, and saw that the urp was bloodied. What're you gonna do, sue God? Stand down, Captain. God and all his blessed saints never got along with Satan and all his devils, but they concurred on one absolute verity—at the end of the day, every man and woman and child was articled to wind up like this, first on the ground, then under it. At least he'd managed to conceal his resurrected affliction from those who loved him healthy.

Delfino called him in for supper and Kip gathered himself at the bole of the tree, climbed to his feet, mussed the trivial liquid into the earth, wiped his lips with the sleeve of his work shirt, and joined his host in the bungalow. Had Delfino looked over at the face of his companion and confidant, he might have fainted dead away himself at the sight of the apparition with whom he dined. But he didn't. They ate, the percussive measure of forks and knives on enameled tin plates telling less about hunger than their abstracted reserve. Kip broke the spell, such as it was, with a question about whether they were going in tomorrow or the day after?

"Tomorrow we get the horses, the perishables, check out all the gear in the garage. We rest a little, then leave at sundown. Best do the trip in the dark."

"How long does it take to get there?"

"Overnight should do it. Pull in Sunday morning when they're most likely least staffed. That's my best guess, anyhow."

"What about on foot?"

"Why you ask?"

"In case there's any problem with the horses."

"Well, we could get in by foot from the road that runs east to west up along the north end of the basin. But we might get caught. Lot of towers over that way. Pretty secured, I think. But if we come in along the edge of the lava flow, nobody'll be watching because nobody'd bother to try penetrating through there."

"Except you."

"Just so."

Better to be talking, thought Delfino. Keeps apprehension more at bay. You talk, you stay calm, stay strong that way. Silence was dangerous, Agnes had always believed. One of her sayings went, —In silence we the tempest fear.

If she'd only known it, Franny would have concurred with Agnes's truism when she got back to Pajarito that night after work to find Marcos more agitated than she'd ever seen him. Up and down their room he was pacing in angry silence, enraged but not with anyone other than himself. "My god," she asked, "what's the matter?"

"I'm an idiot is what's the matter," not glancing up but instead pounding his fists against his thighs as he marched back and forth.

Franny knew she'd been found out. He refused even to look at her. She sat on the end of the bed, waiting. Mary, so infrequently real to anyone, entered Franny's consciousness and pleaded the inevitable. Tell him everything, and tell him now. Apologize from your soul and maybe take the chance of asking if we shouldn't start over, give it a fresh try in a new place where neither of us has a past. Who knows but good might come of it? Franny asked Marcos again, in a tentative voice, what was wrong.

He didn't hear her, or maybe her voice was so subdued by anxiety that it never left her lips. She found herself simply conceding, "Marcos, I guess you know I'm not who I've been saying I am. But I hope you'll hear me out."

"What?" he asked, only mildly distracted from his own thoughts.

"I said, I'm not who you think I am."

"Nobody ever is." Crisp cynicism, unusual for Marcos. Maybe she'd misunderstood the cause of his anger. She sat still, not daring to tip the uneasy balance one way or the other. But it was too late. Marcos turned a very confused, questioning eye on her. "What are you talking about, Franny?"

"You shouldn't call me that anymore."

"Has everybody around here gone mental?"

"I'm not Franny Johnson."

Marcos looked at the ceiling, then back at her. "Great, fine, wonderful. Would you mind telling me who you are, then?"

"My name is Mary."

His unbreathing mouth tensed into a slow frown. This was, he sensed, a moment whose magnitudes of disappointment were of a kind everybody must experience at some point in life, and from which few entirely bounce back.

"Mary Carpenter," she whispered through first tears.

Even if Marcos had wanted to say something—repeat this new name, try it out—he wouldn't have been able to. His voice, along with his faith in Franny, escaped him. He listened to her explanation of who she really was, and how and why she had transformed herself from Mary, a runaway from Gallup, into Franny. He was awed, stunned, impressed, really, by the breadth of her fraudulence.

"I'm the same person, Marcos. I'm exactly the same inside." She didn't, however, bring up Los Angeles, or the possible utopian future that could come with his forgiveness and their fresh beginning.

He sat on the bed beside her, his back to her, elbows on knees and head in hands. The silence welled until she broke it, her voice trembling, "Isn't that what you were angry about?"

"What, that you've completely lied to me about yourself from the first moment we met? You're too good a phony for me to have found out on my own. That isn't what I was pissed about before."

"I don't understand. What's wrong?"

"Everything, now."

"What's going on?"

"Nothing. Everything. I've got to go stop them."

"Stop who?"

"Idiots, all three of us. Me especially." He told her that Delfino and Kip had gone south, chasing a verdict against the government, and that they'd given him the responsibility of informing Carl and Sarah the day after tomorrow. He couldn't tell his parents because they'd call the police, and he didn't want Kip and Delfino to get into trouble with the authorities even before they'd broken any laws. He had to go after them, and she had to cover his absence, no matter whether she was the fucking Virgin Mary or Mary Magdalene.

"That's not funny."

"It wasn't meant to be." He handed her Delfino's documents and said, "Give these to Sarah in two days if you don't hear otherwise from me."

"What am I supposed to tell her and Carl in the meantime, with you and Kip just disappearing like this?"

"You're obviously a born liar, or else the great actress you always wanted to be."

"That's cruel."

"Tell them whatever you want. I'm sure they'll believe whatever you make up."

"Please don't shout."

He turned and stared at her averted eyes. "You're really from Gallup then?"

"Yes."

"Your father, he didn't die in Africa."

Mary said nothing, just smoothed a wisp of hair behind her ear with a quaking finger.

"And your mother lives in Gallup, not Princeton."

"I think so."

"You think so."

"I haven't been in touch with her for a while."

"Why not?"

Nothing. She held back tears because she didn't want sympathy, didn't want to be judged or misjudged by Marcos. Her face was rigid as a mask, her lips white, shoulders quaking. Kip had, in his way, warned her that this moment was inevitable. But he'd never intimated how she was to behave when it came.

"You're in some kind of trouble?"

How she would have liked to laugh. "Other than this, of course not."

"Don't fucking say *of course not*. Nothing's of course or of course not."

A melancholy settled over the room for protracted minutes, then Mary asked, "What do you want to do?"

Marcos answered in so quiet a voice that she could hardly hear him, "I don't know anything except I can't let those stupid old fools go in there and get themselves killed."

"I'm so sorry, Marcos."

"Not half as sorry as I am."

Mary placed her hand on his and as she did there came a knock on the curtained glass of their door, in the narrow alcove that gave onto the long, tiled *portal*. Sunset had palely lit the room through the casements—they hadn't noticed—and now they sat in evening darkness. Neither moved. Marcos instinctively rubbed Mary's hand, which was icy. Another knock.

"Now what," he said.

"Marcos, you there?"

Sarah's voice.

"What is it?" he asked, but his own voice didn't carry.

"I'm so sorry, Marcos," Mary repeated.

"Marcos?"

"Yes," he answered, letting go of Mary's hand and rising to open the door. Sarah stood on the other side of the screen. Drawn to the porch lamp, moths circled and arabesqued above her head. She was sorry to disturb him and Franny, but wondered if he knew where Kip happened to be tonight. She'd been down to the fieldhouse—no sign of him. There was someone here who had traveled a great distance to meet him, Sarah explained, as Marcos saw the face of a young woman behind his mother in the assembling shadows.

PART III

JORNADA DEL MUERTO

Nambé and New York

to Tularosa Basin

1996

They set out from nowhere. The horses chuffed in protest when they backed them out of the rusty van along this unpeopled strait. They abandoned their truck and trailer in a sandy ravine beside the Southern Pacific railroad tracks. Saddled and outfitted, they rode along a grit service road that would take them through Willow Springs and west toward the red Oscuras. Jakes Hill receded, somewhere between Tularosa and Carrizozo, while before them silvergreen clouds crowned the sawtooth horizon. They saw pencil rain fall in spectral columns in the distance, evaporating before it ever reached the ground. They saw the last of the day's small black birds pitching home like little rocks across the wide sky, and heard their meager peeping. Saw paloverde shrubs, solitary green dabs. And pink chaparral and soaptree yucca with its dried dead blossoms that looked like rattlesnake bellies reshaped into tapers. Saw backlit spiderwebs that looked like dreamcatchers woven in rabbit-brush spurs and creosote elbows. Here they passed the corpse of a black rubber auto tire. There they saw tiny dunes of sand populated by little yellow cushion plants in the vague violet shade of a tamarisk grove. They heard crickets trill and a kit fox yap as they caravaned past weathered telephone poles with clear glass insulators still in place from the forties, their wires long since snipped. They saw alkali that resembled frost on the pinkbrown desert floor. They also happened to see a wink of light off in the distance, far downvalley from the sunspout that parodied this magisterial sunset. An obscene glimmer, a tiny chromium glint. Burnished steel that caught the sun and spurned it. Or else the thick glass of a telemetry observation tower. In any case, something even less indigenous to this terrain than the intruders themselves. Either way, they were bathed in a sunset the color of cream pouring into the earth basin. It reminded the young woman of the Annunciation scene painted on an antique retablo she'd noticed on the wall back in Delfino Montoya's shanty bungalow.

Ariel witnessed these lights, caused by nature and man, which prompted the memory of dawn brightly burning in that pool of water on the kitchen floor of the upstate farmhouse, on that relatively recent morning when she'd decided to come looking for Kip. Seemed naive now. But how could she have imagined she'd end up here? Delfino had already told her she didn't belong in the desert. Told her and Marcos in no uncertain terms that this was not how it was supposed to happen.

Nothing had gone right. Sometime after Delfino hit the sack last night but before he awakened this morning, Kip had evolved a different plan, a variant itinerary for them both. Delfino discovered that his brand-new friend had defected, after quietly messing up their gear. The keys to his pickup had been nicked, like the pickup itself, which Kip had furtively loaded with backpack, canteen, gun, map. Weak from insomnia and gutsickness, Kip nonetheless managed to roll the truck down the street in neutral, starting the engine only when he was out of earshot. On the drive north, then east to the spot that afforded best access on foot to Dripping Spring, his thoughts had been a whirlwind of hope. He hoped his expertise in reading topographicals was still sharp. Hoped his diminished stamina would suffice to get him there, and that his bygone genius for moving behind enemy lines wasn't utterly defunct. He hoped, above all, Delfino wouldn't misunderstand his actions, that he would at least mull over the note he left behind. The logic was simple. Kip would set up a siege at Dripping Spring while referring the military police to

Delfino, who could capitalize on this act by bringing press attention to his half-century-old cause.

I've lived off your family's kindness for years now, Kip's note began, then continued,

> *Your brother and Sarah, Marcos, they all love you and even need you. Nobody needs me, as such. We're both war vets of different stripes who wound up on the same side. Give me the chance to help you. Soon as I get there, I'll make sure they find me. I'll throw them back to you, and the show will be yours. Sorry about messing with your stuff. The idea is to slow you down long enough so you have time to think through my proposition. Same way you couldn't talk about your plan with Carl, I didn't feel I could discuss mine with you. You'd have tried to talk me out of it and might have succeeded. Stay there and let me do this for you.*
>
> *Your friend, whether you believe it or not, Kip.*

"Bullshit, crap, and fuckall," Delfino Montoya had exclaimed as he read this, then looked around at the strewn equipment that had been so painstakingly arranged. His natural impulse was to call the police. But, hands lapsing at his sides, he realized he couldn't. Not if he wanted to proceed with his own plan. He began to laugh. Well, nobody could accuse Kip Calder of lacking pluck.

Delfino had just begun to gather up his provisions, intending fully to ignore Calder's devisings, when Ariel and Marcos appeared at his door. For crissakes. Wasted and wired from driving all night downstate and over to Carrizozo through the Valley of Fires, the two explained themselves. Marcos assured his uncle that his scheme hadn't been divulged, he needn't worry—Franny had been sworn to take care of everything and Marcos was more than confident she was up to the subterfuge. As for Ariel, Delfino wondered how Calder could claim, *Nobody needs me, as such,* when his distraught daughter was right here looking for him. Shocked, aggrieved to discover Kip wasn't with Delfino, she demanded to know where he was. He handed her the letter. "Maybe you'll understand this better than I do."

Heart sinking, Ariel read Kip's note. The Montoyas, young and old, looked at each other awkwardly. She slowly folded it, gave it back to Delfino, and said in a low, determined voice, "We've got to stop him."

Marcos asked, "How long has he been gone, Delf?"

"Two, three hours? I don't know. Like I say, I was asleep."

"He can't have gotten far."

"Down here you don't have to go very far to disappear."

"Doesn't matter. We have to look."

Although morning was no longer in its infancy, and Delfino still had it in mind to depart that evening, they drove Ariel's car up and down Route 54 looking for the well-intentioned bastard. But nothing doing. Nor did they dare ask around if anyone had seen a dark-eyed, sickly-looking man driving a shanghaied Ford pickup.

"We know where he's gone," Delfino said, back at the bungalow. "No point wasting more time. I'll tell Kip you're here when I hook up with him at Dripping Spring."

"No way," she blurted, taken aback by her brazenness.

Delfino stood unmoving.

"We might be more helpful to you than you think," Marcos said.

Ariel added, "Don't underestimate the strengths that come from what you think are weaknesses."

"What's that supposed to mean?"

"It means you're not going alone. It'd be plain stupid."

"Look, Marcos, I'm not stupid and I'm not smart. I'm decided, is all. I'd rather go in and find Kip myself."

"Not wise."

"Wisdom never got nobody anywhere except into trouble."

Ariel thought, He's not wrong. Socrates, Cassandra. "Well then, you can go by yourself, and Marcos and I'll meet you there."

"You wouldn't know how to find the place without me."

"That's why we've got to come along. Because without you I'm afraid I'll never find him, and I'm so close."

Though he had no idea that this young woman had never so much as seen this father of hers, or spoken with him, Delfino was moved by her words. Both men looked at her sitting at that same kitchen table, her eyes red, her shoulders dropped in exhaustion but also in a kind of defiant commentary, hair wild from the night's having blown and eddied it during the long drive, car windows rolled down to let in the cooling wilderness wind. It was the end of the discussion. She slept through what was left of the day on the old man's bed, which smelled like damp raffia, as Marcos dozed on the sofa, his legs draped over the arm of the broken thing. When they woke, they found that Delfino had made them an afternoon breakfast of scrambled eggs, toast, and coffee. By six that evening they'd stowed supplies under a dun tarp in the flatbed of a borrowed truck, loaded the horses rented under false assurances into a trailer, and, like a landbound ship of fools, started for their entry point, arriving just before sunfall.

As they moved out onto the dirt road, Ariel sensed that nobody belonged here, not even rocketeers and ranchers. She shook her head to fend off misgivings. No need to think backward when everything was flying forward. But her worried eyes gazed both forward and back with democratic dismay. Who was it who'd written that life is a tragedy for those who feel and a comedy for those who think? It all seemed fairly tragicomic to Ariel at the moment. Prompted by that faraway light they'd seen, the three of them looked around at one another. Nobody said a word. None was going to concede the faintest hint of fear.

It did occur to Ariel to wonder what was pushing her so hard. Was it stubbornness or was it love, something more than a daughter's benevolent passion, or was it pure curiosity driving her now, the need to know? Richard of Saint Victor believed that to love is to perceive. Granna had told her that one, and Ariel liked it. She wanted to see Kip, if only once, in order to *perceive* the man. Kinship was a crazy law unto itself. This was madness, she thought, but all families were steeped in madness. Hers was no exception.

The riders made steady progress. They rode in loose single file, with Ariel following Delfino, and Marcos bringing up the rear with a ginger-colored packhorse on hemp braids trotting behind. They rode at an unhurried pace, so as not to attract attention should anyone happen to notice them. The highway had fallen behind, but there was always a chance that they'd encounter another rider or some kid four-wheeling the outward flats for a lark. Delfino still contemplated ditching his young companions. If he could make a break and lose them, he figured they'd be forced to retrace their tracks back to the main road. But the basin was all long vistas through these first miles until they reached the lava field, thus the likelihood of his being able to escape them was small. So he kept his eye on the path ahead, more or less accepting their presence here. Besides, he had to admit, part of him welcomed the company. Would have been better if it'd been Kip, but it was what it was.

He had seen all this grandeur before. Had seen the primordial sundown, the mountain ranges on either side of the hardpowder basin. Seen the birds jolting to their nests in a cactus trunk or some hidden place on the ground. He'd seen the walking rainstorm and afterglow at their backs to the east, where the sun would rise tomorrow, as always hot and rounding. And yes, he'd seen the flashing telemetry hardware on the southern flats. He knew there was a range center down there, west of Rim Rock. If that idiot Calder hadn't absconded with his map, he could have pinpointed the location. As it was, he had to rely on memory. What the hell—it wasn't like they allow the Bureau of Land Management to publish more than the most obvious unclassified sites in geological survey maps of the area, anyway. Gravel pits, radio towers. As if that were all there was out here. Once they crossed bearing R8E at T8S, from public to military reservation lands, the map Kip had taken probably was outdated, aside from topo contours and distances above sea level.

Between the three riders and the mountains lay the malpais, a badlands of ropy, blistered black lavastone all but impossible to cross, and in the nearer reaches were nasty clutters of mesquite and creosote and yucca whose pods chattered with dried seeds hard as teeth when skittish winds passed through. The cream light shone now like burned butter, collecting in lakes on the desert floor, and as it did, their faces were bathed in deeper dusk. Beyond this malpais, in a stone alley at the foot of those mountains, was the abandoned ranch at Dripping Spring, which they meant to reach before tomorrow's sun.

Kip was on his way in, too, having ditched Delf's truck, and as he walked he hoped that Delfino understood what he himself already fathomed. That Dripping Spring was, at this late stage of the so-called game, nothing more or less than an idea, a point of controversy. Not a human habitat, and certainly not home. Once upon a time, but no more. Maybe Delfino would realize there was no ranch up ahead, finally, to take back. Just petrifying timber, tumbled stone, adumbrations of fences. Whether Kip had overstepped his bounds by hiding from Delfino some necessities for the journey, or whether it'd been a childish act or even a selfish one, barely mattered now. He had enough juice in him to make his benighted way in, hell if he didn't. He knew this was his berserk terminus, just as he knew it was the flagrant fountainhead of the nuclear highway. Why not finish things up in this godforsaken Eden, tasting the desert air like the methodical chameleon does on its noonday rock before it nods off into the nil?

"*W*herth Ariah?"

Mornings were easier than afternoons, when fatigue toyed with her tongue and robbed her of sibilants and other sounds. Yet no matter what time of day, it was baffling which words mutinied and which fell amiably into place. Frustrating, too, to be forced to relearn what so recently was easy as breathing. Try again, try again.

"Where ith Ariel."

Better. Once more, with soul.

"Ariel. Where is she?"

Bonnie Jean, as ever these days, hesitated. Not wanting to say the wrong thing, hoping to keep her mother calm and on track. "Nambé."

"Why's she in Nambé?"

No right answer came into Bonnie's mind, though she took the question as another sign that her mother was continuing to make strides back toward health. Cognizance of what was happening around her, the doctors said. Engagement; recall. Her stroke had been finally assessed as a transient ischemic attack, known as a little stroke in euphemistic medical jargon. The electroencephalogram and CT-scan had revealed some unfriendly plaque, some thickening of her arteries, which Granna pronounced *art of ease,* knowing that Ariel would like the pun. Where was that girl? Her slur bothered the caregivers at the convalescent center, but her appetite for life seemed to have fully returned, and with it the rosy glow in her gin-blossomed cheeks. Back was the twinkle that had been subsumed under the dull cloud shadowing her eyes. Her smile was neither pinched nor crooked, as it'd been during those first days after the stroke. She was hampered but hardly stopped.

"Whereth Sarah?"

"I checked before, Mom. She hasn't come in yet today."

"Didn'd Ariel go . . . with her yestehday?"

This came as a surprise. Hadn't she been asleep during all that? "Yes, she did. You want me to call them?"

Out of nowhere, she said, "Kip Calderth dead. She went to visit hesh grave?"

"We already told you, Mom. He's not dead, and she's in Nambé."

Mrs. McCarthy said nothing. It was coming back to her now. Brice had flown out here a few years ago, hadn't he? To meet up with his old friend. Less clear to her was why Ariel should have such a keen interest in Kip Calder, especially given that her grandmother was here in the convalescent center and missed her company.

"How long's she going to—"

"It's all pretty confusing. Let's just focus on getting you home, why don't we."

"Whereth Brice?"

The impediment sounded biblical, which was just fine.

Bonnie Jean paused a beat, caught her breath. The problem of her private news brownout with Brice bothered her more than she would have liked to admit. To herself, her mother, anyone. Just when you're supposed to pull together with your brother, she scolded herself, what do you do but chide him over something that isn't, finally, your business? He was right, but also wrong about so much. More wrong than right, she thought, though she knew that this attitude wasn't constructive, or even respectful of her invalided mother. Worst of all, it didn't gratify whatever sibling demon lay behind the sentiment, hoping to chew on some tasty bone of contention.

"He's very worried, and like I say, he's coming as soon as he can get away."

"He'll come when he can."

The sentence quite crisply spoken.

"I'm sure you're right, dear. But let's talk about you now. How are you feeling this morning?"

She nodded.

"Want to walk?"

"No."

"They say you ought to walk."

"I'd rather talk."

"Let's walk and talk at the same time."

Daughter helped mother out of the chair, got her four-footed aluminum cane into her right hand, and, taking her thin left arm, escorted her out into the hallway. They strolled slowly, side by side. How well we know each other, Bonnie thought. She's me and I'm her.

Only difference is a couple little nothing, everything things. Who made who—or was it *whom*? She could never remember. Who was old, and who was getting old? Different faces and bodies, somewhat. Different husbands—yes, for sure. Different taste in clothes, because look at her mother's dislike of the housedresses that Bonnie Jean herself found both comfortable and rather attractive. Bonnie loved the Savior on Sundays, but her mother worshiped him every hour of every day of every week. Bonnie didn't much care for alcohol—a watered-down mimosa on her birthday sent her as deep into her cups as she ever wanted to venture—but her mom just plain did. So, sure, there were differences. But Bonnie felt, this day, their kindredness, and said so. "I love you," was how it came out. Very simple moment. The words felt good on her tongue.

"I love you, too," her mother agreed through the difficulty of making her passage up and down the glistening corridor, which was oddly shadowed by her deepening concern over wayward Ariel.

*I*n every creature's death is the promise of your own. Kip hadn't thought of that for decades. It was a truth back in the midfifties, when his father uttered the tenet, and it was still truth today. That the thought, simple enough in its wisdom, had been spoken by a man deeply involved in the production of apparatus that promised death didn't preclude its veracity. To the contrary. Mr. Calder had known whereof he spoke. Walking along this hot sandy road, blinded by the light, his son remembered what had prompted those words.

The buck was already dead. Young Kip and Brice had found him down in Bayo Canyon, big muledeer with an eight-point rack, as Kip recalled, which made him about half their age at the time.

—What do you suppose got him? I don't see any wound.

The beast had bled from its nostrils, and a thick dusty tongue protruded inelegantly over its teeth. Flies walked it and hovered in a feverish cloud above the carcass. Late morning.

—Heart attack, maybe, answered Kip.

—Deer don't get heart attacks.

—You know nothing, boy.

Brice countered, —Do too, boy.

—Anything that's got a heart can get a heart attack, okay?

—Maybe there's something on the other side.

Together they rolled the deer over from left to right, Brice wrenching its hind legs and Kip the forelegs. The animal must not have been dead all that long, since there was still some flex and play in its limbs. The flies rose and scattered, then returned. No sign of any injury, though the boys noticed a bald patch along its tawny flank.

—What's that?

Kip shrugged.

—Maybe it ate something, a rotten buffalo gourd or something.

—Buffalo gourd wouldn't kill a buck and it won't make one bald, either.

—But I mean something like that.

The two kids stood sentinel over the body, silent for a time. A lone hawk voyaged a broad thermal some thousand feet overhead. Kip remembered it had been one drought of a day, hot and mute but for the nazzing of flies, summer's end then as it was now. He'd walked away into the shade of a squat black ponderosa whose top had been lobbed off by a lightning strike, then returned, breaking the silence.

—I got an idea.

—Count me out, said Brice.

—You don't even know what it is.

—Whenever you get ideas about things like this, they never turn out good.

—Chickenshit.

—Like I say, count me out.

—Listen, it's already dead, isn't it? So there's nothing we can do to change that, am I right?

—So then what?

Kip lowered his voice. —You know how they have those trophy
heads up in Fuller Lodge?

—Forget it.

—Well, why not? Look how handsome he is.

—I don't think dead deer heads should be on people's walls.

—Where should they be? Out here where coydogs and buzzards
and flies eat them?

—We ought to bury him is what we ought to do.

Kip laughed. —You know how long it'd take us to dig a hole big
enough to bury this guy? Forget that. My dad's got a hacksaw. We'll
come back down before dinner and cut off the head about here.
Bleed it in that tree a couple days, scoop out the guts and stuff. We
get us a piece of ply over where they're building that addition on the
middle school and saw out an oval for the mount—

—You got it all figured out.

—You with me?

—I already told you.

Without glancing at the corpse again, they began walking west up
the canyon trail toward the Hill. After lunch, Brice accompanied Kip
to the construction site, where they rummaged a piece of wood from
the scrap pile, then returned to the spot where they'd discovered the
deer. Several black crows winged away downcanyon from perches on
the buck's cadaver, and the cloud of flies had thickened.

—Get, go on! Kip shouted, running ahead of Brice.

Kip's friend remained reluctant to participate. Over a peanut butter and chokeberry jam sandwich, he'd asked his mother about those
heads over at the lodge, and how they stuffed them.

—Why do you ask?

—No reason.

—What're you boys up to? she'd answered before going on to explain that taxidermy was a science, even an art. It was something for
people who'd gone to school to study how to do it. Preemptive strike,
she thought.

He more or less repeated these words now to Kip, who stood over the buck, having thrown a length of rope and the scavenged plywood on the ground beside it.

—You told your mother, didn't you, Kip said.

—No.

An endless quarter of an hour passed from the time Kip took the hacksaw to a point midway down the length of the neck—Brice held up the buck's heavy head while staring away at the canyon cliffs, at clouds, at anything that might distract him from Kip's dissection—to a moment when the head separated from the body. Kip tied a knot around the base of the antler rack and hung it as high as he could in the scorched ponderosa.

Once they'd finished, Kip asked Brice, —You sick? You're white as dried spit.

Brice said, —And you're soaked red with blood.

After Kip got caught climbing through his bedroom window that night, he found himself marching down into Bayo Canyon for a third time, though now with flashlights and accompanied not by Brice but his father, who was livid. The apparition of the buck head swaying helplessly in the warm nocturnal breezes was startling even to Kip. Its eyes were blanker than before, if that was possible. The poor thing looked deader than when he'd decapitated it. His father made him bury the buck in the sandy canyon. Kip dug for most of the night to make the hole. After he finished, as father and son were hiking back out of the canyon in light morning rain, his old man uncorked that line about every animal's death bearing the promise of one's own. A week passed before he and Brice were allowed to see each other again, and when they finally did, Kip offered up the saying as if it were his own formulation. They were sitting on the front stoop of Brice's house.

—I'd have helped you dig the grave if my parents let me, you know. I guess your dad wanted you to do it yourself.

—Well, I didn't need nobody's help. I got it done on my own.

—It wasn't a very good idea in the first place.

—You're wrong. It was a great idea.

—What was so great about it? I still think people shouldn't have dead animals hung on their walls.

—They should. Everybody should.

—I don't get you, boy.

—I guess it's over your head.

—What's over my head?

—Besides the sky?

Brice laughed, but Kip didn't, so Brice stopped.

It was then that Kip intoned, in a voice more or less replicating the pastor's at Los Alamos's interdenominational chapel, —The death of every creature is the promise of your own. That's why I wanted to put that buck on the wall, boy. To help us remember.

—Don't call me boy, shouted Brice.

—Remember it, boy, Kip said, though now he himself remembered the thought and its narrative, as he sat under a scorching sun that dazzled and punished all beneath it save for this gemsbok, dead on the desert floor, which reminded him of the buck they'd once found in Bayo. Kip had repeated his father's words then as a kind of threat, but today they returned to him with their original import.

"I'm sorry," he whispered to the present carcass, and perhaps to the one upon which he'd visited such indignity way back. Wagner always liked that story, commended his father for both his method of atonement and the plainspoken philosophy of coda.

What Brice and Kip had discovered, though they hadn't had the knowledge to discern it then, was far more sinister than a hairless patch on a buck's haunch, down there in the canyon where Project waste was laid to rest in thousands of unmarked shallow sepulchers, and where its authors' wilder children played their private games. This oryx gazelle was half bald itself, but surely any connection between it and that dead buck lay exclusively in Kip's imagination, as he, like it, was little more than a footnote in the history of restricted-entry installations.

Kip didn't really want to touch the hollowed shell of this antelope-like creature, but he found it impossible not to. He laid his hand, palm open and quaking before it settled, on the smooth hide so beautiful as to be otherworldly and uttered a helpless petition for all those who find themselves in a place where they do not belong. For Kip knew that he—like this descendant of the original herd shipped by the government out here in the late sixties, from the Kalahari in Africa for the eventual enjoyment of servicemen who got a bang out of hunting exotics—did not belong. Nor did he want to belong, though like the gemsbok he had tried, with notably less success. He pulled out the compass he'd borrowed, or rather stolen, from Delfino, and took a reading. The gemsbok's foreleg happened to be pointed toward magnetic north, and Kip put this small serendipity to use, spreading his map of the Tularosa basin and Jornada del Muerto—of White Sands Missile Range, *Whiz-mer,* the locals called it—on a patch of splintered bedrock between them.

He'd not come as far as he might have hoped. His sense of position was primitive, as he didn't know the area, but from what he could glean, keying off what must be North Oscura Peak due west, peering over the sunken barrel of furred ribs, his hike would take at least another long day.

Sickness came in waves, but he knew he could do it. He'd been in tough places before and got the job done. Besides, he did belong here. He was right where he belonged.

Accustomed to being Franny, Mary was going to miss her. But Franny Johnson was abolished now, kicked like the bad habit she'd become. Lying in bed in Santa Fe, Mary watched a spider spin a corner web. Her accidental confession to Marcos—that Franny was a stitched fabric of deceit meant to cloak an unhappy childhood and dress up the admittedly fading dream of starstruck adolescence—hadn't gone the way she might have wanted. Indeed, yesterday's admission had played out the reverse of how she envisioned it. She hoped that surely Marcos would understand how a screwed-up youth could have led her to such desperate measures. Yes, okay, she lied in the beginning to protect herself, and continued with the ruse because she was afraid. But Marcos would sympathize and forgive, she brought herself to believe. With Kip's fieldhouse finished, and summer at its end, conclusions were in the air. All she meant to bring to a close was her fictitious self, not every single factual thing around her.

Instead, safe to say, Marcos quietly flipped out. Less safe to assume that Mary herself felt inchoate jealousy, or rivalry, or some undefined anxiety toward Ariel, who left with him abruptly on the same night their lives collided. First laying eyes on Ariel ranging tall behind Sarah at the opened door of Marcos's room, Mary was struck by the thought that here was a woman whom Franny, some real Franny with realizable instead of unfounded dreams, might look like. A fine, haunted face conveying all the paradoxes of stardom. And as Ariel's story unfolded, the four of them having moved from the room to the *portal* outside, in the evening air so rich with calm that Mary only wished it might envelop them and wash away all these human crises, her sense that Ariel was a preeminent Franny had the effect of further discouraging her. Ironic, given that Mary wanted to renounce Franny anyway.

The confluences were crazy. Like the made-up Franny, Ariel had been raised back east. Like Franny, Ariel had an educated mother and an absent father. Like the Franny invented in Santa Fe, the persona that Mary had presented to Marcos back in those early months when they first started seeing each other, this Ariel appeared to be determined rather than disoriented. She seemed possessed of a will to know things—though rather than wanting to learn how to ride, or about the artificial insemination of horses, or about how life worked on a pueblo ranch, Ariel was motivated by the dramatic heft of a true tale, starring a father who abandoned everything, thereafter to wander the world. By her very inflections and gestures, Ariel seemed to shine with the earthy elegance that Mary had tried always to inspire in Franny. Standing in the umbra, Mary listened, wilting, as Kip, whom she'd adopted as a surrogate father, was now being taken away from her, too, usurped by his true daughter. She bit her lip, knowing there was nothing she could do to alter what was unfolding before her.

"Franny, you okay?" Sarah's aside had gone nearly unnoticed as Ariel asked Marcos where Kip's daily routine might have taken him, since she and Sarah hadn't found him down at the fieldhouse.

Mary offered Sarah a tenuous nod.

"I'm not sure," Marcos told Ariel, buying himself some time, he supposed, until he could figure out what next to do. It dawned on him how shockingly easy it was to fabricate a lie right here, cool as the proverbial cucumber, in front of his mother. "Did you look around the paddocks and barn? Might be helping Carl."

"Why don't you walk Ariel down there and see," Sarah said.

Too much pulling him in too many directions. He instinctively looked at Franny—no, *Mary*—who said, "We can finish our talk later if you want."

"Okay, then. Later, Franny," thinking *Franny?*—how effortlessly these small deceits multiplied—as he walked alongside Ariel across the yard beyond which the stable lights burned. But to gather so many lies that you create a whole new person out of them?

Ariel was saying something. "Did he ever mention to you that he had a daughter?"

"Kip? Yes, he did, but made it sound like you would never want to have anything to do with him."

"He said that?"

"Not in so many words, maybe. Just my impression."

"That's sad," she said.

"He might've felt sad, but if he did he never let it show. He seemed to think you were within your rights not to bother with him."

"God, I hope he doesn't hate me."

Where the hell was everybody? "Carl?" Marcos shouted down the long corridor as the scoria crunched familiarly underfoot. "Maybe they're in the east field. I know it needed irrigating," he assured Ariel, uncertain whether Carl was there or not, but beginning to wonder whether his promise to Delfino might not be outweighed by Ariel's ambition of finding her father. What if his uncle and Kip were arrested on White Sands, what if they got killed, inadvertently or otherwise? What if they both disappeared without a trace—a remote possibility, but who knew? People are good at keeping secrets, and governments are better, but the military keep secrets at all costs, from friend and foe alike. Even a professional spook like Kip might well change direction if he knew his daughter was here, rather than risk becoming the genesis of some official denial, some motley mystery. Say something, ask her something. "How'd you find out he was your father?"

"He wrote me asking my forgiveness," she said. "But I'm the one who needs to be forgiven."

"How's that?"

"I knew he was sick and I didn't come. Funny, I always thought of myself as a principled person, but what good are principles when you fail to act on such a basic instinct as loving your father? It's a miracle, really, that I have a chance to set things right."

Marcos listened, undistracted despite his turmoil. Ariel's words settled him at once on the question of whether to confide in her.

"Marcos?" Carl was out here after all. His voice was quiet, though he shouted, and his black silhouette stood distant against the field whose borders were erased by late twilight.

"Yey."

"Watch out, it's mucky."

"Carl, where's Kip?"

"What boots you got on?"

"Carl, listen. Where's Kip?"

"I was gonna ask you, damn it. I could've used his help this afternoon. What boots you got on?"

Ariel hovered at Marcos's side in the closing darkness. The round moon had risen into wispy clouds that looked like they'd been combed. White hair gathered up with a luminescent barrette. Its light sparkled like cultured pearls on the flat flooded field. Now Marcos and Ariel could hear water trickling across the hard ground. They ventured out closer toward Carl's far-off flashlight which shone in their direction.

"Not the right ones for irrigating."

"Come help me anyway, you mind?"

"Carl, there's someone here. It's important. Kip's daughter's come to see him."

"What? Look, I'm almost done, just got to close off the feed ditches. He's around somewhere."

"This won't take but a few minutes," Marcos apologized. "Let me help him, then we'll go find Kip."

"I'll come with you."

"No, look, it's all mud."

Ariel did follow him into the blackness of the settling night, but after catching one of her boots in the deepening mire, she dropped back and watched them moving like shadow pantomime figures a hundred yards upslope toward the far top of the enclosure. Water gurgled around her where she stood, as if the earth itself were murmuring some garbled message. So, tell me what it is you want to say, she thought. Nothing but burbles. Old baby earth. She laughed silently, sadly. Something was wrong. He wasn't here. Marcos knew it, she could tell. The planet itself was trying to clue her in. And that girl Franny looked like she'd just witnessed a murder.

"So you say you're Kip Calder's kid?" Carl shook her hand, having walked with Marcos back to where she waited.

"He says he's my dad."

Their faces were illuminated by flashlights.

"Good man, your father. Let's go find him."

They searched Rancho Pajarito for Kip and Delfino both, Marcos feeling rotten for putting his parents and Ariel through all these unnecessary paces. More than once he reasoned himself into blurting out what he knew, but a remembrance of Kip's resolute handshake and his uncle's proud farewell embrace compelled him to go on with his absurd performance.

When Carl finally saw that Delfino's truck was missing, he made the correct assumption they'd gone off together. "Old coots are probably over in Española painting the town," he encouraged Ariel.

"Such as it is to paint," Marcos said, trying but failing to lighten the edgy, somber mood.

Carl said, "I wouldn't worry. Delfino's been visiting from out of town these past couple days, and him and Kip hit it off, so like I say, I'd bet they're out somewhere getting happy."

"Maybe I'll take you up on that offer to drop me back at the Hill tonight, if it isn't too much trouble," Ariel said at last. Sarah persuaded her to have a quick bite with them before Marcos drove her home. As Ariel sat and ate with the Montoyas and Franny, she imagined Kip doing the same these past years. Noticing how Marcos glared across at Franny, who kept her eyes on anyone else at the table but him, she said, "It probably wasn't the best idea for me to drop in on him like this anyway. Tomorrow I can drive back down after I've spoken with him on the phone. Make sure he really wants to meet me."

"Of course he does," said Sarah.

Marcos carried his plate into the kitchen after Ariel turned to Franny and said, "I apologize for barging in on you."

"What's more important than finding a parent," Mary asked in an answering voice.

"Finding yourself, I guess?" Ariel answered in an asking voice.

"Is there a difference?"

"I hope there is, put it that way."

"Franny lost her father in the service," Sarah said.

"I'm sorry."

Mary suddenly left the room after offering her own regrets, confessing she wasn't feeling well. Before she went, she, too, assured

Ariel that Kip would be elated to meet his daughter. Marcos returned from the kitchen meaning to follow her, but decided not to, so sat again. He would later look back on that moment as defining, though hearing Mary's car in the gravel drive might have clued him in then and there on the way things were going.

Within the course of that conflating hour, Kip coughed up blood on the same tree Delfino had once leaned against where the jackbottom loped, way back when, out behind the bungalow where Agnes's widower was now fixing dinner for his guest; and Marcos discovered that Mary's clothes were gone and the dresser drawers left ajar; and Ariel learned from that same Marcos—after they left Pajarito headed west toward Los Alamos but then, down at the intersection where Pojoaque ended and San Ildefonso began, veered downstate instead, past Santa Fe and Albuquerque and Belen—that they needed to catch up with Delfino and Kip Calder before the two men inaugurated another journey; and Carl and Sarah Montoya went to bed and slept, reckoning some of what was transpiring here, not suspecting most of the rest, but aware the sun was bound to rise within a matter of hours for worse or for better.

Nightfall continued to gather, though the sun ahead was still fiery in the cloud notches. They crossed through a dead grove of skeleton pistachio trees planted in hopeful rows and rode down through an acequia whose dried mud bed looked like a mass of broken plates. Illuminating twigs and the tracery of lifeless flowers with its fireworks as they made their way beyond the failed orchard, the bold clear hard dying sun also enkindled windows and metal roofs in the woeful hamlet of Willow Springs. Citron, marigold, clementine sang forth from glass shards and corrugated tin, all contrasted with the pale but deepening purple that settled over everything. To reach the confiscated property would take them all night. Delfino hoped to get there unaccosted, but didn't presume they would. Why should they? While it ought to have been his face that glowed with the most faith, in fact it was Ariel's. Maybe she was credulous, or good at ignoring her terror, or maybe her resolve simply ran so deep that she never considered the possibility they might not make it. Her dark eyes were now darker than the malpais that stretched ahead.

Once they rose up out of the shallow aqueduct, they passed by an abandoned morada, tumbledown and barren, its penitentes long dead and its wooden water tank buckled, sunken on timber knees as if in prayer for the souls of those who'd built it, wrongly certain it would hold up in such a cruel place as this. This holy house was now a place where young couples sometimes met to smoke, drink beer, make love in the litter of moonlight that glanced through chinks in its walls. Here the riders left the semblance of a road behind.

Westward again, having jogged north for a patch, they climbed a rise through a drift of stout cacti each crowned by dull red blooms that looked like perfumed skulls mortified by small spikes. Delfino turned to ascertain how much ground they'd covered. Willow Springs was about a mile behind already. Smoke from a chimney, or maybe from a barrel of trash on fire, lifted like a delicate finger to point at the first stars above. Ahead, a sundog flared so bright in the clouds that Ariel had to hold her palm up before her eyes. Noon at dusk, she thought. The world was like that here. Evening in one valley and daybreak the next valley over. Harsh drab scratchland here, a small lush oasis of stubborn life there, and beyond, pure white dunes or volcanic black or just plain gray desert ornamented by spindly cholla and saltbush like false rosemary. What would Jessica think, or Brice, or David, or anyone else who knew her? No one down here aside from these two men knew her right now, she realized. And they barely knew her, either. She'd had a few weeks of no one's knowing her, or knowing more than some scant part of whoever she thought she was. Not that she could say she knew herself just now. Knowing thyself. Aristotle, old pal, was it even possible under the best of circumstances?

Pretty soon they would be entering the firing range. She felt weirdly exhilarated, oddly honored to be here, grateful for Marcos's kindness toward her, his help in bridging her to Kip. Yet for all this nervous elation, the scene into which they were riding—with its dust-devil swale, its long mountains sinking into lavender shadow, its quills of radiance—didn't seem real to her. Tularosa valley was vaster by far than any stretch of land she, or most anyone, had ever beheld. Mercuric spirit light seemed to pour down into the world with news of things to come. But here there was no virgin for a holy ghost to husband, nor any angels to descend on painted wings. This was a place angels would shun and spirits forgo. Martians might like it here. Or Beelzebub himself.

The crickets were ever-present, and sounded like miniature sleighbells a very long way from snow. A lean mottled mustang, then another, then seven more, wild horses speckled dirty white and brown, started from a gully. The riders watched them scatter and regroup.

"Wouldn't mind trying one of them on for size," Marcos said.

"They'd break you like a twig," said his uncle.

Ariel found herself wondering whether this jostling ride might not cause a spontaneous miscarriage, a thought that made her feel odd, unhappy even. She was startled by how successful she'd been, these past days, at suppressing the pregnancy. Ignoring it, hoping it would pass? Not really; it flitted at the fringes of her consciousness. She'd been thinking about it, just not with her mind.

The three continued west. Heading along the farthest stretch of the lavaflow, they made their way toward its tip where they'd tack west through a nick in the mountains, between the fancifully named Hog Sup Spring and Moya, toward a box canyon nestled against the steep Oscura. This last had sheltered it from the famous blast that occurred a mere eight miles due west, on David McDonald's ranch back in the forties.

More low hogbacks like granite swells thrust upward into the waning light. Under the hooves of their horses crunched the sweet gypsum that looked like baked sugar and smelled a little like it, too. Or warm frost on pinkbrown crockery. For more than an hour they didn't speak. As the darkness deepened, the micaed sky grew closer, or seemed to, lending credence to Wernher von Braun's dream that the postwar rockets he launched from this very valley would "pave a road to the stars." A gentle wind whipped over the desert crust, warm then cool. At the travelers' backs the Sacramentos and last lights of Carrizozo sank into the gloom, and ahead, too, the night took up residence. Full moon rose.

With her free hand, Ariel snapped up her jacket. Where was Kip in all this? He'd been caught off base before. Trained as an insurgent, he'd surely been downed behind enemy lines and in places so dark—in spookdom's sense of the word—that knowing your ass from a hole in the ground made less than no difference to the elements or the adversary. She glanced around, having heard an unfamiliar noise—though none of these noises was familiar—and, being startled, wanted to identify its source.

Nothing there, nothing. She pulled a deep breath through her nostrils, threw her head back on her shoulders, and exhaled upward through pursed lips. An old trick of hers to exorcise fear. She wondered how Granna was faring, hoped she wasn't worried or angry. She wished she could have called from the bungalow but could no more risk telling Granna where she was than Marcos could Sarah. Were Brice and Jessica on their way to Los Alamos? Inhale, exhale.

Composure provisionally regained, she faced forward as her horse walked, following at some distance now the packhorse whose tail whipped like a broken clock weight, Marcos having passed her. As her resolve returned she made faces in the dark, stuck her tongue out at the moon. Orion was up, her favorite constellation, still a little faint across the cold screen of heaven. Orion who always seemed the model of tenacity, never quite closing the permanent chasm that the earliest astronomers had set between him and his beloved Pleiades. Yet he never stopped trying, did he. Never despaired of catching up with the other stars. Arms raised high, legs striding, he marched his way across the black infinities each and every night. She'd learned to tell what time it was, when she was a girl, by the seasonal position of Orion out the farmhouse window. Another neat trick, and sometimes as useful as blowing her fears through pursed lips right back to where they came from.

That made her smile. Good Orion, his sword twinkled and girdle shimmered, still low in the sky. Kip, what are you really doing out here? Can't you for once tackle your own war? Must you always run off to fight the next man's?

Time passed in a fixed kind of way, passed without really moving forward. Ariel guessed it must be ten or eleven, though some few high clouds were still tinted by weird dusk hues, like a desert aurora borealis. She saw shadowy waves of grama grass and black hummocks of primeval rock, forms out on the desert floor that had for eons stood in the same spot, blind sentry guarding ruinous blind sentry, each under the constant watch of the equally blind frontier sun and cadaver-faced moon. They threatened no one, made no sound, yet she knew that whatever fears she'd felt were not unjustified. Not, as they say, just in her head. She made a double-click against the back of her teeth, gently dug heels into her horse, and caught up with Marcos, who asked, "You all right?"

She said yeah.

When he leaned forward to light a cigarette, she saw in his match-lit profile the same look of apprehension she sensed had begun to mark her own face. Had the curious effect of making her feel calmer. "Ride with me a while till it narrows up again," he said.

The intruders were perhaps six, seven miles in before they caught sight of yellow headlamps to the south. You could see things a long way off in this flat if steppelike place, and it was hard to judge distances at night. The lights, however, were moving toward them.

Delf hushed his horse. His companions came up from behind and halted on either side. For long minutes they sat, fixed on the advancing bright-white eyes of the patrol truck.

"This is why I didn't want you to come."

"That them?" Marcos asked his uncle.

"Don't see who else it would be."

"Here we go, then," said Marcos.

"I think you and your friend ought to just turn around and get back out of here while the getting is good."

"No way."

"Ariel?"

"Sorry, can't."

The rugged plain before them was a patchwork of prickly pear, of lechuguilla and razory greasewood. Crosscut by abrupt cuestas, sudden deep gulches, berserk cracks in the pathless earth, it was tough enough to negotiate on horseback and all but untraversable in a man-made vehicle. That much they had going for them, didn't they? Still, the rangers probably had a thousand service roads carved out back here.

Delfino had often crossed this uncharted tract in the early days and was confident that they could make it in the dark without much difficulty so long as they weren't goaded too far off course—in which case they'd never arrive in time to secure Dripping Spring before dawn, square away horses and supplies, paint their signs, and be ready for the delegation that would soon show up, angry and very armed.

The packhorse snorted, unnerved by the lull. The lights sometimes disappeared, then reappeared, like some lidded beast blinking. Ariel asked why they kept turning off their lights.

"They're not. Just dropping into arroyos, coming back out."

More minutes. The lights were distinct now one from the other, and less yellow, more white. One vehicle only; the proximity of the headlamps, high on mounts, it seemed, like plowlights, suggested a Hummer. Two men, five at the most.

"How far off are they?"

"Few miles."

"They're coming pretty fast."

Delfino watched.

"They know we're here."

"Why shouldn't they," he said. "We still haven't broken any law. Just night riders rambling."

Ariel had questions but didn't ask them.

"Okay," Delfino reflected. "Let's cut back. I got an idea."

They retraced their trail several hundred yards, then several hundred more. Ahead, a meteorite stabbed the sky with its silver needle. Alluvial aprons fanned down from the Oscuras into this higher topography, and the three of them soon reached what was a periodic streambed. From there they drove the horses northwest to a hard rise like a curved step that marked the edge of the malpais. Lavastone glistened under the light of the moon, as if damp with dewy crystals.

"We'll cross through here. This's the narrowest part of the lava field."

"Hold on, hold everything."

Delfino waited for his nephew to continue.

"We'd never get through here in the daytime, let alone now."

"We'll get through."

"Ariel?"

"I'm willing if you are."

"Delf, you're sure?"

His uncle was already out into the volcanic stonefield. Ariel and Marcos pushed on, caught him up.

With no inkling that Ariel's father had shared the same thoughts earlier that day, Marcos speculated that Dripping Spring might well be in ruins. He said he hoped his uncle was prepared to find a mess. All those winter snows, drought and rains on and off, and what about the broiling winds year after year? Surely the elements hadn't been merciful, had hammered, chafed, baked, scraped, and finally decimated the place.

His uncle disagreed. "Weather'd hurt it but I doubt it'd take it all the way down. More likely if it's been destroyed, it's been destroyed by men."

Built back at the end of the thirties with the help of laborers from

Las Cruces, the hacienda had been made of adobe over lath. Its architecture had acquiesced to ornament only in the form of some simple porch columns with balustrade and whittled spindles. Otherwise its structure was all simplicity, meant to last. Its white-washed walls were as thick as those of Fort Selden at Radium Springs, Delfino said. The few photographs that had survived their forced exodus were as cherished as any heirloom. In them one could see the raised cistern they used in summer as a swimming hole. One could see young Agnes waving from beside a windmill with *The Kerometer, Chicago* painted on its rudder. A few other adobe structures looked very alike, a barn and stable attached—all built long before Marcos and Ariel were born, indeed even before any of Ariel's parents were born. Delfino had built it as the down-state Montoya ranch, to be passed by his children into the hands of his children's children.

In the absence of heirs, land becomes your flesh, he believed. Land reflects your soul, animates your soul. He carried with him the original deed to the spread and had it in mind, once they were there, to sign it over to Marcos. He could die in peace then, with some dig-nity restored, knowing he'd left an inheritance of earth to his family, just as his father had done.

At the summit of a rock-strewn rise Delfino reined his horse to a halt. This was it. The military range perimeter fence ran along the facing crest as far as the eye could see.

"Last chance to turn back," Delfino told them.

"You're not getting rid of us, old man," Marcos said, and Ariel agreed.

"It's the last time I'm gonna ask."

"Good." Handing over his reins to Delfino, Marcos dismounted and walked back to the packhorse. He whispered into its ear calming singsong nonsense as he unbuckled the leather pouch lashed to the saddlebags and fetched a pair of wire cutters. With the words "Here goes nothing," he tramped across a shallow gorge whose bed was the finest alkali, which crunched underfoot like salt, then up the face of an eroded fault scarp. Scree sprayed behind him. He climbed the last of the little hogback on all fours while Ariel and his uncle watched in the saturating moonlight.

At the crest he knelt, removed his felt dakota, and ran his free hand over the back of his neck. From this vantage he could see for miles into the military reservation, far to the south, and without putting binoculars to the viewfield he ascertained where some bunkers were situated. Some looked forbidding and sophisticated, while others seemed crude, like squatters' cabins. Tricky sons of guns, or lazy. He snipped the barbed wire, making an opening wide enough for them to ride through.

As he walked back to join his companions, Marcos thought about Kip. Hoped the poor devil was all right. At least it was a mild night and, walking, he was under the radar. Riders, too, eluded radar, but without doubt the military had surveillance equipment around here sophisticated beyond what anyone could know. They could probably see your wringing hands from a satellite. Could hear your gulping throat through a digital audio sensor. Maybe, maybe not. Ariel had so far put a brave face on it, but she must be worried sick. She was, he thought as he reached his companions, inspiring, was she not? He had to wonder if he'd do as well in her position, but then remembered that was precisely what he was doing. Birds of a reckless feather. And where was Mary right now? Where had her false wings carried her? No, stay focused. "Let's go."

The klieg-bright moon showed their way. They moved down the near ridge, along the white sand arroyo road, until they found a gentle fold where they could double back toward the forefront of the bluff. Then they came to Marcos's breach in the five-row barbed-wire fence. Even without a flashlight, they could make out a white sign nailed to the post:

Peligro se prohibe la entrada
Campo de tiro armas de fuego en uso

And another, several posts upbasin:

Danger
Unexploded Munitions
Keep Out

Marcos halted and Ariel followed suit so Delfino could enter first. He did, with slow surreal dignity. Jet indigo and dim silver in ranging ephemeral threads were the last colors woven across the sky over the western mountains, colors that clung to the cirrus like psychedelic streamers. The riders, consumed by thoughts as different as the oily pigments ranging over their heads, advanced into a part of the valley that had been sequestered from the public for half the century. Fifteen miles more—much easier miles than those they just negotiated. Ariel couldn't help but glance around, astounded by the secluded peacefulness of the scene.

In the name of Matthew, the name of Mark, in the names of Luke and Saint John. In the name of the prophet Jeremiah, confined by the King of Judah during the war in which Babylon besieged Jerusalem. In the name of Paul who wandered and Noah who would not have but that he had no choice. In the name of Christopher, patron saint of travelers. In the name of any saint possessed of ears to listen, hear my question, I beseech thee. When will the Lord's children ever learn to stay put?

Bonnie Jean, who found herself covering Ariel's watch, argued, "I never ran away from you, did I?"

"You were always a fine young lady, Bonnie. I've never said otherwise."

No denying that. But listen to this. John Howard Payne, who was destined one day for sainthood, good great American that he was, knew whereof he spoke. "Oh yesh," said Granna, whose lispings and liltings off-centered her speech less and less with every passing sentence, it seemed. "John Howard Payne mortalized the idea. *Mid pleasures and palaces though we may roam . . . be it ever so humble, there's no place like—*"

Bonnie smiled, she who always frowned on these routines in the past. How wonderful to hear her going off on one of her crazy jags this afternoon.

—but what she'd like to know was, just when and how had Ariel lost her will to stay home? While Mother didn't express this verbally, the sigh she gave on learning that her granddaughter had probably spent the night in Nambé—given that she hadn't answered at Pear Street when Bonnie phoned to find out how it had gone with Kip Calder—was a sigh that meant, For crying out loud, what's going on with the world?

"I wish I knew," said Bonnie, able to interpret her wordless language.

Millennial madness, no doubt, thought Granna. Things such as this were augured. The sane would act crazy. The crazy would see the light. But this wasn't like Ariel. She wasn't a believer, no, though she seemed to be trying, in her way. She was possessed of common Christian wisdom, wasn't she?

"Remember, I told you she went there last night to find Kip," Bonnie said.

"Nobody will ever find Kip Calder, mar my words."

Granna was amused by the missing consonant, but it made her all the more conscious of Ariel's unhappy absence, since Ariel would have picked up on the vagrant meaning of the phrase, might even have lobbed a little comeback. *Mar your words? Aren't they marred enough, Gran?* And that would have been a sweet kindness, making all this business of recovery roll along with smoothing laughter. As it was, Bonnie caught a glimpse of her grin and gently smiled, tipping her large head to the side like an inquiring cat.

"Like I say, she thinks he's her real father."

"What about Brice?"

"He adopted her."

"I don't believe any of it. I'm worried for the poor girl."

They were sitting on the convalescent center's patio, at the far end. A large glass vase of blue delphiniums on the table, paper cups of cranberry juice, some not-too-fresh meringues. Brice had called to apologize for hanging up and to let Bonnie know that he and Jessica would be coming out next week.

"Home is where the heart is." Bonnie recommenced their game, hoping maybe to fill Ariel's role here.

"Keep the home fires burning," without a pause.

"Land of the free, home of the brave."

Not bad. "Charity begins at home."

Bonnie Jean's smile broadened, an unusual sight. Made her face kind of hurt, a thought that broadened it more. Wasn't this a bit ridiculous, playing games while the universe whirled out of control? Not for a moment. Getting her mother to smile, that was the finest thing. Maybe she should try a little harder to get along with her brother, cut Brice some slack. Couldn't hurt more than that smile did. "When Johnny comes marching—"

"What good's a home if you're never in it?"

"Never heard that one before."

"Bonnie, this breeze's a little brisk. Let's go back in."

"Can't stay put, can we, Saint McCarthy?" Bonnie teased.

Her mother responded with a tangled grin. It was touching of Bonnie Jean to engage in a bit of word-gaming to help an old lady pass the time. All would be perfect if her granddaughter were here and this notion about Kip Calder could be disavowed for the rubbish it surely was. Her life and the lives of her family had always been solid, unquestionable. Yet she felt less certain, now, that things were quite as stable as she'd always believed.

Doubt was a monster she had little experience wrestling. So instead, after Bonnie took her leave, she lay a blanket of faith over herself, over her memories, and wrapped Ariel within its folds as well. After all, tomorrow was Sunday. Day of rest.

*A*ided by the scant shade of a high thin temporary cirrus cloud, Kip rested his eyes. But the cloud passed, and again the sun dazzled and blinded him from its billet in the sky. He pretty nearly couldn't see anything anyhow. His vision had, along with everything else, only gotten worse as the long slow day progressed from Lonnie Moon Peak, or thereabouts, past the wildly misnamed Garden Spring streambed. Garden of rocks and stones and pebbles and sand and dust.

Palms down, he lowered himself onto a dry sedimentary shelf. He unshouldered the beige canvas pack, now soaked brown with sweat. His canteen was light and its water more than warm on his tongue. Knees against his forehead, he sat in a heap. When he looked up he saw that the angel was out there, just as she had been since early afternoon. He looked down at his powdery boots. Didn't remember his feet being quite that small. But there they were, two of them, inarguably measly. Somebody else's feet. Couple of dead marmots.

He spat into his dustbowl palm. Looked like grasshopper spit. Only several streaks of sepia in an otherwise milky froth. Saliva that was mostly air.

He blinked hard and glanced over toward the east again. Yeah, still there. She kept her distance from him, having paralleled his course across the badland. Sunstroke dementia?

Leave me alone, he said, or thought he said.

She made no movement that would indicate whether she heard him or not. She stood, floated maybe, was little more than a white detail on the white horizon. Kip had been trying to shake her all through his second day out here. He sensed he knew that face with its pitiable haunted eyes, but he couldn't place where he'd encountered it before. Had to think harder, think better, more clearly. No friendlies out here, random headings, copy? He said, or thought to say, Keep going, plenty of fuel left. Sure, he was getting some heavy

surges. Incoming, affirmative, and yes the air was scrawled with trac-
ers. But he'd blown down souvenirs along the way, pilotese for hits. It
was give and take all the way. Kip was no rookie, no newcomer to the
blasted heath. He looked for her again, but she wasn't there. Good.

He unfolded the map and spread it out before him. Judging from
where those radio towers were located on the topo and as he sighted
them ahead on the peaks to his right, he'd come in a pretty fair distance, all things considered. He spat again and saw, this time, that
his spit was not brown but red. Ran the back of his thumb over his
gums and tongue and held his hand in front of his eyes, and yes it
was blood. Not good.

Wagner once told him, —The only thing that elucidates history is
blood. Blood inherits and dispenses history better than ideas have
ever done. You can learn ideas and forget them. Whereas blood you
can never learn nor ever forget. Blood's the remnant of all that every
human ever accomplished. Pippers like blood, so do Jollys. Oscar
Deuces love blood, so do Slicks. The machines that kill and the
ones that try to save love blood, is all I am saying. Daisy Cutters
were put here on earth to rid men of blood, and Fox Mikes to keep it
in them. LAU-68s slay your bloody ass while Sandys try to save it.
KIA. MIA. KBA. So many words for so many things, but at the end
of the day there's only one word, and it's either flowing in your veins
or going down with you back into the earth. Dirt knows better what
to do with most men's blood than the donors ever did. Remember
that. And remember to make sure you use your pissant allotment for
positive capable intercept operations, man. You copy, blood? You got
the snot?

Kip's pulse raced in his temples, pounded in his neck, and it was
as if his grandparents and his mother and father and Wagner and Jessica and Brice and the Montoyas and, yes, Ariel, all of them were
risen within him, demanding that he act in a way that would make
them proud. Losing a little blood never hurt anybody. Get up and
get on.

He walked calmly at a thousand feet or ten thousand, who could tell the difference? His blood took on a voice and the voice said simply, Do this. And if he sank to a knee or hesitated, the blood drummed with greater weight and his ears were so burdened with the music of his blood that he found himself paralyzed, shotgun butt hard to his shoulder, double barrels silverblue down the beadline, the ghost in white walking straight into the V of his sights, his finger at the first trigger colder than if he had plunged it, along with hand and arm to the shoulder, into a winter fishing hole up in the high Truchas Mountains.

There was a time in Vientiane, after the West considered the war over and done with, when Wagner and Kip had this bicycle repair shop that served as a clandestine front to help Hmong out of Laos and over into Thailand. A matter of moving them from shithole to ratnest, as Wagner put it. Both men knew it was not healthy to develop a fondness for any of their entrusted wards, given the mission's uneven success rate—the Mekong was a greedy river—and the absolute necessity that Wagner and Kip appear in the eyes of the Pathet Lao to be nonpartisan. Word of a capsized dugout, perhaps overloaded with Lao Sung desperate to get back to Tibet or North Myanmar, not realizing that the Communists would no more welcome them home than tolerate their Buddhism in the new Laos, naturally threw the estranged Ravens into miserable depression. Putting on a brave face, a countenance of ignorance or indifference, only made the job more trying. But imagine if one of the drowned had been, well, the object of an affection. No need to risk double disheartenments when so many individual failures came their way.

Wagner, not Kip, broke the rule once. A woman from Ban Huay Sai who had traveled with her family to Luang Prabang, where he first met her, then down to a safehouse outside the capital. She spoke French and was neither young nor pretty by any orthodox criteria. Her family was huge. Many cousins, many aunts and uncles, many sisters, though no brother. They were diverse in their religious beliefs, which was pretty unusual. Animists mixing with Buddhists and Christians. She told Kip, during the New Year celebration in April, that in her family they were always observing some holy day or other. —*Toujours les Saints, toujours Dieux! A chaque saint sa chandelle!*

A midnight Pathet Lao patrol intercepted their precarious raft just shy of the Thai border. It was July, middle of the wet season. Black low monsoon sky, no stars, and the river running high and inky. Some of the refugees jumped overboard in a panic to escape being towed back to Laos, where they would be sent north to a reeducation camp, never to be seen again. Some were summarily shot. A few were repatriated, Wagner's friend among them.

Neither Wagner nor Kip ever saw her again. She went the way of King Savangvathana and all his beloved family, banished into oblivion after the Congress of People's Representatives decided he best abdicate his ridiculous throne so Laos could become a land of the proletariat, the peasant. When, years later, Wagner himself was disappeared, Kip wondered if he hadn't pushed the Pathet government into it, hoping he'd land in the same camp as she.

Kip would never know, would he. But Wagner would be honored to be remembered, just here and now, out in a desert he'd only read about and never suffered in, as such.

—When you're not sure what you're doing, but you're sure that what you're doing must be done, then you're thinking with your blood, my man, and thus your heart.

His brother Wagner would be proud that Kip remembered all this with clarity. So would his daughter, Ariel. After all, Kip was blood thinking of blood.

Now get on with it, soldier. Down the road.

*T*he voice on the phone was Sarah's, but was not the same nurturing voice Mary was accustomed to hearing. "Franny, I want you to come out to Nambé right now, or else I'm coming to Santa Fe."

Three in the morning. Not like Sarah, either. But nothing had been routine these last twenty-four hours. After leaving the ranch, she spent that night and the following day in hiding. Her only contact with the world was a call from Marcos, on the road to Tularosa with Ariel, reconfirming her promise to keep Delfino's secret. The documents he'd given her during their awful discussion constituted nothing less than a paper time bomb whose fuse could not be lit until the end of this not-yet-dawning day. Mary owed Marcos that much. Delfino's letter and all it meant had to be kept hidden for just a little while longer, and then she'd be free of every Montoya responsibility, whether she liked it or not.

"What's happened?" she asked, innocently as she could.

"Where's Marcos?"

"I—"

"Is he there?"

"He was," she lied.

"Where is he now?"

"I don't know." She was grateful to be able to offer a half truth.

"You know what's happened, and I'd like to know, too."

"What makes you think—"

"You've never lied to me before, Franny, have you?"

Mary mumbled no.

"Don't let me down now."

"I'll come out right away," Mary said, and hung up before Sarah had the chance to say anything further.

A halogen burned at the far end of the long Pajarito driveway, down by the kitchen door. Mary'd driven with the windows open to the biting dry-damp desert air, negotiating the curves along the dusty potholed pueblo road with an abandon that reminded her she was losing control—no, had lost it completely. Sometimes the truth sets you too free.

She made an effort to straighten herself up, appear at least a little calm before entering. The kitchen window was aglow, and she easily imagined Sarah sitting on the banco drinking black coffee, which was how she found her.

Sarah saw her ashen face and reddened eyes but didn't hesitate before asking, "Where are they?"

"Who?"

Silence.

"All of them. Tell me anything."

"Where's Carl?" asked Mary, faltering yet by the door.

"Asleep in bed. Now I've answered you, you answer me."

"I'm not supposed to say until tomorrow."

Sarah glanced up at the wall clock. "It's tomorrow."

"I promised them," Mary shook her head. A further silence, then she said quickly, as if by compacting her words she could make them somehow less real, "Delfino and Kip went to Tularosa. And Marcos went down there after them."

"Ariel, too?"

"I think so."

"What for? Why the exodus?"

"Something to do with Delfino's old ranch?"

"Are you asking me or telling?"

"I don't know." Mary thought, I'm a fraudulent person telling an honest person a mistruth. Great, just great.

"Come on, Franny. What's going on? Not that I don't think I already know."

"Don't call me that," she said.

A truly complicated look plagued Sarah's face. Mary thought she'd never seen Marcos's mother quite this old. Beautiful wrinkled face, weathered eyes. If she and Marcos ever had a daughter—and they never would—she might have looked a little like this in sixty years.

"I just, I wish you wouldn't talk to me like that. I mean, you called me up in the middle of the night and I came right out."

Sarah waited.

"They're going to Delfino's old ranch, Kip and Delfino are."

"No."

"Marcos and Ariel went after them to talk them out of it," and she began to cry, the last thing on this earth she wanted to do.

Worst fears confirmed, Sarah rose, walked to the telephone and dialed Delfino. Nine rings, ten, twelve; no answer. Replacing the handset on the wall phone, she turned toward the young woman and wondered if the right moment hadn't arrived to let her in on the fact that she more or less knew who she was, had known her identity for days. Clifford was the one who had first posed the problem. Mad Clifford, who continued to ask Sarah when Mary was coming again to visit.

"Who do you think Mary really is, Clifford?" Sarah had asked.

"Why, she's my nice niece."

"That was good of her to visit you that time, wasn't it?"

"Very good of her. Very nice."

"You remember when you first came here?"

"No," he said, empty-eyed.

"Me either. You've been here a while, haven't you."

"Long time."

After asking Clifford if he was sure Mary was his niece, she returned to her office and pulled up his records on the computer. Nearest of kin: Russell Carpenter, brother. Home confirmed as Gallup.

Sarah had spoken with the girl's mother not long after Franny and Marcos climbed Tsankawi. Rebecca Carpenter wanted to know where Mary was, whether she was all right, how Sarah had discovered her whereabouts, when could she see her daughter? But while Sarah answered as many questions as she thought was appropriate, she did refuse to provide any address or phone number. At the time it felt deviant, this resolve to side with Mary even as she persisted agilely with her fake identity and Franny persona. But as Sarah told Mrs. Carpenter, not knowing whether she was breaking some law by doing so, "It'll be Mary's decision when she wants to tell me who she is, just as it seems to me it's her decision to be in touch with you. She's fine, but she's got to work this out for herself."

Sarah asked Mary now, "Why did you run away from home?"

"Where'd you get the idea that I ran away from home?"

Sarah thought, Go forward. "Because your mother told me."

"My mother?"

"You act as if you forgot you had one."

"I mean, she's not that easy to find."

"Being such a busy mathematician and all."

Mary said nothing.

"I don't think it adds up, speaking of math. Do you?"

She knew that Sarah knew, though she softly answered, "I'm not sure what you're talking about."

"Funny how sometimes when you're completely certain you understand another person, it's just exactly the moment when you've totally got them wrong. That ever happen to you?"

Mary knew it was now merely a question of how, rather than if or when, to concede the charade. Hers was a tired burden and Sarah might be the last counsel left among her dwindling acquaintance. With a last gasp of false innocence, she asked, "What are you saying?"

"What I'm saying is you're probably going to find that the way back to yourself might be a little more treacherous than simply telling the truth."

"I'm lost," she said, honestly.

"I know, Mary."

Mary sat down on the tile floor, her back against the cool adobe wall. Sarah came over and sat next to her, put an arm over her shoulder. "You must've had good reason to do what you did, Mary."

"I'm not used to being called that."

"Nobody's going to call you Franny anymore, not in this house, anyway."

"Does Carl know?"

"Not if you haven't told him."

"I hope he'll be able to forgive me."

"He'll forgive you because that's his way. Whether he'll understand you is another question. But what he needs to know first is where his brother and son are, and so do I."

Mary drew Delfino's letter and will from her back pocket and gave them to Sarah, who read them with mixed feelings of dread and pride.

Silver above, black below. Never had she been devoured so fully by moonlight. The near world swarmed with sounds. Horseshoe iron scraped and hammered the tuff. Eerie deep whimpers surged from her unsteady horse. The music of a coyote, sharp bluesy bark. Her own breathing gnarled by the taste of sulfur and roses in her mouth.

Deadened by the porous terrain, Delfino's voice up ahead called out, "You with me?"

"Right here," Ariel answered, and a few lengths behind her came Marcos's voice, "With you." Audio guide ropes.

Her back ached, her shoulders were stiff, the insides of her thighs chafed against the saddle. She'd learned to ride as a girl in the up-state mountains along the Delaware—toy hills compared with the colossi here—but this was no bridle path, nor her mount the serene saddle horse she'd grown up with. Under her, instead, was a heavy ranch horse of impulsive spirit who kept her working hard with its sidelong tugs against the bridle and sudden shifts.

They faltered up short and long terraces, down pleats and hollows, stumbling across the valley of extinct firestone. Only a thousand years ago Little Black Peak erupted, flooding this plain, burying Indian fields with blistering magma that eventually cooled into this petrified lode. She wondered how many humans had ever traversed it. Not many. A few traders, settlers. Some lunatics, outlaws, maybe an escapee.

And what was she? Another lunatic escapee? Maybe so. An outlaw? By morning, yes, she'd be considered by some an outlaw.

All she could do was press forward, no turning back. She was reminded of Alice's free fall *down, down, down* the rabbit hole. How Alice, plummeting through the pitch-black shaft, tried to glimpse where she was going but could see nothing in the impenetrable dark. *Ariel in Wonderland.*

A freight train, bound from El Paso up past Vaughn and beyond, moaned behind them on the flats. The clacking of many wheels on the rails played distinct rhythms, and she listened with a detachment that made her realize just how otherworldly her own fall had become. She shook her head. Closed then opened her eyes, closed them again. That was curious, or *curiouser.* What she saw when she closed her eyes was much the same as when they were open. Centipedes of light, pale white phosphenes, flickered like shooting stars.

It was frightening to think of Kip out here alone. Although he'd taken one of Delfino's guns, he neglected to bring along any ammunition. And what in the world had made him think Delfino Montoya would follow his advice to stay home? Kip was, as far as she could make out his pattern, drawn away from others toward an ultimate solitude, a final absence. No compelling argument could contradict this assessment. When all was said and done, despite Kip's confessing yet promising letter in the ledger she carried in her pack, wasn't Ariel just one more of the various others he'd left behind in the course of his continual wandering?

When the last reaches of the harsh malpais had given way to soft desert loam, they dismounted.

"That was the toughest patch," Delfino said. "Smooth as peach fuzz from here on."

"Why is it I don't believe him?" Ariel asked Marcos.

"Because he's lying."

"Swear to god," the man said with a laugh, pouring coffee from a thermos and handing out sandwiches in wax paper, which they unwrapped under a flashlight beam. "Was I lying when I told you I had a good idea about how to ditch them back—"

"Look at that," Ariel interrupted.

"Man," whispered Marcos.

Clusters of tiny topaz lights, not moving like those Hummer headlamps had been, but in stationary twinkling arrays, way down past the farthest edge of the lava field, on the plain between it and the black mountains. Installations, bunkers, maybe enclosed within electric fences or embraced by razor wire—hard to tell from this distance, even with the binoculars. Launching sites, it seemed, and domes housing cameras that recorded high-speed projectiles bulleting over the basin, in simulation of low-altitude warfare, to detonate some target, an abandoned tank truck or retired chopper they'd parked in a fire zone, there to be atomized. No wonder they didn't want Delfino Montoya or any of the other evicted ranchers out here.

Too bad. The three were back on their mounts within a quarter hour.

Sarah was reminded of another such morning as she drove across San Ildefonso pueblo toward the Hill. Mary was fighting for her life in a different way than Kip had fought for his, but she faced unknowns no less intimidating. Maybe more so, given, as Kip himself once said, living is often harder than dying. A lifetime lay ahead for Mary, no matter what decisions she made from this moment forward, whereas Kip seemed to be on a path that led toward relinquishment.

At Pajarito, Sarah had come close to sharing Mary's secret with her husband. Leaving the girl in the kitchen, she woke Carl to tell him she was heading to work early. He squinted at the alarm clock and asked if the spry drifters had returned from their mysterious adventure. Seldom one to hide things from him, she cleared her throat, crossed her arms, and considered what words to use. His face, genial and sleepy before, fell into a rigid scowl when she simply said no.

"Well, where the hell are they?"

One secret or another had to give. Sarah told him about Delfino and Kip.

"Ridiculous," he grumbled.

"What do you want to do?"

"Not a goddamn thing."

"You're not afraid they'll wind up going to jail?"

"Can't wind up in jail if you don't break the law. I don't see them managing to get far enough into White Sands to break the law."

"I think you underestimate them."

"They won't get a hundred yards past the range perimeter. And if they do, getting busted might teach them loons a lesson."

Tough brother talk, but Sarah read his scowl better than Carl might have imagined. She hesitated.

"That's not all, is it," he said.

"Well, not quite."

"What else?"

"Marcos and Ariel went down there to find them."

"Tell me you're joking."

"You want me to bring you some coffee?"

"You're not joking."

"No."

"I'm awake, might as well get up. Did I hear you talking to Franny out in the kitchen?"

"Yeah."

"Well, at least she's got some sanity to her."

She knew her husband to be an understanding man. Allowing people their eccentricities, faults, and mess-ups was one of his virtues, something best learned early by anyone who would presume to work with animals. But unmasking Franny on top of everything else would push beyond Carl's patience. He was the definition of mellow until you got him mad. Delfino and Kip, not to mention Marcos and also Kip's daughter, were enough worry for one day. Besides, once he'd had time to think things over, his first response of hang-it-all diffidence would give way to a much more upset Carl.

"I have to tell Ariel's grandmother and aunt what's going on," she said. "Can't do it by phone, it wouldn't be right. I'll be home early, take the afternoon off so we can figure out what to do."

"All right," said Carl.

"Promise me you won't go doing anything before I get back."

"How could I? As it is, looks like I gotta do Marcos's work, Kip's, and my own to boot."

"Seriously, Carl."

"Don't sweat. I don't know what to do right now, anyway."

The daybreak light was thin and brown. Black Mesa was veiled by a dust cloud. Wind shepherded burrs and tossed bits of bramble. Tumbleweeds bounded across the road in the futile headlights. Mary watched all this, numbly knowing the circle of her conceit had come full around. She felt as mindlessly driven as any of that stuff blown by the wind before them. Everything was out of check, the result of being beholden to too many unraveling promises—Kip's to Delfino, Marcos's to Kip, Mary's to Marcos, Sarah's to Mary. What better place than Los Alamos, she mused, remembering something Kip once said, to arrive with good intentions that might bring about dire consequences?

"I appreciate you coming along."

"Have you decided what you're going to tell them?"

"Well, having got you out of bed to confront you about the truth, I'd be a hypocrite not to let them know where Ariel's gone."

"Isn't it more a matter of your allegiances?"

"You're saying that by telling them where Ariel is, I'm crossing Marcos and Delfino."

"Crossing me, too, kind of."

"You didn't ask me to swear not to say anything."

"It was implied, don't you think."

For a long mile Sarah was quiet. This was forcing her into duplicities, not her stock in trade.

"The Hill must be the only place in the world where if you don't know physics you're in the minority. I'm no physicist by any stretch, but I do believe in the relativity of everything. If space and time can bend, then truth can too, I guess. I'll let them know more or less where Ariel is, more or less what's up."

Mary's turn to fall quiet. Then she said, "After what we talked about this morning, it might sound overbold of me but aren't half-truths also half-lies?"

"Look, Mary. I have another idea. Let's just do the best we can and see what happens. I think the same goes for you with Clifford. Just do him the favor of being his niece. No one in your family's come to see him for a while, except a nephew named Jim."

"My brother." What a strange feeling to say in front of Sarah that she had a brother.

"Nice man. You might want to meet him again sometime."

"I guess for all my father's patriotism, paying honor to his hero brother was a bit much."

"For what it's worth, they used to visit. But then Clifford stopped showing any recognition of your family, until you. It's a long drive from Gallup just to sit for an hour with somebody who's become something of a living ghost. Happens more than you might think. Families tire and fade out of the picture. Your Jim's been by three, four times a year, though. Maybe it's because he's in the military, too. Fellow soldier camaraderie."

Mary had seen him wearing a uniform in Albuquerque at the San Felipe de Nerí festival on her birthday—centuries ago it now seemed. She remembered how young Jimmy used to rib their dad about that black POW/MIA flag. She wanted to ask Sarah about him, and about Johnny. And Rose—did Sarah know what she was doing now? Stifling the urge to learn more, Mary wondered at her own wonder. These names, these people, of course they percolated through her thoughts and dreams from time to time, but she'd come to regard them much as they did Clifford. Distant and distanced enough to have become like characters in a work of drama.

Why was it our minds thrived on forgetfulness? As if the world depended not upon remembering, but forgetting. That she wanted to know new things about those she'd tried with considerable success to forget was something of an internal seismic revolution.

Sarah slowed as they crossed the bridge at Otowi, where the wind walloped crabwise upriver, brawling with gusts that rolled down the canyon ahead.

"That's some storm coming."

"Thanks for helping me, Sarah," Mary said.

Fingerprint-shaped droplets blew sideways over the windshield, soon to gust in torrential squalls so inundating that Sarah had to pull the Jeep over onto the shoulder of the road for a few minutes. Desert deluge, like riding through the carwash, one of Mary Carpenter's favorite Saturday afternoon adventures when she was a girl. She pictured her father in the front seat, her brothers and sister in the back, faces pressed against the windows to watch the soapy tempest.

"There are times when I think things didn't need to go as bad as they did," Mary shouted above the din. "With my family, I mean."

"What brings that to mind?"

"Nothing, the storm just kicked up a memory, is all."

"Bad memory?"

"Good one, actually." Then, "I don't think Marcos will ever trust me again."

Little shadow raindrops crawled down Sarah's face as she looked at Mary. "I guess what you need to think about is whether you want him to."

"He'll be all right down there? With Delfino and the others?"

"He's all right."

The storm strengthened as they continued up the winding pass. At the convalescent center the night staff was signing out. Rain thrashed against the skylight in the main office, and Mary thought anew of the familial joy of the weekend carwash. Crazy, she mused, the things that even seemingly inconsequential sights and sounds could stir up. Franny'd never seemed so removed from her inventor.

"Shall we go visit Mrs. McCarthy first?"

As they walked down the corridor, Mary glanced past open doors into rooms, some dark, others softly lit by bedside lamps. Agony, perplexity, fatigue emanated from those entries, soft murmurs and gentle groans that seared through her. Sarah lay an open palm on her back as they walked, the briefest maternal gesture.

Mrs. McCarthy wasn't in her room. The bed was unmade. The curtains were drawn back. A nightlight gleamed in her bath.

They found her in the east lounge, alone, sitting in one of the deep-cushioned chairs, hands interlocked on her lap, head tilted back to concentrate on the huge panes of glass overlooking Acid Canyon. Water flowed translucent down the windows. But for the early-morning tympany against the glass, the room was embraced by tranquillity. Sarah kneeled beside Ariel's grandmother and said, "Pretty, isn't it?"

Without looking at her, the woman whispered, "Beautiful."

"I understand you'll be leaving us pretty soon."

She turned her head and gazed at Sarah.

"Your daughter's made arrangements with the speech therapist, I saw, and you'll be coming back here twice a week for some follow-up physical work."

"The rain, truly beautiful."

"You can stay if you want, you know. Nobody's pushing you out. You're welcome here."

"Home will be fine."

She had learned to try to avoid words that went flooey in her mouth, ones that might turn *miss* to *myth* or *true* to *shoe*.

"I wanted you to know that your granddaughter—"

"Ariel—"

"You may remember that she came with me down to Nambé to meet Kip Calder?"

"Where—"

"She's with my son, Marcos. This is Marcos's friend Mary."

Mary shook her supple hand and smiled, feeling fraudulent despite having been thoroughly outed. "Hello."

"They've gone downstate for a couple of days and Ariel wanted me to tell you she's fine and will be back very soon."

Sarah looked at Mary awkwardly.

"Good, good," the old woman remarked, as if enjoying the sound of the word, then turned again to the runneling window.

"Good, yes. All right, then. Did you want to sit here a while longer? That rain is so pretty, isn't it."

"You warm enough?" Mary asked.

"I'm fine, good."

"Will you tell your daughter that Ariel's all right or do you want me to let her know?"

"Fine."

Sarah rose to her feet. "I'll tell Bonnie Jean, then."

"Good, you do."

Mary gently stroked a wisp of hair that had caught on the old woman's eyelashes. "There," she said.

"Beautiful," the woman whispered, a rattling stutter at the center of the word.

"I'm sorry?"

"The rain is beautiful, isn't it," repeated Mrs. McCarthy, perfectly enunciating her pleasure.

"It most certainly is, dear."

Sarah took Mary by the arm, and they departed the echoing room to find Clifford.

"K*i-ip*," she shouted, having heard what she thought was a man's voice talking in the encircling wilderness.

Delfino turned in his saddle and said, "Hey, keep it down."

She strained to hear the voice again but didn't.

Marcos rode up from behind. "Let's just get there first," he said gently. "Then we'll find him. You go yelling his name out here and you never know who's going to hear you and yell back."

That was okay. That wasn't wrong. God, she was getting tired. But collected herself again.

Nabor's Tank was the next appointed landmark in this neighbor-less place. It was up ahead in the dark—Delfino could tell by the way the terrain flattened and by the stunted vegetation and the more fria-ble texture of the sandy ground. Even in the middle of the night and all these decades later, he remembered such nuances.

Not much was said for long periods, though now and again they spoke quietly, if only to confirm they were still within earshot of one another. They'd made a lot of miles without a second glimpse of those lights seen earlier. Marcos commented he was surprised they had gotten this far without being stopped. "Maybe they're just wait-ing to see what we're up to before they come try to arrest us," he told Ariel, and she agreed that made sense.

They rode alongside Delfino for a while, listened to him softly whistle an impromptu tune. "How I'd like to have my feet in front of a nice big fire," he said.

"This time tomorrow night you will," said Ariel.

"More likely they'll be *in* the fire," said Marcos, which made her laugh.

At four or so, their clothes began to collect moisture. The huge moon had set. Some matin bird threw itself in bursts through the murk before them, unseen, unheard, noted perhaps by the scant draft it displaced in the otherwise utter stillness. The mountains, their contours discernible now in that they possessed one quality of black, a heavy unrelieved plane of pure lightlessness, while the sky bore another shade, much bluer, backlit, grained with stars—these mountains aptly called *oscura*—ranged close by.

Time passed in jerks and fragments through the night, as one or another of them dozed off, head resting on the leather pommel or rocking forward, chin on chest. The dew that dampened their thighs and shoulders now felt cold on their faces. Gwinn Tank they passed two hours ago, and Nabor's came by now as they cut back up a wash-board road, a rutted trail all but erased by wind and rain, toward Helms Tank, which marked the last leg of the journey. They would arrive around dawn, a little after. Whether they'd arrive alone remained to be seen, but Delfino guessed they were still untracked. Otherwise they'd have been greeted by a cadre of rangers on the western brim of the malpais when they emerged, wouldn't they? He put any hopeful thoughts aside as soon as he conjured them, though. No easier way to bring trouble on your head than to presume its improbability.

Winds began to kick up, harbinger of daybreak. Stretches of sky along the serrated vista—pale, ardent blues and reds—started to gleam. Neon pinks, dim at first, soon would prosper, flourishing toward turquoise, and then the clear horizon would conceive banks of prodigious muscular clouds. Quickening morning breezes coming off the mountains roused the travelers.

"Not far now," Delfino told no one in particular.

First sight of it came in late dawnlight. Marcos fell back with the packhorse. The possibility that Kip might be nearby made Ariel feel suddenly very wide awake. Alert, she breathed in hard and the landscape crystallized before her. But there appeared to be no one at Dripping Spring other than themselves. She tightened her grip on the reins, bringing her horse to a halt, and allowed Delfino to ride up first.

The old windmill still stood, its tail flap looking like the wing of some great russet bird, several windblades dangling, breast feathers ruffled in a blow. That was what she saw before anything else. Then, as they moved across the smooth flats of the low mesa, the rest of the ranch came into view. Its colors were those of the land in which it sat, and so it was discernible mostly by its forms, the collection of man-made angles in a place of natural faults, needles, jumbles, crests, scarps. The porch had collapsed. The tin roof, scalloped like a shell along its fore edges, remained intact but was rusted to the color of a rotten orange. It sat like an origami children's hat, boat-shaped and sideways on its rectangular adobe head. Gutters for rain collection clung to the eaves, and dusty vegetation clung to the rain gutters. Window frames still had traces of green paint on the weathered wood. The house was surrounded by a low stone wall. Delfino tied up his horse, but before he began inspecting the hacienda, he tugged at a pile of metal sheets on the ground at the base of the windmill.

Marcos asked Ariel how she was faring.

"Okay," she answered gamely, climbing down. He helped her tie her horse, and together they got the pack animal unburdened. "What's your uncle doing?"

"I expect he's looking to see if the well's got water."

"You think I can shout now?"

Marcos said, "Don't see why not. We're here, aren't we."

Ariel heard her voice come back to her in echoes after she cried out, "Kip?" Kip-*epp-epp*. "Kip Calder?" forming her hands around her mouth and directing her voice toward the cliffs in the box canyon. Marcos cried out "Kip" with her. They listened but no sound returned other than the aftermath of their own.

"Let's see if we can't help Delfino," she said.

The floor of the collection tank next to the mill was cracked earth, crumbly as Sakrete, utterly porous and useless. Delfino thought water would seep through there faster than through regular ground. Didn't bode well for there being anything wet in the cistern. The three of them peeled back layers of tin siding that had been laid over the artesian well, opened it, and stood back as dank, unmusty but stale air surfaced in a languid burst. That there was any odor at all was a good sign. A dry well would smell like sand, like nothing much. Expecting the worst, Marcos dropped a chunk of stone into the narrow hole. They heard not a damp thud but a small splash. Their faces broke into smiles. Some boiling, some iodine tablets, maybe some filtering through cloth, and the water would be potable.

"Let's see if anything's left inside."

"Just hope it's not a coyote den."

As it happened, the house was unoccupied and barren. When the Montoyas had been forced to evacuate, they hadn't been given much time to pack. Delfino had no precise memory anymore of what they left behind. Had the orphaned belongings disintegrated? Or did they reside now as souvenirs in barracks, or Quonsets, or wherever the people who ran this place lived? In either case, everything was gone and the questions, Delfino realized, weren't even worth asking. The rooms were lifeless voids, covered in fine anemic silt, and were sun-blanched.

Quicker than the gone chattels, morning vanished, too. In the busyness of unpacking and then repairing what was absolutely essential to securing the place—they boarded windows, got the plank door on the front porch to work, barricaded rooms that had fallen into such desuetude as to be dangerous—in the bustle of getting the horses fed, watered, and put up in the scarecrow barn, and paying out their own crude barbed-wire fence around the conclave of buildings, making something of a stronghold, they began to note an important anomaly. And that was this: Still no rangers, no guards, nobody had come out to challenge them, trespassers on restricted government property. Not one soul, including Kip, who Delfino sensed really ought to be here by now, unless he was lost.

"Weird," commented Marcos, who had rigged up a canvas dip pail for the well, which he now lowered to water level on a rope. "I got to confess. Yesterday when we were getting ready, I told myself, It won't be you who unpacks this gear tomorrow night. It'll be some MP laying our stuff out on a tarp so they can take photos of it for the trial. I even heard their questions. Where you folks think you're headed? Montoya stead, we say. Ain't no Montoya stead. Sure there is, up near Helms's ranch by Dripping Spring, we say. Think you better come with us, they say. But at this rate," Marcos went on, "we may wind up running out of food before they even realize we're here."

Ariel, having given up calling Kip's name for the time being, walked over and sat against one of the saddles.

"Still no luck?" Marcos asked.

"No."

"We'll look for him once everything's squared away."

"He's out there. I can feel him."

"Me too," offered Delfino.

"If he is, we'll find him."

They ate in what shade the hacienda offered from the unwavering hard light of postnoon. Exhaustion finally subdued them. Although they'd intended to stand watch in shifts, soon after lunch all three fell asleep in the front room.

Day became dusk. When Ariel woke up, the floorboards under her were uneven, splintery. Her tongue and lips were dry, her legs were sore, her back ached. Her eye settled on nothing familiar. Chinks in the rotted roof conceded tiny divots, creating a small primitive planetarium. Her last thought before dozing had been the same as her first thought now, upon awakening next to the slumbering bodies of these men. Why was she really here? Was she running toward or from frontiers? Perhaps there was truth to the theory that in order to understand who you are, you have to leave yourself behind, wander away from the person you've always known. A matter of perspective.

She stirred while the others continued to sleep, climbing to her feet stiffly, surprised by what a chill marked the air. Hands on hips, she arched her back, leaned left and right, pondering the irony of her having ventured so far only to be less sure now of finding him than she had been the day before.

Maybe this was worse than a fool's game. Risking her job, ditching her parents, not to mention deserting poor Granna, all for an unprodigal father—sheer folly. What could he have to say for himself that would matter? Could Kip truly know one single thing his daughter couldn't very well live without? She looked at Marcos and thought she'd never seen such a blameless face. Maybe should open up to him about some of these confusions. Surely he'd gotten to know Kip during these last years in Nambé.

Walking lightly across the room, her boots in hand, she stepped outside into the muted purple, half expecting to see silhouettes of the men who were going to throw Delfino Montoya off his ranch one final time. She imagined they would have irked expressions on their faces. Pictured the posse lined up as if in an uninspired western, black Stetsons on their heads, their rifles held at angles, chewing cheroots, spitting tobacco. She climbed into her boots, zipped the front of her jacket, and turned up the collar. A peach moon was just now rising on the far side of Tularosa basin.

Toppling jostles of Virginia creeper vines crowded the broken panes along the southeastern face of the building. Hadn't noticed them earlier. Pendant flowers glistening in the thin light. She looked around for kindling. Her boot laces remained untied, trailing behind her as she tramped around what had once been the foreyard. Odd how she had become accustomed to moving around in the dark. Ariel gathered greasewood sticks, staves of mesquite, and brought them back to the firepit they'd built earlier. Kneeling, she lit a match, blew softly into the kindling. The air filled with smoke and then, as if some spirit leapt, the fire danced into fast flames. She fed it with old lumber they'd salvaged from a shed Delfino proposed be sacrificed for the purpose. Fire in the night—Delfino had said it would be one of the best ways to signal their presence. She hoped he wouldn't mind that she'd lit it while he still slept.

A cool draft spilled down the eastern declivity of the mountains. Remarkable how seductive the earth and sky were here, so recurrently dwarfing one's human problems. Long way from home, she thought, yet the basin was oddly embracing in its way. Home is the place where you're most alive, Brice once told his young daughter. She couldn't now remember the circumstances that prompted the paternal adage, but could hear his voice. —Home can be anywhere. On the road, in a rut. Home is wherever you are most at home.

"Ariel?"

Her surprised shriek resounded up the canyon. A silence before they both broke out laughing.

"Didn't mean to scare you," Marcos apologized.

"My mind was a thousand miles away."

"Pretty good fire building for a city girl," he teased. "You planning on burning the barn to make the coffee?"

"Probably not."

"I could use some coffee myself. Besides, I want Kip to see we're here, too."

Ariel said, "The military must already know, so I figured—"

"I'd be shocked if they didn't. Most likely they've already identified us and are running some checks through the computers, seeing if any of us are wanted on other charges."

"Isn't that a little paranoid?"

"Ariel, you're standing at the epicenter of global paranoia. They probably know your shoe size by now, your dental history, your favorite color, whether you put butter on your bread or margarine. They'll swing by when it suits them."

"All I really want to do is hang around long enough to see if Kip shows up, then leave."

"With him?"

"Of course with him, with all of us."

"It's strange talking to somebody's daughter and knowing the father better than the daughter does, but you ought to trust me on this. If and when Kip turns up he won't leave until he and Delfino figure they got what they came here for."

"Stubborn."

"As a jack mule."

The water rolled at a boil and Ariel shook instant into the aluminum pan, then poured the coffee into two tin cups. The fire hissed as if some of the greener fronds were surprised to find themselves being burned.

"We don't know each other, either," Ariel said.

"We don't, but why do you say that?"

"No reason. I guess a person just doesn't expect to find herself in a situation like this with someone she hardly knows."

"I'm not that hard to get to know. A lot of people where you come from would consider my life really boring. I grew up in Nambé, still live there. I want to do what my father's always done for a living. Want to get married someday and have some kids who can either become ranchers or writers or doctors. Just not lawyers. I don't know that many people. Fact is, I know more horses than people."

"People are overrated."

"And horses are overpriced."

"However boring you may think all that is, from where I'm sitting it sounds like unadulterated sanity."

"I didn't say I thought it was crazy. Just boring. You're from New York. That's the opposite of boring."

"My father's a lawyer, by the way. Or, strictly speaking, my legal father, so to say."

"As lawyers go, I'm sure he's one of the good guys," Marcos said. "And if I've learned one thing about Kip, it's never to bet against him. Probably true about both your fathers."

"I wish I'd come looking for him sooner."

"You don't seem to be what my mother calls the *wishtful type.*"

Wishful plus *wistful*—a coinage worthy of Granna. "Wistfulness isn't one of my usual traits, but at least then I would have found him at Pajarito working with you on that fieldhouse, instead of probably not finding him down here in the middle of nowhere."

"Coulda, shoulda, woulda," Marcos said.

"Sarah again?"

"Sarah."

They continued to talk for a while, with surprising ease given the exigency that brought them together there, beneath the growing stars and deepening darkness. A wildcat screeched somewhere up the draw. The bats were out, cloaked in dun velvet, stirring the night. Delfino would soon be rousing.

"Listen, Ariel. I saw a place, couple hundred yards north, where the saddle ridge steepens to a kind of overlook. What I'm thinking is, why don't we hike up and see if there's any lights out on the basin."

They walked by flashlight, Marcos leading the way. Every modest sound—the disturbed stone, the wingbeat of a burrowing owl—registered with grand definition. The climb took what seemed like hours, but when they reached the summit of this foothill saddle and peered out over the night desert, what they witnessed was astonishing.

Moondrenched earth, prehistoric and preadamite. A long garden, the snake offering its pomegranate of knowledge from a perch in the saguaro de vida. Caliban the peccary, Sycorax the scorpion. Ariel lost her footing, nearly slipped into the vortex of this vista.

"Shouldn't do this, most likely," said Marcos, shocked by the immensity of his voice in this rare place. He waved his flashlight like a wand, back and forth, beaconing its sightless eye over the basin floor where another eye might see it. "But if Kip spots us, that's good. And if the White Sands people spot us, that's good, too. Am I wrong?"

"You couldn't be more right," answered Ariel, who waved her own flashlight and began crying out from this aerie. Marcos soon joined her, so that Kip's name flooded the immediate world.

*H*ard to believe that once upon a time Brice McCarthy had lain at night in an apartment in Morningside Heights, his thin mattress on the floor stacked with textbooks, way too wide awake, enduring the difficult music of Kip Calder and his new girlfriend Jessica Rankin making love in an adjacent bedroom. Here and now, as the jet began its descent into Albuquerque, this memory still played devilishly in Brice's head, though Jessica's rested against no shoulder other than his own.

God, though, how they'd loved each other, those two. Kip young and rumpled, strong and restless, brimming with promise. Jessica striding down Amsterdam Avenue in her Dutch clogs and wide-wale cords, holding his hand with both of hers, scads of exquisite heat flowing between them. Brice found such memories painful to this day. Sure, he felt he owned a moral advantage over Kip, given that his politics had proved more sage. He'd been the one to struggle against Vietnam while Kip, like a sheep in wolf's clothing, prepared to ship out any month. But Kip had Jessica. Theirs was a real romance.

Half ideologue, half defeatist, Brice was no stranger to grand concepts. Some of them he even managed to realize, despite himself. Jessica beside him was his wife; to this day he found that cause for wonderment. Their twenty-fifth wedding anniversary, a memorable occasion they eccentrically celebrated on Ariel's birthday instead of their municipal vow date, was behind them. A raucous dinner was held down in Little Italy at a restaurant where Ariel and her then-new boyfriend, David, had arranged everything. Dom Pérignon, antipasti galore, shrimp brochettes dell'Adriatico, fettuccine with squid-ink sauce, Brice's favorite zabaglione with Marsala—a feast of celebration with a dozen toasting friends. Ariel had never glowed with more happiness. And back home that night, he and Jessica made love with the passionate abandon of lusty kids. He looked at her now with no less love, but was aware how these few years since that family meeting about Kip had softly weathered her. The brown hair of her youth, filamented with premature silver from as far back as her days at Barnard, had mellowed to a glowing white that reached her straight, strong shoulders. Her forehead had become more finely lined, and her dark eyes were underscored by half moons of shadow that betrayed the sleeplessness that lately afflicted her.

It was good to be going home to visit his mother. Shame it couldn't be under happier circumstances. Last time he saw her, he'd pledged to return much sooner. Promises most easily made are always the hardest to keep. Ariel was out here, too, somewhere. Didn't want to get in her way, but what he and Jess wouldn't give to see her, talk a bit.

He'd tried phoning Bonnie during the layover in Dallas/Fort Worth, but no one answered. Probably should have let her know they decided to come immediately, even though she'd assured him all was well. Peering out the window into the evening, he saw mountains to the west, dotted here and there with small clusters of pinpoint lights, remote communities separated by vast reaches of uninhabited desert.

Far from the portal that framed Brice's face, thousands of feet below him, Kip Calder waded along in that sere, shadowy ocean. No memories equals no regrets, he happened to be thinking as he strove forward. His credo during the war. What you refuse to remember you cannot rue. Kip's images and those of Brice were naturally distinct, yet resuscitations of people and moments from their mutual pasts twined, like that budding willow they'd leaned against back in Chimayó.

Against the odds, Kip had made progress in his dubious trek. He was stumbling along at the base of the Oscuras now. The map, the compass, the sun, the moon—he was ever the tenable foot soldier. And in truth, he'd been in worse messes than this, had crashed a couple planes behind enemy lines, wended his way through jungle so thick it seemed the air itself had turned vegetable. Here he'd merely stepped on a watch-clock cactus and had several sharp needles penetrate the sole of his shoe, causing him to limp. His foot was probably bleeding in there but he didn't sit down to have a look, for fear he'd be discouraged by what he saw. His lower lip was pasty and cracked, and it hurt as he breathed through his mouth. Had been out here a long time. Two days, was it? What did it matter. He was closing on his destination.

Maybe he was hallucinating again. That angel had disappeared, but now he could swear he heard people crying out his name. A man and a woman. And as the stars began to reveal themselves, two tiny white lights like two more earthbound stars began to shine not too far ahead of him, well below the horizon. Right foot forward, left planted foremost once more, the pilgrim progressed.

Sergeant James Carpenter was the kind of negotiator who could charm the rattles off a snake, but those who refused to be charmed risked getting harmed. That was the word on him at Holloman. He was a follower of rules, no-nonsense, a sharp base MP, not to be messed with. Sometime after midnight, Jim was ordered to duty. Cleared for high-security tasks, he hoped there hadn't been an accident on the range, hoped they weren't mounting a search and rescue. Having been through such ops before, he knew there was little satisfaction in discovering a debris field and dead airman. Twelve of them sat for the briefing. No mishap, but reconnaissance had picked up a single individual, apparently on foot, and a separate group of three, apparently on horseback, that had also crossed onto the military reservation.

This was never welcome intelligence. Often, however, it proved to be small beer. No contact had been made, nor any communication received. Likely scenario was that the intruders were not fully aware of the gravity of their risk. An advance unit was monitoring them at present. Since, by luck, no trials or tests were scheduled, the only immediate liability was their exposure to unexploded ordnance, a problem all would have to live with for the moment. Absent any evidence of espionage, the order was to watch and wait. As everyone at the briefing understood, the area impacted was not particularly sensitive. If some hunters had wandered over the fence hoping to pick off a gemsbok or even a mustang—crazy bastards did that from time to time—the modus would be to escort them back to the perimeter and provide them with a summons that the DOI could follow up on. In the event this was an antinuke civil-disobedience enterprise, another likely scenario, then normal procedures would be followed. Just watch, Jim thought. Bunch of garden-variety tree-huggers. The whole business was going to turn out to be nothing more than a big fat nuisance.

With three troops under his command, he moved out at 0200 hours in a land carrier outfitted with night-vision—didn't bother with the fancy paraphernalia. Or choppers that might create more chaos and drama than the situation called for. They sped along the level interior service road, lighting up the yellow foglamps. It would be a couple hours' drive before they'd come into visual range. The mood among the rangers was spirited. Going to bust some delinquents, always a worthy cause. Jim quashed the capricious atmosphere, however. Men who served under him served with dignity. His silence in the passenger seat inspired the MPs in back to refrigerate.

Last year was the fiftieth birthday of the A-bomb demo model, and they'd anticipated a real ratcheting up of civil disobedience, large crowds of protestors, crews from national television, and what all, but July 16 had come and gone without so much as a serious peep. The usual gang of peaceniks, aging longhairs with their ponytails, antiwar eggheads, disenfranchised ranchers, a few local media types in their double knits and Tony Lamas. Hadn't someone tried to chain himself to the obelisk monument out at ground zero? Escorted him off in bracelets, if memory served, and the story barely made the papers.

Never failed to amaze him how people thought they could change the world through acts like that. Protestors, for criminy sakes. Putting themselves and others in harm's way just to underscore an idea that every man, woman, and child on the planet already understood? Atom bombs are hazardous to your health. So what else was new? Well, the other two outfits were deploying north and southwest of targets, and his team would be going to engage during daylight, after they'd had a chance to run checks up and down the basin towns with the local police, see if anybody was wise to anything.

Quite the breathtaking summer night. The sergeant felt calm with his men, armed and equipped, doing what they'd trained to do. He knew he would need his concentration later, so closed his eyes now and let his mind travel. Times such as this he often found himself wondering where she'd disappeared to, Mary Contrary—the sis he missed. He always suspected she was still in New Mexico, even before Johnny and Rose, the twins, swore they'd spotted her in a crowd at the feast of San Felipe. He supposed he hadn't been the most conscientious brother, given the resources at his disposal. Most everyone was just a couple calls and a few keystrokes away from identification and locationing, unless they were professionally fugitive. He never initiated the query because, well, if she didn't want to be found, he respected her wishes. He remembered too well how Mary and their father had argued, violently, about everything under the sun. Not that he himself hadn't been guilty of bad behavior. Like Mary, he had thought many times about hitting the road, cutting out of Gallup, but he figured there were stayers and players, and he was a stayer. He had apologized to his father long since and they'd made their peace.

He wondered whether Mary wouldn't come back one day, if only to visit their mother. Mary and Mom always got along. He pictured them sewing her costumes for school plays with that foot-cranked, squeaky Singer. That time she trod home from her first waitressing job, in tears because she didn't know where the dessert spoon went, or how to fold a napkin so it resembled a swan, and Mom—who didn't know, either—walked her to the library where they looked all that stuff up in a manual for stuffed shirts. If he could reconcile with the old man, Mary could damn well look in on her mother one day. God in heaven, how families defy logic.

Must have dozed off, since the driver now woke him up. Light was already mustering above, rarefied and tenuous.

"How long I been asleep?"

"Hour, not even. Nothing new happening. Just we're getting up to speed on coordinates."

Information was that the individual suspect would be picked up once his position was secured and the second team could get men into place for an expedient apprehension. The other group of individuals had, according to a preliminary report, established a base camp at coordinates that put them about ten, twelve thousand meters directly due east of the old Trinity blast site on the other side of the mountains—roughly 106 degrees 19 minutes latitude by 33 degrees 19 minutes longitude, it looked like from the shuddering topo spread out on his lap. It was confirmed that they were armed and to be considered dangerous. Their identities were unknown as of yet, and their objectives unclear. No attempt should be made to apprehend them until further information became available. Orders were to secure a perimeter around this encampment. Stay alert and covert, and communicate postyhasty any change in the situation.

Jim confirmed his orders. He had been up through here many times, knew both the valley and the Jornada with the intimacy of friendship, from Bingham to Organ, Oscuro to Engle. He once climbed Salinas Peak with some of the boys and stood looking out at White Sands due south and the malpais to the east. Pure snow and a kingdom of coal to right and left. Truly a wonder, something to behold. Despite what any bleeding-heart liberal protestor might say, the irony was that all the Defense Department agencies that utilized these lands were far kinder custodians than any strip-mall developer would be. Not that anybody would build, let alone shop at a mall here. But still.

He pinpointed their current bearings and located a wash gully up ahead that would let them drive in pretty close without being seen. It'd put them about a mile southeast of the old Montoya ranch near Dripping Spring—or ghost ranch, more like. Quite a ways into the range for a group of protestors or hunters to venture. Wonder whatever happened to the Montoyas. Remember those first briefings at the base, when the rangers were informed about these troublemaking ranchers who felt they'd gotten stiffed way back when. This Montoya'd been a famous curmudgeon for decades. Kind of sad. But everything depends on which end of the telescope you're looking down, does it not, he told himself, and rotated into mode.

The rain diminished. The clouds burned off in castes and tiers. A hundred black-throated sparrows gathered in a tamarisk by the window, their birdsong like bells set swinging by a tacit, spirited wind. A service pole with crossbars looked like an ideogram inked against the lavender sky. The row of yuccas along the walkway mimed green porcupines with spiky quills lit by the ascending sun. A kestrel circled slow as the tip of a minute hand on a veiled clock.

She sat there peacefully, head resting against the back of the cushioned chair, with such a serene smile on her face that the young attendant thought only to place a comforter over her legs so she wouldn't catch cold. Then, standing above the aged lady, she did something she hadn't allowed herself to do since being accepted at the center as a volunteer. It wasn't polite to stare at the infirm, and she'd been a model apprentice, sensitive to the patients and their need for privacy. But no one else happened to be in the room at that moment, and Mrs. McCarthy was, by all appearances, sound asleep. No harm could come of the innocent trespass of looking at her straight in the face. After all, she'd never seen someone this old up close.

"Mrs. McCarthy?" she whispered.

Yes, sleeping soundly.

The girl leaned in near enough to count her wintry eyelashes. She marveled at the ravaged skin, a watercolor version of a river delta painted pink on white paper, the fissures above her apricot mouth. Her delicate nose, the cartilage so thin that the sun afforded it a rose shade, the same color she'd seen in her own hand once when she cupped a flashlight against her palm in the dark to reveal her bones and veins. Eyes sunken, cheeks also. Terrifying, what the years do. The woman's fragrance was soapy and musty at the same time, not unlike spring stink in the conifer meadows after the earth unfroze. Pushing away slowly and silently, the girl's hands yielded the arms of the chair. Sometimes you just wish you could be a painter, she thought as she tiptoed from the room.

Later, she heard the news about Mrs. McCarthy. She cried, of course. Many at the convalescent center did. The woman had made quite an impression on them.

This time it was not Bonnie's niece but rather Sarah Montoya who called her from the hospital to say, in a quiet voice, "No, the news isn't good, I'm afraid."

Telling the family of a death never got easier, Sarah reflected after hanging up. You offered the astringent words—*Your father has died; Your mother passed away this morning; Yes, it's about your sister, I'm afraid she took a turn during the night*—and then your words came back to mock you. *The news isn't good.* How obtuse, how off kilter.

Yet this wasn't the moment for self-criticism. Getting in touch with Marcos, and through him with Ariel, became paramount. Mary drove Sarah back to Pajarito under an implausibly blue sky, the radiance of which Bonnie's mother, Sarah's charge, and Mary's very brief acquaintance would have laughingly celebrated with a chalice of gin and a pull on her cracked clay pipe.

Shalom, she'd have said. *Adíos,* Amen.

*A*riel and Marcos returned to find Delfino making supper. The smell of cooking mingled with the desert perfume of his faithworthy patch of land, raising memories of Agnes here. After a simple meal under the stars, the three busied themselves with cleaning the casita by candlelight. The room sashayed with shadows and quivered whenever a taper flame was brushed by a sudden small breeze. Powdery dust filled the chamber, catching the light and monochromatizing the air. It made Ariel feel as if she were in some vintage movie. *High Midnight,* maybe.

"I'm beginning to feel like this is my new occupation, fixing up abandoned houses," Marcos said, breaking the silence.

"The fieldhouse in Nambé was abandoned. This here wasn't."

Marcos shrugged off his missed shot at levity. To Ariel he said, "So what is it?"

"What is what?"

"Your favorite color."

"Paisley," she said.

"Come on."

"Really, I like them all."

"That's cheating."

"But it's the truth. Truth isn't cheating."

They worked on, taking occasional breaks to step outside and listen to the night. Nothing stirred other than the occasional waterfall of wind down a stone crevasse.

An hour later they stopped. Although it was colder this night than last, the dust they had raised in the sala sent them back outdoors coughing, and they collected around a fresh-stoked bristling fire, sitting in their makeshift bedrolls. Ariel listened to Delfino muse while Marcos drifted off to sleep by the flames that flickered across the old man's eyes. For her it was a way of pushing back the dilemmas she would soon have to face. David more distant than ever. Her pregnancy so speculative that the fetus might as well be residing in another womb. Yet with every passing day it took greater hold of her, whether or not she willed it out of mind. At what moment had it graduated from blissfully undifferentiated tissue, from the androgynous, to take on female or male characteristics? Would it be a girl or boy? Would she or he have brown eyes at birth, rare in babies but not without precedent, given that Ariel herself had been born with them? Jessica had told her that at the hospital they'd tickled her toes when she was asleep, just to wake her up so they could marvel at those brown eyes. Please stop it, she thought, and said "Really?" to Delfino, not knowing what he'd been saying these past fleeting moments.

"This land here," he said, bringing her back into his purview, "was always a land rich in argument, if nothing else. You might not be able to get a good crop, a strike of gold, a drink of cold water, but you could always get yourself a good fight, goddamn guaranteed."

He spoke of this century, the last century, the century before. Fighting and warring made up the history of most populated scraps of land in this fighting earth. Take this particular stretch of gypsum sand and dead playas and craggy lavabeds and broiling summers—you'd think there wasn't much point fighting over such a desolation. But people have come here from kinder places than this, and what for if not to fight. "You know what pyrite is?"

"Fool's gold?"

"Iron disulfide, fool's gold. In the seventeen nineties some idiot French priest comes into this valley and what does he do but turn himself into a gold miner. Lost Padre, they called his strike. The fact nobody ever found either him or his mine never stopped people from killing each other trying."

What they were doing here had been done before. That was on the other side of Little Burro, Lady Bug, Skillet Nob.

A woman named Mary McDonald and her uncle Dan had gone into the range without permission, from up off Route 380. Got all the way in to their ranch, quite near Trinity Site itself—a ranch that had once been the homestead of Mary's father, Dan's brother George, himself a briery ranchman. What nettled the authorities was that Mary and Dan managed to settle into the old place for a good three days before they were discovered trespassing. Niece and uncle had built a fence around the house and when the rangers showed up to escort them out, Uncle Dan brandished his shotgun and Mary sighted down her thirty-thirty rifle and told them to stand away. As fate would have it, one of the guards had unsuccessfully courted Mary back when they were in high school.

In the calmest voice he could summon, he said, —Come on, Mary, now put that gun down.

—Stand back, she says.

—Well, I'm here to take you two back home.

—We *are* home, was what Mary said.

—Aw, be reasonable. You know you can't stay out here.

—We're staying, says Mary and raises her rifle and trains it right in his eye.

—Now Mary, you know you wouldn't shoot me. We go back too far.

—Step past that fence, you'll find out how far back you go.

"That's a good story," Ariel said, seeing that Delfino had paused to think. "What happened to them?"

"Well, they got talked into leaving. Told their case would get A-One priority consideration in Washington. Surrendered their guns and left the way they'd come. They probably had their suspicions it'd be the last they'd ever see of the place, but their hopes were raised just high enough so they left figuring they'd won the battle and maybe were on their way toward, well, not winning the war, maybe, but at least reaching some kind of peace treaty. An agreement they could live with."

"And?"

"Both of them are dead now. One of cancer, one of heartbreak. Government still owns their land. Squatters with the biggest guns on earth."

Delfino sat for a while, watching the fire dance. Then spoke again.

"The best was old John Prather, though. Gave the feds conniption fits. His place was down south, below the Sacramentos. Scrappy land, couple dozen thousand acres of it between what he'd been deeded and what he leased. Like a lot of cowmen down here, his people come over from Texas in the eighteen eighties and built something out of nothing. Less than nothing. Agnes always said Prather was kind of Egyptian, the way he managed rainwater. Dug long earth catch-sinks with nothing more than a team of horses and an iron follow-about plow. He dug a thousand-foot well while he was at it. Anybody out there thinks they know hard work can try that sometime. Let them try and make a living from raising desert cattle. Prather did."

Delfino reminisced about how the United States district court in Albuquerque had, in October 1956, ruled in favor of the condemnation proceedings initiated against Prather by the army and ordered him to vacate his land by the end of March the following year. The government needed to annex his property for expansion of its missile testing and military training procedures. Prather wouldn't budge. He told the army boys to bring in a coffin, said he'd rather die at home than become some tumbleweed blown around by their hot air.

His case had been of interest to Agnes and Delfino Montoya, to people like Hop Lee and cross John Harliss, to all the dispossessed ranchers in the area. Nike missiles were the future, not cows. It was a Cold War whose instruments of mitigating deterrence were being readied in the burning furnace of the Jornada and Tularosa deserts. Old Prather told them to come on over and shoot him. They offered him a couple hundred thousand bucks, plus he could keep his house if he didn't mind living in a live-ammunition zone. Didn't interest him. Some United States deputy marshals were sent in to coax him out, no luck. Held out to the bittersweet end.

"They finally killed him, then?"

"Course they did, but slow-like."

"You mean—"

"Heart or cancer, I forget which."

"You really admired him."

"Admired, hell. I wish I *was* John Prather."

Ariel lay forward in her bedroll to face the tapering fire. Her head was too warm, but her legs were cold, the blankets dampened from night dew. She sensed that by sometime the next day all this was bound to come to a head. The military police had to be onto them. If her augury about Kip's being nearby proved wrong, then tomorrow would still bring a crisis, because she would have to leave Delfino to his own war, wouldn't she? He would understand she had to go look for Kip, maniacal as it might sound. On the other hand, what's a daughter if not someone who takes up the cause of her father? Especially a father who risked his life advocating. No, she'd stay put. Brice the advocate, Kip the advocator—sleep came over her in dark waves that washed these conflicted thoughts beneath them, even as Delfino told more stories.

Stories about how at a moment in history defined by communications, by digitalized and microprocessed interfacing, by information equals power, here where she and Marcos slept on the floor of the desert was a kind of human black hole, where the fracture between what was known within and what was known without couldn't have been more complete. You could look over the long fence, but you wouldn't see anything. And if you did happen to see something out there hovering above the white dunes, it would be incomprehensible to you, and if you tried to explain what you'd seen to others, they would shake their heads and question your sanity. Inside the base, they spoke the same language but kept what they knew to themselves. Stealth—just one of the many black appliances they tested under cover of night out there in their spacious playground—could not have been more aptly named. *Stealth* was the word, and the word was *stealth*. Sometimes you might notice a particular hue in the sunset over the mountains, and you couldn't help but wonder if it was their doing, if they hadn't got it in their heads to recolor the sun, maybe give the clouds a fluorescent shot in the arm. At night, you were awakened from your sleep by something as subtle as the faint odor of borax. You imagined them out there in a distant playa lakebed. You watched their latest secret flying machine afterburning impossible golds and pinks. Saw a fuselage incinerated and a wing twirlingly ascending moonward, after the pilot lost control and bailed out as a quarter-billion dollars' worth of equipment plummeted to earth, the fiery spitball of covert hardware gone down in peacetime defeat. And nutty though they were, the theories about Roswell spacemen didn't begin to cover the point spread. Little green men with pumas' eyes might fly their saucers here, beaming up housewives and family pets, but they had nothing on local technologies. While you and everyone else slept, the real spacemen were at it. And in the morning, if the ore-of-boron odor had been dispelled by frolicsome breezes, you'd wonder whether the whole business hadn't been just one more bad dream. There would be nothing to suggest otherwise. And soon you would forget the whole nightmare and carry on with your life, such as it was.

The freeway north was a hasty light show of shrill crimsons and strident whites. Lit billboards and roadside markers, the radio offering a Haydn quartet. Tankers, buses, long haulers, all the streaming cars—where on earth could so many souls be going at this hour, not yet midnight but late enough? Sleepy Albuquerque no more.

They had no idea where they would spend the night but felt giddy from the altitude, if not from the unordinary frisson of having dropped everything to do what had to be done. Normally they'd be asleep in bed by this hour, but tonight they couldn't be more awake. Granted, Jessica had napped through the second leg of the flight. But Brice was wired, even euphoric. Everybody who meant anything to him was here, one way or the other. Duly acknowledged: All was not as he might have wished. Ariel had not been communicative. His mother's condition worried him, as did his rapport, or lack thereof, with Bonnie Jean. Kip had, like a new moon, dropped into obscurity. Still, Brice felt optimistic, heartened to be with Jess in the old home state, Land of Disenchantment, as he teasingly called it from time to time. New York, rife with its own disenchantments, often swallowed them up with its reliable solicitude. The client lunch. The court appearance. The dinner with friends. The gym. The movie. The equity trade. The Sunday paper, itself a kind of immersion labor. It was good to be away, even under the circumstances.

"Did I ever tell you that the last time I was here I spent the night in Chimayó in the backseat of a borrowed car?"

"I hope you're not proposing a repeat performance."

"Seriously, I did."

"What was the point? Revisiting your wild youth?"

"Hadn't thought of it like that. But maybe you're not wrong."

"I love it when you put it that way," she laughed, switching Haydn to rockabilly and turning up the volume. "Maybe possibly I might just be almost not totally incorrect."

Brice changed the station back to Haydn. Albuquerque's lights were left behind, and the hour of desert between them and Santa Fe intervened.

"Look. Sleeping in the backseat of a car, if you're older than sixteen, smells a little like midlife crisis to me. Next thing you know you're shopping for the red Porsche and the standard-issue twenty-something mistress."

"This isn't fair. I couldn't find a place to spend the night, so I was forced to rough it."

"Actually, it's kind of sweet."

"Sweet?"

"You heard me."

When they rolled past Santa Fe and back into the darkness of the highway stretching through unpopulous pueblo terrain, the idea of reaching Los Alamos after midnight began to seem iffy. As the sign for Tesuque drew into view, Brice realized his allusion to sleeping in a car those few years ago had some relevance. Without warning, he took the turnoff, and when Jess asked what was up, he said, "I think we ought to go back and spend the night in Santa Fe. Rumor has it you prefer beds to backseats."

"Where'd you hear that?"

"Seriously. It just dawned on me they roll up the sidewalk at seven o'clock on the Hill. Nothing's going to be open. Even the motel keepers up there bolt the latches early."

Circling back through Tesuque, they traveled a narrow road by a dark creek, Haydn having given way to Ravel's *Le Gibet*, and half an hour later found themselves checking into the grandest old hotel on the plaza. La Fonda was a splurge, yes, but they took a suite and held their guilt at bay, knowing that tomorrow they would enter another world to share the responsibility of helping with Mother's recovery. Tonight was their night, Brice reasoned, since tonight they could do nothing to ease his mother's burden. Into the wee hours they walked arm in arm around the square and had margaritas at some local hot spot, returning to the inn to fall into bed exhilarated, tipsy, and finally exhausted.

Rather than dropping in unannounced the next day, Brice phoned Bonnie Jean midmorning, but as usual lately, no one answered. Maybe the gray skies and thick rain influenced their mood, perhaps the mild tequila headaches contributed, or possibly it was their waking up so near Los Alamos and the gravity of affliction to be faced there, but as they checked out and retrieved their rental from the underground lot, their prior festiveness dissolved into a kind of unreal mist.

On the road lay real mist, the showers now streaming down at odd

angles, driven by winds that couldn't seem to make up their minds—
if winds had minds—which way to blow. Brice knew these south-
western storms tended to clear as fast as they cropped up so wasn't
surprised by the columns of light that pierced the clouds over honey-
combed cliffs and rain-sparkling ridges of the mesas. But Jessica
stared, awed, at the graduated vistas draped in vapor, popping into
sudden brilliance whenever a cleft opened in one of the cloudbanks,
allowing the morning sun its passage onto plateaus and into their
flanking valleys.

This route was so deeply inscribed in Brice's memory that he
could almost drive it blind, which in a way he did. Questions for his
sister began to bother him, some mistrusting, some accusing, none
of them very genial, and all of them too familiar. The same old Brice-
versus-Bonnie interrogatories that plagued them since forever. Yet he
wondered, feeling this somber mood settling over him even as the
storm lifted and the morning promised a beautiful day, what would
happen if, just this once, he let it slide? Wouldn't it be best for their
mother to see the two of them getting along?

Funny how such a generous idea could make you feel depressed.
Bonnie would chastise him, as always, for having left the Hill and
gone on to build a life elsewhere. She never shelved her judgment
that in disavowing Los Alamos, Brice disowned not merely his birthplace but also the family that continued to call it home. Although he
considered himself more a flag waiver than a flag waver, he knew he
might spend the rest of his life trying to make peace with the place,
attempting to hammer out some kind of personal deterrence pact.

Just because you're forged in the same furnace doesn't mean
you're shaped for the same task. Ask any cog, ask a girder. But as he
and his wife passed the abandoned guardtower and the landing strip
at the edge of town, Brice had an epiphany. One that their mother
would understand. Turning the other cheek, wasn't that the traditional gesture of righteousness? As he drove to his sister's house,
Brice promised himself that no matter what, he wouldn't chide, re-
criminate, or quarrel. Bonnie was who she was. Ariel, too, and Kip.

Father and Mother had both been—still were, really, since death didn't have the power to transform the unique *youness* of any given *you*. Just cuts you off from further variations on the theme. But why brood about death? Here was the house, ever the same. Dusty millers and geraniums on the front steps. The door framing the lean figure of his nephew Sam. Wonder if he'd recognize his uncle. Last visit he displayed no sign of even knowing he had one.

This time was different. As Brice and Jessica strolled up the puddled walk, Sam said, "They're gone."

"Sam, you remember your aunt Jessica?"

The boy had shot up a good foot, was now a young man, all in little more than three short years.

"Hi, Sam," Jessica said, now on the porch, the boy's face behind the screen coming into focus.

"They're at the hospital with Granna."

"Sam, you okay?" Brice asked.

"I'm supposed to stay here," he said.

"All right, then. We'll go over to the convalescent center. I think I know where it is."

"Not there, the hospital."

"Is it about Grandmother, Sam? Did she get sick again?"

"I think so."

"Sam, have you been crying?"

"No," he lied, sheepish.

They stood, the three of them, on opposite sides of the screen door, through a few more awkward moments, before Brice said, "We better get to the hospital."

He recognized her face from a distance down the corridor and saw how pale was his sister, how bent and stiffened by grief, and he knew, without having to ask, that their mother was gone. Bonnie Jean embraced him, weeping, apologizing, her countenance rent by what seemed a mad smile but was instead the most sorrowful grimace Brice ever witnessed. Stricken by what he saw in that face, he felt the weight of his own loss fully hit home. He wanted to weep but somehow couldn't. Even through his own coursing grief, Brice understood his sister's world had changed profoundly, irrevocably, saw that she had lost her mother in a way he himself had perhaps not. Eyes shut tight, he tried to picture Ariel's granna but could conjure only Ariel herself. He asked, "When?"

"This morning."

They pulled away from their embrace. Charlie joined them, shook Brice's hand. "Bonnie, I'm so sorry," said Jessica, as her husband drew her in to his side. A clumsiness of inhibition—or was it the silence that comes when anything expressed seems paltry?—overcame them, until Charlie said, "She had a massive stroke, they think. Nothing anybody could do."

They walked, a sad stricken family, down the hall. He couldn't help but think how close he'd come to seeing her alive one last time. Guilt began working the edges of his thoughts, all too late. The promise he'd made to himself before would have to be observed, now, to a fault. He and Bonnie Jean were the elders and had best act as such. Little mattered more than honoring that and helping to bury their mother beside their father. Indeed, nothing mattered more, with the exception of seeing Ariel. Jessica's thoughts were much the same, and while Brice briefly disappeared to pay respects, she floated the question. "Can I ask, where's Ariel?"

Bonnie nodded as her husband said, "She's been staying at Mother's. Was with her all the time until just a couple days back."

"She's been a real caring granddaughter."

"Where is she? Does she know what's happened?"

"She went down with the lady who works over at the center."

"Convalescent center? Went down where?"

"Went with her down to Nambé."

"The lady at the center, what's her name?"

"Sarah Montoya. She brought Mother in. She was just here."

Jessica excused herself and asked at the nursing station where she could find a pay phone. The receptionist at the convalescent center said Sarah had left for the day, but after Jessica explained who she was, the woman gave her the number for Rancho Pajarito. As she dialed, Jessica experienced her own epiphany, or something more basic than an epiphany, a simple truth that she seemed temporarily to have forgotten, to have let go, unremembered somehow this past month. That was to say, she had lost track of herself, utterly, in losing touch with her daughter. She'd intuited what lay behind Ariel's erraticism, though perhaps not down to any specific problem; she wasn't psychic. But it was becoming clear to her that her daughter's journey away from home was to some degree an invitation to embrace. Why else had she tramped all this way, if not to claim more family, another family? That wasn't rejection. It was a need proclaimed. She could be wrong, of course. She'd been wrong before. But still the idea took hold.

Carl answered.

"You don't know me, but I think my daughter may be staying with you—Ariel Rankin?"

"Where you calling from?"

"Los Alamos."

"You got a piece of paper?"

They dropped by Pear Street on the way to Nambé. Brice spent a few minutes alone inside. He poured sour milk down the kitchen drain and collected from his mother's refrigerator uneaten food—cheese ringed with green halos, a cutlet still wrapped in butcher paper, old relish, an apple, placing everything slowly into a black garbage bag. He watered the plants. He wandered the few rooms, touching surfaces. A few of Ariel's clothes hung in the closet of his mother's bedroom, alongside hers. These he touched, too, with tentative fingers, then withdrew. On his way out, he locked the doors his trusting daughter had left open, knowing as he did that there was little left to protect here beyond memories. Returning to the car, he remembered that Ariel might not have a key, and so went back to the front door and unlocked it.

The place where they headed, usually a place of routine, the workaday, was thrown into its own disorder. Sarah was on the phone, following one false lead after another. And Carl found Franny, or Mary, in Kip's fieldhouse. Sarah had told him she might be down there.

He had seen the world fly into pieces now and again, and this to him was a pretty fine example of things falling apart, like the poet said. Not his poet, but Kip's. He'd appreciated the line when Kip first used it and asked him where it came from.

—Irish poet, Kip answered.

—Friend of yours?

—In a way.

The fieldhouse looked startling to Carl, captured in sunlight as it was. Like some perfect haven from a world where things fell apart. "Mary?"

So he knew. She got up from where she sat on Kip's bed as Carl walked in. "Did Sarah find them?"

"Either they're giving her the runaround or else they really don't know whether they're out there or not."

"Which is it?"

"My guess is runaround. I know you already told Sarah about— everything. But maybe you could explain it to me, too. I don't think I've ever come up against anything quite so strange as knowing somebody who turns out to be somebody else."

Mary sat back down, gathered her hands together as if in rest- less prayer. "My apologies, under the circumstances, probably don't amount to much. Any reasoning there may've been behind my se- crecy seems beside the point with everything else that's going on. I really and truly do apologize, though. I hope Marcos wasn't so angry or hurt by my telling him that he's gone out and done some- thing stupid."

"He may get arrested, they all might, but other than that I'm kind of glad he's down there. Delfino and Kip got no business doing what they're doing. I don't know. I grew up lucky, I guess. Luckier than my brother who always had the itch to move on, make a new life where the old one wasn't all so bad. He'd disagree to this day, but that's him. Delf and Kip are cut from the same cloth. Maybe you are, too."

"Until I met Marcos."

"You might've had better reasons. None of my business, most likely. Screwing up is what most of us do most of our lives, day in, day out. So long as you set things right once you recognize you crossed up, you're fine."

"What if other people don't let you set things right?"

"You've done your job. You can't save them from their messes. But we think of you like family. You're square with Marcos, you're square with all of us. Which isn't to say I'd like to do this again, find out your name is—"

"Mary Carpenter and nobody else."

"Good name."

"That's what Kip said."

"Let's get back to the house."

They walked up together, Carl with his hand on Mary's shoulder for part of the way. Mary hadn't the heart to tell him she was leaving for Los Angeles as soon as she could manage.

Startled out of his sleep by a nauseous cry, Marcos jolted upright. Embers in the small fire glowed like incandescent beads. Delfino snored, he who was supposed to be sentry, curled on the earth in his blankets. Cause for concern. Maybe this really was beyond the man. What did they think they were doing, sleeping unprotected out here? Better cold in the ruined house than warm in the open. Seeing that Ariel wasn't in her bedroll, Marcos hoped she'd simply had the good sense to return inside. His mind flitted as he climbed to his feet and made toward the house to check. Then again, a soft retching whimper outside the theater of firelight.

He turned toward the noise thinking, Kip? All was suddenly quiet, then more vomiting, painful to hear against this tranquil darkness. Maybe some animal.

Instead, by the windmill, Ariel half sat, half leaned, forehead pressed against the wooden wall of the collection tank.

Marcos tripped on a concrete rim of some sort, or rock slab, but didn't fall. Made his way through the black. She was crying.

"Ariel? What's the matter?"

"I'm all right."

He hesitated. "Can I do something?"

"No."

Finding her with his fingertips, he knelt and held her by the shoulders, steadying her. He'd never touched her before. "You're probably sick from, I don't know, maybe the water's a little off. Or from exhaustion, nerves."

She said nothing, ceased with the tears.

"We better talk with Delf about getting you out of here in the morning. I'll come back for Kip myself, or we can phone them, tell them there's a man who wandered onto their precious firing range by mistake."

"I'm not going anywhere," she said. Her body was drenched with sweat. What she wouldn't give to climb into a hot bath. She spat and wiped her sleeve across her mouth.

"You can't very well stay out here like this."

"I'm not sick, and it's not tainted water."

Aware of his clumsiness, Marcos felt her forehead, not really knowing what else to do. "What's wrong, then?"

Her confession that she was pregnant was so softly whispered he misbelieved his ears. His eyes had adjusted to the moonlight now and he could see the travail on her face.

"Don't worry," she said. "It's not like I'm going to have the baby. At least I don't think I am. There's no husband, no fiancé, no boyfriend, even."

"Virgin pregnancy. I thought that was unique to Jesus' mother," which caused her to laugh, or try to. Reminded of his own Mary—

Franny the Judas, or was that too bitter?—he had to wonder whether some betrayer had left Ariel in this jam, different from his, of course, but still a jam. He found himself wanting to help Kip's daughter but had no idea how to begin or even if she'd let him. "None of this is my business."

"Marcos, I'm feeling better now. Let's pretend our talk never happened."

Contradicting himself, he asked, somewhat more gravely than he might have wished, "You're going to get an abortion?"

"Yeah, well, I wanted to meet Kip before I went ahead with anything one way or the other. There was a time when he and my mother could have aborted me, had every reason to. She would have had to go to Mexico to do it, or pay a king's ransom for an illegal job. But obviously she didn't. It's crazy. I haven't even told her yet that I'm pregnant. You're only the second other person who knows. Lucky you, right?"

"You can tell me anything you want, don't worry about it." Marcos thought to ask what made her presume Kip had any insight into the matter, but she seemed to anticipate his question.

"Not that Kip knows about being a parent. Not that he should necessarily even care about me or my mess. I've come so far I barely remember what I was thinking when I left. It all seems pretty surreal."

He patted her on the back. Inept fraternal gesture. Again he pulled his hands away from her in the dark. She hadn't noticed, it seemed, any of these small conflicted movements.

"Have you ever found yourself at an impasse, where you really needed to make a tough decision, a crossroads decision, but instead of making the choice, this road or that, you just dropped everything and took off in another direction completely?"

He was speechless, reminded again of Mary.

"I didn't think so," she answered herself. "You're smarter than that. More grounded, centered. I thought I was grounded, but there's a big difference between being centered and being untested."

"My guess is you're being hard on yourself."

"What makes you say that?"

"Like father, like daughter. Kip told me a lot about his life, you know. I think if he was here he'd tell you that when he left you and your mother for Vietnam, he was anything but grounded, and he's out there right now still trying to prove to himself that he's worthy."

"Of what?"

"Seems to me he's spent the second half of his life trying to make up for the first. Kind of sad, since I think he's a far better person than he seems to think he is. He's helped me in ways I'm sure he's not aware of, helped my whole family. And now he's doing what he thinks is best for my uncle, even though it's turned out to be a pain in the ass for all involved."

"When he left my mother and me, he may have thought he was doing us a favor. For all I know he was right. But sometimes when you think you're doing the best for somebody, you're really throwing a monkey wrench into their life."

Marcos said, "Look, Ariel. I'm usually not so forward, but you might want to think twice about an abortion."

"It's ironic," she said, standing up with his help.

"What?"

"To be talking about this in the middle of a proving grounds."

Without giving any thought to whether such a gesture was grounded or not, Marcos drew Ariel toward him and kissed her. Less surprised than she might have been, she held him close, her breath quickening and shallow but her mind unexpectedly calm.

"I must taste awful," she whispered.

"You don't."

"Besides, we probably shouldn't," though if asked, she might not have been able to explain why not.

"I know."

Hand in hand, they walked back toward the dead fire, woke up Delfino, and the three of them retreated under the fallen casita eaves for the balance of their second night at Dripping Spring.

A week had passed since her mother shared with Rose the secret. That she'd spoken with a woman in Los Alamos who claimed to know Mary's whereabouts. Like Edward Stratemeyer, who under the pseudonym of Carolyn Keene had written the immortal Nancy Drew tales that Rose loved to read to her toddler daughters, Mary had assumed an alias. Rather than thinking any of this weird, Rose marveled at how adventurous her big sister had become. Imagine, taking a pseudonym. It was fantastically romantic, something all of us should do once in our lives. She wondered what Mary's new name was and how it would feel when she walked like a movie star right through the front door of the old house here in Gallup, glamorously triumphant. Stranger things happened each and every day.

"Mrs. Montoya called again," Rebecca told Rose after the girls finished lunch and had been tucked in for their afternoon nap.

The house was warm and quiet. A jar of sun-brewed tea sat on the windowsill. Rose was slicing a small hard lemon to add to it.

"What did she say?"

"She said she thought I should meet with Mary."

"What does Mary think about that?"

"I'm not sure she knows."

"You're gonna do it, aren't you?"

"I should probably talk it over with your dad first."

"What for? You know what he'll say."

"No, I don't. We haven't talked about her for quite a while. Your father's a fair man."

"Not when it comes to Mary," Rose said, then mused, "Funny, here I thought she was in Hollywood or New York City all this time pursuing her acting."

"She was supposedly in Denver."

"And now she turns up in Los Alamos. You see, I must've been right that time in Albuquerque. She *was* there."

"Probably she's in Los Alamos because of Clifford. She was always the most independent-minded of you kids, but everybody needs family."

"Is that what the lady said? That Mary was there because of Uncle Clifford?"

"I just assumed."

"Well, you should go. You could tell Dad you're going to visit Clifford. You haven't been to see Uncle Cliff in the longest time."

"I don't like lying to your father."

"That's my point. It wouldn't have to be a lie. There's not one good reason you shouldn't go and there are a hundred reasons you should. I'll go myself if you watch after the kids."

"It's not your responsibility."

"It is if you're not willing. Look, why don't you ask John to go with you?"

"He's got his job."

"So he takes a couple days off. I'm sure he'd be honored to be asked. I'll do the house stuff till you get back."

"You've got it all planned out, don't you."

"Ma, you have no choice. She's your daughter."

"Russell's gonna be plenty mad."

"You don't know that for sure. You might be surprised. He could think it's the neatest thing his wife's done in years."

Rebecca stirred from her chair. Without saying another word, she walked into her bedroom, closed the door. Rose put ice in two glasses and poured tea into one of them. Half an hour passed, the wall clock ticking methodically, the fridge humming, cutting off, humming again. Then the bedroom door opened—Rose could hear its hinges from where she sat—and her mother returned to the kitchen.

"You want your tea now?" She got up to replace the melted ice with fresh cubes.

"Thank you."

"And?"

"Let's call Johnny," said Rebecca.

*H*e walked dead into the Oscuras. From flats to harsh verticality, gray stone stabbing upward. He walked, stopped walking. He stood wobbling in the center of a light-duty road, holding the map up to his face. White Sands range was depicted in the most sumptuous pale pink, with contour lines in brown and the few trails and roads in puce. He tried to hark but nothing came of the effort. His ears whistled, though there was no wind. He'd passed a second night beneath the stars, shivering in his flimsy skin from the cold, just as he shivered during the day from the heat. Knew he wouldn't last much longer. The basin filled with a dusty sea of midmorning light.

There was a branching here. Twenty-one hundred and eighty feet above sea level, he determined, his head aswim. Farther up this service route were clusters of radio towers. Toward the left, out along the mesa head, was a seasonal washbed that crossed the forking road. If he followed this sandy furrow, it would drop him down to another, apparently smaller road. A shortcut, and the safest route, he figured. From there he'd round the eastern tip of Workman Ridge and head toward Dripping Spring, to Montoya's disputed stead marked with an *X* like pirate treasure.

And then? And then, and then.

He took a drink from his flyweight canteen, kind of blindly folded the map, half-checked the compass once more to be certain he was reading things right, and began down the left crossroad. He caromed like some drunk. One foot, the other. He stumbled, sat down hard. Forearms on upjutting knees, he rested his head on his own flesh sawhorse. His breathing was reedy. His lips were drier than his tongue, but his tongue was as dry as the knuckle that he now listlessly gnawed.

Blood was caked on his wrist. Looked like a morbid Rorschach test. Didn't know where it'd come from, but if he were a diviner he sensed he might be able to decipher its pattern. He knew he was delirious, and he knew probably the blood had merely flowed from his nose or gums and communicated nothing beyond his dire straits, but he liked the improbable delusion that this blood was somehow meaningful, a script legible to whoever might understand the lingo. The army had employed Navajos and Hopi and others from the region to encode secret communiqués during that first nuclear war. Turned out they were good decoders, too. All this blood signage was lost on Kip, trained though he'd been to read the ultimate meaning of a broken branch in the triple-canopy jungles of Laos, and legislate. Read ground movements from his FAC plane and mark estimated enemy positions with Willie Pete bombs, then call in friendly air to lay down the law. But this he couldn't read, nor could he legislate, even had he been so inclined. Here he was so thirsty he'd lick the sanguine symbols off his skinny wrist if they happened to be wet still. But they weren't.

Rather, he laid his chin on his wrist and gazed out over the long terrain before him. The vaporous ghost was back out there, hovering. Otherwise nothing but eternal desert. Yucca spires and the long curve of the horizon beyond.

Impossible to tell where the mirage began and sanity ended, or was it the other way around? Kip trembled, much like the pulsating desert before him, either from fever or fear, it hardly mattered which. He might have fallen asleep for half an hour, baking like mortal meat under the early scorching bulb of sun.

The gentleman in the uniform who appeared beside him had a soft sweet face. That was surprising. There were others, all with guns. The closest said, in a stiff low voice, "Sir, you are trespassing highly restricted military space. I need you to identify yourself and tell me what you're doing here."

Sometimes words just come out of one's mouth. Kip's were, "Don't you think it's strange that feet smell and noses run?"

Nothing.

One of the others advised the man crouched beside this desert comedian, "Better give him some water."

"Not thirsty, thanks anyway. But would you mind helping me stand up? I don't seem to be able to do it myself."

The sweet-faced one grasped his hand and hoisted him to his feet.

"I'll just be on my way, then."

"Why don't you do us all the honor of being serious."

Kip brushed the seat of his pants, a dizzying gesture that nearly toppled him. How many years had it been since he'd purposely forgotten his serial number? A shame.

"How'd you get in here?" another MP asked, reaching out to steady him.

Kip waited through a silence which under the particular circumstances could truly be termed deafening, before answering without humor, "Through the keyhole, like Peter Pan." His feet weren't on. Must have fallen off. He looked down but couldn't see that far. Maybe he lost an eye along the way, too. Really could use that drink of water, but he sensed he missed his rightful chance.

"You are aware you're trespassing on government property?"

"Must mean we both are."

These ventures in levity weren't flying.

"What's your name?"

"What's yours?"

"All right, okay. You understand you're in violation of the law and will be arrested for trespass."

Kip kept looking for his feet.

"Can you tell me what the others are doing here?"

Now he looked around. Delfino must not have been dissuaded by Kip's haphazard decision to take his place. But who were these others? "I don't see any others. Have I multiplied?" Indeed, he was seeing three, five, nine faces where there was only one. Well, no, there were several others, apparently discussing what to do with him. "You talk amongst yourselves," he said. "I've got to move on."

"All right, sir, but first would you mind if we had a look at that map? Might be able to help point you in the right direction."

"Do I look lost?"

No one answered, and Kip saw impatience souring the ranger's countenance. He handed them what they wanted.

"I didn't think so. You know, I was just like you boys once."

The tall fellow studied Kip's map. A thirty-by-sixty-minute series quadrangle of the Oscura Mountains, N3330. Highway patrol had discovered an abandoned pickup truck on Route 380, just south of Lonnie Moon Peak, by an access road that cut into the range toward Workman Ridge and the radio installation at Bug Peak. Registered to a Delfino Montoya; this was most likely their guy. No map annotations that might clue them in on his motives, that is if he had any, or the identities of the others, though they were definitely in on it together—that was clear from the penciled X at Dripping Spring.

"Got ID on you?" the first uniform demanded.

"What for?"

"We're just trying to help you out here. Your name Delfino Montoya?"

That was choice.

"Is yours Kip Calder?"

"Who's Kip Calder?"

One of them wrote down the name in a notebook.

"Nobody."

"You know, you're starting to rub me the wrong way, Mr. Montoya. Who is Kip Calder? Is he one of your three friends?"

"He's no friend of mine."

"This is going nowhere," one scowled.

"He doesn't look too good," said another.

"You don't look too good yourself," Kip managed.

"Let's take him in."

"I don't think so," said Kip.

"You've done enough thinking for the time being, my friend."

They saw no need for handcuffs. In spite of himself, their perp seemed grateful for the water and candy bar they gave him. There were no medics riding with this detachment, but they went ahead and treated his bloodied feet—which were still securely fastened to his legs, as it turned out—with hydrogen peroxide from the first-aid kit in the vehicle. He would have screamed had he any feeling down there, but he didn't.

"I'm pretty tired," he wheezed, before passing out in their custody.

They radioed for medevac. Didn't need to lose a civvy. And plus that, the crazy fucker had guts. Whatever the devil he thought he was doing, this Montoya had definitely shown some serious intestinal fortitude, even if he was a wiseass. Sunstroke, exposure, lack of sleep can do that to a person. He'd probably be okay after a few days' rest. They needed to find out who Kip Calder was, though. No doubt he was one of the three over at Dripping Spring. That could be a different story.

One of the reasons Delfino had sited his house where he did, on this bluff overlooking the draw and plain beyond, was so he could see when company was coming. Now, having dressed himself formally for this long-awaited day, he walked out onto the ruinous ramshackle porch and over to the cold fire. A match under kindling got things going again. He gathered a faggot of shed planks and tendered it into the pit. Wood he himself had probably sawn and nailed into place fifty years and better gone by, now fuel for a fire. Well, it was fine. All right. He would make coffee for himself and the kids. And sure, if these four horseless horsemen of the apocalypse, these four men marching in no rush up the dry draw, were of a mind, they could share a cup with him before returning to whence they'd come. He moved around with a slow nonchalance that would have suggested to any onlooker nothing out of the ordinary was happening here. Not that he was cavalier, but Delfino had lived out this moment in his head so many times that its actuality did seem routine.

Marcos and Ariel lay asleep in their bedrolls inside. Sun had breached the eastern mountains. A dragon-shaped cloud high overhead laced itself in pinks and whites. Delfino fed the horses, watered them. They were hungrier than he remembered his own horses ever having been, and their feed wasn't lasting as long as he'd planned, so he might have to ask the rangers for oats, or better yet just give them the hungry beasts. Then again, no point thinking of them as friendly neighbors dropping in for a breakfast to discuss the welfare of his livestock.

After setting a pan of water on the fire, he gathered the several placards he had painted earlier. Down along the front edge of the dirt yard was the remnant of a stone wall, and now, using rocks and sticks, he propped his *No Trespassing* signs at different intervals along the low bulwark. Knowing that the rangers would see him stirring through their binoculars, just as he watched them approach through his, he left the shotgun inside the casita leaning against the wall by the door. No need to get anybody riled up yet. At least not more than they likely already were. The smoke smelled good. What did it matter that they'd consider him no better than a Mescalero marauder—or hell, even a hair worse? It was right to be back, whatever the consequences.

Once upon a time his breast had harbored a true patriotic heart instead of the crummy thing that pummeled away in there now. He remembered when some suits, company men, had shown up at the Tularosa bungalow, the last time he'd ever been paid a visit by the govvies. Two of them, one uniformed like these fellows now hiking up the hill, the other in a pale gray suit. They informed him the government had determined to lease his land for a further extended period. Would have been in the late sixties.

He refused to take the manila envelope they proffered, saying, —Why don't you gentlemen just tell me what you want?

Graysuit said, —If you'll just read these materials carefully. Do you have an attorney, in other words a lawyer?

—I know what the word attorney means. Do you know what the word necropolis means?

The men looked at each other, thinking, Here we go.

—Didn't think so.

—Mr. Montoya?

—A town of dead people is what it is.

—Mr. Montoya.

—Thanks to you and the people you represent, me and my wife live in a necropolis. All these towns along the basin, except Alamogordo, where your people live, are necropolises. Ghost towns complete with walking, talking ghosts. I count myself one of them.

—Well. If you don't have an attorney, I think it would be advisable for you to contact one. There are some very fine lawyers—

—Soon as anybody's kid is able to walk, he walks right out of this dump, thanks to you. That's how a necropolis works.

—Fine lawyers down in Alamogordo, or El Paso. Go over the offer here with an attorney. I think you will find the proposal very equitable.

—You just think you think.

The officer looked at his wristwatch. He'd run into this bullshit before, and he never enjoyed it. He was young, with a pate shaved balder than a newborn's. The flamboyant mustache waxed into small corkscrews, a style from another century worn in this one by his colleague—who now held a document file out in front of him—did little to disguise that man's youth, either. These were mere children themselves, Delfino realized, marionettes whose wires were pulled by yet others dictating this little local cataclysm, folks who had very probably never even been to Tularosa.

—You think and you believe, he finished.

The same shotgun that presently stood behind the door had stood on that other day, decades ago, just out of sight, and for a moment Delfino had considered reaching for it. Quite the surprise that would have been. Ended things right then and there. His argument wasn't with those two, however, but with puppetmasters he would never meet. He recalled accepting the folder from the outstretched hand, thanking the men—himself suddenly possessed of politeness—and shutting the front door of the house, a house that looked just like the houses on either side of it, houses in turn resembling houses that stood on either side of them, and so on down the block, which paralleled some emaciated trees whose leaves rattled as ever in the sugary gypsumed air.

No leaves rattled here, but the sun brought with it a light breeze, warm and heavy, as the day took hold. The four rangers had fanned out and closed the distance between them and the stead to a quarter mile, give or take. Marcos was up, came out and stood beside his uncle. He saw the figures climbing the rocky rise, too. "Your call what we do," he said.

"What we do is have some coffee."

"Good, fine." Marcos mixed the instant and handed the cup to Delfino.

"Something about Ariel I ought to tell you," Marcos said.

"In a bit."

"It's important."

"What?"

Marcos reconsidered what he was about to say. She could very well speak for herself if she chose. "I'll be back."

His uncle sipped the rotgut coffee, which tasted to him, at that moment, delicious. Best coffee ever passed his lips.

Bearing another cup in two hands, Marcos returned inside to where Ariel lay, still asleep, hair cascading over her face, mouth ajar, her blanketed body curled into a C, like a sleeping cat. How easy it would be to love her. Even though, as he was learning, her life was anything but easy to figure. She was beautiful, but not in any conventional way. Open yet perversely intractable. Pregnant but aborting. Confident but conflicted. A fatherless waif with two fathers.

He would be glad when this confrontation was over. As he knelt beside Ariel, he thought that by now Mary must surely have explained their disappearance to Carl and Sarah. He hoped they could come up with a better idea about how to protect Delfino from his willful fate than he himself had been able to. And here was Ariel, in her way just as stubborn as her father and his uncle. It was becoming clear he should never have committed himself to keeping Kip and Delfino's secret that day in Nambé. Shouldn't have driven Ariel down to Tularosa. Should have phoned the police instead of helping to pack gear and saddle horses. So many shoulds and shouldn'ts. Not to mention last night's kiss between two people literally in the dark about their futures. What had that been? A payback to Mary? Worse, maybe. He meant the kiss.

But what had the kiss meant about him? Could he so easily chuck aside the years of friendship with Franny? More than friendship, of course. He had even thought about asking her if she'd like to take it to another level, half intended to discuss their getting engaged the morning they hiked up Tsankawi, before she brought that flight of fancy crashing back to earth with her talk of moving out to Los Angeles, the two of them. He'd sooner move to Mars. And then her confession, her extraordinary fraud. He didn't feel angry toward her, curiously enough, didn't feel reproachful or vengeful. He'd forgiven her, yes, but in the same emotional gesture had released her as well. She had made up a story and like most stories it had a beginning, middle, and end. It'd been a good fiction, as fictions went. But Marcos much preferred fact.

Ariel's eyes were open, looking at him. He snapped to.

"They're coming," he said, setting the cup on the floor beside her.

"I'll be right out."

At the door, which was dazzled by white-gold sun, he paused. "What happened last night—"

"Don't worry about anything."

"I didn't mean to offend you."

"That's the last thing you did."

"We can talk about it."

"Marcos, I'm not going anywhere. Don't worry. We need to keep our focus."

She was right. Delfino had binoculars clamped to his eyes. He looked frail to Marcos yet at the same time principled and proper, courtly, with his flannel shirt tucked into a nice pair of western gabardine trousers. His turquoise bolo and finest silver oval belt buckle sparkled. Sometime earlier he even managed to spit-polish his boots. There was something noble and woeful about the whole thing.

"Can I have a look?"

What Marcos saw through the magnifying lenses was Jim Carpenter looking right back at him through a pair of binoculars of his own. The sergeant had radioed back to command that he was in visual contact with two of the three. Suspects were male, one apparently in his twenties, medium height and build, jeans and denim jacket, the other late sixties or early seventies, tall, slight build, dressed for a church square dance. Stow the humor. Point was, neither of them much looked like your desperado type. Maybe it was as simple as their having gotten lost. He ordered his detachment not to proceed any closer than two hundred meters until they got a visual on the third man. He could report with some confidence that they were not spies or professional agitators. Fact was, nothing they were observed doing hinted at pro behavior. Had base got any further info on that Montoya guy the other team was tracking?

Negative, he was told. Momentarily, though. Proceed with deliberate delay, his orders were, and he radioed same over to his team. Why not take it nice and slow. Sun on his back felt good. Not impossible these folks simply didn't know the extent and nature of the trouble they were in. Be good to just ease on up there, initiate the dialogue, talk them off the reservation, then let the lawyers duke it out.

Believing this might be the day she would finally meet Kip, Ariel herself spruced up for the occasion by forgoing the dungarees

cinched by a scissored-down belt and moleskin jacket she'd borrowed from Delfino. Instead, she wore only the dark-blue silk dress
that had served as a makeshift blouse these past days, the dress she'd
worn to the center to visit Granna, light-years ago it seemed now.
Awfully creased, but it was the thought that counted. She washed
her face with canteen water and looked at the morning with clear,
bright eyes. Having brushed her hair and collected it into as nice a
chignon as she could manage without a mirror, she rummaged lip-
stick from the bottom of her backpack and applied it, then emerged
from the house barefoot. Marcos thought to compliment her, but for
all her sudden splendor, Ariel was as sharply centered as Delfino on
the impending confrontation. He realized that while she and his
uncle had arranged themselves to different purposes, they shared
equally the spirit of honoring the moment.

She asked Marcos for the glasses and, too, saw the ranger. "We
don't have any way of communicating with them, do we."

"We're telling them what they need to know just by standing
here," said Delfino.

"You think they can read your placards?"

"If they can't they will soon enough."

"You mind if I post one of my own?"

Delfino thought for a moment, then said, "Paint's over there. Your
reason for being here's every bit as good as mine."

In no time, Delfino's *No Trespassing Private Property* notices were
joined by Ariel's *Looking for Veteran Kip Calder.* She'd added the
word *Veteran* in the hopes it would inspire in these military men
compassion toward her father.

"What an insane bunch the bastards must think we are," said
Marcos.

Ariel smiled at him.

"I'd take that as a compliment." To punctuate his point, Delfino
spat into the breeze.

Her movements were studied by the rangers who now determined
to advance their positions. Reported back that they had two males

and a female. After walleting his field phone, the sergeant squared himself, looking up at the three of them, and gestured his peaceful intent, waving hands slowly above his head. The interlopers didn't return the courtesy, so he stopped to resurvey them through his binoculars.

Now close enough to read the quaint placards, he relayed their messages on the closed channel back to White Sands and was ordered not to proceed until further instructed. He communicated this to his men, then sat down on an anvil of igneous in the trench gulch after checking it out for snakes. Unwrapping a stick of chewing gum and pushing it into his mouth, he scrutinized the forescape of tawny sills, stone jointings, and a narrowing apron of sand for the best approach to the site.

Private property, he mused. What kind of witless wonder would want to set up shop in such a place as this? Even if the government weren't putting bread on Jim's table and meat in his Crock-Pot, he would deem this land fit only for the uses to which it was presently being put. Exploding dummy prey and testing high-velocity hardware. At least Alamogordo was on the lee side of natural wrath. Over along this western edge of the basin was different. Beautiful in the harshest ways. But you come here looking to homestead and you ought to be homesteaded straight to the cuckoo's nest. Soup to nuts but skip the soup. Kinda like that.

The secure line came to life. They'd arrested the other man who avowed he was not Delfino Montoya but one William Calder. Delfino Montoya was high probability among the Dripping Spring group. A call from a worried relative corroborated this and indicated the male was his nephew and female this Calder's daughter, though Calder—in custody at the infirmary—had stated he had no family.

It was all coming to complex clarity.

Montoya was on file as having communicated threats to various official individuals over the years with regard to his eviction from Dripping Spring a long time ago. To be considered potentially armed and dangerous, since his name came up on the computer as a buyer of blue-market armaments from right-wing extremist purveyors. They were trying to get specifics on that. The relative's name was Sarah Montoya, his sister-in-law. The younger male was her son, no priors. The woman, name of Ariel Rankin, was being processed. Some things, however, had already been learned about her. Stepfather was an active antigovernment advocate with an FBI file long as your leg, a sheet of multiple protest arrests, and connections to leftist clients. Stepfather's father, Phillip McCarthy, a chemical engineer and scientist, had worked without incident on the Manhattan Project at Los Alamos, but later repudiated said participation. This Calder character, father or not, was also from Los Alamos. His mother was a Cuban national, now deceased, but they were checking into how she got clearance during the war in the first place. Calder had made captain in an elite covert insurgency outfit in Laos, code name Ravens, serving with apparent distinction until he renounced his citizenship temporarily to work underground in Communist Laos on behalf of the Hmong. Now homeless, with IRS records showing no known job affiliation, Calder was legally married to a Vietnamese citizen residing in Hanoi, two stepsons American citizens. For somebody with no family he sure had a lot of relatives.

They then summarized the trespassers' probable objectives and demands.

Great, thought Jim, filliping the gum. Just fucking great.

He was told to go ahead and try to make contact with the intruders, but must under no circumstances be provocative or make any attempt to arrest the individuals until information could be gathered as to whether others were involved. They were already running some background on the lady who telephoned from up north.

Wider awake than he had been since he was called in for this small operation not yet twelve hours old, Jim radioed his team members that he was going to have a little chat with their guests. They were to back him up. Keep their eyes wide open and firearms holstered but at the ready.

Ariel, Marcos, and Delfino watched Jim make his ascent. They could see the three others emerging from their positions on the left and right, and while none of the rangers displayed any aggression in the manner they approached Dripping Spring, Delfino thought it might be prudent to show them he meant business.

"You sure that's necessary?" Marcos asked his uncle, who had retrieved the shotgun and leaned it against the low stone wall.

"So long as I'm not brandishing the thing. They need to know we're not on some picnic."

Troubled by the gun and what it could precipitate, Ariel voiced her agreement with Marcos.

"We don't show we got any protection, they'll just take us away in cuffs, and all we done to get here was for naught. What I think is, we find out what we can about Kip, then Ariel ought to go back with them. That's her purpose."

"We'll see," she said.

In no time, Jim stood facing them downslope from the stone fence. Delfino'd already warned him, when he was yet a few hundred feet away, not to come more than half that distance closer. They could hear each other just fine. Wasn't no noise to disturb them.

"You Delfino Montoya?"

"I am."

"Your friends here, what are your names?"

"Ariel Rankin."

"Marcos Montoya."

While jotting the names on his pocket pad, he said, "You folks realize you're trespassing restricted government property?"

"Sure do."

"You understand that's against the law?"

"May I ask your name?"

"Sergeant James Carpenter," he smiled at Ariel, most polite and friendly. "I've come here to escort you to the perimeter of the proving grounds. We'll be met there by some people who will be happy to take down any statements you wish to make."

"That's kind of you. But we won't need your help when we want to leave. I know this terrain like the back of my hand," Delfino assured him.

"I assumed that's what you were going to say."

"Well, I guess you're a smart fellow."

Not missing a beat, Jim continued, "Not smart enough to know what brings you folks up here this morning, sir."

Delfino asked Marcos if he wouldn't mind walking the copy of his deed down there so the sergeant could see for himself. "Just go partway, lay it on the ground, and for godsakes don't let him grab you," he told his nephew, then louder, for Jim to hear, "Hope you don't mind if I hold my shotgun so we got ourselves some—what do you people call it?—parity. Let's nobody make any quick movements, all right?" With that, Delfino retrieved his weapon.

"Mr. Montoya, no need for guns. We're not here to harm you."

Marcos started down. This is how you get your ass slain, he thought.

"We're doing fine, then. We're not here to harm you, either."

Ariel was shocked by how swiftly the climate had changed. She backed away from Delfino several unconscious paces. Marcos set the deed and its accompanying claim, sealed in a plastic sleeve, on the tan earth. As he turned to rejoin the others, Jim Carpenter advised him, in a gentle voice, "Your mother's concerned about your welfare. You know that none of whatever you're all up to here is worth people getting hurt over."

"So what's my mother's name?"

"Sarah Montoya. All right?"

"What did she say?"

"What do you think she said?"

Delfino was calling him.

"And what about your girlfriend?"

"You mean Mary?"

"I thought her name was Ariel," nodding upward.

"What about her?"

"Aren't you concerned for her welfare?"

"I'm concerned, sure. About everybody's welfare. And while we're talking, you should know there's probably another person out here. He's sick and needs medical attention. The woman with us is his daughter. She's looking for him and doesn't have anything to do with evictions or land claims or any of this other problem. His name's Kip Calder. He's a Vietnam vet. He—"

Jim thought about whether to divulge what he knew and decided to hold his cards. "I'll put a search and rescue out on him right away," and did so in Marcos's presence, raising the VHF radio earnestly to his head and ordering the rescue, though without ever pushing the transmit switch. "Let her know we're on top of it."

Delfino waited impatient and silenced by the vision of this colloquy out of earshot. Marcos began his walk back up the sere knoll. Ariel felt suddenly ridiculous in her dress.

"Hey, Marcos. What do you want us to tell your mother?"

"Tell her everything's fine."

"You want me to lie to her?"

Marcos turned around and said, "You've got all the equipment. Patch her through to me and I'll tell her myself."

"I'll see what I can do, chief. Let's just don't forget who's causing the problem and who's trying to help resolve it."

"Don't call me chief."

Hang tough, zip the lip, stay cool to rule. Jim ran several choice expletives through his mind as he watched Marcos hike away. He didn't much like having to stoop to retrieve the pathetic documentation provided by these neophyte fanatics. The kid seemed level-headed, though, had to admit. Probably loves the codger. Once Marcos was out of hearing range, he reported what transpired. Projection was, all agreed, a minor standoff of brief duration, to be kept from the media. Nobody liked the old fart's shotgun, including, seemingly, the perpetrators themselves. Who knew if it was even loaded? Hardly mattered since they had to proceed as if it were. The girl was entangled in somebody else's fracas and would probably be the weak link. Would have to work on that. Last analysis: What they had here was an elderly local with the same damn gripe they'd heard before. Some folks just won't give up their private past for the common future.

*J*ess remembered an afternoon so buried in the past that she might have questioned whether it really happened had she not borne to this day a scar that verified it did. A sandy beach at Montauk with her new family. Sweet sincere Brice and little munchkin Ariel, then five years old. The waves cascading gently to shore and just as gently receding. Brice, in that faded dorky plaid swimsuit he mistakenly considered hip, had carried his laughing daughter into the green waves, while Jessica herself lay on a towel watching these chancy creatures. She'd slept the night before wrapped in her husband's arms and with her daughter nestled in hers, in the seaside motel bed, breathing in a kind of counterpoint with the swells beyond the window. She loved her family. Loved watching them wade into the water, a small wave, a stronger wave, then several waves so marginal they hardly counted as waves at all.

While she would always value her time with Kip, always cherish the prodigal outcome of their intimacy—darling Ariel herself—Jess had made her peace with his disappearance from their lives. Now her daughter and husband played in the Atlantic, ranging farther out into it until, yes, she realized they were afloat, Ariel's chin on Brice's shoulder bobbing up with each fresh surge, the girl's peals of laughter not quite swallowed by the rushing breakers.

She remembered settling back on the beach towel, sun warming her and specks of fine sand, kicked up by the shore breeze, dancing across her skin. Dear God, if you are and if you're willing to help me out here, she thought, please never let me forget this perfect moment of peace and contentment. Thank you with all my heart.

And meditatively, arrhythmically, the waves continued to roll in, to fizzle and hiss where the sand restrained their progress, then to withdraw before another mouth of brine opened up, curled its long lip into a whitecap of pluming emeralds, and chewed its way down the shoreline. What a banquet! she dreamed, drifting away toward light sleep as a clutch of black-backed gulls squabbled over a rind of discarded grapefruit or some hapless mussel knocked loose from its bedrock mooring.

Maybe she did fall asleep for a fleet second, but no sooner did she reawaken than she knew her prayer had been answered in the most startling, unwanted way. She knew even before she sat up and cast her eyes frantically over the knotty face of the ocean that she would never forget her former contentment, if only because she lost every atom of it in this new indelible, ghastly moment.

The riptide had carried them out with dispatch. Jessica ran frantic along the edge of the water, shrieking their names, crying for help. People gathered, also shouting. The call went out along the shore, its own human wave of hysteria. Several surf fishermen dropped their long rods and raced over to where this young woman screamed that her husband and daughter were drowning.

—They were, they were just there, just a minute ago.

She must have said something to that effect, though it was more than possible nothing articulate came forth.

—Where?

She did hear them asking that question.

—Out there there *there,* out there.

Miles away, an oil tanker slowly traversed the low horizon. Nearer, a few fishing boats pitched, trawlers dragging for scallops or clams. Nearer yet, a dory crewed by one soul, a peapod making trap rounds. All too distant to ask for help. Bathers could be seen along the shore, not many for such a crisp clear day as this.

Then someone spotted them. —Over there! And others in the crowd began sprinting down the beach, Jessica merely among them now, for hers had become their collective fright.

Ariel and Brice's heads were like one speck, a fused trifle in the silver expanse of water. From seemingly nowhere two rescuers had launched, one in a small canoe of sorts, the other paddling hard past the shoals out into the longer swells on a surfboard.

—They're gonna be fine, a woman assured her, taking Jessica's hand as they stood knee-deep in buffeting waves.

A quarter hour must have passed before they were brought back to shore in the canoe, the surfboarder clinging alongside. Some cheering, applause. Blankets. The two were cold and shaken but fine. Some minutes of weeping together in an embrace of joy and surfeit fear before Brice noticed Jessica's hand was running with blood. The wing of flesh between her right thumb and index finger was gashed, and though her memory of tripping over one of the fishermen's tackle boxes and coming down on an open chest of spoon lures was as faint as if it never transpired, the scar from her laceration lasted to this day.

Even now she recalled how preposterous it was that, having nearly lost her daughter and husband to a riptide, she was the one who wound up in an emergency room where she, never in mortal danger like the others, was administered a tetanus shot and bandaged after receiving stitches. How many ironies had been in play that afternoon? She lost count and then interest in counting them, too, as her hand healed and the incident receded, only popping into mind at the least likely moments, such as the present when she noticed how pale her skin was against Sarah Montoya's as they shook hands. And, too, caught sight of that tiny ladder of scarring that prompted her memory of Montauk.

She felt as troubled listening to Sarah as she'd been on that beach. Curious how that same memorable shock—that Ariel'd been snatched by forces over which her mother held no sway—revisited her now. No drowning ocean here, but tides were always at work. She put her hand in her jacket pocket, unconscious of the gesture, and asked Brice if he knew anybody at Los Alamos who might intervene on their behalf down at White Sands—even the name of the place gave her the creeps, resurrecting Montauk in the process. Ariel and the others would naturally be treated better were there a friendly voice pleading their cause. Someone who knew someone who knew someone.

He didn't know anyone, however. Those bridges, never having been built, could hardly be burned during the passing years. His mother, ages ago, might have known the right person, forged the right connection, but that bridge was gone, too, that lifeline lost with a finality Brice had yet to fathom.

"White Sands told me they'd get back in touch as soon as they had some hard information," Sarah said. "I don't know if I trust them, but they gave me a number that puts us directly through to some office where they're following this."

"Did they say anything specific about Ariel?"

"The three of them—Carl's brother, your daughter, our son—have been located, they said. And they promised they're going to bring them out, all very peacefully."

"This is Delfino's doing. He's gonna get a piece of my mind. Like I said before, jail might give him time to think about where his obstinance has got him. Not to mention the others."

"Carl," said Sarah.

"It doesn't sound like Kip's any innocent, either," said Brice.

"They're both hardheaded."

"Hard head's only good if you're a hammer."

The four parents stood beneath the portico eave, hesitant to speak, though a windchime down by Kip's old room idly troubled the whispering air. Helpless and uncomfortable and worried, they looked at one another, as Mary watched on, wondering why generation after generation rushed into parenthood given the crazy folly children brought into parents' lives and parents into children's. She, too, was struggling here, not knowing what to do. The visit with Uncle Clifford had been upsetting because, in her presence, his dementia ebbed. His smile had been strangely ordinary as he fondly told her what a beautiful little girl she'd been, always with a sweet tooth for Toll House cookies and raspberry sherbet. "Eaten at the same sitting," he'd recalled correctly, prompting her to laugh and him to laugh with her.

She spoke up now. "I'm Mary."

"Mary's a friend of Marcos," Sarah said, welcoming a reprieve from Carl's diatribe.

"I'm sure Marcos is looking out for Ariel. He's the most responsible person you'd ever want to meet, and your daughter—"

Her thought wouldn't complete itself so Brice offered, "She's generally pretty responsible herself." The windchime flurried, then was calmed. "So Kip's still alive and well," he continued. "Last time I saw him, he told me he was sick, and looked it. I offered to help but he wouldn't take me up on it."

"He's not that well. But he's definitely still alive."

"Been living with us."

"How'd you meet?"

"Sarah found him damn near dead, sleeping in our barn a few years ago, around Easter. He'd been over in Chimayó for the Good Friday celebration and didn't have anywhere to go afterward, so he just walked until he dropped."

Brice grasped what this meant before Carl finished speaking, as did Jessica. The revelation stirred in them both a multitude of feelings, from compassion to regret to sorrow, for their undaunted confrere. Kip. There was no unbraiding him from the weave without tearing the fabric of their own lives.

"He's become a member of the family," Sarah was saying.

"Kip's hard not to love," Brice half smiled, half grimaced. "I've known him my whole life long. Every time I wanted to hate him, I failed. Every time I thought he was gone for good, I was wrong. He's the most present absence I've ever known."

"He introduced me to Brice, you know."

"I guess that makes us all family, loose knit," Sarah said. "You look exhausted. Let's have some coffee, something to eat."

Jess took her husband by the arm—a protective gesture, mindful of his perplexity—wanting to hold him up, his burden. Not unlike hers, his thoughts strayed from past to past, faltering into this present crisis when called upon. So many images of his mother. Swabbing tincture of Merthiolate on his skinned knees once when he crashed his bike down by Ashley Pond and blowing on them to make the sting go away. How she loved Christmas with its luminarias and her kitchen smelling of eggnog and fresh gingerbread so delicious it made his head spin. The way she always defended Dad after he, Brice, came of age and began to ruin dinners by excoriating the lab, refusing to eat food bought with "blood money." What marvelous loyalty in the face of her own grave doubts. Her instinct to protect the underdog, the misunderstood Kip, the singular Bonnie Jean, her wayward son himself. Her voracious love of Ariel, expressed quietly through little gifts and letters, and her continuing quest to teach the girl about God and Heaven and all those churchy things he abhorred but had instinctively left unimpaired. That last time he saw her alive, humming in the kitchen, *There's a someone I'm longing to see, I hope that he turns out to be . . .* and his farewell kiss, holding her delicate head between palms soiled with tierra bendita from Chimayó. The same healing dirt that Kip had scooped from the shrine that day.

"When did you speak with White Sands last?"

"About an hour ago."

"You mind if I make a redundant call?"

They walked the length of the porch and while Brice telephoned, Sarah made sandwiches and Mary poured out cups of gazpacho. On the stable phone Montoya, too, called around to make arrangements with a couple of other horsemen who'd cover the ranch for him if he found he had to leave for Tularosa basin on the quick.

Having been told that a William Calder was in custody and being brought in for medical attention, and contact had been made with the other three, and that no further information was available at this time—yes, certainly, they understood he was the father of the young lady, and they appreciated his concern and all the fresh information he'd been kind enough to provide—Brice hung up and, in the relative privacy of Sarah's niche office, finally wept a silent stream of tears for his mother, his daughter, his touched friend. Elbows on his knees, face in his hands, his shoulders heaved. In any life, he knew, there were innumerable ways to fuck up, so many wrong paths to choose from, and while his mother's death had been inevitable, the broken promise he'd made to her more than three years ago, that he would see her again soon, need not have been. What good were apologies offered too late? Nevertheless, his attempt at giving thanks to her for what she'd done and what she'd tried to do for him seemed a much less ludicrous endeavor than he might have presumed. Prayers—call them that—for Ariel and Kip wouldn't harm a soul. *Soul?* Listen to him. So Brice added words of petition on their behalf. In the bathroom off the kitchen he splashed water on his face. Weren't deathbed conversions reserved for the dying? What was he doing?

Whatever it was, he felt no regret. If only he could say the same about every act he'd ever ventured.

*T*his room had one window that looked out on a mostly empty parking lot. Its cinderblock walls were painted battleship gray and its smooth concrete floors an amiable blue. The steel door was unpainted. Metal table, metal chairs, a standard hospital bed and good old hail-fellow-unwell-met intravenous tree. Very bright fluorescents. The wall phone connected the occupants to either a nurses' station or guard post down the corridor outside. And yet it was more an impersonal than an unfriendly room, military all the way. Even the waiting MPs were not so unfriendly—just that he didn't want to dialogue with them at the moment.

"There's a lot of folks concerned about you."

Kip didn't have any response, so didn't respond.

The other man asked if he was maybe feeling a little better.

"Yeah," he answered quietly, though his insides were as raw as the day he first arrived at Rancho Pajarito. Felt like a famished mouse was gnawing its way back and forth through his guts. The rippling pain came and went in surges, which made him think that maybe the mouse had to rest, digest a little before starting again to tunnel around in the red dark. Kip tried not to complain. They supplemented the glucose with some pain reliever that was doing its work, more or less.

"Doctor said it was a good thing they found you when they did."

This second man was standing, having entered the room a few minutes earlier. Kip sat on the side of the bed. They'd given him pajamas, garb as simple as the room he inhabited. His feet were bandaged and he had to make do with padding around in surgeon's socks whenever time came to hit the loo.

"The basin's not what I'd call a great place to take a stroll."

"Even if it was legal."

More of the same innocuous jive their colleagues had anted up over the last half dozen hours. For the most part, though he felt silly doing so, he had retorted with his correct name and rank—which had been useful to them—and unmatching serial numbers, which hadn't made much difference one way or the other. For Kip, this reentry into a military habitat coaxed him back toward the tired mental geography of war. The dirt airstrip, its short runway in the mist. Thirsty yellow oxen driven by mountain farmers scarred by chemicals. A beautiful aircraft cartwheeling as its shellstruck flier pulled a nylon elevator, floating into the tiered black jungle.

But Kip knew it was a fool's game. He pushed away all thoughts of battle madness and when that flaming personal curtain lifted, he could almost smell his mother's *arepas,* cornmeal pancakes and maple syrup, as he looked at the blue floor of this military hospital not in Luang Prabang or Pakse or Saravane or anywhere else, but simply here in the country where he'd been born.

"What you said before about people being concerned," he said. "Who do you mean?"

"Your lawyer, for one."

"I don't have a lawyer."

"Just like you don't have a family?"

The other man added, "The people up at Dripping Spring are asking after you, too."

"There's only one person at Dripping Spring, like I already said."

"Three."

"What're their names?"

"We thought you'd like to tell us."

"I'm sure he already gave you the information. It's not like he went there in order to hide."

"He's right," the standing man said. "Mr. Montoya identified himself. So did the others."

"Well," said Kip, neutrally.

"Maybe it'd be best to just fill him in on what we have and hope he'll reciprocate," proposed the seated man, then, to Kip, "Fair?"

Kip shrugged. Gamesters.

"The young guy's name is Marcos Montoya and the woman is Ariel Rankin."

Calm, even serene, Kip asked them why they were lying to him.

"That's the pure, unadulterated truth. What makes you think we'd bother to lie?"

"Because in your position I might be inclined to do so."

"We'll keep that in mind."

Kip lay back on the bed and closed his eyes. They were giving him the straight dope.

Ariel. She was finally here. Not just here, but with Delfino and Marcos at Dripping Spring. Spoke volumes about the girl—or no, about the woman. That she had accomplished such a feat. He knew. After all, he'd just been scraped off the floor of that same terrain. Imagine, Marcos and Delfino knew her, at least a little.

Ironic he should be in military custody this day, given his old instincts—such as they were—remained, as ever, to flee. But the marathoner had been run to ground. On that faraway evening when he'd sat with his father's ledger and begun to pen his apology—an apologia, really—he had unwontedly sought forgiveness. More's the pity he'd been backsliding ever since. His perennial desire to forge an eleventh-hour bond with Ariel might once more be in limbo, but whether he desired to meet her or run to the farthest ends of the earth to avoid her was suddenly irrelevant. Fate had its own sense of humor.

"You obviously know them."

No reaction.

"We can arrange to hook you up if you were of a mind to help them out of their jam—"

That was rich.

"—and clue them in that we're here to accommodate them, if possible."

"They've got a few hours of daylight yet today and it'd be best for everybody if they agreed to come out."

"Whatever the grievance, we can discuss it."

Kip surprised the standing man by saying he'd be willing to speak with Delfino Montoya. Immediately, the seated man rose to his feet and left the room by the door, which was opened from the outside.

"Could I get some more milk?" Kip asked. "More of those graham crackers, too."

Baby food. But even the chocolate the rangers had given him on the flats hadn't stayed down. Reduced to pablum, it seemed.

"You got it."

"By the way, I'd like to speak with this lawyer of mine."

"It can be arranged."

"Am I under arrest? Officially, that is?"

"You can't arrest people unofficially. I'm not sure I get your question, Captain."

He hadn't been addressed by that designation in a long time.

"What I'm saying is, can I ask to leave these premises and legally be granted my request?"

"Afraid not, sir."

"I understand. My lawyer, please."

Kip was left alone with his refreshments and gathering worries. As his guru Wagner would have concurred, these imminent reckonings were merely his wishes finally come true. Too bad he wasn't the suicidal type, an idea that brought an odd smile to his lips, and a question. Why are you so scared? With all the choices having been made and their consequences come or coming to pass, there was nothing to fear anymore. He'd failed too many times to enumerate, his most recent fiasco having landed him in this blinding tomb. Body failing, the last of his health—for lack of a kinder euphemism—fading. For crying out loud, this paper cup of skim milk felt as heavy as slagged ore in his hand. Chewing the crackers was labor and swallowing them a strain. The starch in these jammies abraded his sunburned skin. His injured feet throbbed beneath the physician's dressings with more authority than the shy beating of his heart. Death, mercenary or merciful, had hovered at his shoulder for many years now. So what was the problem.

The problem was this. Everything had always been Kip, Kip, Kip. Even when he tried to be generous, the Kip fix was in. His chaplain behavior toward Franny had bordered on emotional slapstick. Who was he to preach? Besides, Franny received the fatherly concern he'd always denied Ariel, and while he meant the tenderness he hoped was expressed, it was misdirected. The fieldhouse sheltered whose head from the sun and snow if not his own? His invitation to Brice those few years ago, what was it but a dead man's trying to stave off death by thieving the life's breath from another man's happiness? Even Delfino was to be robbed of his desperate revolt in the name of fraternity. And now Ariel had tracked down her travesty of a father. At least she would have the chance to see what little she'd missed out on. Wake-up call. The disappointment would be healthy for her. Odd idea, that by letting your daughter down one last time you'd be doing her the biggest favor you ever managed.

Ariel would have been saddened by all this self-condemnation were she aware of it, but she was caught in a swirl of thoughts very different from these. Rereading Kip's letter in the ledger, hoping to draw strength for the standoff, she'd come to other conclusions about him. Her day had transpired in slow minutes. A governor from the last century proposed, *All experience gained elsewhere fails in New Mexico,* and Ariel could now only agree. Lew Wallace's awful novel *Ben-Hur,* once the most popular book in America aside from the Bible itself, had been a childhood Christmas present from Granna, and his aphorism came courtesy of her grandfather Calder, whose journal she'd not only been studying but had begun to supplement with her own nervous thoughts. Leaf after leaf of invitingly blank paper lay in the binding behind the pages her grandfather and Kip had used. All in the family. And what, she thought, sitting in the shade as the precarious afternoon inched along, was more vulnerable than empty pages? The person who would presume to fill them?

Marcos ferried to and fro between Ariel and his uncle. Ever since he'd traipsed back up the scree gulch a second time with the news that Kip had been found—the rangers had pulled back a hundred yards, not trusting Delfino to lay off the shotgun—he noticed Ariel withdrawing a little. Sitting beside her, he watched her write in her notebook. She didn't seem to mind that he read over her shoulder, an oddly intimate allowance. The afternoon chickenhawks ellipsed way upstairs, and she made note of it in the heavy ledger on her lap. The freight train ran diminutive along the floor of the clay basin, whispering in its tracks, and she made note. Marcos sat beside her and said he was as torn as she about what to do now, and without much thought, she made note. *Marcos and I don't know what to do.*

For his part, Delfino stood sentinel at his stone rampart. At the edge of his thoughts loomed one that was outrageous, maddening, in fact, grievous. They'd made it in, set up temporary camp, been confronted, handed over his documentation and demand—all had gone according to plan. The one thing he hadn't over the years predicted was this strong, growing realization that even if they gave him Dripping Spring lock, stock, and barrel, he would never be able to bring the place back to life. Fact was, Delfino Montoya was an old man. He'd hitched every hope to the prospect of one day standing right here, and now that he was, he understood he was as razed as the very stone rampart on which his foot rested. Momentum was all that carried him forward.

The sun moved down toward its evening berth. They watered the horses, had something to eat. The army guys had made their contact and, it seemed, were content to wait and see. None of these tactics could work for long, all of them on both sides of the fragile fence knew that, and Ariel made note.

"Do you believe there's a reason for everything?"

"That's out of the blue." She glanced up from her writing and looked into his eyes.

"Not really."

Ariel thought about it for a minute. "No, I don't," she said, knowing she was being merely counterintuitive and didn't in fact have any answer one way or the other. See what he's saying.

"You believe in ghosts?"

Ariel laughed. "Marcos, the sun's crisping your brain."

"Probably."

As they sat out of earshot, Delfino scanned the vertical ridges up behind them through his binoculars.

Remembering that curious moment only a few infinite weeks ago back at the farmhouse, when she could have sworn her cat Buddha nuzzled her where she slept on the warm bluestone wall, Ariel said, "Probability is, ghosts don't exist and there's not a reason for everything. But for argument's sake, let's just say they do exist."

"I know they do."

"Okay then. Why?"

Marcos thought about Doña Francisca de Peña. Or rather, about his ghost who he'd come to believe was Francisca. "Because they're dead but don't want to leave off living. I've seen a hundred foals that didn't know for hours they were alive. Their mothers had to lick their eyes open for them to see. Same way you have to spank a baby to make it realize it's got to breathe. No reason the reverse doesn't happen. Some people just don't know their life's over."

She sensed she'd begun to understand the blue from which these thoughts were arising. "You think there's some chance your uncle Delfino is risking becoming a ghost?"

"I never thought about it that way."

Time passed—hollow, absentminded, tranquil—as she wrote *never believed in ghosts* in the ledger and sketched a willowy phantasm next to it. "By the way, I don't," she said, breaking the silence.

"Believe in ghosts?"

"Not on your life. I love ghost stories but I come from a family of scientists and lawyers and atheists and none of them believe in ghosts. My grandmother's a Rock of Ages Christian, and I'm sure the only ghost she believes in is the Holy Ghost."

"Too bad."

She liked Marcos. "Maybe so. But what about Delfino. You think he's trying to get himself converted into a ghost? Some words from you could make a difference. Tell him you prefer a living uncle to a dead ghost."

"Aren't you worried about Kip?"

"Talk to Delfino and I'll get to see Kip."

"You could leave right now."

"Something tells me Kip would want me to stand in for him here with you and your uncle. Does that sound crazy?"

"Probably. No, yes, definitely it does."

"Maybe the sun's getting into my head, too. I don't know. Why is it too bad not to believe in ghosts?"

"Let me ask you a question. It'd be a way of responding."

She noticed the shadows lengthening.

"What are you doing sitting in the dust by a fallen-down ranch house with the likes of me and my uncle, caught in the middle of something you hardly know a thing about?"

Ariel folded her hands on the open ledger.

"I'm asking in all innocence," he added.

"Nothing's innocent."

"Ariel."

"You really want me to say I'm chasing a ghost?"

Delfino was calling them, his voice interrupting the larger silence that had strangely settled in over Dripping Spring.

Ariel finished, "You'll have to tell me about your ghosts sometime."

"There's just one."

He stood and extended his hand to her, which she took.

"You're serious, aren't you," coming to her feet. She brushed the dust off her dress after dropping the pencil in the ledger to mark her place. "Man, woman, or child?"

"A woman," he said. "Are you coming?"

They walked side by side into the dirt yard. Delfino extended the field glasses to Marcos with some urgency.

"They're behind there, too," he blurted, his chin raised toward the Oscuras.

The younger man trained the glasses on granite terraces and pediments whose capitals still shone in slantlight even as their bases were beginning to swim in pale muddied purple. More rangers. Of course they'd surround them. Made perfect sense.

"What's your thinking, Uncle?"

Delfino pursed his lips. "Same as ever. Except I think you two oughta clear out. You did a kindness helping me get here, and I'm grateful. But you should turn yourselves in and go be with Kip."

"But what about you?" Ariel said.

"Like I say, I'm right where I need to be. You're not."

Marcos looked at Ariel. "I think he's right, at least about you turning yourself over. I sure as hell have to stay, though."

"You're eating my food, Marcos. You're in the way now."

Delfino's nephew pushed his hands into his back pockets. He understood his uncle's comment wasn't selfish but rather a spin at protectiveness. Ariel's idea that he talk his uncle down from the ledge, so to speak, was a good one. He'd wait for the right moment and give it his best shot.

As if materializing out of thin air, Jim abruptly added his thoughts to their deliberation. "I think Mr. Montoya's got a good point." The three turned to face the sergeant who had climbed the rise with non-chalant stealth and now stood thirty paces from the rampart return-ing their stares, though with immeasurably greater composure. Instinctively, Delfino grabbed his shotgun and just as instinctively Jim unholstered his handgun, saying, "Easy there. Why don't you set down the musket—"

"Twelve-gauge Remington."

"—and I'll do the same."

A quiet breeze mussed the sand at their feet.

"You first," Delfino said.

Knowing he was covered, Jim played the gambit, laying aside his weapon on a bench of stone.

Delfino followed suit.

"There's someone on the field phone who wants to have a few words with you."

"Am I coming to you, or you to me?"

"Either way."

"Bring it up here, then."

And Jim did.

Candid high-desert light of such tough clarity. Bonnie sat under it alone. Her husband was at his job. Sam had gone off with friends. She communed with her brave geraniums and pretty petunias. A lit-tle green lizard kept her company.

She looked around the patio and thought about all the work that had gone into making it such a nice refuge from the world. Charlie had come up with the idea of designing those herb beds using tires off the car when they bought the new radials.

—No need to go throwing them out, he'd said. —We lay them along the back fence, fill them with topsoil, and presto you got planters.

Sometimes he really got things right, did her husband. Mint prospered in one tire. Sage, rosemary, and verbena in the others. Maybe painting the tires white had been an extravagance, but it looked very professional to Bonnie's eye. She glanced around at other perfections. Thistle in the bird feeder, so shiny and black. The concrete deck hosed off by her younger son just this morning. Her cup of Sanka on the round glass table. She could remember each and every thing that had gone into creating this small Eden. Every bush pruned to the shape she liked. The garden hose wrapped in a tight circle. Of course, the cedar fence could stand to be restained, but they'd get around to it in time.

In time. That was the point. Just like the Hill where she was born, Bonnie was getting on, and anything that remained as it was when she looked at it last was good. Gone were the days when she and Brice ran around on the muddy April roads from Sundt house to the clapboarded and rustic Tech buildings where the physicists worked. Gone the days when her mother taught school to the handful of first-generation Los Alamos children. Her older son, Sam's big brother, was gone, and all she had for him was some stupid beeper number he seldom checked—he didn't even know his grandmother was dead. But look, she thought, the rufous hummingbirds came around each year. One even now sipped nectar from the lilies. The sage she could smell in the sunlight would flourish again next year, if frosts didn't kill it at the root. And as the sages said, you couldn't count on anything staying the same. Plants, animals, people. The first scientists who settled this mesa were not coming back, any more than the Anasazi before them.

Well, she didn't know what she was thinking. Trying to think. Maybe just hoping to keep it together, her fledgling sense of what it means to be parentless. Generations come in waves, and so long as Ma was alive the distance between Bonnie Jean and the shore on which she herself would eventually break seemed farther away. She never thought like this before. We were all just waves coming to shore, Bonnie reflected. How many waves had beached since Creation? Trillions, tens of trillions? On the other hand, what did the numbers matter, anyway? She and Charlie and Brice and Jessica and Kip were next, and nothing could stop it or even should. A life was enough, Bonnie Jean thought. Seventy, eighty years, what more do you want? Dogs are happy to get ten. Some butterflies make do with a day. The milk-bonnet mushroom, so fresh in the morning, melts by noon. People who wish they could live forever are nuts. Pretty as the garden is, good as her husband and children are, nothing remains inspiring forever. Especially nothing you think is yours. You want something so bad you can taste it, and then you possess it, and next thing you know either you're its possession or you forgot what drew you to it in the first place.

The funeral would be held in a few days. Brice had gone downstate, but promised he'd be back to help carry the casket and make the graveside speech. Jessica and Ariel would be there, too, he'd assured her, though assembling the family wasn't going to be as easy as it might've been under other circumstances. Brice had asked his sister if she wouldn't mind working out things with the minister. They both knew where their mother had wanted to be laid to rest. Really, in Bonnie Jean's imagination the funeral service was already accomplished. It was just a matter of reenacting a few hours of ceremony, then a dinner among familiar strangers. But where had that lizard darted off to?

As she rode the switchbacks up to the Hill, Rebecca Carpenter remembered that last phone conversation she had with her runaway daughter, and how disturbing—disabling, even—it had been to hear Mary's buoyant assurances about life in Denver. She knew her girl better than her girl might have imagined. Had always known what transpired under the roof of her Gallup house. The war between Mary and Russ still rang in her ears, caused her to freeze up even today, thinking back. Mary'd done the right thing cutting out, but made a mistake lumping the whole family together with her father.

How to convey such an idea to her without undermining Russell was another story. Maybe some wounds never do mend.

"I'm so nervous," she told Johnny, who was at the wheel.

"Who wouldn't be. So am I."

They first paid a call on Clifford, who had aged since last they saw him but seemed chipper this afternoon as he shuffled along the corridor. And he was downright ecstatic when they mentioned that they'd come also to visit Mary.

"She here now?" he asked, a broad toothy smile erupting across his white face. They hovered beside the aquarium.

"Not now," his sister-in-law said. "But if she wants, we can bring her by tomorrow."

"You do," Clifford said, turning his attention back to the fish.

They checked into a motel in Los Alamos and telephoned Sarah Montoya at Pajarito. With Carl and Brice having left for Tularosa, she'd decided to let the center run itself for a few days, and taken up overseeing ranch matters until things got resolved downstate. Johnny told her, "We're here, if Mary would still like to see us."

The difficult delicacy of her role had never been more apparent. This collective upheaval was beginning to wear on her. She asked for their number at the motel and promised to pass it on to Mary.

"We're only staying the night. So please let her know as soon as you can."

"Your uncle Clifford is doing well, don't you think?"

"It was good to see him," Johnny said. "Tell Mary our fingers are crossed."

Mary was sitting right there on the banco in the kitchen and heard Sarah's half of the conversation.

"Here's the number. Their fingers are crossed that you'll call, your brother said."

"Jim?"

"No, Johnny."

"Johnny's with my mother?"

Sarah nodded.

"Guess this is it, then."

"Whatever kind of rapport you want with your family from here on out is up to you. Not that you haven't held the key all along."

Mary ran her hand over the back of her neck. Having made the decision to return the silver necklace Marcos had bought at San Felipe de Nerí for her twenty-first birthday—she'd placed it, with a note, in his dresser drawer, along with the other jewelry he'd given her—she nonetheless felt oddly naked in its absence. Unprotected somehow, exposed.

"Let me ask you a question, Mary. What's to prevent you from trying to follow through on what you originally planned to do when you left Gallup?"

"I'm not good enough."

"That's not what Marcos says. You're the best actor in that company, according to him."

"No offense, but how would he know good acting from bad?"

"Franny Johnson wasn't such a bad performance."

"It couldn't have been worse."

"All I'm saying is, why not follow your dream, see what gives. You're young, pretty, smart. Reconciling with Gallup might free you to go on. As it is, you're not where you wanted to be."

She didn't speak.

"Marcos told me you suggested that the two of you try swimming in a larger pond than Nambé."

"Los Angeles. He wasn't interested."

"Some people, I'd venture to guess most, don't think in terms of small ponds versus big ones. Nothing wrong with believing either way. But you know it's not how Marcos thinks."

"He's ambitious."

"For his horses and family, yes. For you, too."

"He's going to be one of the best at what he does."

"But for him it's different. He doesn't much care if anybody notices, whereas you have to. It's fundamental to what you want to do.

Just because Marcos is the way he is doesn't mean you shouldn't take your own leap of faith in yourself."

Sarah left the room to give Mary privacy as she placed her call to Los Alamos. Afterward, looking for her, Mary instead found Jessica out in the yard sitting beside a ruined fountain, a marble artifact of Spanish design that must have looked magnificent as an architectural centerpiece at the turn of the century, but now was something of a nostalgic eyesore. A salamander was gyrating along through its murk of standing water and brown leaves.

"Hello," she said.

Jessica started.

"Didn't mean to bother you, but have you seen Sarah?"

"No, Mary."

"Would you mind telling her I've gone to meet my mother and brother, and that I said to thank her for everything?"

"I'll tell her."

"Good, then. It was nice to meet you."

"Sounds like you're not coming back."

The salamander, a tiger common to the valley, reefed itself on a sandwich of floating leaves. A dragonfly settled on a nearby raft of Russian olive twigs.

"I don't know if I am or not."

"Mary, we've never spent a moment alone together and we don't know each other, but I gather that you and Kip are pretty close. What's he like?"

"Kip," she said, watching the salamander briefly sun itself. "I can tell you he's a gentleman and a good soul, because he is. And that he was always trying to steer me in right directions. But I don't think anybody could sum him up. Another turn of the screw and he could have been a saint or maniac, there's that kind of edge. I don't know. I think he figured me out more than I ever did him."

"I know the feeling."

"He's okay, right? They found him."

"He's going to be all right, apparently."

"And Marcos and the others?"

"Still out there."

Mary sighed. Like Bonnie's lizard, their salamander vanished without leaving any evidence it had ever been nearby.

"Everything's going to work out," Jessica tried.

"I'm sure," said Mary, turning to go. "You'll tell Sarah."

"Tell her what?"

"That I'll be in touch," and she left. Marcos's mother watched her walk to her car, looking through the window in the greatroom, where the phone rang and, without preamble, Carl told her they were about to get to see Kip in the base hospital at Alamogordo. Reportedly he was dehydrated and burned worse than a bug under a magnifying glass and his feet were all fucked up, but otherwise he was good as gold.

"Why don't they just go in and bring the other three out?"

"Seems Delfino's armed. I'll get back to you."

Sarah joined Jessica by the fountain. "Keep meaning to clean this out, make it presentable, but it seems I never get the time."

"I like it the way it is."

"Just a tar pit. Probably find dinosaur bones in there if you looked hard enough."

Jessica said, "Nothing's resolved, then?"

The other woman shook her head, noticing that the cottonwood trees were reflected on the dark face of the stagnant fountain water.

"I feel awful for Brice, losing his mother and now this, but with Ariel out there in the middle of nowhere—I don't know. I've never felt so helpless."

Sarah rested her hand on Jessica's forearm.

After talking with Carl, Delfino gave Jim back his field phone and, in dreamlike suspension, retrieved his shotgun from where it rested against the stone wall. He held it not in a threatening attitude but like some third arm, off to the side, oddly casual, numb to any possible consequences.

"I thought we had a gentlemen's agreement about the weapons, Mr. Montoya," said Jim.

Carl had read him the riot act, and though Delfino found it hard to disagree with anything that was said, he felt caught between the need to see this through and the urge to chuck it all in. As his brother had pointed out, he'd gotten everyone's attention. More than he'd managed to do ever before. What now? He needed to think. Hard with all these people staring at him.

"Delfino," said Marcos. "Let's put down the gun. He's talking with you, with all of us."

"You really have my father?" Ariel asked.

"He's doing fine," said Jim, ignoring Delfino's shotgun. "And yes, I can get you through to him just as easy as I got Mr. Montoya through. But we need to work on some understandings. We need for you to come on down out of here. As it is, nobody's been hurt and any charges they might want to bring against you would probably be minimal. Everything'll be fine. You'll get a good hearing for your grievances."

"This is just the kind of pretty talk I heard before. Kip's fine, I'm fine, you're fine, we're all just doing fine here today."

"Mr. Montoya, I'm not the government. I didn't write the law. I'm trying to defuse what's obviously not a great situation. There may be ways of getting your land back, but this isn't one of them."

Delfino looked down, then up.

"I'm just here to tell you this way won't get it done."

Despite himself, Delfino began to believe the sergeant.

"What did Carl say?" asked Marcos.

"Later."

"Later," Jim echoed, then asked Marcos, "Meantime, what are we going to do?"

"This place is his, it's his call."

To Ariel, "You want to speak to William Calder?"

"She's here to do just that," said Marcos. He'd begun to see himself as a kind of translator. No one was speaking quite the same language as anyone else.

Ariel watched mutely as Jim took a look at his own weapon lying dormant beside him on the stone. Confrontation was not in his orders, but humiliation at the hands of some civilian—whether his claims carried weight or not—wasn't in his nature. Marcos looked at Delfino's profile, attempting to read through the diminishing options. Delf gazed past Jim, out over the basin, wondering what Agnes might do if she were here with them.

"I would," said Ariel.

Jim thumbed in some numbers on the keypad, made the request, signed off. After several minutes the callback came, and he said a few words into the receiver, then took a step toward her handing over the field phone like an awkward calumet.

"You mind?" he asked Delfino, whose shotgun was pointed more at him than not.

Ariel took the well-worn leather-cased radio into her hands as Jim stood back.

"How do I—?"

"Press the talk button to speak, release it to listen back. Channel's clear, go ahead."

Ariel looked like some seeker clasping a possible grail, yet doubting its authenticity.

Visibly trembling, she said, "Hello," holding the earpiece hard against the side of her head.

As she might have expected, no one returned her greeting at the other end.

"Anybody there?" somewhat more forcefully.

The voice was reedy and strained and faraway. "Ariel?"

"Yes?"

"Ariel, it's your—I'm Kip."

"Kip?"

"Can you hear me?"

"Yes, yes."

How she wanted to say, *Yes, Dad,* but couldn't invoke the word.

"Ariel, are you all right?"

So this was his voice, what he sounded like. Tenor, somewhat melodic, a bit sandy. Thinned, she guessed, by his ordeal.

"The question is, are you?"

"Delfino and Marcos are there with you?"

"And the military police. Where are you, though?"

"Ariel?"

"Yes."

The transmission wasn't clear throughout, instead was flooded with static before going ungarbled again.

"Listen to me. If they make some kind of offer to let you come down to see me in exchange for your giving up on Delfino, don't do it. You're there for both you and me now, doing what I wasn't able to. Can you hear me?"

"I hear."

"Don't do it, Ariel. You hear?"

Other voices, none too happy, spoke behind Kip's.

"I hear," she repeated just as Jim decided to take back the field phone and cut off the transmission.

"So," said Jim. "You satisfied?"

"Satisfied with what?"

"With the fact that what you need to do is come out of here so we can all sit down and talk about the problem like adults?"

Declining Jim's invitation, she turned to Marcos, who'd asked, "Are you sure?"

She nodded.

Delfino wondered aloud if the sergeant wouldn't mind leaving them alone for the night. They'd gotten as far as they were going to get this evening. Jim, retrieving his gun and turning his back on the three intruders, acceded to the request without saying so much as a word. They watched him, a slow deliberate man, retreat across the short mesa forescape, then down the slope as sunset light played, a thousand beaming fingers signing mute messages across the Tularosa floor. It was then, standing before his decrepit sanctuary— once his pride and future, but now his undoing—that Delfino came to a hard insight.

An idea, in spite of a lifetime of hope otherwise, can unravel and come to nothing. So simple, yet so unbelievable.

Ariel, Marcos, Jim, and his adjuncts camping nearby—none of them was responsible for Delfino's original disappointment, his aspiration stretching over decades, his present contingency, or his newfound despair. He'd outlived most of his enemies. The officers and staff who'd originally come to Dripping Spring during the war to evict him and Agnes were to a man buried in plots hither and yon, in Missouri and California and Utah, not one left walking. Most of the ranchers were gone and all their treasured livestock. Agnes and her brother, gone. No one left but Delfino Montoya and these few busted buildings, some of whose planks and beams he would burn later that very evening to warm up canned peaches after they finished their meal of dehydrated mixed vegetables and jerky. The moon would shine through these widening chinks and gaps tomorrow night and in the next century, whether or not his hopes were dashed, until this habitat was beaten back down to dust, as it was so destined.

The three retired, Delfino having insisted on taking first watch. Nothing would calm his troubled mind, and he sat by the door listening to Ariel and Marcos breathe as they slept. A wave of shame passed through him for having brought them here.

He quietly climbed to his feet, lifting the shotgun from where he had set it. The air seemed deficient and his own breath came to him uneasily. Outside, the feathery edges of everything were emblazoned by starlight and the moon. As he wandered toward the rampart, stones crunched underfoot, soft round noises, though he strode as lightly as he could.

The world never favors plans, preferring instead moment by moment to unwind itself of its own volition. Destiny is the sum of choices you make in this flashpoint existence. But just because you're the merest, tiniest fleck in the tempest that is this world doesn't mean you haven't the capacity to resist. It's your earth to walk through. Get up and walk. You'll be done soon enough.

Something Agnes might have said. Or read somewhere. But no. It was Delfino's spontaneous philosophy just now, and Agnes was behind the thought because Agnes lived on inside him. If only he could share a few words with her, get her take on what to do. One thing was certain. She would want him to look out for his brother's son and his friend's daughter.

"They're nearby. I can feel them," Ariel whispered, placing her hand on his shoulder.

"Jesus. Don't scare an old man like that."

She hooked her arm through his free one.

"Thought you were asleep," he said.

"I heard you go out."

"Sorry. Tried to be quiet."

Standing side by side with him, Ariel could feel how gaunt he was, how tenuous, really.

"You're gonna have to leave here and meet with Kip in the morning," he told her.

"That's not what either of us wants. I'm standing for him now."

"Well, it's what I want."

"Can I ask you a forward question?"

"Nothing to hide on a night like this."

How dare she ask him such a thing? she thought, even as she said, "Why is it you don't have any children?"

"What?"

Too late to stop now. Besides, hadn't she come all this distance to put such questions squarely before herself?

"I mean, I'm assuming you don't have children or else they'd be here with you. Or maybe they don't agree with you about this—"

Delfino said, "We tried to have kids, my wife and me. We couldn't."

"But you wanted to?"

"We'd have had a dozen if it'd been in the cards for us. But it wasn't. End of story."

Ariel waited before pressing further. A meteorite stole across the sky, faintly perceptible in the deep blue.

"Did you ever think this ranch might be like a child, one that was kind of kidnapped from you and your wife?"

"No, can't say I ever thought of it that way."

"Probably a stupid idea."

He hesitated, said, "Probably."

"I guess your life would have turned out a lot differently if you'd had all those children you wanted."

"Guess you're right about that."

"Let's just say the ranch was a child. Even if you'd been able to raise it to maturity, you know there'd still come the day when you'd have to let it go."

Delfino shifted his weight and hitched his shotgun up onto the saddle of his hip. "What's all this talk about children, anyhow?"

"Just thinking aloud."

"You never had any, did you?"

Ariel laughed uncomfortably.

"You will, though."

"I never thought of myself as much of a mother type."

"What type do you think of yourself as being?"

"I don't know."

"Oh, go on. You're way too smart not to have some idea about who you are."

"I thought I was the one who was supposed to be asking you the forward questions."

"Go ahead."

"You got to know Kip a little. Why's he so afraid of me?"

"That's how you suss it out."

"You see it some other way?"

"He told me he thought you might be afraid of him, or disgusted with him, or like that."

"Not disgusted."

"Afraid, though."

"Everything's worthy of fear."

"That's probably why you're so courageous about things."

"Oh, no you don't. I'm terrified. About everything. There's nothing I'm not afraid of right now. I've never been so afraid in my whole life. You don't get to take that away from me."

"Not trying to. I happen to disagree, is all."

Beautiful old man, she thought, as she'd thought before—or no, she'd thought something like that about Granna. Too bad Agnes hadn't been able to bear them their dozen kids.

"I don't like your gun," she said.

"Neither do I."

"Look, Delfino. I'm trying not to be afraid of Kip."

"You should be, and shouldn't."

"That's not saying much."

"That's saying it all. Any good thing in this life is to be feared and not feared. Doubted and trusted. Anything you're not afraid of isn't worth the time even thinking about. I'm a whipped dog. You should listen to me because of that, if nothing else."

They heard movement out toward the north, beyond the farthest skeleton outbuilding of the old rancho, and also some scuttering stone down in the basin below where the sergeant had withdrawn hours before. Neither spoke to the fact, other than perhaps through a separate conversation of tightening grips and involuntary catching of breath. Each was either too afraid or too dauntless to speak to these little incursions, it didn't matter whether or which.

Delfino did, however, shock Ariel by asking, "Why would you even consider scrapping your kid?"

"What do you mean?"

"You know what I mean."

"Marcos told you."

"No, sixth sense. I saw how nauseated you were riding in here, even though you tried to hide it. Saw you getting sick and then well again real fast. I might not have kids of my own, but I been around. Anybody planning on having a baby wouldn't do what you're doing."

Ariel sighed.

"So, why scrap it? Doesn't make sense."

"That's a pretty personal question."

"I thought we were having a forward talk. What's to lose?"

Ariel didn't ease her grip on Delfino's arm. "You mean by your asking that question, or by my having a kid?"

"Kid."

"Pretty much everything. My life, my freedom, my days."

"Nights, too. So I hear."

"My nights."

"Your mind."

She laughed. "Yes. Definitely my mind."

"What else."

"That isn't enough?"

"I'm sure there's more. Like your loneliness, selfishness, things like that."

"Did Kip ever tell you why he did what he did?"

"Ask him yourself. What I do know is that he wouldn't want you to walk his same path. And by the way, Ariel?"

"Yes?"

"Ranches aren't children. I appreciate the idea. But they're just rocks and wood and nails and glass and boundary markers."

"You don't believe that."

"Starting to."

"Maybe it would be better if you thought about it both ways."

"Meaning?"

"Meaning that if you—" but the voices behind them cut through the night like the onset of a sudden fever. No sooner did they turn around than someone spoke loudly from down in the wash ravine to the south, and someone else—Jim—shouted a universal order for calm. Marcos came running from inside the house, crying out Ariel's name and his uncle's. There was a flurry of buffeting against the air. Ariel reached out for Marcos and caught his hand before another hand shoved her from behind, toppling her forward onto the parapet and knocking the wind out of her. Different dark forms struggled above her. There was moaning. Somebody shouted. Shocked calm, fresh chaos. She'd lost any sense of where Marcos could be, though Delfino Montoya was there, stumbling with her, tripping as the shotgun he dropped discharged its own brisk flare while the moon breached the ridge hard by Sierra Blanca.

PART IV

THE FOREVER RETURNING

New York, Tularosa Basin, Los Alamos

to Nambé

1996–2000

Singing and pennywhistles and gusts of laughter. Three generations of merrymakers sat at a long table centered by a big frosted cake. A pile of forks and stack of plates stood beside an old redware bowl heaped with melting vanilla ice cream. *Happy birthday to you*— roughly harmonizing their way through the familiar tune—*happy birthday, dear Miranda,* and after she blew out all three candles, cheers resounded in the room. Miranda clapped and giggled, her blue eyes beaming, as her father began to cut the cake. What a party. Sarah took the family photographs, which would be preserved in an album for this girl to view years later with an altogether different cast to those eyes. An adult's knowing look, one that would register memories of her birthday in that first March of the new millennium. Later that evening, Sarah would upload digital images of the best shots and e-mail them to Miranda's grandfather Brice so he could share in the celebration.

He would easily recognize most of the faces on his laptop screen. Ariel and Marcos and all the rest of the family, including Jessica, out visiting for the grand occasion. Some of the others he might not know, never having met any of the new ranch hands or the foreman, Diego Chavéz, who'd come on at Pajarito to take over where Kip had left off. But whether or not he recognized Diego, he'd be reminded again of Kip Calder, the honorary Montoya whose suggestion it'd been to give their granddaughter her name. Miranda Montoya. Had a nice alliterative lilt to it, a good music. Not to mention its origins, like Ariel's, in *The Tempest*—another way Kip, who'd never fancied his daughter's name, had made one more fond compromise with his own revered child. Fine and dandy, though Marcos insisted that he was going to name their one on the way, and it wasn't going to have any goddamn literary allusions. Kip Montoya? Maybe, maybe not.

But look at this. If there had always been a strong likeness between Kip and Ariel, little Miranda was a beautiful, feminine reincarnation of both. These photos of Miranda revived memories not only of Ariel back when she was this young, but of Kip back when he was vibrant with health, ready to take on the world. The images from those insane desert days three and a half years ago were as sharply clear as these of the birthday party on Brice's screen. First seeing Kip in that claustrophobic military infirmary was like something straight out of Kafka, he'd thought at the time, and said as much. Granted, Kip had committed a federal offense and his accomplices were resisting being taken into custody on similar charges, but that didn't mean he could be put to work luring the others out of Dripping Spring. Not legally. The fact he'd baited and switched, agreeing to talk to Ariel Rankin and Delfino Montoya, implying he might be able to help the MPs but then instead urging his daughter and friends to stay their course, rankled the hell out of his captors. But it was their own fault. Their risk and loss.

Kip might have flown off the handle in any direction at the sight of his so-called lawyer, Brice McCarthy, so it'd come as a relief when he tried, failed, then finally managed to stand and awkwardly embrace him, Kip's intravenous tube and infusion bag getting joggled in the process. The door was locked behind them, a very unnecessary precaution.

"So this is my lawyer."

"*Pro hac vice,* unless you have another one."

"What a world."

They smiled.

"How're Ariel and the others?"

"I've been trying to find out, but I'm in the dark, too."

"Are we out of here?" Kip asked.

"First I have to get a judge to review charges and set bail. You look awful."

"Never felt better."

"Come on."

"I feel like hell, but I'm not the priority. You think you can work out something so Delfino can leave with more than just promises that the DOD will reconsider his case?"

"I read his letter and documents on the way here with Carl. It looks like a straight uphill battle to me."

"That's the kind of case you liberal lawyers are supposed to take on, right?"

Brice warmly smirked at his old friend. Creep. Next thing you know Kip was going to call him *boy,* just like he used to when they were punk kids.

"Obviously I'll try to help Delfino. Ariel's my first concern, though," Brice said. "They tell me you spoke with her."

Kip nodded, a bit sheepish about having urged her onto a heading Brice and Jessica wouldn't necessarily have advocated.

"What'd she say?"

"She said she was fine."

"Did she want to surrender?"

"No," Kip murmured, then felt compelled to confess.

Carl, who'd been allowed into the room and had stood quietly by the door, said, "Kip, I thought I knew you, but you're just as crazy a fuck as my brother."

Kip stared at the blue floor until Brice broke the lull. "If I know Ariel, she would've stuck it out with them anyway. Not in her nature to abandon people," forgetting for the moment just how abandoning of him, Jessica, and her grandmother his daughter had recently been.

Did Kip hear a gibe against himself in Brice's words? Perhaps not, but even if one were intended he wouldn't for a moment defend himself against the truth of the innuendo. What did begin to bother him was the possibility he'd urged Ariel to remain at Dripping Spring because it would delay their reunion. Pathetic, if that were the case. He hardly knew anymore.

Brice's proposed journey out to the former Montoya ranch site in the role of negotiator never transpired, of course, since while he and Carl were conferring with Kip, the order was passed on to bring the standoff to an end later that same night. White Sands had ascertained through background checks that the cache of arms the intruders had with them in the mountains might run a bit deeper than that sole shotgun the old man carried around. Seems he'd bought some pretty fancy, if outdated, hardware over the years. "If they brought his whole gun cabinet with them, they could put on quite a show," Jim's commanding officer told him. Everyone agreed the best course would be to storm them while they were still asleep, or at least drowsy, in predawn, when the light was weakest.

Delfino knew what was happening even as it went down. White heat in his shotgun saturated the charge after the firing pin struck the primer. It flamed through the flash hole, igniting the powder. The pressure behind the cartridge rose so fast it began to bloom, blistering hot. The brass end of the casing swelled until it filled the steel chamber walls of the barrel, and the case neck expanded so as to ram forward the buckshot housing. The only thing free to move, in the face of all this pressure, was the load, which accelerated from the gut of the gun. It was born in a flash of heat, spinning like a mad dervish. Its blast pierced the air. One thousandth of a second passed before some of the shot tore like tiny nettled wasps into his flesh.

All this occurred under a setting moon. Silver light from the Remington offered brief, brilliant illumination, then everything lay veiled under starlight once more. Delfino clutched at his neck and shoulder in disbelief. Ariel, having taken Delfino's hand when he reached out, toppled with him as he collapsed on the stone fence. He was gibbering when she pulled his head into her lap and shielded him, enfolding the man in her arms. Feeling the warm wet slick of blood on her hands and face, she screamed for help, and Marcos yelled at the men to hold their fire. Jim was shouting the same order. Someone jumped, someone else dropped to a knee. A third sprinted forward to crouch beside the fallen ones by the rampart, while Marcos, who held a rifle, threw it, good and hard, down on the ground and himself ran to where these men and this woman were standing or kneeling or writhing under the night sky.

Delfino Montoya was injured by what would prove to be one of his own shells. The gaping, mangled wound looked dire under their flashlights, though it appeared worse in the field than it soon would to the surgeon in his operating room, which was bad enough. The girl, whom Marcos embraced even as she embraced his uncle, was splattered with blood that turned out not to be hers but the old rancher's. The whole fracas took mere minutes, but those minutes were concentratedly terrible. The aerovac got there more swiftly than in a dream. Marcos sat beside her, and Delfino lay in the rear of the same chopper receiving emergency medical aid as Ariel watched Dripping Spring recede beneath them, a mere disarray of ruins and boundary markers getting smaller and smaller under the first pinks of dawn ascending the Sacramentos.

What happened would always seem unreal. Delfino was rushed into surgery, Marcos and Ariel were taken into the infirmary. Led to different rooms, they were checked over and found only to be exhausted and dehydrated. Each felt bewildered by this separation from the other.

"You did this knowing you're pregnant?" the doctor chided.

Not like he was wrong. It had been madness, but with purpose. He'd never understand so she took his criticism silently. She really wanted Marcos to be here. Of anyone, he understood.

Within the hour they were moved to a conference room in another building. Carl was allowed to talk with them, and soon afterward Brice came in, having made calls to Nambé as well as back east to colleagues for legal advice. He'd already expedited scheduling hearings with local authorities for the next morning. After hugging his daughter, Brice asked the obvious question—"What the hell did you think you were doing?"—and heard straightforward answers about what had brought her and Marcos Montoya to this juncture. When Kip lit out on Delfino, and Delfino refused to abandon his plan, there really wasn't much Ariel and Marcos could do other than turn them in or follow along. Brice didn't foresee too much difficulty arranging their release on bail. Kip's, either. Delfino, assuming that he came out of surgery okay, would be more complicated. But given the history of similar strife in the basin and the old man's record of lawful behavior, Brice figured he would, when the time came, be able to bargain for parole in exchange for a plea of guilty. Surely the White Sands attorneys would prefer leniency to drawing the attention that would come from putting an elderly evicted rancher in jail. It wasn't necessarily what Delfino was going to want, but it seemed the only responsible strategy.

Ariel listened, but her mind was elsewhere. Her interrupted talk with Delfino contended with the immediate present. God, she hoped he was going to be all right. What he'd said about her being courageous beleaguered her. She wasn't courageous. In fact, she was the least courageous person she knew. That's how she saw it. Right or wrong, the time had come to take another step at least in the direction of Delfino's sanguine thought. She asked to see Kip.

"He's not looking good," warned Brice, all too aware he'd soon enough have to tell her about her grandmother.

"Neither am I," glancing down at her torn, bloodstained dress.

"Let me try to get authorization," Brice said, and left the room.

"Your father told me the story during our drive down," said Carl, watching Marcos's eyes on Ariel and hers on him and thinking he'd never seen Franny and his son exchange looks like that. "Not everybody gets to have two fathers."

"Does that mean I'm lucky or cursed?"

"If it's cursed, it's a good kind of curse," said Marcos. "You'll see."

With a uniformed man at his side, Brice returned. He put his arm around Ariel and said, "I'm proud of you, proud you're our daughter," and she left with a backward glance at Marcos and one more at Brice.

She was led out of the building and back to the infirmary, down a corridor until they came to his door. After unlocking it, the MP stood aside. When she entered Kip's room, father's and daughter's eyes met, and what they saw was so familiar yet singular that it was as if they glimpsed for the first time their own reflections in a mirror. Each was overwhelmed by the resemblance, yes, but also by the intense, actual presence of the other. For some inconceivable reason, Ariel thought of her best childhood pal, Buddha. Buddy?

"Ariel," Kip said, and she walked to him.

"Dad," the impossible word coming through so readily.

The warmth of their embrace, the ease of it. Kip whispered her name again, and she laid her head on his paltry shoulder and said his full name, both perhaps by way of convincing themselves they were really here.

Thin as a shade the man was, and smelled somehow of juniper vanilla, smelled like a newborn. Maybe she was weeping; the room was suddenly a blur. For minutes neither spoke. When Ariel finally stepped back, holding Kip's hands and looking deeper into his ravaged and sunken eyes, she heard him say—did he truly?—"I love you," as if these were the simplest words he ever articulated, whereas in fact he never expressed them to anyone other than Jessica Rankin, long ago. Ariel voiced the same three words to him. Then again. And once more. Each time uttered so dissimilarly that the phrase seemed to mean three different things.

Later she would view this as the moment when she decided to forgo an abortion, to take her developing progeny to term, her girl or boy, and let the rest of the world set whatever course it wished. She helped Kip onto the bed and sat beside him there, holding his narrow hand. What could they say? Everything, nothing.

They glowed in each other's company. Kip was reminded of Emma Inez, Ariel of that tattered photograph of a young man with his closest friend, arms over shoulders with Shiprock looming in the distance. Rarer than love at first sight, it felt to each of them like they had solved an irresolvable problem, or found they could suddenly speak Chinese or play virtuoso violin. While Ariel looked the worse for wear, and Kip worse yet, neither recalled ever having witnessed another person so full of spirit.

"You should lie down," she said. "Here, let me help you."

Kip allowed her to arrange his pillows, then took her hand as he eased himself back on the bed. Without asking, she dipped a wash-cloth into the pitcher of ice water on his bedside table and daubed his forehead. Not at all used to the touch of another—or was it sim-ply the cold?—he flinched a little, then relinquished his fear. It was not the cold. This was his daughter, trying to tend to a sick, face it, dying, man. Would he presume, after every single thing he'd denied her, to take that away from her now? From himself, as well? He would not.

Ariel wondered if he was feeling well enough to tell her some sto-ries, the most provisional memoir, some images for her as she began to paint for herself a picture of his life. "Tell me anything—the least things about yourself would be more interesting than you can imag-ine. I'm here to listen."

And at that he did gather some memories and began to describe them, leaving out the invented stuff about being a lighthouse keeper and driving stolen cars across the border. He was only amazed by his lack of fear, not to mention of that inveterate will to run away. Why had he run in the first place? he had to wonder, as he tried to tell Ariel what his life had been like after he left her mother.

"Do I have any sisters or brothers?" Ariel asked, remembering her conversation on the subject with Granna.

"No blood kin."

"You have no family?"

Kip shook his head. "No, not really. No, in fact."

"Just me, then."

"Just you."

They smiled at the revelation, then Kip turned the focus on her.

"And you? You're not married," holding up her ringless hand.

"No."

"Boyfriend, or how do they call it now, a significant other?"

"There've been a few, one in particular these last couple years who I thought might be the real thing, but that's over."

"Tell me about your growing up," he asked, and she did her best to portray herself, though as her narrative progressed it dawned on her that she'd never truly thrown herself at life emphatic, firm, aflame— whatever right word might measure up to the dense passion she'd felt these last days and weeks—until she set out to search for him.

She told him as much, and when she did, something that had been lurking still, bothering him, came to the fore. Had she looked for him and not found him those few years ago, after he gave his father's ledger to Brice in Chimayó?

Ariel admitted she hadn't.

He asked, "Why now, then?" and she finally came up against the very question she'd traveled here to have answered. It was as if the oracle were querying the supplicant rather than the other way around.

"Because I'm going to have a child," she said, simply.

"You are? That's wonderful."

"No husband, no wedlock. Still wonderful?"

"Wonderful no matter what. But Ariel, I'm not making the connection, why you came here now if before—"

She squeezed his hand and said, "Because I needed to see my father in order to know whether I should ever be a mother. You gave me up for the longest time, and you had your reasons. I couldn't do that. It would have to be all or nothing for me."

"I'm so sorry about everything, Ariel—"

"Me, too."

"You deserved a better father than I could have been."

She thought for a moment, and said, "When I was a little girl, I was the opposite of you and Brice. You two ran up the mountains and down the canyons, and even after you grew up you just kept on flying straight into the teeth of life. So much of my flying's been done in my head. Nothing wrong with that, but you should know I don't hold anything you've done against you."

"You're quite a young woman."

"I used to love Robert Louis Stevenson. He wrote something I always thought was wise, and maybe I think so even more today. It went something like, To love playthings when you're a child, to lead an adventurous and honorable youth, then to settle when the time comes into a green and smiling age, is to be a good artist in life and deserve well of yourself and your neighbor. Separately, maybe we haven't been the best artists of life, but put us together and you've got something deserving well of ourselves and each other."

"Thank you, Ariel. For finding me."

"I'm just sorry I didn't—"

He put his finger to her lips.

"Just think," he said. "A child."

She sat with him another hour, leaving only when he fell asleep. As she was escorted back to join the others, she realized that almost everybody knew her secret except Jessica and Brice, though no one besides Kip, of course, was aware she had determined to go ahead. She would confess, or rather shout it to the rafters, as soon as the right moments proposed themselves.

*I*ncorrigible, exquisite Granna McCarthy was buried with her Bible and her pipe, laid beside her husband in a simple service. More mourners turned out than her family expected. Middle-aged former students, church friends, even some people no one recognized. Her inspiring nets had been widely cast. While in his eulogy Brice spoke of faith and loyalty, he felt profoundly troubled by his own bad faith and disloyalty in having neglected to follow through on his earlier promise to visit his mother. In the weeks that followed, while seeing Ariel through the trauma of gain and loss as best he could, Brice found himself shuttling between New York and New Mexico on red-eye specials, having committed himself to extricating his daughter and the Montoyas from their legal tangle. He stayed in the guest bedroom of Bonnie's house when he was up north, and in the Tularosa bungalow when downstate. He sometimes visited Pear Street to pass some thoughtful hours there. He knew this was a displaced case of better late than never, but so be it.

Arraignments, bail, conditions for release—all the prelims transpired swiftly, which maybe gave him false hope the rest would as well. After a lot of wrangling, the charges against Ariel and Marcos were dropped, as were those against Kip. The latter was too ill to stand trial, and the former two, it was argued, had been at Dripping Spring not for the purpose of committing a crime, but to help mediate.

Delfino's was a tougher problem, one that had everything to do with his shotgun having discharged, resulting in the endangerment of government officers. That he had nearly blown off his own head didn't matter. He was lucky to be alive, but nobody forced him to do what he did. Brice was surprised to discover, however, that a lot of these White Sands people sympathized with the old-timers. Couldn't doctor history, but the ranchers sure had gotten a damn raw deal back when. As it happened, no one had the stomach to put Delfino Montoya away.

The compromise they hammered out involved his committing to drop all further claims against White Sands or any governmental department or agency attached thereto, and never to trespass on the range again. In exchange, all charges against him would be dismissed, and under strict range supervision, the remains of his wife, Agnes Montoya, would be reinterred at the site of the couple's former homestead. On his demise, Montoya himself would also be allowed a permanent resting place at Dripping Spring. Kip had asked to be buried there as well, and his request, too, would be granted, but that was to be that. "We're not running some cemetery here, Mr. McCarthy," one of the lawyers said, to which comment Brice wanted to retort, "That's precisely what you're running here, sir," but restrained himself in the interest of settling his clients' affairs. Nor would there be visiting rights for anyone wishing to place flowers of commemoration in the future. Just wasn't in the cards. They were bending all the rules as it was.

Ariel reluctantly flew back east, knowing she had bent more than a few rules herself. She'd completely neglected her job, for one. Welcomed back to her manuscript-strewn office with greater forgiveness than seemed justifiable, she tried to reenter that world which only weeks before she'd inhabited like a sociable character in one of her more benign books. But it wasn't her world anymore. She was sorry to resign, but did, and as she cleaned out her desk and bade goodbye to her colleagues, she was overtaken by an intuition that while she had no firm idea of what she was doing, the gesture was sufficient unto itself. She who never moved rashly was now expelling her past with heretical dispatch, and against the chances of no certain future. At least in borrowing her parents' car—the Dart was still in Los Alamos, poor dusty warrior—and driving to the farmhouse, collecting David's things, boxing them up, and sending them back to him, with "Forward If Necessary" written on the box, she declared one future finished. In a moment of madness, stone-cold sober on the back porch, gazing out into the hills of sugar maples some of whose leaves were just starting to turn, she dialed his number one last time, to let him know her plans. Not that she expected anything from him. To the contrary. A canned voice told her the number had been changed. Then another said unlisted.

During that aberrant September and into early fall, she seemed to live for word of Kip, of Sarah and Delfino. Above all of Marcos, who called most every night after she returned to New York, to hear about her day and tell her about his.

"Is the criminal of the household in?" he would begin.

"Speaking."

Or else, "Is there a con around?"

"Who's asking?"

"A pro."

"Pro con?"

"Not very."

Shuck and jive, meant perhaps to disburden the darker story behind their having met, not as any mockery of Delfino or Kip, rather as a language of bonding.

He called from the kitchen. It wasn't hard to imagine him beside the refrigerator decorated with Polaroids and postcards, sitting on the hardwood counter—Sarah wished he would kick that habit—smoking a cigarette (that one, too) after everyone else at Rancho Pajarito had gone to bed. He asked her how she was feeling, whether the morning sickness had abated now that she'd entered her second trimester.

"Seems I'm over that part of the pregnancy."

"Great."

"I'm glad I went through it for a while, though."

"Why? You some kind of masochist?"

"No, listen. If I hadn't gotten sick that night out at Dripping Spring, I wouldn't have told you I was pregnant, and it was a good thing I did."

"Not that I was much help."

"You were, believe me."

"I'm not sure how."

She said, "Trust me. Telling you, knowing you knew, was unbelievably helpful."

"So, Ariel?"

"Yeah?"

"You fat yet?"

Mocked them away from sweet talk, though as more weeks passed they found themselves speaking often about what they loved, why they cherished what they cherished—all the things that had brought them to these affections and affinities. Ariel read him passages from the Calder ledger, surprising both of them one evening when she shared Kip's letter. Marcos told her about Franny Johnson, who'd turned out to be Mary Carpenter, and Ariel filled him in about David Moore and why she was about to become a single mother.

"Aren't you obligated legally to tell him he's going to be a father?" Marcos asked, noting as he did how the question made his stomach churn.

"In fact, no. But more than legally, sometimes I still think I owe him the moral courtesy—except then I remember I already did that. When he left, the issue was dead, literally dead, done with. He mailed me a check for the procedure—"

"Abortion?"

"—abortion. I found it in the mailbox when I got back and I threw it out. I've tried to reach him, but nothing doing. He's known all along how to get in touch with me if he had any interest in the matter. He doesn't. There's nothing to talk with him about. Does that sound cold?"

"More sad than cold."

Ariel agreed with Marcos. It was sad. But there was no changing what happened. You wove with the length of thread fate spun out, did your best to weave well. If others laid scissors to the fabric, you patched the damage and hoped it wouldn't happen again. If it did, you patched the damage once more.

In November, just before Kip was diagnosed as terminal, Marcos visited him in the fieldhouse where he'd taken up residence again in the wake of Tularosa. He wanted to tell Kip about Ariel, about his feelings for this woman whom he now knew more as a voice than a flesh-and-blood person.

Kip welcomed him, exchanged small talk about this new horse or that, then asked what was up.

"I'm going to New York. To visit Ariel," Marcos said.

"Sounds good," said Kip.

"You don't mind?"

"Mind what?"

"You're right, never mind."

Kip wasn't going to be very helpful, so Marcos shifted subjects.

"Do you miss Mary?"

"I miss everybody, Marcos. It's a sign of getting old."

"Come on, I'm serious."

"I miss Ariel."

"So do I," Marcos said—out of his mouth before he knew it.

"I've noticed."

"You don't mind?"

"That's the second time you've asked. Mind what?"

"Something's going on between me and Ariel."

"No reason it shouldn't."

"We're completely different, though. She's a city person. I'm a pueblo valley horse breeder."

"The only woman I ever fell in love with was a city person, and when we met I'd come from these same sticks as you. You know it doesn't matter."

When Marcos flew east to see her in Manhattan, Kip's words would carry resonance. His room at the Gramercy Park sat empty throughout his stay, while he and Ariel spent long nights talking about all and everything, holding hands, crashing side by side atop the coverlet on her bed. Faces close, they breathed each other's breath until they half fainted from intoxication.

Accompanying her to an obstetrician's appointment the morning of his last day in town, he was asked by the receptionist, "You're the father-to-be?"

"No," he said, at the same instant Ariel said, "Yes."

"Yes," at the same time Ariel said, "No."

Which was the moment, the intimation, that led them beyond talk and handholding, so that after walking slowly, enveloping each other as they returned to the East Village and up the creaky stairs to her aerie, then closing the door behind them, they undressed one another and, kissing, kneeling, embracing on the braided rug, collapsed gently together into a wraith of passion. Marcos asked, running his large, tender, work-rough hand over the mild swell of her belly, if this was a wise idea. Lying on her back, dark hair framing her serious face, she turned her head toward him, ran her hand down his cheek, and whispered there'd never been a wiser idea. They made love with an innocent ease that proposed it would happen again, a hundred times, a thousand times, over the years.

She rode with him to LaGuardia the next morning and they walked together to the gate, hugging so closely that they half-stumbled sideways, and with every step kissing. When he asked her if she had a photo of herself, she gave him her driver's license and they kissed in such a delirium he nearly missed his flight.

"How'd you get that?" she asked him before he boarded. She nodded toward the scar on his forearm.

"I was really young, first learning to ride. Got on a horse way beyond my abilities. It's ugly, but I kind of see it as a badge of honor."

She ran her fingertips over the distressed skin, as if stroking silk. "It's beautiful," she said. "Safe journey home."

Everything moved quickly after Marcos left. She invited herself over to Chelsea that evening and, as she'd done so many times in the past, made dinner with Jessica. She announced her plans, savored her parents' words of support. Within the week she gave notice on her apartment, put her belongings in storage, and moved west to Pear Street. At Christmas her parents joined her in New Mexico, passing some time themselves with their friend Kip as the first snow fell over the finger mesas. The childhood pals celebrated their shared birthday together surrounded by family, and by friends who'd become family.

As winter progressed, Ariel marveled at how Kip, readmitted to the convalescent center as a Los Alamos Hospital outpatient, became infatuated by books. Bedridden for most of the day, he couldn't sit as before with others watching television. Instead, in January he traveled with Don Quixote and Sancho Panza, in February with Ishmael and Ahab. Ariel brought some of Granna's books from Pear Street, and he devoured them, a famished man at a feast, liking some better than others. His daughter could never predict his responses.

He had his own take on everything, unswayed by any canon or decorum. Keats's "Ode on a Grecian Urn" provoked wicked laughter from the frail man as he read aloud to Ariel,

> *"Ah, happy, happy boughs! that cannot shed*
> *Your leaves, nor ever bid the Spring adieu;*
> *And, happy melodist, unwearièd,*
> *Forever piping songs forever new . . .*

"God in heaven, what a load of slobber," continuing,

> *"More happy love! more happy, happy love!*
> *Forever warm and still to be enjoyed,*
> *Forever panting, and forever young.*

"Listen, Ariel, take it from one who knows. Nobody in their right mind wants to be forever panting. Let alone forever young."

"But that's one of the most famous poems ever written," she argued.

He was being harsh, but she couldn't dispute the underlying logic—horse sense, Marcos later said—and so did not. No one could say Kip Calder wasn't wildly spirited in those last months before he finally succumbed to cancer. The way a flame sometimes surges into abrupt brilliance just before it gutters and goes out.

Kip survived to see his granddaughter born. Both he and Ariel were in the same hospital. The waiting room was a wonderful havoc. Jessica, Brice, Bonnie Jean, Sarah, Carl, Delfino. The patient and impatient. Marcos was there beside her holding her hand as she went into labor. Miranda was about to be a March baby, just like her mother.

Ariel could have sworn she heard one of the delivery doctors whisper, *Stock the pond with mermaids.* Well, maybe not. Dilating, swirling, spinning, she lay back against the wet sheets and pressed her knees away from one another and thought of the pond upstate yielding to an early spring thaw, its deep quilt of ice melting, snapping and crackling in barrages of succinct commentary about what it was like to be water once warm and supple, and then frozen, frosted, hardened to the point where any animal or any boy on his snowmobile could cross it without fear of drowning, then to be liquefied again by the warm equinox. And she thought how crazy it had been for her even to consider forgoing this melting moment of her own, this melting away from self toward selves. Marcos was saying something to her, that he loved her, that she was doing great. And the doctor was speaking, too, but she didn't really want to listen. She wanted to think of how the peepers would soon be multiplying along the shallow shore of the pond, and how during the night a clumsy skunk, hobbly and hankhaired, might drop by for a sip of water. Bluebird, phoebe, tree swallow—they all will be nesting soon, and the grass will be spongy, marvelously cold under bare feet. Windows will need washing, and the peeling paint she'd thought to scrape the year before will lie like white potato chips along the walls, even as cracks and pennynail rust stains present themselves. She recalled again that moment when she'd seen herself reflected in the pool of water on the kitchen floor and started and pushed and clenched her fists as the birthing began, and she forgave everyone who'd ever done her the least harm, because none of it amounted to anything compared to this good, living present.

And the room continued to make itself known to Ariel, its heavy lights, its voices of urgent encouragement. She never felt so much like a universe, a spring overflow pond herself. Everything was so utterly stretched beyond the boundaries of probability, and the pain was beautifully everywhere running through her.

So this was what it was like to give birth. No, what it *was* to give birth. One breathing in, slowly, slowly. Two out, slowly, slowly. The nurse said the child was crowning. She never felt so euphoric in her life, looped on all this air, buzzed by breathing in and out. She wanted to remember everything and told Marcos she wanted never to forget this day and he said she wouldn't as he held her hand and told her the baby was a girl, a beautiful little girl, and before Ariel could think of another thing Miranda was gently laid on her mother's chest and Ariel took the first look at her daughter who seemed to look at her right back.

*L*a Cienaga was moving, but the traffic was slow for such an early hour. Going to be a hot one. The hazy sky above the palm trees was already florid, though the sun had only just risen. They said the Santa Anas would be blowing again today. Yeahboy, a scorcher was in the cards, and wind to drive the heat right through your mind, but it wouldn't matter. The eucalyptus scent in the air this morning was perfume from some fine heaven, balm for the soul. And besides, she'd be in air conditioning until long after that same red sun had flown away over the wide Pacific.

Had no idea what was on the docket. The acting agent had left a message like always, nobody ever quite connecting person to person. Messages on machines got the job done, so why personalize when the system worked fine. She had a location address and contact name and all was well with the world. This was not going to be Jane Austen on the silver screen or a sitcom or anything more than a commercial shoot, so no need for major apprehension. The agency had asked if she had any cuts or bruises on her hands, so she surmised it might have something to do with soap. Detergents, or else moisturizer. Possibly just a matter of holding up some product. Paid the mortgage between real gigs, and it was a mortgage now, on an apartment in Santa Monica, not some frittering West Hollywood rental. Covered private coaching, too, which she worked at with dedication.

Every so often she wondered if she and Marcos mightn't have made a go of it if she'd simply met him over the counter of that restaurant as forthright Mary Carpenter from Gallup, New Mexico. In the honest hours, awake in bed at night, listening to the mockingbird sing its countless songs outside her window, she knew it wasn't so. He'd hate it here. Hate the blatant billboards, the cars, the commerce. Hate the parties and having to be on when other people were also being on, watching you be on. Whereas she lived for the marvelous game of quarry and chase.

While she'd dated a few men after moving out here, nothing had gotten serious. It would happen, she was sure. The whos and whens were unknown, but the right man would eventually cross her path— end of story, run the credits, lower the curtain. She couldn't swear it might not befall her this very day.

That's how it happened for Marcos. She knew, absolutely knew, the first she laid eyes on Ariel, what was going to develop. These things you feel in your bones, no explaining otherwise. Was she happy for him? Probably yes, definitely yes. But her pleasure or suffering regarding Marcos and his family was peripheral now, had to be. Sometimes when Sarah phoned her—funny, she was one of the few who seemed to call when Franny was actually home—and filled her in on Pajarito doings, it all seemed a million miles away. Other times, she couldn't get enough scuttlebutt. Sarah continued to refer to her as Mary, though she went by Franny Johnson out here—a good name, like Kip once said, different from anybody else's, distinctive. She didn't mind Sarah calling her Mary, though. Nostalgic to hear it. Franny wondered if Sarah made the calls on the sly. Not that she was devious, didn't have a deceitful leaf in her tree. Her purpose was without doubt admirable. Sarah considered Mary a commitment and wanted to follow her progress, was all. She'd never forget that time Sarah urged her to push forward with her aspirations, though in darker moments she questioned whether, even subconsciously, Marcos's mother hadn't wanted her to move on. But, well, never mind. Move on she had, and that was that.

Last time she saw him was probably the last time she would ever lay eyes on Marcos Montoya, at Kip's memorial. More Irish wake than dirgeful funeral, since Kip himself had planned the party ahead of time. By April his condition had so deteriorated that no further medical therapy was prescribed beyond pain management. His nine lives had been used up, and no chemo could change that. Ariel had

acted as his amanuensis, writing down his final thoughts. The festivi-
ties were to take place at the old adobe fieldhouse, summer solstice.
There was to be champagne and caviar, music and dancing, the
works. Nobody was to be excluded.

His plans were followed to the letter. The revelry lasted deep into
the Nambé night. Hard to imagine she and Ariel danced together to
some Frank Sinatra song on the record player they'd set up beside
the icetub filled with bottles of bubbly. It was not unlike one of those
jazz funerals where the band tours the streets riffing out the melody
of a man's life come to its end, a noisy triumph of redemption, drum
and cymbal applauding the deeds now all done. Ariel's baby lay in
her bassinet, surrounded by doting relatives and friends. She was
cute as the proverbial button, Franny thought, and slept through the
raucous wake like an angel.

All the while, the man of the hour lay far from these noisy festivi-
ties. Ariel, dancing now with Delfino, had acted as sole witness to
the burial. He was settled in the sandy loam alongside Agnes Montoya's bones at Dripping Spring. Just where Delfino himself, dancing
a little drunkenly with Marcos's fiancée, would someday be laid to
rest, according to his own hard-won wishes.

At midnight, the music having been silenced, Marcos set off
fireworks—again Kip's orchestration—that lit the starry black sky in
a shower of sparks, then vanished in threads of light coming back to
earth. And as Franny stood beside her uncle Clifford, whom she'd
driven up from Gallup to attend, she wondered if anybody other than
herself would ever make the connection between Delfino Montoya,
his two companions, and Sergeant Carpenter. The world was ever a
small place, like they say, but since Franny had never disclosed what
she knew to either family, it hadn't grown smaller yet. What good
could come of her telling anyone about the chance convergence?
Clifford probably would appreciate it, she thought. He seemed more
spaced out than ever, but also much happier now that her parents
had brought him back home to live. Next time she went out to visit,
maybe she'd let him in on the secret. Just the kind of thing Kip

would have found amusing. Dear Kip who'd tried his best to father her through the bad old days. She would always be grateful that he'd taken an interest, pushed her in the right direction. Sarah, too, and Marcos in his way, as well. She'd always think of herself, like Kip, as an honorary Montoya.

But look, here she was at the studio. Time to lay aside these memories. Time to shine.

In Bandelier the parched brush had accumulated. The fuel load was high. Park service workers, some of whom had been around for the fire on Burnt Mesa back in 'seventy-seven, which took out entire ponderosa forests that hadn't burned for a century, didn't like what they saw. Wheatgrass had sprouted up fast under the spring sunshine, and throughout the monument—up on Escobas and over toward State Road 4—gambel oak thrived in sere acorned thickets, narrowleaf cottonwoods with them, chokecherry and desert olive, piñon-juniper woodlands that promised choice kindling for a lightning bolt or dropped cigarette. They used to pursue a policy of outright fire suppression back in the old days, but controlled burning was the new methodology, the science of which was simply to cheat a potential blaze out of the woodland fuel that would allow it to jump from tree to tree, mesa to mesa. Just as the surgeon cuts to cure, the park service burned to prevent fire.

There had already been some wildfires around the state. When Marcos and Ariel Montoya made the millennium pilgrimage to Chimayó, one fire was raging down in Ruidoso and another near Farmington. April had been a month of winds this year and though there had been some showers the river was skinny, and the mountains, usually still covered with deep fields of winter snow even now, were nearly bald. Chimayó valley was tawny with dust, and the murder of two pilgrim youngsters from the Hill cast a pall over the annual celebration. The promise of calamity hung in the drought-dry air.

Ariel, well along with her second child, left Miranda in Delfino's care, watching in horror the television news about what had begun to transpire in Los Alamos. Sarah had phoned minutes before from the center, breathless, more apprehensive than Ariel had ever heard her. They were evacuating not just the convalescent facility and hospital, but all fourteen thousand people on the Hill.

"Make up every spare bed we've got and get Marcos to clear out the greatroom. We've got to put up a lot of folks," she said. "And tell Carl to make space for more horses."

"How many?"

"As many as he can manage."

"Should we come up there to help?"

"The police'll just turn you back."

"Sarah, are you in danger?"

"They're saying people's houses are already starting to go up on the northwest edge of town. I'm leaving now."

"Sarah?"

But the line went dead and when Ariel redialed she got a fast busy signal. She ran down to the barn where Marcos was working with Carl. Together they dashed to the upper pasture and could see it, the massive plume of gray obscuring the Jemez. Carl tried to call Sarah from the stable, but by then a recorded message was advising that all lines were currently busy, please try again later. Bonnie Jean did manage to get through to the ranch, and Delfino told her to come straight down with Charlie and Sam, there was plenty of room.

The wind got worse, and within hours all hope of early containment had vanished. Los Alamos had not seen such an exodus since the days of secret practice drills in the forties and fifties, rehearsal evacuations trialed to get Hill personnel and families away from the then-fledgling nuclear lab as quickly as possible in case of enemy attack. Down the canyons thousands of cars and trucks now streamed, even as up those same roads crew after crew of engine companies rushed from Española and Santa Fe and beyond. A firestorm, as Brice would believe but never tell a soul, revisiting the birthplace of other firestorms. Mathematics and probabilities mounting some kind of iniquitous backdraft.

The acrid stench of smoke rose high and wide, seeping toward Santa Clara with the fire following behind, and smoke settled across the wide pueblo terrain beyond the Rio Grande as far as the Sangre de Cristos themselves. One after another, families began arriving at Pajarito, where the Montoyas helped unload horses, dogs and cats and caged birds, a dozen children of all ages, another dozen women and men, friends some of them, others friends of friends. The night was going to be long, but hopes were high that the thing would be under control by morning.

It was not. Flames fanned by winds that they themselves created worked their way through lifeless homes, up and down streets razed like flinted tinder to the ground as crews ran out of water, and the fire raged from block to block toward and then past concrete bunkers berthing explosives and others housing fireproof containers of radioactive inventory. White Rock nearby had thus far been spared by the widening inferno, and with it innumerable drums and fiberglass chalices of asbestos, PCBs, plutonium waste. But the next day brought no relief. Four thousand scorched acres became sixteen, then twenty; a hundred annihilated houses were soon two hundred. Then three dozen more. Blackened chimneys and charred swing sets and rubbled foundations. Residents watched their houses being destroyed over and again on newscasts. All they could do in Nambé was wait. Sarah had completely lost touch with half her staff, and her patients had been distributed to shelters or sent home to their families as the fish swam unaware in the long aquarium tank whose aerator had gone off with the power failure, resurging at the behest of a generator good for another day.

It seemed as if the world were on fire. An hour east of the Hill another blaze burned, Manuelitas and Canoncito near Las Vegas covered in flames. And another down where Delfino used to live, Cloudcroft and Weed, the towns with the pretty names Ariel had seen on her map, years ago now, when she drove from El Paso to

Chimayó, in the forests above Tularosa, which sank in smoke as three thousand acres were scorched in a handful of hours.

Meantime the fire on the Hill was given a name, Cerro Grande, as the destroyed acreage neared fifty thousand, and questions began to be asked about the tritium and uranium and plutonium remnants in the brush and soil of those canyons where Brice and Kip had once played. Then, not as quickly as it began—a week had passed since Sarah made that first urgent call to Ariel—the fire faltered under calm skies, firefighters grabbed the advantage, and the largest fire in New Mexico's history was over.

Family by family they left Pajarito, as did thousands from other refuges, some returning to find scorched shards, others to houses that reeked of smoke and fire retardants but were still intact. The workers handed them Teddy bears as they boarded buses for the tour of their town. Some horses were repastured at other ranches, some were bought and sold. The convalescent center remained unscathed, while Bonnie's place, though not burned, lay under a carpet of ash, looking for all the world like an outlandish cocoon. Her geraniums, her patio, the evasive lizard—gone. But she and her family were among the fortunate ones.

Granna's house was another story. Little remained but the foundation and the wrought-iron grille on her screen door. A pan, a pot, the ruined battleship of her old Frigidaire. Ariel and Bonnie walked its ruins together, Bonnie weeping, Ariel in disbelief. The little library, burned to nothing. The bed in which the woman had slept for so many years, first with her husband and then by herself, scorched beyond their ability to so much as find it. The photos, the family album, the memento of a hike up Turtle Mountain way back when, an oblivion of charcoal. The bottle of gin she'd left behind, burned and melted.

When they were asked by authorities if they wanted to rebuild, and asked what had been lost and what they assessed the damage to be, they couldn't correctly answer the questions.

"What would Granna want us to do?" Ariel asked Bonnie Jean.

"I wonder," she said, wiping her eyes as they stood on the pavement of the street, its trees now skeletons, its sidewalks thick with melancholy wet ash mud, stinking of defeat.

"I have an idea," said Ariel.

Her aunt listened, straightaway agreed, and though they made their decision without consulting Brice, they knew he would concur.

"Nothing," Bonnie told the FEMA adjustor.

"Sorry?"

"We mean we want you to do nothing here. Nothing at all."

"You want to sell it, you mean?"

"Never."

"You want help cleaning up the debris?"

"Good of you to offer," said Ariel.

"But we'll take care of it ourselves," Bonnie finished.

He looked at them. "That's it, then?" he said.

"Yes," they said. "Thank you."

Later that same day, and on a number of days that followed, they came back with Marcos and begin to pick through the remains, clean up the lot so it could renaturalize. They found relics here and there. The brass knocker from the front door. A little glass pig she kept for good luck. The bone-handled knife used to carve Thanksgiving turkey when Brice and Bonnie were yet kids, now singed beyond purpose but identified and soon to become part of a tiny McCarthy museum in her daughter's house.

"It was a miracle no one died," Ariel said one afternoon as they worked their way across the lot, Marcos beside her with a shovel covered in soot.

"Well, some did, many did," Bonnie Jean said quietly. "They might not know, but they did, no doubt."

Eventually the lot would become a homemade memorial park. Around the seedlings and small bushes they planted in the raked soil, a blade of grass sprouted, and another before that summer ended. Then some wildflowers, and then some more.

She had come to think of the river as a friend. Walking the narrow dirt path beside it at dusk, as now, was one of her most cherished indulgences. Her mind cleared. Her heart slowed. If she needed to ponder a problem, she could. If she wanted only to listen to evening birds and scuttling stream stones and contemplate nothing whatever, she could. Whenever she was able to grab an hour at the end of the day, while the grandparents or Uncle Delfino looked after little Miranda, or Marcos took over fathering her, she loved walking east along the shambled bank to Conchas Park, where weathered poplars and cottonwoods jutted forth, their roots exposed because the loam had given way under quickwash from hard rains. The Chimayó lowrider gang that used to party here had moved on, leaving nothing behind except for a rusting oil drum knocked onto its side, their bonfire barrel now a cylindrical sculpture some coydog might nose for prey in the night before trotting on. Otherwise only the running water, rustling leaves prodded by lazy air, birdcalls, and overhead the vast purpling heaven and its first faint stars.

Conchas Park, conscious park. She heard the crunch of earth underfoot, turning back toward home this evening, heard her small rhythmic contribution to nature's improvised music. She heard her breathing, which came more easily now than it had when she first moved in at the ranch after the wedding. Ironic that living in thin air made your blood grow richer. But hers, she thought, was richer in ways that had nothing to do with altitudes above sea level. And this unborn life inside her, this gift of her love with Marcos, this boy—as the sonogram promised—whom her husband had finally named Chase because he imagined him a venturer as Kip had been, was his blood equally enriched? When he kicked, as just now, was he dancing to the quiet rhythm of her stride, as his father once had danced in Sarah's womb? Yes, surely it was so.

The sun had gone down half an hour ago and she saw the moon meagerly reflected in the murmuring water. She picked up a stone and tossed it, watched the quivering white orb shatter then regather itself on the river's face. She was unafraid walking this lonely road, though really there was no reason for her to feel safe. The dark was gaining quickly, the clouds over the Jemez having lost their afterglow, so she moved along a little faster.

Thin air. Funny, that reminded her of Marcos's ghost. He never abandoned his conviction that it was a ghost he'd seen back when he was young. Sometimes she teased her husband about it, but got no laughs from him, as he refused to take it in the spirit intended, so to speak. He was sure he had identified her through research he'd done using antique deeds on the place from the Rancho de Peña era. For such a practical, down-to-earth man, his insistence that he had encountered the ghost of Doña Francisca, the only daughter of the man who first settled this spread back in the nineteenth century, seemed, well, just seemed out of character. Everything else Marcos did or said made such sense. It reminded Ariel of Granna somehow, the fervency of her belief in the altogether unprovable.

Yet, walking in this twilight, seeing the mists on the river, she could imagine how such a vision might come to pass. Desert air, this lean desert air, was chilly tonight, while the creek water ran warm from a long fall sun. The fields were wet from irrigating, the ground tepid. Wasn't that the meteorology which would produce these skeins of pale haze, these fog strings drifting like spectral tapers across her path? It was, she was certain. This must surely have been what Marcos saw all those years ago.

An owl hooted. A magpie shifted on a branch overhead. Ariel walked even more quickly, and as she did she began to think about the notes she'd been adding to her new ledger, the one she now used, having filled the Calder volume. More noticings, more notes.

How would she evoke what she witnessed here before her? Mist-figures taking on clearer shapes, and one in particular rising toward undeniable form down the path a hundred paces or so, not far from the aluminum gate that would let her back into the lower pasture and on toward the fieldhouse, where her husband and child waited for her. If Francisca was somehow still in Nambé valley, could it be possible beyond just wishful thinking that some small part of Kip was, too?

With rosetilla of Chimayó, Ariel mused, she might have tried to help him remain a presence. With rosetilla the aster, *ambrosia concertiflora* that flourishes along the riverbed, herb of the toad, *yerba* that cures men, women, and beasts whose bodies were suffering. Maybe Francisca prepared for him the traditional mash of *yerba del sapo* and salt and asparagus berries and steeped it in a bowl of creek water and set it out for him under a Navajo willow. Perhaps his *médica* choreographed his respite from absolute death, knowing somehow that her lover's great-grandson's wife would be grateful.

Ariel unlatched the gate, shivering from the deepening chill. At the far end of the paddock, protected by coyote fences, stood her adobe, hidden safely in the moonshade of deleafing cottonwoods—the fieldhouse where Kip had spent so many of his best days. She walked past the stud barn through the vivid meadow fog that floated in fragile bundles across the scape and when she reached the corral fence, an *añil* cloud stopped her in her tracks. It looked for all the world like a woman. Whorly embroidery running the length of her skirt, a silk blouse under a wispy jerkin, *flor* boots soft as slippers, a sombrero banded by silver disks that caught the early starlight in enchanted glints. Flowing from the earth beside her was a condensation, the synopsis of a man, radiant in his handsome mist, as real as Doña Francisca de Peña had ever been or would be. There were others, too, moving about in a fantastic dance. And though Ariel knew the forms and shapes were the work of nightfall haze and her own imagination, as she made her way across the pasture she believed they were also as real as any imagined thing need be. They were family of the roundish earth, *nambay-ongwee*, like the Tewa before them—Doña Francisca de Peña and Kip Calder, clubfooted Gil Montoya and prayerful Granna, Agnes and Grandfather McCarthy, her beloved little Buddha. Though they no longer lived, their mists would be remembered.

When she opened the fieldhouse door, she was greeted by the same amber lamplight she remembered from Chelsea, back when she watched the appalling pigeons on the ledge and countless people passing by on the sidewalks below. And to think she and Marcos lived in this old fieldhouse now, which they'd expanded some, modernized some, but which still had Kip's fingerprints, quite literally, on its adobe walls. Just as Kip continued to live inside Ariel and Miranda and, soon enough, baby Chase, they lived inside the consequence of his labor of love down here in the lower pasture. The delicate balance was struck.

Marcos kissed her. She took off her barn coat, apologizing for staying out late. The river was so beautiful tonight, she said. The starlight on the water. The clouds rising out of the earth. After dinner, the day nearing done, she asked if she could read them something she'd written, before Miranda was put to bed. Marcos answered yes, and the girl settled down in her father's lap to listen, though she was still too young to understand. And when Ariel opened Kip's old ledger and read, "Doña Francisca de Peña never believed in ghosts, and even after she became one herself she couldn't help but have her doubts," she glanced up, and Marcos said, "Keep going." So she did.